I0635899

At Her Pleasure

A Mistresses of the Board Room series novel, Book #4

Copyright © 2023 Joey W. Hill

ALL RIGHTS RESERVED

Cover design by Scott Hill

SWP Digital & Print Edition publication November 30, 2023

Digital ISBN: 978-1-951544-27-0

Print ISBN: 978-1-951544-28-7

SUMMARY

It was a night for doing stupid things...

Ten years ago, Mick should have arrested the drunk, angry woman vandalizing a cemetery. Instead, on that cold night, he yielded to her pain and rage, and let her go. Now a former cop, he's come to New Orleans on business—a job which brings him face to face with the woman he never forgot.

Cynbad Marigold is a successful businesswoman and a formidable Domme, a Mistress who chooses men who need enough pain to appease her limitless craving to inflict it. Most of them safeword before she goes too deep, but when Mick reappears in her life, he doesn't want safety. In uncovering the shocking depths of his own darkness, Cyn realizes she wants to give him the home he needs—safe in the shadows of her soul.

Whose darkness will take them deeper—and will their bond keep them from going too far?

AT HER PLEASURE

A Mistresses of the Board Room Novel

JOEY W. HILL

CONTENTS

ACKNOWLEDGMENTS

Writing BDSM romance well is only partly about mechanics and terminology. Understanding how and why each person practices BDSM helps to bring characters to life. While I am a submissive, I have my own preferences, so the places my characters go don't always call to me personally.

For that reason, I am grateful to online communities like Fetlife, and individuals who share personal insights into their desires. For those of us interested in learning about them, even if that kink isn't our kink, it enriches our understanding of what power exchange relationships are all about. To an author wanting to "get it right," it's incredibly helpful!

I also want to thank my readers who post content to the JWHMembersOnly Facebook group, inspiring ideas that work their way into my stories. For Cyn and Mick's book, a nod goes to Sandra P, whose mention of the "sexiest tease" she's ever seen kicked off one of the events in the book. Another thanks goes to Jessica G, who shared a titillating video of modeled male corsets from Innova Corsetry. Finally, appreciation to Jackie M, who mentioned the old school Scottish discipline "belt" (tawse) some time ago, but it resurfaced to become a part of this story.

A concluding note and warning: Cyn is a sexual sadist. The more extreme BDSM practices in this story have been researched, hopefully avoiding any major mistakes, but if you are a reader interested in pursuing edge play, use great common sense, research what you are doing, and find an experienced mentor you trust to guide you. Stay safe and take care of one another—the maxim for *every* relationship.

CHAPTER ONE
Ten Years Ago...

Mick's radio crackled. "Possible D&D at 5th and Woodside."

Drunk and disorderly at the cemetery. Probably kids, or a homeless person off their meds.

"65 Adam to Central responding."

"10-4, 65 Adam. Caller says the subject is a woman."

So not kids. More complicated, but not urgent.

He kept his head on a swivel as his cruiser purred down the streets. His headlights swept over trash piled up over the storm drains. Most of the streetlights were out. Broken by kids with a good throwing arm, eager to earn their props with the local gangs.

In one of New Jersey's top-rated cities for crime, his precinct covered its worst neighborhoods. If a kid here made something of him or herself, they deserved a Bronze Star. And a fistful of Purple Hearts for the scars, inside and out.

People clustered in the ample shadows. Some froze like rabbits as Mick rolled past, but he didn't stop. His sergeant said to wait for the calls. *Don't go chasing trouble.*

To distract himself from the overwhelming urge to ignore that advice, Mick picked out a song on his phone and played it on low volume, humming along under his breath. He wasn't much on religion, but it had been one of his mother's favorites. "How Great Thou Art," the Elvis Presley version.

Having music in his head that meant something to him gave him breathing space, reminding him of the reasons for flowers, puppies, the smell of a woman's hair. The firmness of her touch.

He'd much rather have that than her softness. Soft was oozing mud that sucked him down and held him under, making him disappear. He wanted an insane mix of torment and tenderness no one but him would call a woman's love.

Ah, well. As his Irish grandfather would have said, "Feck it out, boyo, and get on with it." His grandfather had used the "throw" meaning of "feck," but he probably wouldn't have disagreed with "fuck it out." Mick's dad was one of eleven kids, after all.

He had an active dick, too. But Mick's grandfather had been true to Mick's grandmother. Mick's father had whipped it out for any woman who caught his eye.

At least the darkness that plagued Mick wasn't that kind. Just the opposite. If he found his blessed female torturer, she'd command his devotion until they both dried up and blew away into dust.

Loose gravel from potholes crunched under his tires as he pulled into the cemetery. No other vehicle in sight. As he parked near the caretaker's shed, he noted a battered wheelbarrow next to it. Since the landscaping around the parking area had long ago been stamped out, he suspected the only thing the employee did was mow and clean out weeds and fallen branches.

Gang members avoided this place, maybe because they had family here, and even they had respect for the dead. Or they didn't care for the reminder of how many of their crew were planted in the plots.

"65 Adam, 10-84." He was on site.

"10-4, 65 Adam."

Dispatch would wait for him to evaluate the scene and request backup if needed. One experienced cop on the midnight shift could handle an unarmed homeless person. In this precinct, his five years on the job made him a veteran.

Thirty acres wasn't big for a cemetery. Some older sections, dating from the sixties, had more impressive stones, but today it was one step above a potter's field. People buried here couldn't afford what it cost to die, but as a big fuck-you, they did it anyway.

A few gnarled trees had stubbornly endured, growing big enough to spread their branches over the graves. Their profiles were menacing, but also protective. He could respect that.

No sign of flowers, silk or otherwise. If anyone left some on the markers, they were stolen fast. Was the thief wanting them for his girl or mother, but lacked the cash to buy his own? Did he apologize to the dead, or tell himself they didn't care?

Before Mick switched off the car and got out, the song on the player changed. "Gone, Gone, Gone" by Phillip Phillips. As he strode down the path toward the shed, he held the beat in his mind.

Drawing out his flashlight, he passed the beam over rusty tools resting against the wheelbarrow. Cigarette butts overflowed a sand bucket.

He paused, listening. Nothing. Then he caught a raised voice on the breeze. Followed by shattering glass.

He radioed in another status, still holding off on a request for backup, and proceeded in that direction. Some of his fellow officers didn't like visiting the cemetery after dark. It wasn't all superstition. The shadows were thick here, and the wind animated them, moaning through the trees. It could distract a cop from real world dangers.

Mick was good at separating fact from fiction, and the older gravestones soothed him. They'd weathered enough storms not to be bothered by much anymore. Which suggested the occupants had settled in and found peace.

Or maybe not.

"How does that feel, you fucking bitch? How does it feel to you?"

He topped a crest and paused next to one of the crooked trees. The scene ahead was backlit by the city's grayish night sky and the cemetery's dirty post lights, planted along the walking paths.

He'd seen a lot of things, and took most of them in stride. This was different—not the act, but the tone, and the woman doing it. He stood motionless, unnoticed.

She was grinding herself against a headstone. Not for pleasure. She shoved against it, hips working like a man thrusting into a female, as brutally as possible, while hitting the top of the stone with her clenched fist. He marked the broken beer bottle clutched in her other hand. She brandished the jagged weapon at the grave.

"You should have a spiked dick shoved up your ass every damn day you're in hell, you useless, piece of shit cunt." She gave the stone one more vigorous thrust, then stepped back. "Get up out of that box. Bring me another beer, bitch."

Her harsh laugh held despair. Dropping the broken bottle, she walked over to a cardboard six-pack of cheap brew. Three were left. Her jeans and T-shirt were baggy, but when she bent and twisted, her body was a lean wire, underfed but tough muscle. The flannel shirt open over the T-shirt was too light for the chill in the air.

Clutching the new beer, she collapsed next to a smaller headstone. As she twisted off the top and tipped the bottle to take a big swallow, she slid her arm around the stone, like it was a person. "You're so stupid," she informed the marker, tapping the top of it. The bottle made a light clink. "You don't have to kill yourself to disappear. You just have to not matter to anyone. At least not more than their own fucked-up lives. Then you can disappear into yourself. The soul has no bottom, Cissy. It goes straight fucking down. All the way to hell. It's warm there. Quiet, I think. Quiet."

Her voice was young. Not much over eighteen, but age was only a physical distinction. Most kids here had cynical eyes that had seen too much. Even so, their youth had a heartbreaking way of resurfacing under the right circumstances.

Not this one. What he heard in her voice slid up his spine like sharp nails, followed by teeth set to his throat.

The witches of Fate, those beautiful sadists gathered around their cauldron, had taken a man with an overdeveloped urge to fix a fucked-up world, and given him other, murkier needs.

The older guys ribbed him, asking Mick if he had any chest hair, just because he was still in his twenties, but he suspected they teased him as a concerned reminder he wasn't a hundred years old. Their shrewd cop eyes saw some of the same troubling things he saw in his own mirror.

The dangerous, unhelpful thought came to him that the woman humping a headstone could handle his darkness. Maybe better than her own.

Damn it, he knew better than to let himself go there on the job. But apparently it was a night for doing stupid things.

Resting her temple on the gravestone, she propped the beer on her knee and rocked the bottle back and forth. He noted the small headstone had no weeds and was edged by a little pile of smooth rocks. The same couldn't be said about the bigger one. Trash was mounded around it.

She took a thoughtful sip of the beer. "I pissed on her grave, Cissy. I want it to stink like that stairwell we hid under that one time. You remember? If I ever have money, I'll pay a hundred drunks to shit on her every day. I'll buy you the best skateboard in the world. I'll put it down there with your bones. You tell ToyBoy to decorate it, like he did his. You two ride them wherever you want. Heaven or hell. No limits."

She started up abruptly and threw the bottle at the other stone. It shattered, spraying beer. "You goddamned bitch. Didn't we hurt enough for you? I should have fucking eaten my way out of your womb. Torn you apart from the inside out. Suckled my first and last milk from your tit while you bled out."

When she went after the gravestone again with her fists, Mick saw she'd cut herself. Or was beating her fists bloody.

Fuck. Okay, show over. Time to break up the volatile family reunion. As he advanced, he clicked on his flashlight again, capturing her attention.

People startled by the police reacted in a variety of ways. Fear, confusion, apprehension. She whipped her head around and bared her teeth.

"Fuck off," she snarled.

Or that.

As he weighed his options—de-escalation, subduing the suspect, calling for backup—another reaction sat down in the middle of that debate and just stared. *Goddamn.* He'd seen her face before. In a mural, painted under the 10th Street overpass.

The graffiti artist had put blocky purple lettering alongside it. *Artemis, Mistress of the Hunt.*

Jet-colored eyes caught the flashlight beam and reflected gold sparks. She had thick lashes, prominent cheekbones and a jaw like a feral cat. The dark brown hair pressed down by her watch cap was a rebellion of curls reaching her jutting shoulders.

The artist had been killed four months ago, shot against that mural while he was adding to it. Flecks of his blood would forever be mixed with the paint.

A few drops of rust-colored beer were on the girl's cheek.

In the painting, Artemis had her bow raised and aimed at the viewer. Whenever Mick looked at it, he felt anticipation. The eager hounds clustered around her long, slim legs had emaciated bodies. Not from lack of food, but because he imagined every spare calorie went toward the Hunt.

Her eyes bored into a man's soul. They challenged him, asked if he had the balls to hunt *her*, see what it was like, two predators matching wits. If he caught her, what kind of fight would it be?

The girl's proud mouth curled in derision. He wanted to kiss that mouth when it was snarling, wanted to feel the snap of her teeth.

He yanked himself away from the weird melding of art, myth and female. He shouldn't be fixating on a drunk young woman in a cemetery, one who'd barely hit twenty, if at all.

7

One who was in obvious pain. But as soon as he met her eyes, Mick knew she held the nourishment he craved.

It was a shame he was going to have to arrest her.

The "Gone, Gone, Gone" song was still in his head, the lyrics feeling far more personal than they should be.

She did a short lunge at him, like at an animal she was driving away. "Get the fuck out of here. This doesn't concern you."

She might be buzzed, but she wasn't drunk. Her eyes were sharp. No slurring of her words. Her aim at the gravestone had been accurate and delivered with force. He expected what had made her stagger away from the bigger headstone and collapse against the smaller one was the weight of the emotions she was carrying.

Or physical hunger. Her face was too pale and thin.

However, confronted by a threat—or maybe he was just an annoyance—she was standing sturdy, feet braced, fists clenched. She wanted a fight.

The jeans were loose enough to conceal a gun or knife. The gang tat on the side of her neck was faded, and that crew had been swallowed up by a new one over a year ago. It hadn't been touched up, which meant she'd left them, not an easy feat here. While she wore no other gang markers, she had to be armed. Any woman with sense would be.

He'd held his ground at the lunge, but it had brought him a hundred percent back to the here and now. He kept the flashlight focused on her hands and torso. He'd unsnapped his gun holster when he left the car, but he'd probably let her kill him before he'd draw on her. After the week he'd had, he just couldn't bear the idea of it.

Yep, he was fucked in the head tonight.

"You're causing a disturbance, ma'am. And trespassing. No one in the cemetery after dark. If you move along, we can leave it at that."

Her teeth showed again. "I said this doesn't concern you, motherfucker. *You* move along and we'll leave it at that."

"Okay." He put the flashlight back on his belt. "Turn around and get on your knees. Lace your fingers on top of your head."

Her pretty mouth twisted into a barbed wire shape. "You don't have a big enough dick to get me on my knees."

"Does anyone?"

The grim humor startled her. Made her blink. That was when he moved.

She'd imbibed enough to slow her reflexes, and he had the element of surprise. He took her down, putting her on her stomach. She screamed at him, pushed with more force than he would have expected for her size. While she bucked, she scrambled for any glass or rock in reach. He stopped that, getting her arms behind her, her wrists zip-tied at the small of her back.

Most people, unless too far under the influence, called it quits once restrained. But she was just getting started.

As he pulled her to her feet, she hooked his leg with her own and dropped them to the ground again. She squirmed away and bounced back up, but instead of running as he expected, she kicked him in the thigh. If he hadn't rolled away fast enough, she'd have found his balls with the toe of her ratty sneakers.

Only then did she bolt, but the maliciousness had cost her. He grabbed the cuff of her jeans and yanked, bringing her down again.

He dodged the kick to his face and went for a full body tackle, using his greater size and weight against her back to mash her into the ground. Her head snapped around and she sank her teeth into his arm.

"Son of a…"

He yanked the arm away and adjusted to keep the rest of him out of range of feet or teeth.

"Pussy," she spat beneath him. "Fighting me like a cop instead of a man."

"Honey, they're one and the same."

9

The watch cap had come off, the tangle of brown curls framing her angry eyes, lowered brows and distracting mouth. He drew in a breath.

She should smell like beer and meanness, and she did. But the meanness turned him on. And her hair smelled like baby shampoo. Fucking baby shampoo.

"Don't you fucking try anything." He pushed up on a knee and patted her down, finding the sheathed knife tucked beneath her waistband. No gun. He put the blade into his belt, then eased back. Keeping a warning hand on the bound wrists, his knee on her butt, he stared down at her. Her body was vibrating with rage, but her eyes were glassy, and she'd gone eerily silent.

"You want a fair fight?" he said abruptly. "Is that what you want? One fucking fair fight in a whole life that hasn't had one?"

What was he doing? Her eyes rolled his way, her expression caught in the same *WTF* zone, with a big dose of *what is this asshole trying to pull?*

But zero fear.

She was a scrapper, but that didn't tell him what her actual fighting skills were. His training, not to mention his weight and height, might mean he really couldn't offer her a fair fight. But she didn't look like she felt that way.

In this world, a woman with her looks hooked up with someone for protection. He'd bet good money she hadn't done that.

He took a measured moment to reconsider his actions, to acknowledge if he ended up dead from being this much of an idiot, he deserved it. Then he cut the zip tie, stood and backed away. "Get up."

As she rolled to her knees and stood, he kept his eyes on her and clicked the button on his radio. "65 Adam. 10-85, situation resolved. No arrest made. I'm going on dinner break, 10-63."

"Roger 65 Adam. Dinner break confirmed."

Her eyes were wary, but interested. Behind a whole wall of distrust. Still no fear.

"You didn't answer the question," he said. "Do you want a fair fight?"

"What's my other option?"

"Get your ass home. Or I haul you in on trespassing and drunk and disorderly conduct."

A sneer. "I'm not drunk. What are you calling a fair fight?"

"Hand to hand, whoever pins the other for eight seconds. Like a rodeo. No hitting in the face or genitals. Everything else fair game."

"You can follow those rules. I won't. It's not a real fight if there are rules."

"Winning a fair fight means you can respect your opponent when it's over."

"Respect is like ruffles on a dress." She barked out a laugh. "Worthless and pretty. Much like you."

His lips quirked. "You think I'm pretty. Be still my heart. Is this fight happening or not?"

She didn't move, so he took that as a yes. He unholstered his Glock to drop out the mag, then re-holstered it and unhooked his belt. He set it aside, pocketing the mag in his trousers before he started unbuttoning his shirt.

Her eyes went to daggers. "Is this how you get bitches to fuck you? You get me pinned down, cop, and try to put your dick anywhere, I will tear it out by the root and□—"

"Stop." His growl brought her up short. "This isn't about that. You have my word. If I get blood on my shirt, I have to explain it."

"So what are the stakes?" she asked.

"Just a fair fight. Whoever wins, you go home. I go home. That's it. Unless you'll let me buy you a sandwich and a cup of coffee. You look like you could use it."

When she gave him that scornful look rather than an answer, he left that hanging, and nodded down the slope beside them, toward a scrubby patch of grass, a shallow pit that had once been a gazing pool. "We'll go there."

"What's wrong with here?"

He glanced toward the smaller gravestone. "This will get rough. We don't want to trample her grave. Right?"

Her gaze flickered. Despite her disdainful expression, he also noted her eyes coursing over his shoulders, bared by the tank beneath his uniform shirt. He knew he was pleasing to a woman's eye, even without the uniform's appeal.

"Pretty enough for you?" he asked.

"Get over yourself, fuckhead."

He almost laughed. His ever-present restlessness was a form of claustrophobia, and this bit of craziness he was indulging in with an angry, savage girl felt like he was breaking out. Hell, he was putting his job on the line here. Might as well enjoy the torching of his police career.

He gave them both one more chance, though. "So what'll it be? You going to get on home, or you want a chance to kick my ass?"

"When I win, you give me back my knife."

When. His lips twitched. "Long as you don't try to use it on me. You do, you're going to jail."

She shrugged. He took the lead, heading down the slope, carrying his shirt, belt and weapon. He kept her in his peripheral vision, so he knew when she started following.

Broken wine bottles marked their trail. She'd scared away any winos using this as a nighttime drinking spot. He suspected she scared the hell out of most men.

He liked that about her.

Reaching the pit, he put the belt out of easy reach and turned to face her. He expected some sharp-tongued trash talk, more verbal foreplay, before they got into it. Instead, when she stepped inside the perimeter, she looked like she'd been waiting for a violent free-for-all the way other people dreamed of a winning lottery ticket. Or true love.

"Don't forget□—"

He was going to remind her of the safety points she'd flat out told him she wouldn't observe. Instead, she charged, her eyes lit with the only mandate she planned to follow.

To hurt him as much as possible.

He   liked   that   about   her,   too.

CHAPTER TWO

She hit him full body, no holding back, a cat leaping on the head of a pit bull, all claws extended.

She probably still believed he was bullshitting her and had a perverted motive. Her world had no room for trust, let alone for a stranger and a cop. But though he'd given her ample opportunity to cut and run, she hadn't.

She wanted the fight.

She did have some training. With the added mix of street instincts and fury, she proved within the first few seconds she could hold her own. He blocked a right hook, but couldn't stop the redirect that landed in his ribs. She was agile, fast and brutal, not letting up, the flurry of moves as hard to stop as a defense line blitz.

Unless he fought harder, dirtier, and didn't hold back as much. He didn't want to fight her. Or rather, he did. He wanted to fight her until he won. But then he'd back off and do what he really wanted to do in the face of her overwhelming personality, the chaotic energy that cried out to his own.

He'd kneel to her. Submit.

She wasn't mature enough yet for that move, not ready for it. Maybe neither of them were, but the idea called to him anyway.

She was getting madder, that glorious rage fueled by and into what they were doing. He could feel it as he countered, pinned and let himself be shook off.

"Don't you fuck with me," she snarled. "Fight me. Goddamn you, really fight me."

He had no time to tell her he was giving it his all, in the most acceptable way possible. Which meant working to stay ahead of her while restraining himself, because he wouldn't risk truly harming her.

14

He'd offered her a fair fight, and she'd told him she didn't want that. She wanted blood. He'd seen that, but thought this would help her turn from it.

That kind of thinking was undeniable proof of how fucked his head was, how much he'd ignored his trained instincts about violence and a person's capability for it. Those instincts returned in full force when, at the height of her wrath, her hand landed on a shard of thick glass the size of a slice of cheesecake.

In a blink, their sparring area turned into a battleground.

Driven by whatever had brought her here, the anguish that had her violating one tombstone and holding onto another like the person buried beneath it, she whipped her hand forward. The point sliced open a path up his chest, hot and burning, and passed so close to his throat it scraped his pounding jugular.

He shoved her back and struck the pressure point at her shoulder that would force her fingers to loosen and drop the glass. But her eyes had gone wide, and her fingers had already opened. She leaped even farther away from him.

"Fuck. Oh fucking hell."

She looked like she was considering whether she should bolt, and then she did, scrambling up the short hill. Served him right. He didn't want her arrested because he was a dumbass.

He dropped to one knee, hand over the wound, which was sopping wet. It was all right. He didn't think she'd damaged anything below the skin layers. As he tried to calm down, get his heart rate under control, he probed the injury. The deepest part was over his pectoral. She'd started there and swiped upward. His collar bone had jarred her strike hand, so the weapon had only grazed his throat.

"Here, sit down." He lifted his head, startled to find she'd returned, clutching a backpack.

"Shit, shit, shit. Let me see." She tore the already cut neckline of his tank. He winced as she cracked open a bottle

15

of water from her pack and poured it on the cut. After studying it, she reached into her backpack and pulled out a paramedic go bag. Saline solution came next. Now it was time for him to curse.

"I reached the muscle layer. You need stitches," she told him dispassionately. "You should call for some help."

She placed a pressure bandage over that part of the cut, reached for his hand and placed it on top of the pad, a nonverbal order to hold it. Her fingers were cold but firm.

A firm touch.

Her brown eyes were worried, and she flattened her hand on top of his to add to the pressure.

"I'll be fine. No call for help. I do that, I have to report what happened. You go to jail, Mistress."

Her brows lifted. "What did you call me?"

"Mistress. Of the Hunt. Like Artemis."

She grimaced. "That damn mural. I'm going to get a spray can of black paint and cover it up."

"Don't do that. Was that ToyBoy's work?"

"No." He saw her realization that he'd heard her talking to the gravestone, but she moved past that. "He liked doing skateboards, small stuff. The painting was Balloon's."

"Balloon?"

"That was his street name. He liked balloons. The 5th Street gang put holes in him the same night they did ToyBoy."

She gave Mick a critical look. "You're really built, but the rookies usually are. Older cops get fat."

"I'm not a rookie. I've been on the job five years."

"Long enough not to have done a dumb move like this," she observed.

His lips twitched again. "Yeah, I guess."

She lifted the pad to give the wound another look. "Let me use your phone to call 911. I'll bail when I hear the sirens. Make up some shit about an attacker who jumped you and I was a bum who made the call and then ghosted."

16

"I'll be fine. Get going."

The stubborn set of her mouth was far too distracting. "You're not giving the orders," she told him. "You've been on your ass at least eight seconds. I won."

He watched with mild alarm as she pulled out a suture kit. "How do you have a paramedic's bag?"

"I stole it," she said matter-of-factly. "Same way I keep it stocked. Not my first time needing to patch myself up or someone else, including stitches. I read up, learned how."

Interpreting his look as a doubt of her abilities, she lifted the hem of her shirt, high enough he saw the frayed elastic band of a black bra. As well as a thin scar that ran from the V-point of her ribs to her hip bone.

"I did a pretty good job, but this was shallow and done with a sharp knife, a clean cut. It'll eventually fade out."

"Hopefully in time for bikini season." His voice was tight as he suppressed the surge of anger on her behalf. He curled his fingers to keep himself from offering a soothing stroke to that harrowingly long line across her flesh.

"Yeah, I've been really worried about that." She rolled her eyes. "You're not going to be as lucky. I got you pretty deep and it was jagged glass. I'll stitch you up and douse it good with antiseptic, but if it gets hot or you get feverish, don't be stupid. Get to an urgent care."

"Got it." He knew she was right, but if he could help it, he wasn't letting this come back on her. The best way to do that was to let her stitch him up. "Appreciate it," he added courteously. Then chuckled at the absurdity.

She shook her head. "You're fucked up, man. This is going to hurt. You want one of my beers?"

"I'm on duty, so no."

"You're on dinner break."

"Blowing a breathalyzer still counts if you drink during meal break. They frown on that."

"I bet that's not all they frown on." She rose and moved toward his duty belt and shirt. He tensed as she bent to pick them up. Even though he had the mag for the gun in his trousers, there were extra ones in the belt. Her knife was also there.

Her gaze lifted, met his. Ignoring the mags and the gun, she retrieved the sheathed knife and hooked it back into her waistband beneath the hem of the shirt. The move gave him another glimpse of her pale flesh.

She brought the rest back to him. "Pull out your flashlight and shine it on your chest so I can see what I'm doing."

Before he complied, he moved the belt and holster to his other side. She was opening the kit, but she noticed. "Damn, I was planning on shooting you after I finished stitching you up. Way to thwart my evil plan."

Her mild tone was a contrast to her intent gaze as she lifted the tissue forceps, used the needle holder to pick up the curved sharp, and went to work.

She stitched him up as efficiently as any paramedic he'd seen. His flashlight hand twitched a little with the first needle insertion. As he felt her attention, watching how he handled pain, her interested look made things tighten in him, lower down.

The shadows covered it, or at least he thought they did. When she finished up and set the suturing tools aside, she put her palm firmly over his erection.

His head came up and their eyes locked. She pressed against his cock, fingers curving over it through those damnably thick uniform pants. "You like the pain." Her voice was oddly flat. Lips parted. Moist. He could feel the heat of her breath. See her teeth. His arm throbbed where she'd bitten him.

He saw no need for anything but raw honesty. "I like taking the pain a woman can give out."

"What would you have done if you'd won the fight?"

"Whatever you wanted."

She swallowed, drawing his gaze to her throat. For the first time, he saw confusion in her beautiful dark eyes. As

18

he'd suspected, what was there wasn't yet mature enough to acknowledge what he was voicing, but something deep in her understood. He wondered if she'd live long enough, or have enough of her spirit survive, to learn what to do with it.

He wanted that to happen.

She returned to tending him. He grimaced as she applied the antiseptic and taped bandages in place. Thanks to the length of the cut, it took two of the large squares. When she was done, he rose. He wasn't lightheaded, which meant his blood loss had been minimal. His steadiness seemed to reassure her, too.

"Pack up your shit," he said. "My mealtime's about over and I need to show you something."

He stripped off the ruined tank, put his uniform shirt back on, tucked it in, and hooked his belt in place. But as his gaze went up the hill, he thought of something else. He'd make time for it, even if his sergeant gave him shit about pushing the limits of dinner break. "Hold on. Don't leave. I'm going to the caretaker's shed."

He strode away. She might ignore him and ghost, but he was still going to do what he intended. At the shed, he picked up the rusted sledgehammer next to the old wheelbarrow. When he started to shoulder it, the stitches pulled against his raw flesh, so he gripped the neck and handle and carried it in front of him.

She'd get pissed if he tore them.

When he came back, she was still at the dried-up pond, though she'd packed up her bag and had it hanging on her shoulder. As he headed toward the gravestones, she came up the hill to join him. She stopped at the smaller one, watching him with wide eyes. He was grimly pleased to do this, to show her how he could put his strength into her service. He paused long enough for her to see his intent, to tell him *no*, if it wasn't what she wanted.

Instead, she squatted on her heels and put her arms around the stone again. He saw enough of it to read the name

Cissy, and a birth and death date that said she'd died in her teens. A sister, he assumed, because of the proximity to the mother's grave.

He gauged the distance was enough to keep the girl safe from flying debris, then swung the sledgehammer.

He modified the stroke to protect the stitches, but he was going to do the damage needed. He was destroying more than stone here. In three swings, he turned the larger headstone to rubble. He didn't look at the name.

"Will anyone replace it?" His voice was rough, thick.

She shook her head. A blinding mix of emotions possessed her countenance. It was like staring into the sun until his head ached and his eyes ran with tears. The pain beyond her rage made her look incredibly vulnerable. Artemis standing over the fallen.

"C'mon," he said gruffly. "Let me show you what I wanted to show you."

He headed toward his car. A glance back confirmed she hadn't moved. She was staring at the remains of the gravestone. He stopped and waited for her.

After a few moments, she lifted her gaze to him. Her face had gone back to that neutral mask, her eyes unfathomable. She moved in his direction.

When they reached his car, he opened the passenger door for her. "I prefer to drive," she told him.

"Sorry, only cops get to drive cop cars. Be happy you're riding in front."

She settled into the seat with a sniff, her arms around the backpack. But as he circled around, she leaned forward and pushed the siren button, giving him a wicked look as the noise nearly shattered his ear drums and blue lights flashed in his eyes. He got in, giving her a reproving look, and switched them off. He wanted to smile, but the light had shown him the hollows in her cheeks, the feral animal look.

A mysterious and strong young woman, but a hungry and poor one. Probably a breath away from being another ToyBoy or Balloon.

He dropped his phone in the well between them, and when he did, his finger accidentally brushed the screen and activated his playlist.

The next song was an old hymn sung by the Statler Brothers. He guessed she'd be surprised to find he had that stuff on his music player. But when she turned her face toward the window, *he* was surprised to hear the lyrics come from her. A discordant recitation, halfway between speaking the words and singing them.

"'He walks with me, he talks with me, he calls me my own.'" As she glanced his way and saw his expression, she shrugged. "I've slept in a church basement a couple times."

"Yeah." He turned out of the lot and left the cemetery behind. As he drove through the dirty streets, he noted the still-present people in the shadows, tracking the car. She had her head down, a thinking pose as she turned the watch cap in her hands.

"So do you usually do this kind of thing?"

"No. Not really."

"So why did you tonight?"

There were a lot of reasons, but he went with simple and somewhat true. "Something happened on my shift, a few days ago. It's been in my head, messing me up some."

An understatement. It had doubled the agitation he carried within him. His life felt like a jail cell, and the pressure to break out was intense. He wanted to challenge the state of the world, the intolerable limits of his own mind. He needed to roar, to rage, to run. Hunt. Chase.

Which was sort of what he'd done tonight.

As she digested what he'd said, and considered what he hadn't, he wanted to touch her hair. That beautiful mouth. Ask for the privilege as he knelt before her, aching to earn her trust, the right to care for her. He wanted to drive right out of town, take them both somewhere far away.

Here tonight, maybe he'd given her a glimpse of what could be different for her. She'd never know how much he ached to join her on that path, but fortunately *he* was mature enough to know how insane an idea that was.

He pulled into the side lot of Paulie's Garage as her head came up. "Why are we here?" she asked suspiciously.

He fished in his pocket and removed his personal keys, pulling one off of the ring. He pointed to an old Cadillac behind the chain link fence. "That belonged to my uncle. He died a few months back."

His last living family member who knew he existed or mattered. Which uncomfortably reminded him of what she'd said to Cissy.

"It still runs." He cleared his throat and offered her the key. "Backseat sleeps pretty good when you can't afford a hotel. You asked what I would have wanted if I won. I didn't lie, but there's something else I want even more. I want you to get out of here. Pick a direction and drive. Go somewhere you've always wanted to go. Somewhere warm. You look like you've been cold so long you don't bother shivering anymore."

Her aggression was going to run afoul of the police again, and cold fear, aching through that wound in his chest, told him where that could lead.

"You're welcome to tell me to fuck off. To eat shit, but I'm going to say what I have to say. You have a lot of energy, but you also carry the kind of mad that turns into prison sentences. I know you can do better. You're smart as hell. Don't destroy yourself, don't let your demons take over. Find a way to manage them, use them for something good for yourself."

Her eyes were smoky as a smoldering fire. Deliberately, he curled his fingers around her wrist, the hand closest to him, still gripping the backpack. The touch sent electricity jolting through both of them. She twitched. He pulled her hand free of the pack and laid the key in her palm.

She touched his fingers, a bare second of contact, then she shoved out of the car and stood beside it. Waiting for him to let her into the locked gate.

After he did that, he walked her over to the car. She gave him that wary cat look. "You going to call it in stolen?"

"Maybe, when I wake up tomorrow for my shift and have to pretend I don't have a foot-long cut that hurts like a son of a bitch."

She pressed her lips together, her eyes swirling with that ice cream sundae mix of reactions he'd probably dream about for the rest of his life. "You liked the pain," she said.

"You liked giving it. You also liked tending it." He met her gaze. "Don't lose that combination. Bye, Mistress of the Hunt."

CHAPTER THREE
Present Day

Cynbad Marigold ignored most dates other people considered significant.

Wedding anniversaries. Yeah, she'd never have to worry about that one.

Birthdays. What was the point of marking every year you got older?

Date of death. She hated it when people put fake flowers and homemade crosses where car crashes had been, or TV news people marked the anniversary of multi-death tragedies, year after year. It had happened in the past, on that day, during *that* specific year. Move the fuck on.

Death came to everyone. You didn't have to marinate yourself in it, like raw meat preparing to be cooked.

All that said, one date punched through her armor every year. It turned her head into a fucking angst swamp.

Which was why instead of pulling into the paved lot of her preferred BDSM club on a balmy New Orleans night, she should be turning around to go home. Text Ros and the others and tell them she wasn't feeling it.

A Domme who preferred sadism on the far ass end of edge play had to be more cautious about her state of mind.

She'd set up a session with Sy, but he served at her pleasure. It was a Mistress's prerogative to send him a brusque, "Changed my mind. Keep your dick on hold until I reschedule." She could sit on her back porch and drink a glass of wine. Look at her yard.

"Cyn's an outstanding Mistress, especially if you want a real sadist. But don't expect more. She's an emotional dumpster fire."

She'd overheard that from a group of submissives, hanging out in the club's social area. None of the little shits had ever had a session with her, but the one who'd spoken had probably been fed the opinion by one who had. Probably a one-off who'd wanted that "more" from her, and had some ill feelings after she shut that shit down.

Despite her annoyance at being reviewed like the latest movie release, she didn't disagree with the assessment. She was a special kind of messed up, but she'd never claimed not to be broken. Broken things could cut. Or kill.

She remembered the glass carving into the young cop's chest, the blur of motion, the blood welling up. A drop had landed on her lips. Over the years she'd wondered if that taste was why she couldn't forget him.

She hadn't paid attention to his badge number or name plate before he removed his shirt. The registration in the Cadillac's glove box had expired, so she'd deduced it was his uncle's name. Paul Doyle. Which gave her nothing. She didn't pursue it. She didn't want to know more about the cop. Yet she hadn't stopped thinking about him for a decade. And he was in the forefront of her mind tonight.

Damn it, she wasn't cancelling. A last-minute bail because she couldn't get her shit together was rude. It was only acceptable as a mindfuck, to increase her sub's suffering in the right way.

So she chose a song on her music player. Settling back, she drummed the steering wheel to match the rhythm of Gretchen Wilson's "Redneck Woman." As the chorus built to the *hell, yeah!* she tapped her booted foot and slapped her thigh to the beat, bringing that energy inside her, pushing the rest out.

She imagined Sy's back, a brown canvas ready for her marks. She heard the sucking in of his breath as she made contact with her whip, paddle or cane. She'd taste the perspiration collected in the hollows of his spine. Nectar, created by pain she administered.

Her subs were full-blooded, testosterone-packed alphas. Strong-willed men who needed submission and wanted the agony she could give. They made her work to top them. She tightroped the line where a misstep turned predator into prey. She could make a man believe she'd made that stumble, then show him a power he hadn't anticipated.

Like she'd shown that cop. Except, to this day, she believed he'd seen that about her before she had.

It was okay. She was fine. Later tonight she'd do the porch thing, and get mired in the past, if that was what her fucked-up brain wanted to do. Right now she was going to go see the women who were her chosen family, kick some good-looking ass, and enjoy her evening.

She left her truck and headed into Club Progeny. Though it was busy in the foyer area, she didn't have to push through the milling people. They saw her and moved out of her way. As they did, she noted the banner for the upcoming Ladies-in-Charge Night. Earlier this evening, management had hosted a formal presentation about it, put on by a contract planner they'd hired to set up and run the event. Vera had said she'd attend, so Cyn had passed. She dealt with enough meetings at work. She didn't sign up for one on her off time.

She'd go to the event, though. A Dommes-only party, with whatever male and female subs the Mistresses approved as guests, would be worth attending. She'd need to decide who to approve as her plus one. Or two, because she often preferred two full sessions on the same night.

The public stations were already in use. Mistress Doris had a sub strapped to a web. The big man with a thick beard wore a filmy negligee she'd pinned up, revealing a way too small pair of lacy panties on his masculine butt. His erection thrust out the top in the front. Doris was scolding him for such unladylike behavior.

Humiliation through feminization wasn't Cyn's kink, but when Doris hit his upper thighs with a paddle, making him grunt, sensation rushed through her own thighs and her pulse increased.

Yeah, she was ready for Sy. She was glad she hadn't left. Giving in to her weaker impulses was never the right choice.

As she reached the steps to the VIP lounge, Led Zeppelin's "Immigrant Song" burst out of the speakers.

She flashed the DJ an appreciative look, and Tardis pointed a gun finger at her, turning it to a thumbs up. She let the rhythm take her up the stairs. The ladies were in their usual booth, but the first person she saw was Sy.

He sat with three other men, but he'd been watching for her. His golden-brown eyes sparked with anticipation, but he wouldn't come to her until she was ready.

He looked damn good. A double-wrapped studded belt hung low on his jean-clad hips, and he was shirtless. His dreadlocks rested against broad shoulders and a muscled back. Over the tribal tats circling his right biceps was an inked invitation. *Baby, Let Me Be Your Demon.*

Though the club lighting didn't make it obvious, she noted the faint teeth marks above and below the text. She'd put them there during their last session.

If a sub considered bloodplay a hard limit, she was definitely the wrong Domme for him.

Sy had a diamond stud in one nostril. Beneath the jeans, he sported a barbell ladder and Prince Albert ring in his cock. Electricity applied to the jewelry was something he dreaded and craved. His strong face would crease with the effort to bear as many shocks as she wished to inflict upon him. Which was always more than she actually did, because he would beg for mercy, using his safeword, before she reached her own threshold.

Which was fine. A sub had to have that capability for her to consent to a session with him. When he wanted irreparable damage, the temptation to give it to him was too great, the effort to pull back too unbalancing. Having to make the call herself to protect him pulled her out of her Domme-space and made her cranky. So a sub who fucked up like that didn't get more than one chance with her.

Sy had been a regular for a while, and they provided one another a good time. Which didn't match most people's definition of a good time, but it worked for them.

He was playful and had a mouth on him. He never let a little pain—or a lot—stand in the way of using it. Those beautiful upper body muscles were honed by being a talented drummer, doing gigs on Bourbon Street and in the Frenchmen Street clubs. He'd also served some time for assault, bar brawls getting out of hand. He didn't take shit from anyone and he liked a fight.

He was absolutely her type of sub. Their session was scheduled forty-five minutes from now, so she'd let things build while she caught up with the others.

The booth inhabited by Ros, Abby, Vera and Skye had a good view of the dance floor and the public play stations. Acoustic tiles buffered the VIP area, so conversations didn't have to be yelled over the music.

Rosalinda Thomas was her boss, CEO and co-founder of Thomas Rose Associates, a successful boutique marketing firm that attracted clients worldwide. Abby was CFO and the other founder. Skye did tech and communications, and Vera handled HR and legal matters. Cyn was VP of accounts.

The five of them made up the company's executive team who, with TRA's nearly fifty employees, kept the successes coming and the waiting list for their services expanding.

The women were also all Dommes. Anyone who knew this world would look at them and recognize it.

Cyn slid into the booth next to Vera. The HR exec wore a vintage plum purple suit, the fitted skirt above the knee. Perched on her head was a pill box hat with a half-veil. A double strand of pearls, matching earrings and crocheted lace gloves completed the look. She looked like a black woman prepared to go to church—in the 1930s.

She'd recently let her fade grow out, so her black hair was curly and thick around her face, and fell to her shoulder blades. A half dozen silver rings lined the shell of one ear.

Cyn checked out her shoes, purple and white checkered pumps. She wore seamed stockings.

"How many hours did all that take?" Cyn asked.

"When dressing well is a habit, it doesn't take long," Vera sniffed. "Though having twenty versions of the same outfit makes it pretty quick, too."

She angled a pointed glance at Cyn's silver lace nylon tank that clung to her fit upper body, and black slacks over square-heeled boots. The right boot had an anklet that looked like a pronged choke collar—it was. The boot toes had silver tips.

"Careful, Vera," Ros said, amused. "She looks in a biting mood."

"Some serial killers bite," Vera responded.

"Which is why I never tell you bitches what I do when I'm not here or at work." Cyn signaled the waitress and the woman acknowledged with a thumbs up. She knew Cyn's preferred drink. "No accessories after the fact."

"She's always looking out for us." Abby's catlike eyes twinkled. Her Hollywood starlet beauty—red hair, hourglass body—was a contrast to her head for numbers, which belonged on the neck of a pasty accountant type.

Cyn made a face at her. "So how was the presentation?"

"There was a slide show. With very stimulating graphics."

With a wicked grin, Skye signed the first statement, using the voice software on her phone for the rest. No one at TRA considered it ironic that a woman who was mute was their tech and communications guru. Skye whimsically traded out celebrity voices on the digital method. She also had a throaty Southern female voice she considered "hers."

Her looks leaned toward computer hacker sexy. She had a moon-shaped face, and her spiky blond hair, cut short on one side, a straight silky fall on the other, framed sharp dark eyes. She wasn't fat, but she liked spending time in front of her screens, so her curves had a lush softness.

They'd all learned how to sign with her. When she tag-teamed subs with the other women, it was a useful way of communicating without tipping the submissive off, if they didn't want him in the loop.

"Some of the public sessions they're planning are heavier on the pain side," Ros added. "Mick, the event coordinator, recruits his planning team and volunteers from the membership. I suggested he get your thoughts."

Cyn frowned. "I'm busy."

"You can talk to him later this week. There's time." Ros lifted a brow. "I thought you'd want to contribute, since you gave that guest presenter on Sadism such a hard time."

"She said you should stop a session when the sub starts to cry." Cyn rolled her eyes. "For some subs, the session doesn't really begin until there are tears."

"Psychopath," Vera said pleasantly. "You'll want to talk to him. He's nice to look at."

"A sunset is nice to look at. It's function that makes a man worth the time. Dom, sub or switch?"

"We couldn't tell." Abby rotated her glass of non-alcoholic mango juice, drawing patterns on it with wet fingertips. A toothpick speared through three blackberries served as a garnish.

Cyn lifted a brow. It was rare this group couldn't recognize a person's power exchange preference.

"The information wasn't offered." Ros's blue eyes gleamed with speculation. Those eyes could make a man lose his train of thought or turn his balls to ice, depending on her mood toward him. Her intimidating professional demeanor, the successful CEO who'd come to New Orleans from the New York corporate world, only added to it.

She also adored shoes. Her shoe closet was a bigger investment than her Garden District home. Cyn might tease her about it, but damn, the bitch wore some great ones. Tonight's were pointed-toe slingback stilettos, with color blocked ivory and black squares that matched her snug black skirt and ivory blouse. Her white-blond hair with dark tips curled up at the shoulders.

"Mick's organized BDSM events in multiple states and apparently does an outstanding job everywhere he goes," Vera put in. "I asked the hostess if he had listed a play designation, and she said no."

"The female subs who wanted to volunteer surrounded him like a flock of birds," Skye said, still using her digital voice. "He was very attentive and gentle with them, like a nurturing Dom, though he didn't take it past a certain line. When speaking to Mistresses, he was respectful, in that way that catches our attention. But no overtures accepted."

"How was he with male Doms?" Cyn asked.

"Total hetero vibe, like beer drinking buddies," Ros said. "Not into men."

"How did they feel about him?" Cyn dipped her head toward Sy. Or, more specifically, the men with him.

Skye *had* tag-teamed subs with the other women, but no more. She, Ros and Abby all had men they called their own now, and they sat with Sy at the nearby table.

Lawrence, a former Navy SEAL, had started off as Ros's hired bodyguard when Cyn's boss pissed off a local gang lieutenant. From the first, the rest could see where it was headed between the two of them. Lawrence was a loving and protective service sub.

Neil was Abby's husband. He had served with Lawrence, but was still an active SEAL. Like Abby, Neil was a Dominant, something that mystified Cyn, but it worked for them. Maybe because of the additional variables that schizophrenia threw into the mix.

Around the time she and Neil had met, Abby had been diagnosed with late onset schizophrenia. What she'd dreaded all her life had morphed into a tough challenge she managed daily with their help. It hadn't decimated the math part of her brain, though she worked from home part-time.

31

Tiger, Skye's man, was a six foot plus biker who ran a successful area garage. Once a member of a one-percenter motorcycle gang, he'd left it behind with difficulty to live a legit life. Cyn understood the cost and effort of that, though she'd never let him know.

She didn't talk about her past.

Her question about the men's opinion of Mick had put a frown on Ros's face, the first flag in the amiable evaluation. "Lawrence and Neil thought something was off about him. Tiger said it more bluntly." She glanced at Skye.

Skye could use her software to modulate the moods she expressed with the digital voices. What came forth now was a more serious tone. "He got cop *and* criminal vibes from him. Equally strong.'"

Some Dom, some sub. Some cop, some criminal. Eluding definition by some of the sharpest people Cyn knew, with the best instincts. No wonder they were intrigued. Since she and Vera were in a position to enjoy him if he did like a Mistress's hand, he bore closer scrutiny, though the odds were on Vera's side. Cyn's demands were more than most male subs were seeking.

"You said he's nice to look at. Give me those details, since we're clueless about the chocolatey center."

Female eyes lit up. "Good body," Vera confirmed. "About six feet, broad in the shoulders and chest, though not as big as Tiger."

"No one is as big as Tiger."

Skye grinned at that.

"*Nice* ass and thighs," Vera continued, with an expressive eye roll. "Blue eyes, dark hair. Dressed business casual, black slacks, blue shirt. Chest hair, thank Goddess."

Cyn arched a brow. "How did the package look?"

"Noticeable and nice," confirmed the HR manager primly.

32

When Ros shook her head in mock reproof, Cyn scoffed. "Oh, like you bitches didn't notice. Having your own man candy doesn't make you blind."

Abby offered one of the blackberries to Ros. "Agreed. I'm married, not dead. Curious scar."

To show Cyn the location, Skye put her fingers up to her collar bone and moved them in a diagonal line to the top of her breast. "Neil said it looked like it was made with a serrated knife," Abby said.

Or glass. Cyn saw it in her mind, the shard ripping across flesh. The term, "someone walked across my grave," was a little literal in this case.

No. Today's date was fucking with her head. He'd been a Jersey cop, not a roving kink party planner.

A cop who'd done something no cop with any intentions of having a long career in law enforcement would have done.

"His necklace reminded me of that jewelry artist you like, Cyn," Ros said. "He must have already been browsing at the French Market."

Shit. Don't ask. Don't ask. "What did it look like?" The words were a cavernous echo in her head.

"Skeleton on a silver cross," Vera noted. "Not a crucifix. The skeleton is hugging the cross."

Andra Day's "Rise Up" was playing. Tardis had some fucking bizarre timing. It was getting hard to breathe, just like the lyrics said. Unfortunately, she had sharp-eyed friends.

"Cyn?" Vera ventured.

"I want to loosen up on the dance floor. I've got a session with Sy." She pushed the expresso shot the waitress had brought her to Vera. "All yours."

"Only if I want to be up all night." Vera passed it to Skye. "Here. You don't sleep, just like her."

"I do when I have the right sleep aid." Skye signed the response, sending a fond glance toward Tiger. Though he wasn't close enough to hear the conversation, the look was enough to capture his attention. His lips tipped in a half-smile, all for her.

Ros was still focused on Cyn. "Do you know Mick?"

"I might have crossed paths with him. But if it's him, it was years ago. So no. I don't know him."

He'd been defined by what he'd done for her that night. Ten years gave her nothing about him now. One thing she was certain hadn't changed, though, because that kind of thing didn't.

He liked pain at a woman's hand.

She still remembered the steel erection, the look on his face, when she'd said it straight out.

"You liked the pain."

"You liked giving it."

"What would you have done if you'd won the fight?"

"Whatever you wanted."

"I don't know who he is now," she repeated.

As she left them, the women exchanged glances. "If it is him, he made an impression," Ros mused. "She doesn't like to talk about her past. She's only given us snapshots from her life in Jersey."

Abby took a sip of her mango drink. "So was he part of the darkness, or was he a light?"

Vera gazed at Cyn's retreating back. "Maybe both."

Cyn took Sy with her to the dance floor. She liked rubbing against him, not letting him use his hands, but allowing him to prove how creatively he could convey his desires without an obvious bump and grind. He was a very good dancer, and she liked that, too, watching his muscles ripple and flow, and his graceful footwork. Because she could touch him as much as *she* wished, she slid her hands over him. Cupped, curved, dug in.

When her nails scraped his collar bone and followed the same diagonal track as Skye's finger, she recalled how often she'd lain in bed, tracing that route on her flesh. She'd fantasized about putting her teeth on the cop's collar bone, on each inch of the cut, tasting the mark she'd left upon him.

She'd move down from there, biting the sensitive area around the nipple, making him gasp and steel himself against the pain. Or lean into it. She'd have his hands bound above him, body stretched out for her, nowhere to hide or retreat.

It was time. She spoke into Sy's ear, so he could hear her over the music. "Wait for me in the room. Strip and assume the position I prefer. I'll be there when I'm tired of dancing."

He nodded and backed away from her. His jaw was tight with anticipation. His cock was already hard, evident against his jeans. It would only get harder as he knelt in the room, waiting for her to arrive.

She twisted, turned, beat out the rhythm with feet and the rocking urgency of her body. Her desires rose with the music, becoming more urgent.

"Be Mean" by Joe Jonas. A club favorite. When the whip popped in the song, the dancers liked to jerk, as if feeling the sting. Then they'd laugh and dance some more.

Eyes were on her, nothing special about that. Everyone indulged the visual human feast Progeny provided. Unless a Master or Mistress ordered a submissive not to look.

Would the cop obey such a command? Over the years, as she'd embraced her Domme core, she'd considered that question. The mixed Dom, sub or switch signals the women had felt from Mick had been present back then as well. But he'd definitely hungered for what all beasts craved. Sustenance, and the freedom to embrace savage instincts. He'd looked at her like she could provide those things.

But he hadn't taken them. Or asked for them.

Oh hell, she was full of shit. Strip away the embellishments the years manufactured, and it was simple. A cop had helped a kid, too mired in rage and grief to know how close she'd been to the point of no return.

After she'd been in New Orleans a few months and found work in a used car dealership, she'd been earning enough for an impulse purchase. She'd bought the skeleton necklace off of the French Market artist. On one of her rare weekends off, she'd gotten into her car and driven eighteen hours to Jersey. Straight to the cemetery.

Cissy's grave had still been tended, no weeds. More smooth stones had been added around it. Seeing that had made her skin prickle, and her chest get tight.

She told Cissy she'd found a place so very different from where they'd been born and raised. And promised that one day, when Cyn could afford it, Cissy would join her there.

Then Cyn tucked the necklace under the stones, leaving a bit of the chain visible. If it was ever noticed, it would be stolen. But if the cop found it, she intended it as a simple message. *You gave me a different world. Thank you.*

She'd returned to her car and headed back toward New Orleans. She was at the cemetery less than thirty minutes.

A few years after she started working with Ros, Cyn went back to Jersey again and had her half-sister's remains exhumed. She was here now, at Metairie Cemetery. The crypt was a small one, but clean and neat, with a sleeping lamb statue on top. There was room for Cyn to join her, whenever Fate said her time was up.

She'd stood by the grave during the exhumation, not wanting Cissy to be afraid. On that visit, she'd noted the stones had been scattered, and the weeds were overgrown again. No cross. Some wino was wearing it, or had traded it for liquor.

She told herself that was okay, because she was taking Cissy to a world of sunshine, music, dancing, good food, and people who spoke in lazy drawls.

And that was the end of that.

Except now he might be here. This was what Fate did. Its motives were its own, and it used wishes for target practice.

It also apparently threw people into each other's path just to see what entertaining fuck-ups would result.

No. This was beyond even the normal crazy shit Fate pulled out of its ass. That jewelry artist made bunches of necklaces, and other people had scars on their chests.

In that exact spot, on that same diagonal track.

Yeah, right.

When she reached the corridor to the private rooms, Cyn took a breath. Most of the action was on the main floor, or already behind sound-buffered closed doors, so she was alone. She listened to muffled thumps, a short note that might be a yelp. A deeper hum could be moaning. The sharp tap was a whip crack.

Some occupied rooms were silent. The play might be about holding it in, letting the energy build under pressure.

A footfall, a disruption of the air behind her, told her someone had entered the hallway. And stopped.

Perhaps it was a sub, recognizing her as a Domme and respectfully waiting until she advanced to the room she'd reserved. But no. As the silence built, that prickling feeling scraped her skin like a vampire glove.

It was him.

She knew it, the way she knew his gaze had been among those she'd felt on the dance floor, a different weight to his regard. A connection that could be felt in a crowded room after ten years of separation.

He'd bled for her. She'd tasted him.

"You filled out good, Mistress. Still lean, but not so many sharp angles. No longer sparking like a frayed wire."

She'd played his voice in her memory countless times. It was more gravelly, but it had the same sure authority, a man who asserted, confirmed, reassured.

But not one who commanded or ordered. Those words didn't come to her mind when she thought of him, though she'd felt his resolve, his determination to see done what he believed should be done. Boundaries hadn't been what mattered to him.

If she turned, would she see that he'd filled out too, become more solid, stronger? He'd looked in his mid-twenties when they met. *Pretty enough for you?*

She didn't turn. If she saw him, she couldn't do a session with Sy, and she needed to do that. In a flood, a smart woman didn't let go of what kept her above water. The session with Sy would provide that.

She felt him move a step closer. As a kid, when she'd ridden the school bus and someone sat down next to her, she'd feel the compressed space between them. She'd stare harder through the dirty window, ignoring how close they were, avoiding conversation or connection.

A hand touched her waist. She had her arm wrapped over her stomach, so his fingertips overlapped hers. No man touched her without permission. Particularly not here. The jolt that passed through her suggested she was still that frayed wire.

"Touch without express consent is against club rules," she said. "If I report you, you get suspension, at the very least."

"By the thumbs, ankles or my dick?"

Her lips pressed against an unexpected smile. She remembered that dry humor. But it was important to keep the past in the past. That night, enshrined in memory, was everything she needed it to be. Nothing else could match it, or be as special. She refused to tarnish it.

She didn't turn around, but she tilted her head in his direction without capturing him in her gaze. "I have a session," she said.

His breath fluttered against the side of her neck. "I'll wait for you, Mistress. As long as it takes."

She walked away.

Well, goddamn. Mick watched her go, with hip action a mermaid would envy and the don't-fuck-with-me attitude of a mob boss.

When Rosalinda Thomas had said he should talk to one of Progeny's sexual sadists, Cynbad Marigold, a shiver had dragged up his spine like female fingernails.

Until he'd left Jersey himself, he'd tended Cissy's grave. Cissy Marigold. It hadn't been hard to find her sister's name. Cynbad "Cyn" Marigold. She had a sheet, but not as extensive as he'd expected. One offense. Stealing, age eleven. She'd taken off from a mini-mart with some groceries, including baby formula.

In the desk sergeant's notes, a handicapped older sister—mildly mentally impaired and with an underdeveloped arm, half the size of the other—had come to get her. Cissy. She'd brought the store's owner with her. Maybe because of that and Cyn's age, and the precinct having way bigger crimes to handle, Cyn had been released.

Nothing else after that. And nothing after the night Mick met her, confirming his hope she'd left the area.

He'd never expected to cross paths with her again. He'd contented himself with the potential and possibilities of her happily-ever-after. With what he'd done with his life since then, it was better to leave it that way.

But seeing her again? She'd surpassed his best fantasies.

When he came up behind her in the hallway, he had his first close look, though he'd caught tempting glimpses of her on the dance floor, winding among the sensual sea of humanity. Pressing up against a man who made Mick's hackles rise in territorial reaction.

She wore black slacks and a snug silver lace tank with a mesh back. Black bra. He bet during a session she stripped it off, letting the tight points press against the lace. A sub would be tempted to look without permission, giving her a reason to swoop in and tear him a new one.

When he'd patted her down in her loose jeans, she'd had a narrow ass. It was still narrow, but the cheeks had rounded and looked damn good. Two nice handfuls for a man with palms his size.

Her dark brown hair now shone, the abundant curls falling to her shoulders in artful disarray. He couldn't see the gang tattoo, but he wouldn't be surprised if she'd had it removed, no trace left other than some subtle pigment difference. A person would have to know about it to realize anything had been there. Had the scar on her stomach faded as she'd said it would?

When she'd tilted her head in his direction, he'd seen a flash of a brown eye through the strands of those curls, and a pert, fox-shaped face. He remembered her feral look. Seeing a hint of it still there made his body hot and tight. He wanted to go after her, get on the hunt.

And goddamn, she still used baby shampoo. Or something that smelled an awful lot like it.

If she'd grown up soft and girly, he wouldn't feel so gut punched. But everything he'd imagined her becoming, shaped by his own selfish desires and needs, she'd become.

She looked like she could give a man the fight of his life.

The room she disappeared into was private, no viewing window. He couldn't watch, couldn't see the kind of Domme she was. Fuck, he didn't really need to, did he? His throbbing dick already knew.

She hadn't turned around. He wanted her to see him. Look at him. Before the night was over, he was going to make sure she did.

Then he'd know what to do next.

CHAPTER FOUR

Since her preferred submissives were hardcore masochists, Cyn could be in a bitch of a mood. It made the session more of what they both wanted. She could feed off the man's willingness to take it, to please her, and bring herself balance again.

As she pursued all the things she'd anticipated doing to Sy, like any good session, it expanded into even more. When it was done, he was quiet and hazy, the smart mouth conquered like his body had been.

She sat in a chair, him on the floor next to her, leaning against her leg because she'd decided to allow that. She wanted hard male flesh against her strumming nerves. She hadn't given Sy the privilege of her orgasm tonight.

She'd dropped a damp towel on his thigh and put a bottle of water next to him, as well as a small cooler. She watched him clean himself with still trembling fingers.

If she did a session with someone who needed more touchy-feely aftercare, she had backup Mistresses willing to do that. Before Tiger, Skye had been her go-to, since she liked cuddling. Now Vera handled it, if she wasn't otherwise occupied. If she was, there were staff subs Cyn trusted for the task.

To the unaware, it might not make sense, the type of sub who wanted the meanest Domme for his session, but craved aftercare in the opposite direction. But if a person tried to make sense of everything that drove people to be what they were, that shit would make them crazy.

The point wasn't figuring out why; it was accepting it and determining which man's interests best matched her own. If he challenged Cyn how she desired during a session, did his job and satisfied her, she'd ensure he had what he needed, too.

Sy and she were a good fit, even on the aftercare. No Vera required.

Cyn nodded to the cooler. "Open that."

The cantankerous metal flip latch required mental and physical coordination. When he managed it in seven seconds, it told her where he was in the grounding process.

Inside were two beers. He held one to his forehead, cool glass against sweating flesh. Taking it from him, she rolled it between his shoulder blades, enjoying his body's quiver.

"Tell me you're okay, Sy."

"Yes, ma'am."

She gave it back to him. "Drink some more water, then open the beer and take three swallows."

The first beer told him she was pleased with his service. The second would signal she was cutting him loose.

After a good session, she liked to go for a drive. The later, the better. New Orleans was an all-night city. She'd cruise the streets, watching the more adventurous tourists around Jackson Square. Roll near Frenchmen Street, hearing live music still spilling out of the dives. Though she'd have to circle around Bourbon, since vehicle traffic was blocked off from the street each night, she could still come close enough to inhale that funk of bodies, stale alcohol, urine and vomit. The music and glittering lights couldn't conceal it, but they didn't really try. It was part of the charm.

She'd circle back to the riverfront, pass the Aquarium and Harrah's, and roll into the warehouse district. Mardi Gras World's big complex was here, where the artists stored and worked on next year's floats. Not far from it was Skye's loft apartment. She and Tiger typically stayed there during work nights, and out at his place on the weekends. The multi-acre property had a barn and a test track. He'd turned the barn into a home garage for his motorcycle collection and to indulge his passion for chopper work. The track let him test the results.

Skye had bought herself a sweet little Harley, though plenty of times when she and Tiger rode the backroads, she preferred riding on Tiger's big muscle bike, her hands resting against his denim clad hips or broad shoulders.

Cyn stuck to loops through the city. Being city-born, rural spaces made her uneasy. A mugger coming at her with a knife or gun, fine. Such things were part of her world. Dealing with furry night creatures, eyes shining through the trees? No thank you.

She was cool with places like Audubon Park, though. Or cemeteries. New Orleans had a lot of good ones, a different kind of forest with their mazes of old crypts, and she knew how to get into them at night.

When Sy could stand and was dressed, she bid him good night and gave him the second beer. Weariness showed in the set of his shoulders and mouth. As she trailed her fingers over the fresh bite over his tattoo, he pressed his drummer's callused hand over hers.

In that touch, there was appreciation, and an acceptance of who and what they were. Not just Domme and sub but friends, in a hard-to-describe way. Explanations were a dead-end road. Shit didn't have to make sense to be right.

He'd rest well tonight, his demons temporarily at rest.

As they left the room, he headed toward the locker area. She studied his gait, his awareness of his surroundings, her last check to make sure he was ok. She didn't note any flags.

Her sessions took two hours or more. She thought about returning to the lounge. Ros and Skye might be in private rooms with Lawrence and Tiger, but Abby and Neil would have headed for home. Whatever sexual energy they gathered at Progeny would be exercised in a more controlled environment.

After she hooked up with a sub for some play, Vera might come back to the lounge for the same reason Cyn did—to see who was around. But Cyn wasn't in the mood.

"Want to take a ride?"

Her heart thudded once against her ribs, hard. He was still here. From the sound of his voice, he was further down the hall, probably sitting in one of the chairs left along the corridor. A place for a Master or Mistress to sit if he or she decided to step out of a session. Cyn had done that plenty of times, an act of detachment while her sub quivered with overwhelming need behind the door, her absence driving up his anticipation of what she'd do next.

If she had clothespins on a sub's balls or nipples, or ginger root up his ass, he'd have no cues on how long he'd have to endure it. Would she leave those things in place too long, or be out of range to hear his discomfort escalate?

Neither of those things was ever true. But why deny herself the pleasure of the mindfuck, listening to and feeling the desperation and worry coming through the wall?

He'd said he'd wait for her. Had he been here all this time?

"You going to look at me?" Humor gripped his voice. "I'm still pretty enough, though less pretty than I was. Sorry to say, no uniform. If you liked that kind of thing."

In her memory, he'd been hers. Her response to him now wanted to translate that ownership to the here and now. Which could be bad for both of them, because her feelings toward him dwelled in the realm of her most brutal instincts.

The dotted line in the middle of the road was a suggestion they all agreed meant something. Until they didn't. It still existed inside her, that person who would pick up a broken bottle and lash out, damn the consequences.

She pivoted, suppressing the strange impulse to shut her eyes then open them, like a birthday girl prepping for a special surprise. Which she had zero experience with, except through indifferent attention to TV sitcoms.

He had a beard now. Dark, like his hair, though the light made a few strands glimmer. In the cemetery, she hadn't been able to pin down his eye color, but Vera had confirmed blue. In this light, it was the bluish cast of steel. In sunlight, it might lighten to the color of faded jeans that held a man's ass just right.

44

She moved away from his face, not ready to take in all the details there. His dress shirt enhanced his eye color, and the fabric stretched to show his well-defined chest and shoulders. Sleeves crisply folded back from his forearms. The cuffs of the black slacks brushed laced oxfords, but she noted the polished footwear had thick rubber treads, not hard soles.

Though he'd stood up, he was beside two facing chairs, as if he'd pulled one over to brace a foot on it. She pictured him leaning back, relaxed, scrolling through his phone while waiting for her. Or studying the ceiling, using the flat expanse to project reflections on the past, present and future.

She marked the length of thigh, straight hip, the hold of the slacks around the groin. Fit men looked so damn good with a belt cinching their waist. As her eyes traveled back up, she wanted to see two things.

Since the shirt was open two buttons, the first was available to her gaze. The cross with the skeleton hugging it, resting at the valley between his collar bones.

The significance of him finding it, that he'd tended and visited Cissy's grave, that he knew she'd left it for him, was now undeniable.

"You know that's grave robbing."

"You left it as a message for her. But you wanted me to find it."

Her five-seven height and three-inch boot heels closed the gap to his six feet, but he *was* bigger and stronger-looking. He should have seemed smaller without all his cop trappings, the uniform and gun belt.

He was tracking her, every step, every movement. She was being consumed by all his available senses. If it was clear what he was, what he wanted from her, she'd have told him to lower his gaze, denied him the thorough perusal. But this was the best part, figuring out what he most wanted, what he dreaded but needed at the same time.

45

His face had more lines, like he spent a lot of time outside, and he was in fighting shape. The angle of the hip, hands loose at his sides, showed he was prepared for whatever came at him.

Except maybe her.

Instead of walking toward a chapter in her past, she felt like they were picking up the story right where it had left off. As she drew closer, she saw the scar. It had the sheen old wounds did, the pinkish tinge at the borders, the deep color at the main seam.

Though rage had driven the act, the result was she'd left her mark on him. A personal mark. She wanted to see it, touch it, put her teeth to it like she had in her fantasies.

"What did he give you?" He'd tilted his head toward the room she'd left.

"What you can't."

The shape of his mouth didn't change at the deliberate taunt, his voice remaining even. "Was it what you wanted?"

"For tonight. For this moment."

"Good."

She put her fingers on his chest, over his shirt, feeling the man beneath. The scar. "I've heard touching without permission is a reportable offense," he said.

"If you didn't arrest me when I did this to you, you won't file some weak-assed complaint for a simple touch." Her gaze flicked up. "And if you say something stupid, like I was just a kid then and you gave me a pass, I'll walk away. After I punch you in the nuts."

"No touch from you is simple, Mistress."

The skeleton and cross brushed her knuckles. He hadn't moved, absolutely still under her hand. That an important message, too.

"Is Mick your actual first name?"

"Yes."

"So you're not a cop anymore."

46

"I left that not long after we met. Didn't seem to be the best fit for me."

"But party planning was?" She withdrew her hand and stepped back. Not far.

Mick slid one hand into his slacks. "I do security-related jobs for a friend. Kink events integrate well with them."

When he glanced down, drawing her attention there, he was offering her what he'd removed from his pocket, one of the yarn voodoo dolls sold at the tourist traps. She had a blue bow in her hair, and was clasping a skateboard.

"While you were in session, I remembered seeing this at the souvenir shop near Harrah's. Figured I had time to get it."

He knew what today was. Of course he did. If he'd tended Cissy's grave, he'd looked at her date of death often enough. Her heart started thudding against her rib cage again, a prisoner beating fists against the bars, demanding supper. Too hungry to be wise.

"I don't wallow in the past." Her sharpness was defensive. It annoyed her.

"I get that." He continued to hold it out.

She couldn't explain how his understanding pushed past her safeguards. Any more than she could explain how she accepted the gesture of comfort she wouldn't have accepted from anyone else.

She took the gift, her nails scraping his palm, his open fingers. The doll had a crooked smile, crooked eyes. Whimsical and sweet, with a touch of the macabre.

"Want to take a ride?" he asked again.

She met his gaze. Hell, those blue eyes packed a punch. "Where are we going?"

"I have a spot in mind you might like." His gaze pointedly tracked the path Sy had taken. "If you're not too tired."

"Sleep is a sign of weakness."

"Or a basic physical requirement to function. And live. Like food and water. Damn, woman. You look good."

47

"Tell me something I don't know."

He bent forward and inhaled, making her blink. "I like your shampoo."

She chuckled. "Yes. I'll take a ride with you."

"Great." He tilted his head toward the closest exit.

As they moved toward it, he fell in just behind her in that way men did, usually to put a hand to the small of a woman's back. He didn't, but his proximity made it feel like he did. She didn't normally appreciate protective gestures, but feeling him that close wasn't offensive to her.

Under the light outside the door, she sent Vera a quick text. *Good session with Sy, bailing for one of my drives. See you at the office.*

Mick had stopped at her shoulder, and read the screen. After she hit *send,* he plucked the phone from her hand and pocketed it.

"So no one knows you're with me. Or expects you to show up until tomorrow." He showed teeth, like a wolf. "Which means I can take you where I want, do what I want."

He put it out there as they stood in view of a busy parking lot, both aware she could blow him off and go back in.

His energy told her he was initiating a scene, here and now. No safe words, no pre-agreed structure, nothing guiding them but the past and the strength of their desires.

She locked gazes with him. "You could try. Anyone know where *you* are, or expecting you to show up somewhere anytime soon?"

"No."

"So if I leave your corpse wherever you're taking me, I have time to develop my alibi."

An attractive curve came to his mouth, but it didn't dilute what was in his gaze. "I've dreamed of hunting you for ten years, Mistress. Fighting you again, overpowering you. Does that scare you? Losing control?"

He wasn't taunting her in that passive aggressive way some men did. *"You have to have all the control because you're afraid of a real man."* Male Doms got the same crap. *"You can't get it up for a woman who stands up for herself."* All of it bullshit. It was why they found gathering spaces like this, where they understood what it was really about.

"What's your scene now, Mick? Dom, switch, sub?"

"In a world about open boundaries, everyone always wants to classify themselves. I've done some of all of it."

She laughed. "You've perfected some evasive bullshit. Beyond fucking, what's the thing you want to do most?"

When his attention slid back over her again, she could see the amount of time he'd spent imagining her naked and wet. An intriguing shudder went through her body, and his gaze darkened.

"Primal play. As far as fucking you, I want to earn that." That dangerous light in his steady gaze grew fangs. "Did he fuck you tonight?"

"No. I fucked him." With a strap-on, while the choke collar she'd transferred from her boot to his cock dug into his erection, with the help of her grip. When she pulled it off of him and let him come into a condom, Sy had blacked out for a couple seconds. She'd roused him by trailing light fingers up and down his spine. The body woke up first, the nerves coming to life and then firing up the brain.

She didn't let herself twitch a muscle as Mick slid a finger along her jaw. "If you try to kiss me, I will bite you."

"What if I bite you first?" he asked.

He shifted his hand to her arm, clasping her firmly enough to suggest she was being brought to a vehicle, and that she'd have to fight to escape him.

Her body tightened up. With no rules, no safewords, one of them could end up seriously hurt. She'd learned to stay away from these kinds of risks, had learned to play within the boundaries, even as she flirted with them.

With Mick, she didn't have to worry about it. Because she trusted him. Which was stupid, because what she'd told the women was true. She didn't know him now. Even as she was pretty sure she did.

As she'd said. Things didn't have to make any fucking kind of sense for them to be right.

"Is that your thing?" She dragged her feet enough to increase his grip and earn a warning look. "Finding a girl to fight, and overpowering her? Or looking for one to overpower you?"

What she'd learned about watching primal play at the club told her it was normally important for the top to win. Otherwise, it wasn't much of a charge for the bottom.

But he'd just said classifying things, putting a structure to them, wasn't his thing. The unknown, the unpredictability, whetted her appetite too. Stirred her blood.

She sized up men as potential sparring opponents, even in scenarios where that wasn't likely to happen, like client meetings. It gave her some good fantasy material during the boring parts.

Mick had acquired something more, beyond police training. He had the right tension and look in his eyes, that awareness. He was capable of whatever the moment called for. Having grown up in a violent world, she recognized it. Which she suspected was why he'd set off Tiger's radar. Exactly what had he become once he'd stopped being a cop?

Security-related jobs for a friend.

Ten years could turn a man into a monster. But there was the wrong kind of monster and the right one.

"You don't look like you've gotten any more cautious," he responded. "You also look like you want a challenge outside those SSC walls."

"How 1950s of you. Telling a woman what she wants."

"It isn't offensive to tell someone water is wet."

"I'm more of a RACK girl. Risk aware, versus safe and sane. Or PRICK. Personal responsibility in consensual kink."

"Shocking. I'd never have guessed." His gaze locked with hers, pure heat exchange. "Dreams of fighting with you have gotten me harder than any sex I've had since."

A childish, nonsensical chant went through her head. *The sky and his eyes are blue; water is wet...and so are you.*

Yes, she was. His voice alone was doing it. The words were just added foreplay. "So you're no longer a virgin. That's good."

He chuckled. His fingers were tight enough on her now to leave bruises. She didn't mind. "I don't do role play," she added, notwithstanding the pseudo-kidnap scenario they were working.

"Me, neither."

"No woods."

They were moving toward the back of the parking lot, weaving around cars. "Wasn't where I had in mind. But why not?"

"Too much nature gives me the creeps."

"Okay."

They'd reached the rear of the lot, and he stopped in front of the perfect vehicle to contain a captured victim.

Mick drove a motorhome.

It was an old model, thirty feet long and sporting a few dents. The dull ivory paneling had a three toned golden stripe down the side. It looked like something out of an eighties movie. "Is this home?"

"It's where I live." He opened up the side door. As he pocketed his keys, he gestured her to precede him up the steps to the interior. Once there, the parking lot lights coming through the narrow windows positioned up high showed her a horseshoe-shaped seating area around a table. She assumed it could be lowered and covered with extra cushions to form a bed. To her right was a kitchenette and the driving area.

She moved into the aisle in front of the table so he could come in behind her. A shadowed area in the back had a sizeable bed, with storage areas above and below it.

He pulled the door shut behind him and twisted the latch. Her instincts kicked in and she spun, but the area was cramped and he knew the layout. She could fight in unfamiliar terrain, but he was too damn fast.

Plus, the sparring at Roughnecks, her preferred MMA gym, stayed too much on the civilized side these days. Knowing he was going to push them both past that had her adrenaline surging.

Déjà vu. In a blink he'd hooked her foot, taking her down to her stomach, and had one arm pulled up behind her back at a breakable angle, if she struggled too much.

"Figured you would have learned to counter that move," he noted, his voice a menacing purr.

"I thought I'd toss you a bone before I make you eat your teeth."

He grunted on a laugh, but when she tried to throw the hold, he didn't ease off. Pain sang through her shoulder. Would he release her if she pushed it, risking dislocation or a break? She didn't know which answer she preferred.

Yeah, this was going to get fucked up.

Energy was building between them, to as yet unknown proportions. "Tell me a safeword," he said. "Though I don't really give a shit."

"How about 'fuck you'?"

"Only if it means that's what you want to do next. Safeword?" He pushed, sending another shot of pain through her. She bared her teeth.

"I don't safeword, because I don't submit."

She raised her hips to grind her ass against his bent thigh and the part of his groin she could reach. She was wet clear through her panties, her nipples stiff against the friction of the floor.

She hadn't let herself come with Sy because some part of her knew she'd been waiting for this. She planned to keep waiting, letting it build. Deny them both until she was ready, because she had theories about Mick she was eager to test.

"That's as close as you'll get to my ass tonight without losing your dick," she told him. She tried another move to break his hold, but he shifted with her, countering.

"Don't bet on it." He'd eased the arm to a more comfortable position, but before she could take advantage of it, he'd produced handcuffs. He slapped one on her wrist and clicked the other end around the pole support for the adjustable table. "You try to mess up my stuff, I'll come back here and hog tie you. Sit tight until I get you where we're going. No woods, Mistress, but no one else will be around."

He had his thigh against the base of her ass, his knee pressed between her legs, a hand on her back. He moved his other hand into her hair, curling in tight. When he bent down, she snapped at him, but he stayed out of range. Her neck pulse was a rapid drumbeat, her limbs quivering.

"Get your ass behind the wheel and get us there," she told him.

He put his face to her hair and drew in a deep breath. His hand tightened on her scalp, delivering real pain and the threat of pulling out some hair, but she was tuned in to the nuances. It was part of what made being a Domme her drug of choice. Men expressed themselves physically, and the more they felt, the more their power and strength bled into it. The challenge was determining what was going through their minds, their cocks and elsewhere.

In that act, he was telling her something undeniable.

I've missed you so goddamn much. Dreamed of you.

Nothing back then had suggested a future where they moved forward together. Having them cross paths like this was exactly as it was supposed to happen. It gave it power and promise, and the two of them permission to embrace it however the hell they wanted to do so.

He shoved himself up and kicked her right leg out wider. He pinned the left to keep from getting his face mauled by the heel of her boot, and zip-tied the right ankle to the support leg of the narrow couch on the other side of the aisle. Now she couldn't push herself up or roll over.

"Didn't trust me not to mess up your shit?"

"I have a Precious Moments collection to keep safe."

He withdrew her phone from his pocket. As she watched, he started to power it off.

"Before you do that, can you text my friend Vera? Tell her I've been kidnapped by the psycho party planner in a motorhome he stole from a *Criminal Minds* set."

"I'll do that, first chance I get." He pocketed the phone again. "Comfy down there where I walk and wipe my feet?"

"Suck my dick." She lifted her hips as if offering.

His teeth flashed. "Good Demi quote."

"Show me yours."

She lost the insulting tone, turning it into the smooth burn of whiskey. She was here to play.

Her gaze moved over his thighs in the black slacks, his hips, belt flat against his trim waist. The noticeable not-flatness beneath the zipper. "I want to see how hard having a woman tied up and helpless makes you."

His blue eyes rested on hers. "You're not helpless. That's what makes me hard."

"I didn't say explain it. I said show me."

He shifted back a pace, his ass pressed against the arm of the facing couch. His feet straddled her bound ankle. He unbuckled the belt with a clink of noise, unfastened the slacks, and took the zipper down with a quiet snick. Reaching into his underwear, he cradled his cock and balls, pressing them against snug black cotton.

"Want to see actual flesh? Maybe shoved between those pretty lips?"

"If you want two inches taken off the top." She gave what he was showing her a critical look, even as her body got slicker, more restless. "Don't worry. You'll still have enough to give me a decent fuck."

"Mistress, you do know how to give a man a backhanded compliment." He removed his hand and refastened his slacks. When he buckled the belt, she imagined wrapping the strap around his wrists, making him fight the hold so hard he'd have deep red grooves when she finally freed him.

As he pivoted toward the front, she had the opportunity to bring up the booted heel of the free leg. She thumped against his upper thigh, but he'd anticipated her, shifting out of the way to grab her ankle and calf before she could hit more sensitive areas. He pinned the leg back to the floor with a heavy foot, leaned down and slapped her ass. Hard. Fucking bastard.

"Shut up and lie there." His tone was ominous, his eyes a match for it. "Think about what I'm going to do to you."

"I'm going to think about all the ways I'm going to fuck you up."

"Already there, honey."

Satisfied, she laid her head on her forearm and watched him take a seat behind the wheel. The engine started with a coughing roar, diesel kicking in, and he put it in drive.

Despite what he'd said about wiping his feet, the floor she was lying on was clean, as were her surroundings. Nothing too new, but all of it cared for. She detected a lemon scent, fragrant and light, which made her wonder if he cleaned with pure juice, rather than a chemical cleaner. Then she noticed a lemon tree with bright yellow fruit and dark green leaves tucked into an alcove between the kitchen and living area.

She went counterclockwise from there, exploring her perimeter. She saw a closet, door closed. The storage bins under the large bed in back held folded clothes. Her attention moved to the couch, where he'd leaned when he showed her his cock under straining cotton. What would he have done if she'd reinforced her order to do as she'd told him, take it out and show her? She licked her lips, anticipating that view.

Behind the clear doors of the cabinets mounted over the couch, she saw a few books. In this lighting, at this angle, she couldn't make out any titles except one. The words stamped on the spine were a reflective gold. *Huck Finn.*

Next to the books were pastel-colored knickknacks. She squinted to bring them in better focus. Fucking hell. He *did* have a Precious Moments collection. Only a few pieces, but still. She assumed they were super glued to the shelf so they wouldn't be dislodged by the vehicle's rockier movements.

In the kitchenette he had a coffee pot, with a loaf of bread and some fresh fruit stored in the cubbies.

He'd said this was where he lived, but he hadn't called it home. Beyond the one shelf of books and the out-of-place figurines, she had few hints of his history or interests. A couple file boxes stored under the table seating were marked with the labels "Taxes" and "Kink Events."

Had he fucked women here? Entertained friends? Traveled with family? It didn't feel like it.

Mick could see her in his mirror, and she noted he was keeping an eye on her. He knew to monitor someone who was bound. Because he had her rear view in the rear view, she gave him the finger and wiggled her ass at him. "Could have left me a pillow to take a nap." She raised her voice to be heard over the engine.

"I'm a gentleman. I'll stick one under your hips before I rip off your panties to fuck you."

"Not in this lifetime. Why aren't you a cop anymore?"

"I wasn't a good one."

He made another turn and the motorhome bumped over gravel, or a poorly paved lot. Her teeth clicked together from a deeper-than-expected pothole.

He shut off the engine, and the safety lights along the aisle went dark. No outside illumination came through the windows. In the resulting murk, she could barely see Mick's silhouette as he rose.

Her fingers curled in the cuffs, metal biting into her flesh.

It was like going into a Halloween haunted house. The ticket holders were funneled through dark hallways and rooms as people jumped out at them in costume. Just entertainment, no "real" risk, though the really good set ups had the right combination of sensory input and deprivation to tap into people's fears. Fear of the dark and unknown, of the violence that waited closer than they acknowledged, but the subconscious knew was always possible. Right around the corner, waiting to leap on them.

As Mick loomed over her, that prickling apprehension trickled into her chest, her mind. She was more aware of her cuffs and the zip tie holding her leg. What made it real was knowing he *was* dangerous. It wasn't an act. She could feel it from him, and not knowing what he meant by "I wasn't a good cop" only increased the uncertainty of what lay ahead.

"I've thought of doing so many things to you." The gravel in his voice raked her skin, rough and right. "Some nights, I'd hurt myself so the ache wouldn't drive me fucking insane."

She let the things she knew about him twine around the things she didn't, and steady her voice. "So are you going to take the cuffs off and make this a fair fight?"

In her head, she was hearing Evanescence's "Bring Me To Life." Eyes like open doors, inviting him right down into the darkness of her soul. What was there was coming to life.

Wake me up.

"Who says I give a shit about fair? Someone told me it's not a real fight if there are rules."

He merged into the darkness, a wide wall descending upon her. He squatted and touched her thigh, palm skating up over her ass, but a breeze would have had more weight. It was what the contact said that mattered. He could touch her however he wished. Do what he wanted.

He knew what she could do with her free left leg, but maybe he'd thought she wouldn't try it twice. Either way, he was ready. As her heel flew up, he caught her calf again. This

57

time he shoved the leg back to the ground and planted his knee on the back of hers, putting uncomfortable pressure on her kneecap, pressing it into the hard floor. Pain shot through her thigh muscles as she fought the pin. Leaning over her, he cut the zip tie on the other one. Then he removed the cuff from the table support.

She tried to buck him off, flip over. He had all the leverage in this position and cuffed her wrists behind her back, the click and rasp of her breath loud in the silence.

"Just you and me here, baby. No one to hear you scream."

She laughed. "I'd let you kill me first."

"Yeah. I remember that about you." He jerked her to her feet, grasping her by the elbow, but he didn't let her stumble or knock into anything in the enclosed space. He took her to the door, pushed it open and guided her down to the ground. His movements were swift but sure. He didn't let her fall.

They were outside the city, along a rural route. He'd parked under a bank of trees on one side of the untended lot. As he took her across the broken pavement, she saw one flickering, bug-encrusted light, shedding indifferent light on a faded sign. *Fall Maze, Lafayette High School Fundraiser.*

The date was last year. Possibly to keep the grid for future events that hadn't yet come to pass, the bales had been left in place. The maze was positioned on the rear border of a fallow corn field, the brown stalks rustling in that eerie way empty husks did, inspiring horror movies.

In the distance, she saw a square of light in a Monopoly-sized rectangle of a house. The owner of the field, she assumed. Frogs croaked, and she caught the faint whiff of marsh that infused the air almost everywhere around NOLA. The road appeared sparsely travelled at this time of night. If anyone noticed his motorhome, they'd assume a traveler headed for Florida had found a place to catch a nap.

Mick took her past the sign and into the entrance of the maze. She fell back to break his grip. He moved with her.

She tried to kick, and he used the move to yank her forward, putting her off balance. Again, he didn't let her fall. He ducked away as she spat at him and shoved her a couple steps ahead, separating them. When she spun around with the kick, he was out of range, but his expression showed admiration for her form and balance.

He removed a key from his pocket and showed it to her. "I'm going to take off the cuffs. Turn around."

She gazed at him through narrowed eyes before turning away. A different kind of stillness descended as he unlocked the metal bracelets, his fingers brushing hers. Then he stepped back.

As she pivoted, he was folding the cuffs over and tucking them in the back of his belt. A very cop-like move, even if he wasn't one anymore.

This time he hadn't put much distance between them. She could have made that kick work. He reached out and trailed his fingers down her throat, stopping at her sternum, just beneath the scoop neck of her tank. "Do you like that?" he murmured. The touch was once again lighter than air, while waking up every nerve. His fingers brushed the silk cord of her necklace, a polished jet stone carved with a rune for the goddess Freyja. A gift from Vera.

"I want to learn everything you like, every kind of touch," he said. "I've imagined so many."

When she talked about the things she liked, it was about what she was doing to the man under her control. Not the ways she wanted to be touched. She didn't let those thoughts come into her head. But she was letting him touch her.

He pushed her, shoved her, overpowered her. But backed off when it mattered. A significant combination.

"So, primal play." She stepped away and he lowered his hand. "Is this where I chase you?"

"Not how it works. You want me to chase you." His voice rumbled in the dark like an approaching engine, stroking her nerves in all the right directions, as well as a few wrong ones. "You want me to work for it, show me how difficult it will be to catch you. But I will."

That silky, menacing edge infused the words again. "When I do, you'll fight me hard and dirty. You won't go down easy. Or at all. You're nobody's bitch."

From what was vibrating off of him, she knew the clock was counting down. But eventually he'd be playing on her clock, not on his. "What do you get out of it?"

"I want a woman to fight me, fight back. I want her to do her best to kick my ass. I want her to fight with her last breath. It turns me on, feeds the beast."

She'd experienced the wrong side of what he was describing. She'd actually fought for her life. She'd experienced the right side only once, with him. A hint of the possibilities, before he'd given her a chance for a life beyond day-to-day survival.

He was offering those possibilities to her again. So she was done with questions. She backed up three steps. Adrenaline surged anew as the planes of his face altered, all the small muscles tensing. Showing readiness.

Yet, still watching her, he reached into his shirt pocket and withdrew a cigarette and lighter. The flame deepened the shadows in his steady gaze.

"What are you doing?"

"Having a smoke. When I'm done, I'm going to find you. Take you down, light up another and burn a circle on your perfect ass." The blue eyes gleamed, reminding her of Sy's tattoo. *Let Me Be Your Demon.*

"I'll sign it for you, with my knife," he added. "No holds barred, Mistress. No rules except what's inside us."

She glanced up. "No moon, but there's the dog star. Better hope he and all his buddies can help you find me."

She slipped away as he was studying the sky. She knew he purposefully kept his attention there so he wouldn't see which direction she'd chosen.

So he would have to track her.

60

CHAPTER FIVE

Mick gazed at the stars around Sirius, listening to her disappear. A quick, purposeful stride that faded.

Walking the line he lived offered him moments of perfect freedom to indulge his most basic instincts. They also taught him what a prison the most vicious ones could create. Long before the door slammed to keep him in an actual cell.

When he'd inhaled the scent of her hair in the motorhome, he'd understood the popularity of shifter fiction. Right now, given the chance to transform into a wolf and hunt her down, he'd take it. He'd like to be able to scent the air and find her fragrance from miles away.

Maybe he had. He was here, wasn't he?

He drew on the cigarette, listening like a wolf might, all senses tuned to a telltale rustle, the change of frog song, a sudden silence as she passed their way. Then the warbling started again.

With more resources, she could and would have laid traps for him. He'd chosen this place because it held few options except evasion and navigation challenges. The props the high schoolers had used to enhance the experience—scarecrows, pumpkins, a cup of hot chocolate afterward—were gone, leaving a desolate-looking place with the scratchy, sinister sounds of the corn.

He liked traveling the backroads, and had noted the locale on his way into the city, stopping to get a closer look. As he'd used his drone to scope it out from the air, finding it was about the size of a football field, he'd thought about chasing a woman through here. He hadn't realized how quickly the opportunity would present itself. Especially with one he'd imagined running to ground a million times. One capable of doing him real damage.

A lack of props wouldn't stop her from seeking out an optimal attack point. She wasn't a runner.

When she'd touched the scar she'd given him, she'd about driven him to his knees. Had she felt the ripple of nerves under her hand? He wanted her to reopen the wound, deepen it. Reach his heart and the black, trapped soul inside.

Christ, dial back the Irish melodrama, Mick.

He ground out the cigarette and pocketed the butt. He might be a lot of things, but he wasn't a litterbug. Indifference and cruelty were linked, demon twins in the womb. He'd had to embrace both qualities often enough to know how close the partnership was.

Indifference to someone else's life, their suffering, their time, their needs.

He would never be indifferent to her. Never.

He chose a path on the left, littered with a fine layer of shed straw. Most bales in the stacks were tied together and staked to keep them vertical. As the twine had broken from weather or wear, some had fallen or were more lopsided, allowing narrow views between the columns. Crushed beer cans and the occasional discarded condom suggested teens hung out here. No cigarette butts. Farm kids also knew how susceptible their surroundings were to flames. Carelessness would lose them their no-parents hangout spot.

Tonight, they were alone. He listened for another moment, a powerful-looking man with still eyes. Then he moved forward, a silent stalk.

Time to hunt.

Cyn's blood was humming, and her senses were as sharp as the knife Mick had used to cut the zip ties, in one smooth stroke. She'd been wired after the intense session with Sy, as she always was, but this gave her a new gear.

She noted the frog song, the direction and strength of the breeze. Occasional cracks between the straw bale towers gave her glimpses of other parts of the maze. The taller ones had been anchored so they couldn't be easily toppled.

When he started hunting, he would be swift, and he'd be paying attention. She needed to find an opportunity to turn the tables and put him on the defensive. The chase was the foreplay. The fight was the main event. When the hunt part was done, she wanted the upper hand.

So she paid attention to any movement in the shadows or changes in sound, ahead or behind her. She discovered a rear exit to the maze. A set of bales had been pushed out of the way, giving her access to the field behind them. She exited, deciding she would circle around and come back through the front or another access point, to give her an advantage.

But the corn field terrain wasn't tamped down the way the maze was. Uneven and muddy from recent rains, it made her rethink her plan. Knee-high foliage also grew between the maze and the cornstalks and she wasn't interested in meeting what scuttling creatures might inhabit it, any more than they'd be pleased at being stepped on.

She backtracked, pausing to listen before she slipped into the maze again. When she inhaled, her stomach flipped. A subtle trace of cigarette smoke told her he'd passed this way. She also caught the lingering scent on his clothes and skin. Bergamot, rosemary and cedar. Maybe some vanilla.

It was intriguing and arousing, the two of them circling one another in semi-darkness, but she still wanted that advantage. So she tested the rope anchoring the nearest straw bale tower and figured it would hold. Putting her feet in between each bale and using the twine holding them to haul herself up, she reached the top, eight feet from the ground. As she slid onto the surface formed by two towers, she moved slowly, trying to blend with the eerie wind and corn symphony.

She stretched out on her stomach. The expanse was flat but prickly through her shirt. Her eyes had acclimated to what little light there was, so she could make out shapes and track movement. She noted the motorhome in the distance, the dull ivory sides captured by the flickering entrance light.

She moved her gaze over the pathways enclosed by the bales. Nothing. If he thought she would seek a higher vantage point, he could be gliding close to the bales rather than walking down the center. It would make him part of the shadows.

Or he could be on top of his own set of bales, watching for her. Though he'd be heavier, those recent rains would give the bales more weight, that and the rope anchoring making it possible for him to do what she was doing.

She perused the top of every tower, the sides, taking her time, her hands folded under her cheek. There. She saw a shadow move, at a turn two corridors over. She kept her gaze pinned on him, but even after being sure she had him, he almost managed to disappear twice.

How did a man learn to move like that, a part of the night itself? A more important question: *Why* did a man learn to move like that?

Maybe he practiced for primal play. *Yeah, maybe.* But instincts for hunting and killing, developed through experience, had a different stamp than those practiced for role and game playing, no matter how seriously it was taken. Neil and Lawrence had the former kind, so she recognized them in Mick.

He was coming her way. Cyn debated her strategy, and decided she'd let him go by, so she could launch a rear attack. Her lips curved at the obvious double entendre. Here she was, without her best strap-on. Would Mick go for being fucked in the ass? It would be fun to find out, and get creative with it.

She'd said she didn't normally do role play, and he'd said the same. However, she did have a prison rape scenario that sometimes flitted through her mind. Him in his cop uniform, cuffed against the bars of the cell, fighting her, the prisoner, as she dropped his pants, and drove a nice slick dildo through his tight sphincter. Listening to him roar from the burn, threaten her, telling her just what he'd do when he got free. Hunt her down and...

So many possibilities in that *dot dot dot*.

He'd passed by, and she slid to the ground while the frogs or crickets burrowed in the bales were still silent from his presence. As he made the turn and disappeared to the left, she flattened herself against the tower, so she'd appear part of its silhouette. Peering through the crack, she waited to see him pass on that side. But not hearing his footsteps when she expected to do so alerted her.

She slowly turned her head back toward the direction he'd disappeared, and there he was. Back at the end of her alleyway. The tilt of his head and set of his shoulders suggested he was staring at the shadows that cloaked her.

She didn't move, and he started in her direction, casually. She wasn't fooled. He knew she was there. Maybe he'd scented her the way she'd scented him.

She exploded into motion, tossing a laugh over her shoulder as she ran. At the end she turned right, then, out of his sight, took another immediate right. It would bring her back on a parallel track with the alley where he'd spied her.

Because she was fast, she intended to flatten herself against the bales again before he saw her. He'd assume she'd gone left or kept running, entering another part of the maze further down.

She'd made it to her chosen spot, almost even with where she'd lain on top. Before she could take cover in the shadows, the bales exploded, their ties cut, and he came crashing through. When he caught her around the waist, they both hit the ground, but she scissored up, twisting loose.

That night long ago, he'd moved so fast. He moved faster now, but she'd learned far more about fighting since then, too. Extensively trained in MMA, she could hold her own. Plus keep it to a fight, not a death match. No need for broken bottles anymore.

They faced one another, circled. When they came together, she wondered if he felt the same electrical charge she did, like lightning dancing over Olympus when the gods battled. It *was* a dance. A series of holds, broken by pulling loose at the right angle, or using a pressure point strike, as he'd done that night, to get her to drop the bottle.

He used his size to put her in the dirt and pin her down. She hit his chin with the heel of her hand, wrestled her body free by shoving against the ground with her legs.

The primal play she'd witnessed at the club used modified moves to keep the participants from doing one another worse harm. Kicking with the flat of the foot, or dropping a closed fist like a stone against the body, rather than giving it the propulsion of a punch.

Neither of them cared about that, but she noted he still refused to hit her above the neck. She used elbows and fists to hit wherever needed to drive him back. He was good. Damn good, even holding back.

She had outstanding endurance, but so did he. Eventually he found a hold she couldn't shake, his arms banded around her just above the wrists, holding her arms pinned against her torso. He lifted her off the ground, leaning back so she could only kick at the air. All she could do was rake his thighs with her too-short nails. She thought longingly of her claw rings. Engraved and pretty, they were wicked sharp, able to puncture or tear flesh.

As she kept struggling, he began to tick off that eight second rodeo count. She made sure the description fit, fighting with all her strength, trying to kick him, knock her head into his, bite any part of him she could reach. She had the satisfaction of hearing the strain in his voice.

"One…two…three…four…"

A grunt as she slammed her boot heel into his shin. It would leave an impressive bruise. She whipped her head around in a different direction, looking for contact with the

66

bridge of his nose or an eye socket. He swung her toward the bales and straw stabbed her cheek instead.

"Christ... Five...six... Damn it..."

She pushed against the bales, hoping to shove him back, put him off balance, but instead he put her face down on the ground, landing hard on top of her, holding her fast with sheer body weight and male determination. Déjà vu again.

"Seven... Eight."

"You better not be looking to me to yield," she panted.

"No." There was an odd note to his voice. He lifted off of her and she rolled over. As he was pushing himself to a sitting position, she was already on her knees, throwing the punch toward his jaw, fast and straight.

He caught it in his fist.

For a long moment, they stayed that way, staring at one another, breath rasping. She couldn't tell which of them was trembling. She refused to believe it was her, and wasn't sure what to think if it was him.

Her heart was drumming in her chest with the exultant energy of a high school band at a homecoming game.

Yet another thing she'd never experienced. She'd tried to break herself of the habit of crafting insipid analogies out of TV and movies, rather than real life, but then she'd realized there was nothing wrong with having a rich fantasy life. Nothing at all.

Mick let her go, fingers slipping off of her white knuckles. As he rose, he offered her a hand. The stiff courtesy to it had her accepting, putting her hand in his and rising to her feet.

He let her go and stepped back. One. Two. Three. Eight steps before he stopped.

Then he dropped to one knee. "I yield, Mistress."

His face was strangely quiet, but she didn't make the mistake of assuming he was calm.

"The night we met," he said, "this was my plan. I was going to wrestle you to a stalemate, or until I won. I knew I had to win, for you to want the next step. I would yield to you, because that was what we both wanted."

A faint smile touched his lips. "I was going to ask you, 'What can I do for you? How can I make it better? How can I protect and serve?' Because I wanted to fucking help, even as I also wanted to take you down first."

He lifted a shoulder. "You weren't ready for it to go that way. But it was in my head. Nice to finally be able to share."

He was right. She hadn't consciously known she was a Domme that night, but the sexual identity had been there, roused by their interaction. It had never gone fully dormant again. Trying to figure out how to get a roof over her head and food in her belly had been a greater priority. However, by the time Ros formally introduced her to it, Cyn had a full-color catalog in her mind of things she wanted to do to a man submitting to her.

It was in that world she'd found room for herself to breathe. A new way to express her emotions, break away from what held her back. She built herself armor to help her get what she wanted, rather than a wall that prevented it.

So taking control was familiar ground. Taking control of him? That was uncharted territory.

He waited for her, on his knees, his gaze still locked on her. It made her ready to do battle. A different kind this time.

"Stand up," she said. "Hands stay at your sides."

Her shirt was ripped, so she pulled it over her head and dropped it to the ground. The Freyja pendant settled against bare skin, the stone brushing the joining point of her bra cups.

As she moved toward him, he tracked her upper body, shifts of muscle, quivers of soft flesh.

"You like my breasts, Mick?"

"I like all of you, Mistress."

She put her hand on his chest. His shirt was dirty and ripped, too, so she yanked it open, scattering buttons and exposing his chest. The scar twitched over muscle like a

68

disturbed snake. The skeleton and cross rolled to one side, then settled back flat.

"What things did you think of doing to me? Tell me something you thought I'd like."

"Hoped." His voice was deeper in the dark. "I wanted to be right, because that meant I was already inside you. You were already inside me. As if, when I was thinking about it, you were looking at me, whispering in my ear."

He leaned forward enough to do that, his breath against her cheek.

"Touch me this way.

"This is what I want.

"Do it like this."

"Don't move." His desires pressed upon her like a wall, She didn't know if her will could hold them back, which meant they were too close to what she wanted, too.

When she held the cross and skeleton, his voice rumbled through his chest, under her knuckles. "I thought about you buying that, leaving it for me. What it meant." That light smile touched his lips, creating a swirling warmth in her chest, a tightening of nipples and a dampening of her body. "Then I told myself you didn't give it that much thought. You just liked it, and left it for me and Cissy."

"Yes." She traced the scar from the starting point at his pectoral, following it up to his collarbone. His body quivered under her touch.

"Most people see that scar at my throat, and they think that's where it started. Not…"

"Over your heart."

She kept stroking the scar, noting how his muscles tightened, his attention upon her getting more intent. It was having that effect on her, too.

"Are we done with chitchat?" Whether he was or not, she was. "Take off your clothes. Everything."

When she stepped back, he unlaced and removed his oxfords first, then the thin socks. Through his naked soles, he'd feel the gravel mixed with the packed dirt.

His slacks got pushed down next, though he removed a small flashlight from the pocket and offered it to her. As he bent to remove the pants, the skeleton dangled over his furred chest, his thigh and calf muscles flexing with the movement.

To take off the boxers, he had to guide the elastic waistband out and over the head of his thick erection. She drew in the sight as he put the clothes to the side and straightened. His fingers were curled at his sides, hinting at the self-restraint he was exercising.

He'd yielded, but his primal desires hadn't abated. A lion didn't lose the desire to hunt just because he took a break to fuck a willing lioness. The two needs were wrapped together, drawn from a similar source.

He was complicated. But he'd serve her. What she felt from him simmered, a conflicting mix.

"Clasp your hands behind your back. Fingers interlaced."

She often denied a sub the right to look at her when she was studying him. But with what she had in mind, being able to look and not touch was going to be more difficult for Mick, and that was what she wanted to test.

For her part, she looked her fill, clicking on the flashlight to help her. Christ, he was beautiful. The quality cut of the clothes hadn't misled her eyes. The broad shoulders and wide chest tapered to his waist and straight hips. The velvet skin of his cock was stretched to smoothness, the head flushed. His balls looked like a weighted handful. He groomed himself but kept hair there. He also had a nice mat on his chest, narrowing to the gleaming trail past his navel. His arms and legs were dusted with dark strands.

She moved around him, taking her time. She put her fingers on his back, learning the landscape there, and dug her short nails into his neck, under his ear. His pulse accelerated under her touch. He dipped his head toward her.

70

He had an ass she wanted to mark with her teeth, all day long. The slight shift as he looked her way offered a flex of the left buttock. She imagined burning a brand into the flesh, leaving it dark and angry. Something permanent.

But she wouldn't be the first. She noted several shiny round scars. Bullet holes. A burn on the back of his thigh had left a scar the size of her hand. Leaning forward, she put her palm over it. As she did, she pushed her thumb into the seam between his buttocks, stroking.

"Spread your legs wider."

When he did, she caressed his sac and played over the perineum. She was right about that weighted handful. His buttocks quivered, and a ripple went through the burn scar. She noted other marks. Knife, maybe.

How had he turned his body into this scarred battlefield?

He'd knotted his hands at his back like she'd ordered. She noted there was more tension in the left shoulder than the right. An old injury there, she suspected.

She stepped back. "Down on your stomach. Right cheek to the ground and put your arms out to either side, fully extended. Every inch of you pressed flat."

When he did it, she knew when his cock contacted the gravel, straw and dirt, because his movements became more tentative. She straddled him and sat down on his ass with a comfortable thump. She braced one foot outside his legs, one between them, and used that booted foot to spread his legs wider, with an insistent push. She wasn't heavy, but over a hundred pounds of woman sitting on his ass put pressure where she wanted it. She heard the muttered curse.

"Do you want to know how I choose my subs, Mick?"

"I don't give a shit about your boy toys."

She chuckled. "I call it a flag test. If you stay hard through the minimum level of pain I like to inflict, then we can play. If you don't, you're not what I want."

"A pass-fail." His strained voice held a wry note.

71

"Yes. Shut up now." She removed the Freyja pendant, palming the smooth, flat stone in her hand. About the size of an egg, it had some weight to it.

It didn't take much to hurt a man's testicles. It just required access. She dropped her hand holding the pendant down between her legs, to where she could reach what was between his. "This is one of those moments when a man might wish his balls weren't as impressively big as yours."

She swung the stone by the cord and hit him where she intended. The impact made him flinch, but he held, through that contact and the dozen times that followed. She savored every shudder.

When she considered him properly sensitized, she set the stone aside and used her fingers, doing a flick against the tender area. A harder flick, then a pinch.

"Fuck…"

She settled herself more firmly on his fine ass, knowing his cock was getting up close and personal with the gravel. It probably felt like ground glass.

"Plenty of Dommes like fancy toys. I like them, too. But the most creative ways to torment a man come from what's close to hand. And my imagination."

She pushed up with a heavy thrust of her weight against his ass that won her another grunt. After tucking the Freyja pendant in her pocket, she removed her boots so she could shed her slacks, leaving her in her silky panties and bra. She pulled the boots back on.

He'd adjusted his head so he could see her. His eye flashed beneath the longer strands of hair over his brow. Sliding a finger under the edge of her panties, she tested her wetness, then brought it out to show him the glistening digit. She squatted and painted a heart on his ass cheek. Then she smacked it, not playfully. The angled strength of the blow would vibrate uncomfortably through his testicles.

"Do you have a safeword, Mick?"

"Same as yours. Fuck you." His gaze glittered. "Only reason I want you to stop what you're doing is if you're going to put my dick inside you."

"It's so sweet that you think that's a possibility."

She tucked the flashlight in her boot and slapped him with the keys again. Harder.

Ignoring his oath, she straddled his thigh, putting her knee against his abused balls and perineum. When she took a good grip of his ass cheek, she started rubbing herself against the back of his thigh, letting him feel the silk crotch of her panties whisper against him. She purred at the hard muscle against her clit, then shifted to straddle both thighs, pressing her mound against the base of the buttocks.

"Wish I had my strap-on, so I could fuck you into the gravel. But this will do for me, here and now."

She pushed against him like she would if she was fucking him, massaging her clit against the seam of his ass, knowing every thrust rubbed his cock against the unforgiving ground. His muscles stood out as he endured it, his teeth clenched.

What made it even more delicious was that he wasn't bound. He could turn over at any time, try to stop her. Come up with a safeword phrase, like "Stop that, you fucking bitch."

He wouldn't. She was as certain of it as she was that his dick was harder than the gravel. It was in the incendiary lust in his blue eyes as they kept flicking toward her. He was ready to choke and fuck her at the same time. But he remained still, a ticking bomb only she could trigger.

Oh, God…just rubbing against him, watching him take the pain, was spiraling her toward release. Her body throbbed and she wanted him inside her *now*.

She'd waited for ten years, no reason to lie to herself about it. Abruptly, she moved back to her heels and stood. "Clasp your hands behind your back, fingers interlaced."

As he obeyed, she noted the shudder. Movement from any part of his body rubbed his cock against the ground. She adjusted his knotted fingers so the knuckles were where she wanted them, pressed against his lower back.

She also retrieved the cuffs he'd had on his belt, verifying the key was still in his pocket. After she put the cuffs on him, she had another order ready.

"Roll over onto your back. Show me your cock."

"Only if you show me your cunt."

She put her booted toe against his ass and pushed, hard. It scraped him forward along the ground, and then rocked him back again as she removed the pressure. Probably no more than a half inch, which didn't sound like much, unless one considered how it felt to shove a half-inch splinter under a fingernail.

His breath whistled through his teeth. "You've gotten meaner, Mistress."

"I'll take that as a compliment. Turn over. Keep your hands the way I put them."

On his back, with his weight resting against them, the cuffs would dig into his wrists, his knuckles into the small of his back. As he awkwardly managed the roll, it was her turn to suck in a breath.

His cock had been scraped, enough that she could see the redness, plus a tiny, beaded strand of blood. But he had passed her flag test. Her whole body contracted at the size of his erection, hard and thick as one of the corn stalks, jutting up defiantly from the unforgiving earth. A true masochist.

Keeping her weight on her back foot, she slid her other one over his cock and pressed it down against his belly. Just holding it down, telling it who it answered to. Violence, blood and fire burned in his gaze. Need, in its rawest form.

She picked up his boxers, using them to wipe the dust and a few bits of gravel off his cock, giving him a healthy stroking at the same time. He didn't thrust into her hand, but the effort not to do so was visible in the quiver that passed through him, head to toe.

"You're pleasing me, Mick."

"Thanks for not saying 'good boy.' That would have pissed me off." His voice was tagged with a full-on growl. If he'd bared fangs at her, she wouldn't have been surprised.

"I don't fuck with boys." She set the boxers aside and straddled him again in the panties and bra, her boots. She had a pocket inside the boot, a place to store a condom if she was in the mood to let a sub orgasm. Or, far more rarely, if she wanted to ride him to completion. When she took out the protection now, his gaze lasered onto it.

She thought about asking if she needed to use it. She was careful enough that, if she wanted to bareback a partner, as long as he was equally safe, she could do so. But she didn't want to ask Mick. From the shadows in his gaze, she already knew the answer.

He couldn't tell her it was okay to leave it off.

It was annoying that it bothered her. She hadn't lived in chastity under some random possibility she'd meet him again. What was in his expression went beyond that, though. Whatever his reasons for having to use a condom, they deeply bugged him.

She'd look at that another time. Or not at all. He was here for a couple weeks at most. No need to get bogged down in emotional bullshit. She adjusted, bent and licked the tiny blood-speckled spot on his cock, tasting his musky heat. As she laved the abrasions with her tongue, she soothed, right before she scraped him with her teeth and made him flinch again.

"Fucking hell, Mistress…"

Breathy, almost reverent.

Binding his wrists had ballooned that raw energy inside him to a more intense level. He was a dangerous beast, but when it mattered, he was well-mannered. He didn't try to push against her lips, though she could feel the pulse throbbing in his cock. She didn't put him in her mouth, just teased him, spiraling licks around that impressively standing erection.

When he was swallowing groans and his powerful body was shaking, she rolled the condom over him, clasping the base in firm fingers. The head had been slick with precum, the shaft hot and rigid in her grip. Contracting muscles fluttered in her lower belly and cunt, her flesh soaked with need. Moving the elastic of her panties to the side, she posed just above him, his tip teased by her slick folds.

She waited to see how he would behave. He swallowed back what she had no doubt would be a direct order to fuck him. Even in his agitated state, he knew that was a mistake.

"Torture me all you want, Mistress." His voice was strained.

Her tone was frost. "Do I need your permission for that?"

He shook his head, the shoulder with the old injury twitching. That position, knuckles stabbing into his back, metal cuffs against his wrist bones with her sitting on him, would be getting progressively more uncomfortable. But torture was an endurance sport, and she had an experienced sense of what a man could suffer for her without permanent damage. "I'm here for you," he said.

The absolute right answer. She sank down on him.

It was good that she was well-lubricated. A little hum came to her lips as she took every considerable inch of him. Her head dropped back. She was in her own world, setting the pace. He was here to serve her. And he was doing a very good job.

"Mistress…" A harsh rasp, his gaze roving greedily over her face and throat, the thrust of her breast, the movement of her hips on him. "Oh, fuck…"

"You don't get to come, Mick," she purred. "This is all for me. I want you to leave this lot as hard as you are now. I want you to curse me for torturing you. I want you to be willing to do anything to be in my cunt again. Including not coming until I say you can."

"You're killing me, Mistress."

She rose and fell. Oh God, he felt so good. But she kept it together enough to answer him. "That's how it's supposed to be. Your life is in my hands, Mick. Isn't it?"

He managed a jerky nod. It was taking all his focus to obey her and not release. Any other man would have had no choice, but Mick refused to let himself disappoint her.

She didn't know how she knew that, but she did.

"You don't have my permission to die, either. Even if I do my best to kill you."

She put her hand on his upper abdomen as she rode him, leaning forward to increase the dig of the metal against his wrists, the stab of his knuckles into his lower back. She stroked, clenched, rose and fell, becoming more aggressive.

She took her time, denying herself even as she kept feeding on his frustration, relishing the tension in his bunched muscles. The climax spiraled up faster than it usually did for her, so she was having to push it down, tell herself to wait, to wait…

"You want to come, Mistress. I can feel it. Your cunt is sucking on me. Let it go. Let me see it."

His mouth tightened over a swallowed curse. He'd realized his error. Her lips curved. "Eyes shut, Mick." At his mutinous look, she stopped moving. "Or I slide off and finish this with my own hand. Behind the straw bales, where you can't see me."

His eyes closed tight, but what came from his lips was her favorite endearment.

"Yes, I am a fucking cunt. A cunt fucking you, as long as I want." She was breathless, and though his eyes were shut, the angle of his head suggested he was reaching for that sensory input, pulling it inside to keep. It felt as if he'd swelled to twice his size, the friction against her sensitive, slick tissues catching her on fire.

"Oh…" The orgasm rolled over her, arching her back, her throat, making her thigh muscles clench against his hips. A cry broke from her, the long, low sound of a woman being well-serviced by what a man could offer her.

Something even more than what she was used to, than what she allowed. Than she wanted to admit.

The waves kept coming, helped by her fascination with his incredible struggle not to come. She'd been sure he would lose that battle, but he didn't. Even during the aftermath, she kept testing it, drawing out those waves, savoring every last ripple of sensation, every tight muscle of his jaw, around his eyes, in his neck, shoulders and chest. At last, she leaned forward, and breathed on his parted lips.

"Open your eyes, Mick."

They were glazed, fierce. She pulled herself off of him, reaching down to remove the condom. As she did, she caressed his shaft, then rose, standing over him, a foot on either side of his hips.

"You have a choice now. To do without, or roll over and come by rubbing yourself against the ground."

Shock crossed his gaze. Followed by a primitive animal hunger, impossible to describe or translate, though she understood it, deep inside. It took him nearly thirty seconds to be able to speak to her in anything resembling human communication. But when he did, heat washed through her.

"What does my Mistress want?"

Another absolutely right answer. "To see you roll over and come."

He drew in an erratic breath. Had anyone ever been this cruel to him? She wanted to be the first. Needed to be the first. She wanted to believe that wonder in his eyes, the amazement that someone understood, that someone needed what he needed, in a way that didn't make it self-serving on either side, was a first-time experience.

She'd come pretty close before. She'd been lucky that way, in her choice of male subs. But she'd never had something like this. Something that reached inside her and found what this did.

He turned over. Without his hands, he was scraping his face against the dirt and gravel. He couldn't protect his cock except with the lift of his hips, which stretched his upper body and scratched his nipples against the ground. Since they'd been taut with arousal, that would hurt more, too.

She retrieved his belt and moved in front of him. When she sat down Indian style, she adjusted forward, lifting his head to place it in the triangle her thighs and crossed ankles formed. The gravel bit into her ass through the silk of the panties, but that was fine. Her own pain threshold was way above handling mere discomfort.

He would be able to smell her pussy in its post-climactic state, feel her labia pressed against the crown of his head. His mouth rested on her ankle.

It was an incentive, since what he'd endured for her was about to get even worse. A shudder went through his back, then he lifted his hips, lowered them, dug in, working himself against the ground. She leaned down to stroke her fingers through his hair. "That's not gravel," she whispered. "That's my cunt you're in, Mick. Fuck me with every ounce of strength you have. Show me what kind of man you are. How much pleasure you can give me."

He made a pained grunt, but began to thrust determinedly. If he could shovel the gravel out of the way with his cock, take the pain of that, beneath he might find the more forgiving, rain-softened earth. Still not comfortable, but it would have the kind of friction that might help him get to that release. She didn't expect he was looking for that, though. He wanted to do as she'd commanded, no tricks or cheats.

Another raw grunt tore from his throat as she doubled over the belt and struck his back. On the next strike she released one end and lashed him with the tongue, delivering a targeted sting to his flexing ass.

A masochist could come merely from imagining a Mistress inflicting this level of pain. But when enduring it, the body had different ideas. She knew when a man wasn't going to be able to get there, no matter his determination.

Offering mercy wasn't in her nature, but he'd impressed her. And if she let him damage his cock too much, it would be no good to her.

"Stop," she said.

His breath was wet and heated against her ankle, a frustrated series of gasps. "No. I haven't done what you said."

"When I say to do something or not to do something, to stop or go, and you obey, you are doing what I say. That's all that matters."

She retrieved the key from her boot. When she bent forward to unlock the cuffs, he tried to push her hands away, even with the restricted reach of his fingers. She smacked them lightly, a reproof, and removed the restraints. As she set them aside, she noted the grooves around his wrists she'd hoped to create.

"Turn over, Mick."

He didn't move, his forehead pressed to her leg. "Who do you serve?" she asked. "Your ego, or your Mistress?"

His eyes shut tight, his lashes brushing her ankle. A shudder went through him, so deep it brought a frown to her lips. Finally, he turned over like she'd commanded.

More scrapes on his cock. His still entirely erect cock. The precum was stained with blood. Not much, though. Pain could hurt plenty without causing serious damage. She'd explored and tested that concept extensively.

"Unclasp your hands and put them on your chest."

He did it, reluctantly. Head still in her lap. She stroked his chest, his jaw. She eyed his abused cock. "I want to see it spurt for me, from nothing more than my voice. I'll be disappointed if it won't."

His eyes had so much going on in there. Darkness, light, fury, frustration, and suddenly…tenderness. Or was that coming from her? An unsettling thought. She lifted one of his hands to touch her mouth to the red mark on his wrist. His fingers twitched, stopping short of contact with her face.

"I want to touch you," he rasped.

"No. You can imagine that later, when you're by yourself."

"I've done that for ten years."

"Don't move anything." Slowly, she put his palm against her face. He obeyed her command, letting her take over the movement, but showing that unprecedented mercy, she rubbed her face against his fingers, brushing her lips against the tips. "You will come for me," she said. "Start pushing into the air. Imagine it's my breath before I suck you into my mouth. Getting you wet before I slide you into my cunt."

He lifted his hips, and her gaze went back to his cock. She loved to watch a man fuck the air, from the front or the back. If she could have both views, so much the better. She liked the mirrored rooms at the club. But this worked, too.

"Keep doing it." She nibbled on his fingertips, sliding her tongue along his palm, even as her attention stayed on his cock. While his hips worked, the shaft moved up and then came back down on his abdomen, a light thump that changed to a slap against his contracting stomach muscles as his movements became more assertive.

"Mistress...fuck..."

"Yes. You will come for me. I want to see it. Right now. Your seed belongs to me, Mick. Show it to me."

He convulsed, shoulders pushing against her crossed legs. She brought his hand to the side of her throat, curving it over her there as she put her free hand back in his hair. Pulling hard, she tipped his face up and leaned over him, staring at the straining muscles, his wild eyes. Viscous white semen fountained out of his shaft, spilling over the head and dripping onto his stomach as he groaned, caught up in the response. His hand alongside her throat spasmed, a strong squeeze.

"No..."

81

She didn't know what that meant, but he grabbed her upper arm with his other hand, holding on as the reaction intensified. She wouldn't treat it as an infraction. He was grasping something solid in a storm. She could be that for him. As well as be the storm itself.

She curled her hand over his other set of biceps, holding onto him as well, a closed circle, until the climax ebbed. It left his body limp on the uncomfortable ground, but he stared at her as if they were drifting on clouds.

As if she were someone he hadn't met before. As if the person she'd been had come together with a whole new being, forming something unexpected to him. Startling, tilting his world.

She knew the feeling.

She told herself she would dismiss it, as soon as the moment was over. He was gone in a couple of weeks. This could be a lot of fun until then.

But the word *fun* was far off the mark of what she was feeling. She should be smart enough to back away from this.

But backing away from a threat wasn't her style.

She was a hundred percent certain it wasn't his, either.

CHAPTER SIX

They got dressed, saying little as they walked back to the motorhome. He produced a shirt for her from the plastic tote under his bed. Curiously, it was a woman's, a dark blue cotton shirt with floral embroidery along the V-neck.

He pulled a shirt out of the narrow closet for himself. He'd tucked their ripped clothes into a trash can under the kitchenette sink.

As he shrugged into the shirt, buttoned it and folded the sleeves back to his elbows, she noticed him watching her pull on the one he'd given her. Something bothered him about her wearing it, but she didn't think it connected to whoever had left it here. For one thing, it smelled new. Was he used to providing clothes for women he chased?

She removed it, folded it back up and put it on the table. Moving past him to his still open closet, she passed her fingers over the soft fabric of the eight shirts hanging there. Blue, brown, black, gray.

He was close. She leaned back against him as she chose the black one and pulled it out, then moved away from him in the close quarters to shrug it on. She left it open, the long tails fluttering around her hips. When she put her Freyja necklace back on, his gaze followed the settling of the pendant between her breasts, cradled in silky cups. "Back to the club?" His voice was still thick.

Opening his refrigerator, she discovered bottled water and a small number of fast food containers. She withdrew one of the bottles and cracked it open, taking a swallow before offering it to him.

"Do you want me to drive? It's not a cop car."

"I'm good." Amusement passed through his gaze. He drank about half the bottle before handing it back. His calm assurance said she could trust his self-evaluation. Most of her subs didn't realize how carefully she watched them after a session. No one under her care was going to tank from sub drop or attempt to drive before their faculties were fully under their own control.

Regardless, she still chose the narrow-cushioned seat behind the driver instead of the passenger seat beside him. As he sat down in the driver's side and turned over the engine, he glanced back at her.

"Shirt looks good on you."

"Yes, it does."

His lips quirked. As he pulled onto the road, she rested her head on the back of his shoulder. She couldn't tell if the gesture was for him or for her, but it didn't matter. She acted on her wants and needs. She didn't analyze them. That was a trip to the seven circles of Hell she didn't care to take.

He dipped his head in her direction, but kept his hands on the wheel, not trying to reach back and touch her. She studied the capable fingers and corded forearms. Put her head on his shoulder again and watched the world roll by.

When they pulled into the club parking lot, she was almost dozing, but she came fully awake. He rose and took her hand, leading her down the aisle toward the door. She put her other hand on his belt, tightening there until he had to descend the steps to the ground. But once there, he turned and offered her his hand. His grip was firm and sure, his gaze direct. The drive had finished the grounding process.

"You don't have to walk me," she told him. "I'm just over there."

"Fifty steps toward a cliff is an interesting walk, especially if the edge is at twenty-five." He closed the door. "You might want the company. It'll give you another chance to grab my ass. Bite me. Or kiss me good night."

The banter was another positive sign, but she sensed turmoil behind his eyes. She was tempted to plunge into that storm, but it was time to seek shelter.

The club stayed open until four in the morning, or until everyone left, whichever came first. A few cars remained in the lot. It was a nice night, not too humid for a New Orleans early morning.

Mick had looked where she'd pointed. A Porsche, her Ford truck, an Escalade, a Forerunner, and a raspberry-colored Mini Cooper were grouped together. The last sat among the larger vehicles like a cat toy. "If I guess which vehicle is yours, I want a kiss good night," he said.

"If you say the Coop, I'll kick you in the balls and you'll never see me again," she advised. "And I don't give a shit what you want."

His teeth flashed. "Thanks for helping improve my chances of winning. If I guess wrong, what do *you* want, Mistress?"

She swept her gaze downward. "While you're here, you treat your dick as mine. It doesn't get anything without my say-so."

He pursed his lips and glanced toward the vehicles. "The Escalade."

He'd chosen the one most would assume was hers. It was vaguely disappointing, and for more important reasons than the loss of a kiss. She told herself that missed opportunity was preferable, because she rarely kissed subs.

She was telling herself a lot of things tonight.

When she moved toward the vehicles, he followed her. Past the Escalade and to her truck.

Its jacked tires required a hefty step to the running board. The engine ran loud, and a gun rack was mounted in the rear window. Though she had various firearms, it didn't hold a long-barreled weapon. Instead a braided single tail was coiled over the prongs.

Cyn turned around at the driver's door. As she'd slipped her hand into her pocket for her keys, she'd encountered the skateboard doll he'd given her. Her thumb stroked it.

Mick was a foot away, looking at nothing but her.

She moved in, curling her hand behind his neck. She didn't have to bring him down far in her booted heels, but it was enough to satisfy the desire that he had to come to her. For her. As he'd come for her in the straw bales, stalking her. As she'd had him come for her, nothing more than her verbal command making his cock spurt.

"I want you to treat your dick as mine," she reiterated. ""I want you aching. All while you give the Ladies-In-Charge event better than your best."

His gaze heated, challenge accepted, even as she knew he'd issued his own. He'd lost the wager, but the kiss wasn't a proposition. It was a dare.

Since she didn't back away from a dare, she brought her mouth to his.

When was the last time she'd kissed a man? And had she wanted it as much as she wanted to taste Mick now? It didn't matter. Even if she'd never tasted her favorite dessert before, the smell of it, the look of it, told her how unforgettable that first bite was going to be.

She caught his bottom lip, felt him wisely steel himself to take the cut of her teeth. Then she fully covered his mouth with hers, exploring the shape, the firmness of his lips, the way they moved and contoured to hers.

Whether Dom, sub, switch or none of the above, a man showed his ability as a lover by letting the woman take a subtle lead on a first kiss, telegraphing her needs before he eased ahead, proving he could dance the dance with her, accepting the keys to unlock the pleasure she'd offered.

Mick had rested his hands on her hips, but now one moved to her upper arm, stroking. From there it went to her throat and jaw, her hair, learning her, how she moved and fit with him, the responses of her body.

She put herself fully against him, absorbing how solid he was as she slid her palm over his pectoral and rib cage, her thumb passing over the base of the scar she'd left upon him. She could feel the ridge through the shirt, the pointed press of his nipple, the rough texture of chest hair.

But all of that was like branches moving in the wind, flirting with sensation. The root of it, what gave them nourishment, grounding, was between their mouths. She took more, exploring heat, wetness, firmness, softness, the promise of sex the mouth could deliver. On her cunt, her breasts, her nipples, the back of her neck and knees, her feet.

She'd make him worship every inch of her with his lips and tongue. She'd bind his wrists behind his back, make him do that worshipping on his knees, until his thighs and core muscles were screaming. She'd make him go slow, so slow, taking the pain for her pleasure. Like he had tonight.

She added ferocity to the kiss, and his palms landed on either side of her against the truck door, before she could order it. As her need rose, he'd anticipated that she'd want to deny him touch. She slid her hands down his back, and yes, just as he'd said, took a healthy grip of his ass, rock hard muscle.

When she donned her metal claws, she would pinch a man's bare ass, nips that got sharper and sharper until the skin was on fire. Every new pinch was excruciating, making him bite back cries.

She'd tease him. *"But it's just a pinch, baby. A big, strong man like you doesn't mind a pinch."* When she was done, he had tiny blue and red marks all over his ass.

That was a pleasure for another day. Another day soon. Thinking of their limited time didn't bring her any joy, but she'd work with what she was given. She returned her hands to his chest, her palms flattening, fingertips pulling in one last brace of sensations before she drew back. She ended the way she'd begun, with a sucking, wet clamp on his lip. Then she released him.

"Fuck. When was the last time you kissed someone?" he murmured. "And where is the poor happy bastard buried?"

She managed a smile, even as the dark thought came that she really couldn't remember the last time she'd kissed someone like that, if ever.

"You lied, Mick. You knew which vehicle was mine."

He didn't deny it, though he read her tone and stepped back, sliding his hands into his pockets again. "Yeah, I did."

"Who told you?"

"No one. It just looked like you. A redneck woman, ready to kick ass and get dirty. Doesn't matter whether she's from Jersey or Georgia."

"So why did you lie?"

"Because I wanted you to win."

"Because you like having a woman punish you." She gave him a cold look. "So it was self-serving."

Coolness entered his gaze. "I'm into pain, not punishment. You know the difference. I want to suffer for you."

"Still. Neither of us wins, because you lied. I don't care what you do with your dick. Maybe next time we see one another, I'll change my mind about that."

His jaw flexed. "When will you be back here?"

"The day after you leave."

He gave her an exasperated look. "We need a consensual non-consent scene for LIC. You want to do it?"

She opened the door of her truck. He took a step closer, his male energy curling around her. Though he didn't try to stop her, the aggressive desire was there. She should call him on it, but her mind was screwing with her. It was considering something appalling, like inviting him to grab a coffee, talk and catch up, like normal people who hadn't seen one another in a long time.

She didn't do normal. Or public play. "No. There are other Mistresses who can do it. They can also tell you which subs are willing to bottom for it."

"Do you do CNC, privately?"

Not anymore. "Sure. If it works for me and who I'm with."

He'd picked up on her hesitation. He braced a hand against the side of the truck. "Is that lying thing a double standard?"

She got into the truck, settling into the driver's seat above him. "Fuck you, Mick. Go crawl into someone else's head."

"Hey." He caught the door before she could slam it. Genuine regret crossed his face. "Sorry. If it's not your thing, or brings up bad stuff, that's okay. I shouldn't have called you on it like that."

She couldn't keep him out of her head. It really was time to go. "Let go of my door."

A tug-of-war tension was between their two holds, but then he let her close it. She started up the truck with a roar. He'd gone so still while watching her. She wondered how he did that with energy boiling inside him, wall to wall heat.

Her blood was an oil fire on water, her swimming below, lungs on fire, looking for space to emerge and take a deep breath. *Shit.*

She lowered the window and gestured. He stepped onto the running board and gripped the outside handle to keep himself there. She grasped the collar of the shirt and tugged.

Reaching through the window opening, he touched her face as she put her mouth on his again, opening his lips to the stroke of her tongue, the edge of her teeth. He welcomed and tasted her in return, hand cupping her skull.

Her hand moved to his throat, a light squeeze to keep him there as she stilled and took a long, indrawn breath. She held her mouth against his, then swept her tongue over his once more, a tease before she drew back, hand still screwed in the collar of his shirt. "If I agree to do the CNC scene, you're my bottom."

He reached in and gripped the seatbelt, she assumed to pull it out and buckle it over her. She stopped him. "I don't wear them."

"Wear one for me. Just this once. I wouldn't want anything to happen to you before that night. Call it my self-serving side."

The humor amid the darker emotions swirling in his eyes had her lips relaxing into a smile. He was interesting and a challenge, she gave him that. She held up both her hands, amused as he maneuvered further into the window to pull the belt over her, snap it into place at her hip. As he did, she took another nice inhale of him.

When he pulled back, he slid his hand along the belt's track, fingers brushing the curves over the bra cups. He then adjusted the shirt so they were covered.

She gave him a *really?* look. He grinned before he stepped off the running board. "Saving lives, Mistress. Don't want any distracted drivers out there."

Rolling her eyes, she hit the button to raise the window. As she put the truck in gear, she suppressed the idiotic urge to wave. Instead she drove away without taking the second look she wanted, though she did pull off a covert glance in the side view mirror.

He was still watching her. It stirred pleasure within her, but it was mixed with uneasiness. He'd picked up that she was lying about doing CNC, and how his needs meshed with hers made it possible he understood the reasons.

Yet she'd decided to do it, and he'd agreed to be the bottom for it.

It wasn't a big deal. Tomorrow, she'd tell him she'd thought about it and decided no. But for tonight, she'd think about all the things she could do to him, his beautiful body and captivating mind, if she could inflict whatever she wanted on both.

She decided not to go home. She went into work. She kept a change of clothes in her truck, since it wasn't the first time she'd spent the night somewhere else.

Thomas Rose Associates was housed in a three-story, ten thousand square foot home built in 1860 in New Orleans' Garden District. It had been designed by Henry Howard, the same architect for the tourist magnet Corn Stalk house.

She took a shower in the full bath on the third floor, where her office was, and used her bag of toiletries to do her make-up and hair. She decided to wear Mick's shirt open over her sleeveless fitted shirt and charcoal gray slacks. No, she wasn't doing the girly sniffing thing. Not exactly. She let herself have a passing whiff, to remember more acutely the taste of his sweat on her lips, the musk of his climax, the heat of his skin.

When she went into her office, she examined the voodoo doll Mick had given her again. She remembered Cissy's crooked smile, the vaguely out of focus eyes that still seemed to see so much.

On her desk, Cyn had a several stress toys. One was heart-shaped, given to her by Sy as a joke. The other was a voodoo doll. She could put her thumb on its stomach and make the rubber eyes pop out, back in, back out. A good stand-in for customers or others she might actually want to squeeze until their eyes popped. She put the skateboard doll next to it for company, packed away the thoughts about it that would interfere with productivity, and got to work.

She reviewed each project team's progress, sending them direction for adjustments and course corrections. She verified she had what she needed for her client meetings and follow-ups today, and for the rest of the week. When she heard movement below and coffee smells wafted up, she saw it was seven o'clock.

Leaving her office, she headed down the spiral front stairs to the kitchen break area. Through the crescent-shaped window over the front door, she could see the long armed ancient live oaks that embraced the building. During the spring, the azalea bushes were so heavy with blooms one had to look to find green leaves. Benches, fountains and statuary were scattered over the black iron-fenced grounds. The more outdoorsy staff enjoyed working in those spaces. When Cyn glanced out her own front facing window, she'd often see Vera there on her laptop.

The five-woman executive team had their offices on the top floor, while the project and sales teams occupied the first and second. The foyer was a spacious area containing a large reception desk. The staircase curved along the right wall.

The colorful Dianne Parks painting behind the desk depicted the French Quarter in bold colors. Carriage horses patiently waiting for passengers, street players and vendors scattered around them, historic building facades in the backdrop.

As work environments went, it was pretty top notch. When she thought of how she'd gotten here, Cyn always felt incredulity, combined with an irritating little poke from Fate. *See? Without my twists and turns in your life, where would you be?* Since she was in a reasonably good mood, she didn't tell it to fuck off.

Cyn had been working in a dealership as a service manager. Her boss had called her into his office to ream her for not overselling services and padding maintenance visits with things the clients didn't need. He didn't care how much long-term or new business that lost them. People smart enough to know they were being screwed didn't hesitate to post reviews complaining about it.

When he dismissed that, saying short term gains kept them employed, she told him he might be okay with treating people like shit, but she wasn't. He'd fired her. *"Get the fuck out."*

When she marched through the waiting room, head held high, Ros had been sitting in it, dressed in a tailored business suit that likely cost six months' rent for Cyn's ratty apartment. Her silver and white Jimmy Choo heels would have caught any woman's attention, while her legs would snare any man's. Her expression suggested she'd caught a good bit of the exchange. Cyn managed a barely polite nod when their eyes met, but kept going.

A few minutes later, while Cyn was waiting at the bus stop, Ros rolled up next to her. "I decided to take my business elsewhere," she said. "I assume you have a place you'd recommend?"

Cyn gave her a wary look. She was in a pisser of a mood, but before her tongue could get her into trouble, Ros added, "I'd also like to talk to you about a job. Will you join me for coffee so we can discuss it?"

Ros had taken them to a diner she liked. The owner had personally come out of the kitchen to tell her about the specials. "We have a good BLT today."

He was a handsome, bullish-looking man with tawny skin, dark eyes and a good smile. His short hair was dark and thick. "Are you making it yourself, Fernando?" Ros asked.

"You know I am."

"Then that's what I want. But you'll be the one to bring it to the table."

A light smile played on his lips, his brown eyes heating. "Of course, ma'am."

After the waitress brought them coffee, Ros took a sip before she spoke. "I'm from New York originally. I recognize a Jersey girl when I hear one. How many jobs have you had since you came to New Orleans?"

"Six."

Cyn's lack of degree, and probable inexperience in whatever kind of work Ros did, meant a job offer would be entry level. Cyn was fine with that. She'd proven six times how fast she could rise in the ranks. To get hired, Cyn had learned to adapt to her audience. If Ros had a concern about the number of jobs, Cyn would spout some convincing bullshit about how she'd been trying to find her niche, broaden her experience base, to bring her best to the job she really wanted. Blah, blah, blah.

Most potential employers didn't want to hear the truth about why she was fired as often as she was hired. And up until now, what the job was hadn't really mattered, beyond being legal, keeping her fed and off the streets, and bringing the usual futile hope she'd be dealing with fewer assholes like the prick who'd just fired her.

Yet as she met Ros's gaze, Cyn realized whether it was the fight with her boss, or she'd accumulated just enough money she was no longer a breath away from homeless, she wasn't going to be less than who she was anymore. Not just with Ros, but with anyone.

Every thought would be spoken as she felt it. No more lies in order to live or worse, to get by or get along. She wasn't a nice person, but she was fair. And when it mattered to her, when the people and the company mattered to her, she'd not only get the job done, she'd fucking knock it out of the park. She might not be what they wanted her to be, but she'd be what they needed. Because that was more important, even if she was the only one who knew it.

"I have a hard time with incompetence. Laziness, dishonesty. People doing only what's in their job description."

Ros lifted a brow. "What else should they be doing?"

"Whatever's needed for the company to succeed, because that takes care of everyone. Including the customers."

"So you quit when that gets too frustrating?"

"No. I step in, try to tune it up, fix it, kick the asses that need kicking, suggest replacing what doesn't work. Unfortunately, that's most often whoever's managing or owns the joint. So I get fired."

Fernando was headed around the counter with Ros's sandwich. Noting it, Ros lifted one finger. He stopped, turned and put it back on the pass through. Though he smoothly returned to other tasks and supervising his people, Cyn noted he kept a portion of his attention on them, waiting for Ros to gesture again.

It was impressive, and more than just a man fawning because she fucked him. Recognition stirred Cyn's gut, something undefinable but familiar.

Ros's gaze held hers as she tapped the side of the cup, her other fingers still curled around it. "So you've never quit a job."

"No." Cyn shrugged. "I can tell you where I've worked if you want to check. I'm okay with them telling you whatever they want about me."

"Their version will be different from yours."

"No doubt. But if you can't read between those kinds of lines, we wouldn't be having coffee and you'd be in the waiting room, happy to be overcharged for your service work."

"Hmm." Ros nodded toward the counter. A moment later, Fernando slid the plate in front of her. Cyn had said she'd stick with her coffee, that she wasn't hungry. She tried not to inhale the fresh tomatoes and toasted bread. The scrambled egg had a garlic pepper scent.

"Fernando makes the best breakfast in New Orleans," Ros said. "If you know anything about restaurant competition in NOLA, you know that's saying something."

"Yeah. It looks good. I'm fine with my coffee, though." She said that right as her traitorous stomach growled, loudly enough to be heard by her companion.

"Fernando, Abby will be joining us shortly." Ros typed in a text and glanced at Cyn. "We pick up the meal tab for our interview candidates."

"I don't need charity."

Ros's blue eyes went sharp. "You don't look like you do. But you're hungry, and a plate of food will be in front of you in a few minutes. For the car to run well, it has to have fuel. Right?"

Fernando backed a couple paces away from the table before turning. Once again, the cues caught Cyn's attention.

Ros noted her scrutiny, her interest in the byplay. With a feline smile, she slid a piece of her toast onto the saucer of Cyn's coffee cup. "We're going to get along just fine," the female CEO said.

Had it been that which had brought Cyn into the fold, as much as the eventual job offer? Probably, but it was more than that. Cyn didn't see Ros as a surrogate for the type of mother she'd never had, but the CEO projected confidence that belittled no one, and was steadfastly loyal to her people. The women that populated the top floor were Ros's inner circle, but anyone in her employ was family, unless they lost that privilege through shirking, dishonesty or other weaknesses on the same list Cyn had detailed that day.

So Ros had Cyn's allegiance, no matter what. This place, these women, they were her center and what mattered. Though this thing with Mick had taken her by surprise, unearthing things that should remain buried, he would be gone in a few days. She needed to remember that.

She needed coffee.

Well before she reached the kitchen, she heard a baritone, humming like a bee with credible Barry White aspirations. Bastion was here.

Management, project and sales team efforts were what kept TRA a leader in marketing services to a select clientele, ranging from million-dollar corporations to up and coming small businesses. Even the occasional promising street artist. However, as far as the vital office operations and admin that supported them, no one doubted who was responsible for that.

He was in the kitchen, all six feet plus of him.

Bastion Lake was built like a pro athlete in top condition, and dressed with Tom Ford style. Today it was fashionable jeans stressed with a light sheen, paired with a belt whose antique gold buckle looked like a studded flower. A thin felt coat stretched over his shoulders and nipped the waist, flanking his hips and powerful thighs. His dress shoes had gold toe tips. His black locs reached his waist and were tied back with a clip matching the belt buckle.

"Sloppy as ever," Cyn greeted him. "Did you even brush your teeth when you rolled out of bed?"

"Come give me a tongue kiss and you'll find out."

Even at normal pitch, Bastion's voice could vibrate a person's bones. He was a bisexual Dom whose scene energy could surpass even her own. Bastion would often take two subs in the same session. Occasionally he joined the women as a guest at Club Progeny, but he had other haunts he preferred, perhaps because Progeny's membership cost was steep, and the man was a clothes horse. He also liked his jewelry. Today he wore a ruby ring, the stone clasped in a bronze lion's roaring mouth.

"Tongue kiss," she scoffed. "In your dreams."

He'd known she was coming. Though he routinely compared it to motor oil, her preferred K cup brand of coffee was ready and prepared the way she liked it. She gave him a nod of thanks and moved to the window over the sink. Vera was pulling into the back parking lot in her bronze Aston Martin DBS V12. An in-your-face broadcast of her passion for James Bond films. Or rather, the men who played James Bond. She was jonesing to see Idris Elba in the role, probably to augment her fantasies of topping him in an opulent dungeon playroom.

People were far more than they appeared. Vera was their spiritual person, a Wiccan priestess who'd performed weddings and led pagan holiday events in the New Orleans area. Her steadfast moral center made her the right fit for administering TRA's HR and legal requirements. When their group had faced more personal challenges, like Abby's illness, Ros's threat from a local gang, or Skye's decision to love a man who had ties to a violent world, Vera could be relied upon for her calm grasp of the bigger picture.

Initially Cyn had viewed Vera as an enemy for just that reason. She saw so much it felt like a privacy invasion to meet her gaze or shake her hand. But the unexpected warmth and comfort Vera brought to her insights made them palatable. Mostly. She could tell you that your soul was damned, but leave you feeling loved and cared for anyway. No matter what, a person wasn't alone, even if, like Cyn, they preferred to be self-sufficient in every way.

Cyn was an acquired taste, she knew. The people who worked under her knew she was tough to please, but when they did the work and showed the right initiative, she was fully in their corner. Over time, she'd populated her department with creative yet thick-skinned individuals who could excel because they thrived off the challenge of hard work and high expectations. When they succeeded, she made damn sure they were rewarded for it.

Yes, she scared newbies and interns, but so did Ros. There were bets among the executive team about who scared them worse. Cyn was competitive, so she tried to keep the edge on Ros there.

"You been here all night?" Bastion had come to stand by her. Vera was crossing the parking lot. She wore a marmalade orange blouse and hip-hugging blue skirt with a silver chain belt draped over the gathered front. The belt had matching blue and orange beads. Her heels were blue. Seamed stockings again. Vera might be the only woman in humid New Orleans who routinely wore hosiery to work.

"God, why would anyone want to spend that much time coordinating in the morning?" Cyn sipped her coffee. "No. I got here about four o'clock."

Bastion slid a glance over Cyn's slacks and form-fitting tank. "Black women look outstanding in primary colors. Unlike you pasty white girls. But I give you credit for monotone without monotony. With your astonishingly consistent black, white and gray spectrum, we can't tell when you're wearing the same outfit as yesterday and doing the walk of shame. Tell me that's not on purpose."

"Tell me why you think I'd be ashamed of fucking someone all night? I'd bring video to work if Vera wouldn't have baby cow pies. And I occasionally wear colors. You said my red blouse looks vampire hot on me. All I need are fangs."

"You already have fangs."

She *had* changed out jewelry, tucking the Freyja pendant away and pulling one out of her go bag she hadn't worn in some time, but she carried it with her, always. Sometimes holding it for a few minutes in the morning before putting it away and choosing something less personal. Because the people around her noticed shit.

As Bastion proved by reaching over and picking up the skeleton hugging the cross. She'd bought herself one, telling herself she liked it enough to buy two, one for her and one for Mick slash Cissy. It wasn't like she'd bought a damn broken coin or something unreasonable like that. Her skeleton also wasn't the same as his. The artist preferred to make each one different.

"This is new."

She shrugged. He let the necklace go to pick up the tail of the black shirt at her hip and finger the fabric. "Nice quality. This is a man's. It doesn't smell like you."

"You're being creepy, Bastion."

He chuckled, taking a swallow of his chai tea. Cyn didn't care for the taste, but she liked the smell, associating it with him and times like this, early morning with just a handful of people in the building. People she felt comfortable around.

She had shifted so she was brushing his shoulder, leaning a little. It had taken a long time to get there, but the first time she'd done it, Bastion hadn't made a big deal of it. Just kept drinking his tea, much like now. He never initiated it. Never rebuffed it, either.

On the rare occasions she sought that contact, he seemed to pick up on the underlying reason and responded like a caring Dom. Not meaning he treated her like a sub, but tailoring his reaction to his understanding of her needs.

Vera had disappeared around the building, probably taking the side stairwell up to their offices. She'd be down for some coffee herself soon. They had a small break area on their floor Bastion kept stocked, but they liked to touch base with him. And all of them often used this breakroom during the workday to connect with staff. No ivory towers for Ros's executive team.

"Sy give you problems last night?" Bastion asked, moving to the coffee maker to prepare another cup. "That boy's mouth can get him into trouble. The good kind, usually, but his weekly beating keeps him straight."

"No. We had a good session."

"Just wasn't exactly what you were looking for?"

More like an appetizer to the main event. The thought bugged her. Being with Mick had been explosive enough to change her inner view. As if she'd been wanting something different for a while and hadn't realized it. She didn't like it when her subconscious fucked with her.

Her mind was like the maze even now, moving in random patterns, bypassing the exit to cycle over the same thoughts and sensations. His mouth and hands, his scent, the things he'd said, how he'd responded to her. The strength of the past holding them together.

"Did you hear about the Ladies-In-Charge presentation?" she said, instead of answering.

"LIC?" Bastion's eyes danced at the sexual implications of the acronym. "I heard the presenter was two handfuls of eye candy."

"You should come with us one night to meet him, Bastion," Vera noted, joining them. "Cyn probably knows more about his schedule, since she was out half the night with him."

100

At Bastion's significant look at the black shirt, Cyn rolled her eyes, but fired her response at Vera. "Did you employ a drone to follow me, Miss Bond?"

Vera took her coffee from Bastion with a smile, and sniffed at Cyn. "I saw your truck when I left, and I was concerned. Security told me you left with Mick."

"We know one another from years ago," Cyn told Bastion as his thick black brow winged up. "We went somewhere to catch up."

Bastion glanced at Vera. "Sounds like the top layer of the truth, like cake icing."

"You have finger bruises on your wrist," Vera noted, brushing her manicured nails over Cyn's arm.

Cyn remembered how Mick had gripped her wrist during their sparring. She'd fought him. Fought hard until he'd had her decisively pinned. Then he'd helped her up, stepped back. And knelt.

What happened after surged into her mind, but before she could let it swamp her, she gave Vera the truth. Maybe still just that top layer, but the truth all the same. "Remembering the past can be dangerous."

Vera gave her a concerned look. "Did he try to hurt you?"

The question startled her. They were used to how she sparred at Roughnecks, and how intense her sessions could get. Sometimes she let a sub get his hands on her. The way she drove them meant things could get crazy, in all the ways she liked, testing her wits and strength.

"No more than I tried to hurt him. It was all fine. Where's the look coming from?"

"He feels...unpredictable. Like there's something there, really dark and waiting. Just be careful, all right?"

"He's okay, Vera." Cyn didn't want her friends worrying. "He did me a solid a long time ago. I don't want to talk about it, but he's fine. I trust him."

Bastion looked as startled as Cyn had felt at Vera's question. "You're right," he told the HR manager. "I need to

101

meet this one. I've never heard those words come out of her mouth so unqualified. Even for us."

It grated, but it was a fair assessment. Bastion and Ros's team had more of her trust than Cyn had ever expected to give anyone. Except Mick.

She'd trusted Cissy, but that trust had been built in the trenches of the hell their childhood had been. A childhood Cissy hadn't survived.

Cyn had, and part of the reason was she never gave her whole trust to anyone. You could love people without fully trusting them. It was better for the relationship. No unreasonable expectations.

"I know how sneaky you all can be," Cyn said lightly, and turned the topic to work. "What time's my interview with that new kid you want to bring on board?"

"The one three years younger than you?" Vera teased, though her gaze remained thoughtful.

"Don't bait me, old lady. Aren't you going to be forty soon? You should retire before you need a walker."

"Ten o'clock." Vera gave her a dagger look and Cyn grinned. The phone on Bastion's belt started to vibrate, a call forwarded from the front desk. But as he picked it up and headed toward the foyer, Cyn was aware of the look he exchanged with Vera, still containing that *what the fuck* astonishment.

"I stopped by your office on the way down," Vera noted, fortunately capitulating to Cyn's desire to change the subject. "You had a fax from Ben O'Callahan. About sous vide cooking?"

"There's no privacy here." Cyn picked an apple out of the large fruit bowl. "Did you read it?"

"I skimmed the first page, since I saw his name and he's Kensington & Associates' lawyer. I wanted to make sure it wasn't something you needed my help with. I'm confused. You don't cook."

"You should have read it more carefully. It's not about food."

Vera processed that, then her eyes widened. "You two need to be on a watch list."

"We're on yours. The world is safe."

Ben O'Callahan was a Dom sadist on par with Cyn herself. The joke at Progeny was if the two of them ever tag teamed, they'd have an ambulance on standby for the submissive foolish enough to volunteer for the session.

Luckily, Cyn preferred to be a solo act. No room for anyone else's demons in the room with her and her chosen submissive. Ben had always seemed to be the same.

Cyn winked at Vera and left the kitchen, heading up the side stairwell to return to her office. She had work to do, though with the hours she put in, she stayed well ahead of deadlines. Which gave her time to plant her elbows on her desk, stare at her computer screen and think about last night. Pore over every moment, and what the next encounter might bring.

He'd agreed to be her bottom for the CNC scene. She'd told herself she'd turn down the offer today, tell him to find another Mistress for it. She should do that now. The club had set up a temporary email for him. She could send a message to it, so he'd have time to find a replacement.

She picked up her phone and found two texts waiting.

One was work-related. Polly was pregnant and going to be late because of morning sickness.

Work from home today if it's easier to get it done, Cyn typed back.

They didn't have enough offices for all the employees they had now, but rather than add facilities, they'd implemented a staggered schedule where the employees, full time and contract, were here three days a week, working from home for two. Everyone had what they needed to be productive, here or at home.

The next text was from Mick.

103

It *said* Mick, not a random unidentified phone number. When he'd taken her phone last night, the bastard had put himself in her contact list.

The number had a New Orleans area code, which suggested he was using a burner. An odd decision, because an event planner would presumably want to accumulate contacts for repeat business.

She opened the text. It had an animation, a skeleton with a top hat dancing in the rain. He was exuberantly twirling and dipping an umbrella in the puddles as his bony feet splashed through them. On his third turn, a piano dropped out of the sky, squashing him with a comic plume of purple dust.

Her burst of laughter made her swallow wrong, and she had to reach for her coffee to clear her throat. The only time she really laughed like that was when she was with Vera and the others. When she was expecting it. She read the text as she coughed.

You're a hell of a fighter, Mistress. I need a freezer full of bagged peas for my bruises. Come have lunch with me.

She typed a response without hesitation. *Got meetings. I work for a living.*

But her finger hovered over the send button. After this morning's interview, she didn't have any more meetings.

She deleted the message and sent him a different one. *Come to the address I'm sending you. Eat something beforehand if you need it. Don't wear underwear.*

She followed it up with an interoffice message to the top floor women, Bastion and her project managers, letting them know she was taking a long lunch. Long enough she might not be back today.

Again, she reminded herself he'd be gone in a few days. That sword cut a lot of ways, but could also point toward a forward charge. There was no reason to hold back on everything she'd imagined about him over the past decade. Was there?

Practically, what she had in mind would also allow her to test out the wisdom of doing a public session with him. The CNC scene she hadn't told him she wasn't doing.

She turned back to her computer and hit the gas on finishing up. She wanted to get there ahead of him.

CHAPTER SEVEN

Soon after Cyn left for lunch, Vera appeared in Ros's doorway. "Got a minute?"

Ros looked up from the monthly sales report. She wasn't a hands-off CEO. She was still the face of the business and landed most of the corporate accounts that allowed them to take riskier, smaller projects. She also represented the occasional client herself, to stay in tune with the latest in marketing developments, and because she enjoyed customer contact. Her one nod to being CEO was she could cherry pick who she wanted to personally represent.

"What do you have? Abby already sent me budget projections to review, so anything will seem easier. Even legal matters."

Vera gave her a half smile and took a seat in a guest chair. "It's about Cyn and Mick."

"So I'm not the only one who thinks that's why we won't see her back today." Ros's humor died away at Vera's troubled expression. "We've been hoping someone would inspire her to explore a relationship outside the club. I know he's not here long. Is that why you don't look happy about it?"

Vera shook her head. "That's a concern, but no. It's Tiger's reaction to him. Neil and Lawrence felt some of that, too. It bugged me, so I did some digging. You know everyone who comes to Club Progeny gets vetted, even if they have reciprocity from other clubs and groups."

"I'm aware." Ros's jewel-like blue eyes sharpened.

"Well, he didn't go through the vetting. He was vouched for by one of Progeny's co-owners, your friend Tyler Winterman. You know he holds majority interest in The Zone down in Florida. He told management that Mick had already been cleared through them, plus a dozen other clubs, so the effort wasn't needed."

"Mick's here for a short time and the staff is busy arranging the LIC event," Ros noted reasonably. "Tyler didn't want them spending redundant time and energy."

"Maybe. But Tyler doesn't encourage club management to skip steps, or play the 'I'm the owner who doesn't have to follow the rules' card. If anything, he goes the opposite direction. It bugs me."

"Worries you," Ros corrected. "Because of her."

Vera crossed her legs. "She's getting tighter, more closed in. Since the near misses with you and Abby, and after you two and Skye paired up."

Ros frowned. "She hasn't acted like…"

"No. She seems fine. I have no doubt she'd say so herself and believe it. Cyn doesn't think she has any complicated layers, but we both know she's a black hole, even to herself."

Ros tapped her pen on the desk, like a slow metronome. The thoughts hovered in the air between them, the shared history and experience with the woman in question.

"I've never seen a man cause her emotional disruption," Ros said. "But that can precede good things. A relationship like I have with Lawrence. Or Abby and Neil, Skye and Tiger. So…"

"I agree. But there's something about him. It's like a snake waiting under a rock. I'm not so sure she knows what's under the surface."

"Well, she's Cyn. She dives deep into subs. He may not be a clearcut bottom, but they went off together last night and she had bruises today, so he's the kind of power alpha masochist she likes."

"You noticed." Vera gave her a tight smile.

"I'm the boss. I notice everything," Ros said loftily. "Cyn will dig into a man well beyond the six feet of a grave. If there's something there, she'll find it. On her terms, which usually involves pain. If he can't handle that, he'll back off."

"What happens if she can't handle it? She doesn't know how to back off."

"That's why she has us." Ros met her gaze. "Whether she has full faith in it or not, we have her back. Always."

"Yes. True." Vera rose. "I have no recommended action. Just wanted to voice my gut feeling."

"Which I respect, and you have given us a course of action. We'll all keep an extra eye on how it goes."

Vera nodded. "All right. Thanks for the ear. I better get back to reference calls. Cyn liked the new marketing hire."

"Don't bother with the calls, then." Ros chuckled. "She hasn't been wrong yet about anyone she approves. She has good judgment."

"For a lot of things, yes. I just... There's this part of her that's unfinished, if that makes sense. A part she locked away somewhere, and I have this uneasy feeling he has the key to it."

"I'm aware. Cyn and Skye are close in age, but Cyn has always seemed like the baby, because of how volatile her emotions can be."

Vera's lips tugged. "She'd give you that death look of hers if you called her that."

"I know." Ros smiled. "Doesn't make it any less true."

Her phone buzzed and Bastion's voice came through. "Ros, Gene Trelwood is on three to talk about his account."

"Understood."

Vera made an "ok" gesture and slid out. Their business was done, nothing more needed. Not yet.

However, after Ros finished her call, she rocked back in her chair and turned toward the window, considering. She trusted her HR manager's instincts. Because she did, she picked up her phone and dialed. When the caller answered with a greeting, she came right to the point.

"Dale, I need a favor."

Mick left his motorhome at the campground he'd selected, hitching a ride into town and picking up a trolley that had a stop near the address Cyn had left him. On the way, he sat on a bench by himself, listening to tourists chat excitedly about what they were going to see today. He watched service workers, like maids, waitstaff and contractors, reading or scrolling through their phones. Some gazed out the windows as they listened to podcasts, music or audio books.

One of them didn't do any of that, a middle-aged Latina woman with expressive eyes in a fleshy face. She wore jeans and a smock over a purple T-shirt with a dance club logo. A plastic bucket of cleaning supplies rested next to her white, thick-soled athletic shoes. She probably worked at one of the hotels. She was people-watching, likely for the same reason he was. Clearing her mind before facing a demanding environment. Their eyes met, and she offered a reserved smile before her gaze moved on.

Cyn's text was sending him to a warehouse in the industrial district. He'd done a quick search and found it was owned by an LLC, with Cyn the sole owner behind it. The layers hadn't been that difficult to push through. She wasn't trying to hide herself. The LLC was likely for tax purposes.

Mick got off at the stop and walked the several blocks to the warehouse. It was humid today, but a breeze filtered through the buildings from the nearby river. In the young oak trees lining the sidewalk, he saw the inevitable strands of beads hanging from branches. This place was close enough to the casino, restaurants and hotels that tourists had passed through, leaving the colorful additions.

He thought of the voodoo doll he'd given her, and the skeleton necklace she'd left for him and Cissy. It was the kind of macabre whimsy New Orleans was known for. He'd worn the necklace ever since he'd found it, and whenever he looked at it in the mirror, or focused on how it felt against his chest, that scar, he thought of her. He'd liked imagining that skinny, angry, hungry girl in baggy clothes, standing in some cheap marketplace, finding the necklace and thinking of him.

Though he'd accepted the possibility she might have stolen it, it didn't change his attachment to the trinket.

The warehouse was a nondescript place, no signage. If she'd become a serial killer, it was a suitable venue for her victims. Biting back a smile, he punched the code she'd given him into the security panel and heard the door buzz.

When he entered the building, he came face-to-face with a snarling wolf, nearly ten feet tall. As he blinked and settled from that start, the door clanged shut behind him. From the dozen or so parade floats he saw, including the wolf, he deduced she must rent out the space as overflow storage for Mardi Gras organizers. She was smart that way. He knew she'd pulled in six figures last year through investments and her salary and commissions at Thomas Rose Associates.

The girl in the cemetery had come a long way. But as he well knew, revisiting a memory could bring you right back to the person you'd been. What you'd felt and wanted. Worried about and feared. What you'd lost, that nothing in life would ever replace.

"That first night, when I saw you, you reminded me of a wolf. You still do."

He turned toward her voice, though he didn't see her in the shadows clustered around the floats. She never sounded uncertain, never fearful. Even back then. It fascinated him. If she lost control, it was to anger. She refused to be cowed. Everything she was came through her tone, and it changed depending on what the moment required—or she desired.

What he heard now was the sultry drawl of a Mistress. "I want to see how you handle submitting, when I control the setting. Did you eat lunch?"

"I wasn't hungry." Remembering his initial text, he added, "It's what you do. Offer to take someone to lunch."

"Figured. Don't do that shit with me. I'd rather you send me a text saying what you really want. What did you really want, Mick?"

"I wanted to see you." He'd woken with an ache inside. She was the knife that would cut even deeper into that desire.

"Why?"

"You know why."

"To fuck."

"No. Yes."

Her shoes made a crisp scrape sound on concrete, moving past the wolf, behind it. Now her voice came from the other side. He shifted, keeping his back to the door, aware of every echo, where it came from, what caused it. Light filtered through the warehouse's high windows.

She was goading his predator instincts. Ceiling fans rotated in the rafters, bringing him the scent of paint and plaster from the floats, metal and dust.

"You've asked about my reputation at the club," she continued. A statement, not a question. "What do they say?"

"You're an amusement park's scariest ride. One trip is usually enough. It's not just the pain. You find out what their threshold is and blast past it, farther than they thought they could go. You do it with mind fucks or a force of will they can't resist." That they didn't want to resist. "Most end up safewording, because others tell them that's what you wait for, to end the session. Your mental and physical stamina is the stuff of legends."

Her scoff raked his ears. "And that's your thing. Pitting yourself against me, testing yourself?"

"No."

"Why not? Think you'll get tenderness from me? The romance novel, the beast changed by the beauty's love? You're not *that* pretty."

"Come out of the shadows, Mistress."

"Answer the question."

He turned in the direction of the voice. "There's a Washington Irving quote. 'He solicited not her tenderness, but her esteem.' I seek your esteem, Mistress. That's a bigger gift to me."

111

It was truth. But he also knew, though she avoided softer emotions, she had them. He'd felt it, when she put his palm on her face, or laid her cheek on his back during the drive back to her truck. She walled herself away from softer things. Except in those rare moments, she saw tenderness or care as a weakness, a trap. It didn't matter if it could bring her pleasure or a different depth to the relationship. She didn't want that depth.

Even so, years ago, he'd glimpsed her limitless need to be with a man who could let her dive as far into that side of herself as she needed. A part of him had answered, like the sun yearning for the moon. It might be the only thing he could point to and say, *yes, I did that right.* Something that wouldn't be forgotten by the world.

She'd stayed in his head ten years. And he'd stayed in hers. Last night had proven that feeling hadn't been wrong.

He avoided softness as well, but for other reasons. He couldn't indulge the fantasy that he deserved tenderness or care. It was why he wasn't looking for a Mistress to punish him for his sins. That was self-serving. He just sought pain. He could give her that.

"Tell me the real reason you don't choose an orientation at the clubs." Her voice was flat like an interrogator's, nothing revealed. His gut stirred with apprehension and anticipation of where she wanted to take them.

So he gave her a different answer, one truthful enough to fit this moment. "I'm seeking whoever speaks to me, in whatever language calls to me. Sometimes that's made me the bottom, sometimes the top. When I look at you, Cyn, I see someone who saved herself because she had to, because she had to become something more than what she came from. I want to honor that strength, surrender to it, even as I want to give you everything you had to deny yourself to get there. Does that make sense? I can't classify that."

A long pause.

"I know what I need from you, Mick. What do you need?"

He put it out there. It was also mostly the truth. "I need someone not afraid to give me pain far beyond where others go." Someone who wasn't afraid to leave a scar. "A Mistress who will leave me bleeding, let me mop it up and get myself to the ER, while she toasts herself on a job well done, knowing I'll come back for more of the same."

Her throaty chuckle teased the base of his spine, spreading that tingling sensation over his buttocks and into his balls. "Skye said the female submissives flutter around you like little birds. You care for them, watch out for them." She paused. "A part of you longs to nurture your Mistress, but the kind of Mistress you want rejects that."

He hadn't considered it that way, but he couldn't deny it. "Whoever made us this way is the original sadomasochist. I expect you know that as well as I do."

She passed through a spot of light. She wore trim slacks and a sleeveless top, the same kind that clung to her modest curves, showing off the smooth muscles in her arms. Like a man, she seemed to prefer the same outfit day-to-day, a fashion that fit the club or the office, and the clothes had style and quality. Her curly hair was soft around her face, a hungry, blood-greedy look in her brown eyes.

She'd disappeared again, but left a question floating behind her. "Can you still take pain like a man, Mick? Even after last night, and all those frozen peas?"

"That's for you to test, Mistress. If you give me that honor."

"Drop to your knees and take off your shirt."

Light fell upon her hands as she stepped forward, though the rest of her stayed cloaked. She was threading a collar through her fingers. Two or three inches wide with silver studs, links and chains. She could hook any number of tethers to it to hold him in place.

She wasn't going to ask him what he wanted, what limits he had. They were adults. If he wanted it to stop, she'd know it. If they did a CNC scene on Ladies-In-Charge night, all limits would be up to her. He suspected she was testing the idea here. So he'd better not fuck it up.

He slipped the buttons of the shirt. Her voice cut through the air. Yep, knife sharp. He felt it on his skin.

"Pay attention. I said kneel and then take off your shirt."

The anger, the desire to fight back, swelled. Instead, he held her shadowed gaze—at least where he thought her face was—and knelt. The floor was concrete and uncomfortable. Without the colorful and festive army of floats, this would be the kind of place a crime lord would bring an enemy. That bite of concrete through aching knees would be the last thing they felt before a bullet emptied their brain matter onto it.

"With the club's resources, why do you have this place?"

He unbuttoned and shrugged out of the shirt. With her eyes on him, the fabric slid off his shoulders like the passage of her hand there. He took his time with it, expecting that would please her, too.

"This is where I come when I don't want to make DMs nervous. Or have to worry about club rules."

"How many subs have been here with you? Trusted you enough to take that risk?"

"Only a couple. Maybe it's not trust but stupidity."

When he put the shirt to the side, she emerged from the shadows. The slacks and sleeveless shirt outlined her sleek body, no spare fat. Her breasts were small, firm curves. She didn't give a damn about looking womanly, but nailed it because she channeled female energy at its highest power. His Artemis. She was the sexiest woman he'd ever seen.

Then he noticed her jewelry. She had a skeleton pendant like his, except the bony figure had a more feminine look, and a pewter daisy behind its nonexistent ear. A girl skeleton.

Like the pendant from last night, the cord was long enough to let the skeleton dangle between her breasts. Above it was a second necklace on a chain. The silver dagger twined with a thorny rose, several crystals in the design.

He moved his attention over the slope of her ribs, her waist and flare of hips, the long legs. He thought of them wrapped over his ass, insistent, driving him in deeper.

His emotions bucked, water white capping from a rising wind. Especially as she came closer, her gaze traveling over him in the same way, down his throat, over his bare chest and shoulders, his abdomen. Every inch of skin and fur. The snarling wolf was behind him, and he felt like curling his lip at her, threatening with teeth.

Her dark eyes on his, she held out her hand, in front of his mouth. "Do it. But don't use your hands."

He bit down on the side of her palm, tasting her, feeling the bone and sinew, all of it his to tear into. He kept his teeth clamped there as she gripped his hair and twisted tight. While she did that, she bent and brushed her lips against his temple, his cheek bone.

His grip eased and her hand was free, on his chest, pushing him back to his heels. He'd left teeth marks on her skin. He wanted to taste her the same way, leave evidence of himself all over her.

"Eyes down," she said. "Head stays up."

He did it because he wanted to. It let him fully absorb the sensations that accompanied her putting the collar around his neck. Her knuckles brushed his beard and the hairline above the collar's hold in the back. She buckled it with sure fingers, making it snug, then hooked her finger in one of the rings and tugged. "Look at me, Mick."

If he tried to explain what kind of forces were swirling through him, he'd turn into a monster and do something terrible. A shudder ran through him. Her hand was on his shoulder, feeling that earthquake.

"If you make me repeat myself, you'll regret it."

He lifted his head, but stopped when he was gazing at her abdomen. Disciplined, firm. He thought of a crepe myrtle tree, the slim trunk stripped of bark, so smooth and silky to the touch. Would that be how she would feel, naked?

"What do you want, Mick?"

She'd already asked him a version of that question. She knew there was more. He hedged.

"I thought you didn't care what your subs want."

"I don't. But I want to know what to deny them."

His smile brought pain. And words he'd never spoken to anyone. Maybe even to himself.

"I want someone who knows me. Really knows me. All my dark places. Understands just how deep my need for pain goes. I need someone who knows how to hurt me badly enough I feel like I might be dying, but I'm not. When I get out of bed and do my job tomorrow, sore as hell, that pain will feel like those little ripples after a climax. Reminders I can savor. Is that fucked up?"

"I don't deal in judgment." She paused. "When you call me Mistress, it's not how my subs mean it. You're still calling me Mistress of the Hunt. Why are you fixated on Artemis?"

His gaze finally lifted. "I'm not one of your subs. I'm just yours."

Her mouth tightened. "Do you have an answer to the question?"

"There was a vulnerability to Artemis the others didn't have. It suggested she needed someone's care, someone at her back, someone to hunt with her." Mick pushed past the flash in her gaze, the denial. "As well as to be someone for her to hunt and bring down. He might be her match, but at the end of the day, when the hunt is over, what he most wants is to be the predator she captures for herself."

Cyn hooked her fingers in a link and pushed his chin up with her knuckle. As he spoke, his gaze had shifted to her mouth, her throat, and her gesture told him she wanted him to meet her eyes again. But his lids felt heavy. He didn't know why. For her, though, he managed it.

116

He was glad he'd made the effort, because he'd ignited a fire in her brown eyes that brought heat to the ice he carried at his center.

He knew the dangers of letting it melt, and told himself not to put that on her. He could keep it separate, unthawed, and give her everything else.

He wouldn't be here long. *Give her everything you want to give her.* Not what that fucked up part of him was screaming for.

Screw that. Do it. Show her what you need.

It wasn't about what he needed.

Her hand slid to his carotid. She stroked, putting pressure on it. She was good at that, too, not cutting off the blood flow, but inciting that dizzy feeling. He swayed and her hand was on his shoulder again, firm and strong.

Slowly, his head dipped. He rested his forehead against her upper abdomen.

Here. This was the spot. He would stay right here and hold it together. A sigh lifted and lowered his shoulders, and he put his arms around her hips. Curled his fingers into her waistband, dug in hard. She was a buoy in a storm.

His Mistress stiffened at the uninvited intimacy, but after a bated moment, she curled her fingers in his hair again. Stroked his nape, for at least a dozen heartbeats. Then her patience with him expired. She tightened her grip and pulled his head back.

He let his arms drop. It was enough. Any more, and that monster would be loose, and he wouldn't be able to contain the agony inside it.

Inside   him.

CHAPTER EIGHT

Mick's move, resting his head against her abdomen, curling his arms around her tight enough to suggest she was keeping a drowning man above water, startled her. But her desire to keep standing there, just stroking his head, was even more unnerving.

She didn't like to get into a rut, a routine. She liked to change things up. There was no need here. The terrain between them had terraformed over ten years, and was waiting for them to explore it.

Even so, a tornado of knives could come through at any moment, cutting everything she'd built for herself to ribbons. She had to stay sharper than they were, keep her armor thick.

She moved back, lifting a finger to keep him where he was. Going to the switch panel, she chose the spotlight she wanted. The warehouse safety lights and upper windows offered enough illumination to get around, but she wanted to see his reaction to the options she had.

Tape on the floor carved out a circle among the jungle of floats. Though he probably thought she rented out the warehouse for storage, the floats were hers. She bought them at auction, retired from parades across the country. A late-night Internet hobby. She liked the dark circus atmosphere it created.

The spotlight shone on a pillory inside the circle. The device was cold and unforgiving metal. She could lower the post to put a man on his knees, if that was where she wanted him. Uncooked rice scattered on concrete could be unforgiving.

The custom piece had been crafted by Jon Forte, another New Orleans Dom. Cyn had sat in Jon's giant home workshop, watching him make the final modifications for her, welder's helmet in place, his midnight black hair tied back on his shoulders. His wife, Rachel, a voluptuous blonde thirteen years older than him, was a physical therapist and part-time yoga instructor. She was also his devoted submissive. Their love was like a swimming pool of joy. Anyone in their proximity was immersed in it.

Cyn might have said that sarcastically to Vera, but she didn't feel it that way. Though she wasn't admitting it to anyone, it had been peaceful and lovely to be around.

Just like Ben, Jon worked for Kensington & Associates, which was a manufacturing and acquisitions firm. Jon was K&A's tech and engineering VP.

Matt Kensington, the CEO, worked out at Roughnecks, too. Cyn routinely challenged him to a sparring match, and Matt always refused. With an annoying old school gallantry, he wouldn't raise a hand against a woman.

It rubbed Cyn the wrong way, but she kept her snark mostly contained, because K&A was a client, and because Matt and Ros were long time friends.

Matt was also good at fencing Cyn's biting remarks. She could respect that, even as he got on her nerves. He looked at her as if he knew something about her she didn't know. Arrogant asshole.

She was self-aware, even if she preferred to ignore what her self was aware of, most of the time. Whatever pushed her buttons about him had to do with her, not him. It didn't stop her from wanting that fight. All good things came to those who could wait. Their banter on it always had an edge on her side of things, but she played nice. Tried to.

She wasn't great at waiting. But she was far better at it now than when she and Mick had first crossed paths.

Cyn crooked a finger in his direction, keeping her gaze on the pillory. "Come here."

It didn't surprise her that he rose to do so. Some subs would have crawled on their knees, because she hadn't told them to get up. Simon Says.

Mick wasn't crawling to anyone. But he would kneel before her when she desired it.

The top piece of the pillory was locked in the upright position, leaving the bottom ready to receive a man's wrists and neck. When Mick stood at her shoulder, she nodded toward it, a mute command.

Mick didn't hesitate. He laid his wrists in the concave slots, his neck in the center one. The pillory's current height gave him a thirty-degree bend, his back and ass muscles flexing.

The wrist openings had tracks that could be loaded with accessories. Like a strand of barbed wire knots. Right now the tracks were empty, so when tightened they felt like metal cuffs. The neck opening wasn't adjustable, protecting the occupant from strangulation, though she kept a sharp eye on her sub's condition, in case he sagged against it, putting dangerous pressure against his windpipe. If that happened, a release button dropped the bottom and allowed her to ease the unconscious sub to the floor. Since she'd used it more than once, she'd appreciated Jon's awareness of her need.

She moved to the pillory and pressed the button to lower the top piece. It did so at a gradual pace, giving the occupant time to adjust his wrists and neck position if needed to avoid having his skin pinched. Unless that was what she wanted. Sy had carried an angry red and blue mark on his throat for a couple weeks.

The pillory settled, a satisfying thunk happening as the bolts went into place. Jon could have created a silent locking mechanism, but she'd wanted the psychological effect of a man hearing that point of no return, knowing he was dependent on her mercy.

Moving to her supply cabinet, outside of Mick's field of vision, she retrieved one of her claws. The metal piece curved over her forefinger, the ring snugged behind her first knuckle.

Cyn returned to him at a saunter, savoring the bare back, the tense ass, thighs and shoulders. Bunched biceps. Were his fingers curled into fists on the other side of the pillory's hold,

120

or loose? She guessed a half curl. Mick was the type of man who kept his options open.

She slid one fingertip along his back, up the valley of his spine, to his nape, curving her hand over it and tracing the opening around his neck.

Then she dragged the claw over his shoulder. With very little additional pressure, she could draw blood.

A quiver went through him at the unexpected sensation, and he shifted his feet. She moved her touch to his waistband, following it to the front, and unhooked the slacks, loosening them enough to see bare hips. No underwear.

"You follow direction. Why don't you wear jeans?"

"I would have worn them if you wanted that. Casual business attire just works better for most things I do."

She left the slacks hanging precariously above the treasure of his naked ass. Moving to his front, she stroked through the longer strands of his hair on top and tugged. She passed that sharp tip close to his unblinking eye, pricked his lip, then combed it through his soft beard.

Reaching down with her other hand, she gripped his left one, guiding his fingers several inches to the right of where his wrist was held. "Feel that tiny knob? Don't push on it."

He explored the shape. "Yeah."

"That's a safety mechanism. If you push it, the bottom will drop open, letting you go."

"I'll bet it annoyed you to have to include that."

"It did. So I tell my subs not to use it for the wrong reasons. It's to save their life and dignity, if I pass out at the wonder of seeing their bare ass."

"You've already seen my bare ass, so I don't have to worry about that. Though it would hurt my feelings if another sub's ass caused you to swoon and mine didn't."

She chuckled and moved back to the light panel. As much as she loved the pillory and what she could do with it, it wasn't her ultimate destination for him.

She switched on another spotlight. The St. Andrew's cross had been her first piece of equipment. She'd built it herself, with Jon's guidance. She'd made it with pallet wood, three glued plank layers for each crosspiece. The center bolt and floor anchoring hardware made it overbuilt, but she'd known the strength of the men she'd put on it. It wasn't about being pretty.

Over time, the unpainted, unfinished top planks had been seasoned and smoothed with sweat and blood, but a sub could still find splinters when his fingers clawed at the wood, seeking a purchase to bear what she was doing to him.

While she was building it, the cop—Mick—had been the first she'd fantasized about putting on it.

The way Mick gazed at the cross confirmed this was where she wanted him for the bulk of this session.

She pressed the switch to draw back the bolts and raise the top, releasing him. "Go to the cross. Put your hands and feet where the cuffs are."

He complied. As he moved in that direction, he didn't keep his pants from sliding lower. She'd unfastened them, so he wouldn't touch them. By the time he was there, she could see the upper rise of his buttocks and a tempting hint of the seam between them.

She closed the distance between them again. "Take off the shoes and socks. Still no hands."

He used his toes with smooth agility and a lot of muscle movement. When she came closer and tugged his slacks all the way down, she noted a slight shudder as the zipper scratched against his erection. Unintentional discomfort or pain was a bonus that pulled her deeper into the things she wanted to do.

He kicked it all to the side, getting it out of her way. "I assume you don't pick up clothes," he noted.

"Do I look like your fucking maid?" she asked pleasantly.

A grim chuckle as he glanced at her. "No. She wears a frilly black and white number."

"How cliché."

"I'm a man. When it comes to sex, there's no such thing as too many clichés."

"Look straight ahead."

Stepping behind him, she took a deliberate step back, no physical contact and taking away his ability to see her. While she silently studied the view, every enjoyable inch, she monitored his reaction. As the moments stretched out, his tension increased. He wasn't comfortable with someone out of view behind him. Just like most cops. Or seasoned criminals.

He'd learned to adapt to it and contain the reaction, but he was as alert and aware of his surroundings, of potential threats, as a wild animal. Being close to that kind of energy stirred her blood. Like she'd found a mate.

In a purely temporary way.

"What do you see?" His voice had gotten throatier, deeper. She wanted to take that sound, turn it into something physical and stroke herself with it. Climax around it, with it vibrating through her tissues.

"A canvas." His lifted arms and spread legs, shoulder width. His back, broad between the shoulders, rib cage narrowing to waist, the flare of buttocks and hip. His hands flexed. He kept his palms and wrists pressed to the wood like he was bound. Eventually, she might command him to dig his nails into it, see if he could find splinters.

She cupped his ass with one hand. Drawing closer, she reached between his thighs and feathered her fingers over his testicle sac, the heavy weight of it hanging between his braced legs.

A brief tensing, because he didn't know if she'd use the claw. That uncertainty made her shiver, a man's apprehension combined with his determination to accept what she wanted to do to him, without knowing what that would be.

123

The wood could break, if the man was strong enough and what she did to him spiked an adrenaline surge that high. Mick looked capable of it. She loved that cross, but the possibility was a pleasant charge.

Memories were the only thing that lasted, and the good ones embellished themselves over time.

"I've taken pictures of my canvases, before and after," she murmured. "I've thought about making cards out of them. Like charity organizations send out, paintings done by tiger paws or the sweep of a dog's tail."

The sweep of a flogger, the red patterns it left behind.

His half chuckle was tight. "What goes through your mind, while you're doing it? Hurting someone like that?" His muscles quivered under her hand, his head resting on his stretched arm.

These are my marks. It happened. They're there, even when they disappear. On you, in you. With you.

All that went through her head, but she only said, "'I was here. I did that.'" A weird smile twisted her lips. "Do you think they'd keep that card, like they would a birthday greeting from their grandmother? Or congratulations for a wedding or a new job?"

"I would." He dipped his head, momentarily forgetting her command and trying to look behind him. Then he remembered. "Actually," he mused, "I'd probably throw the others away. Except from my grandmother. She'd curse me from Heaven." He paused. "Do any of them…your canvases, ever ask you what you see when you look at the pictures?"

No, they didn't. She didn't have these conversations with her subs. Nothing suggesting a personal interest beyond the session. Sy was probably the closest to being a friend, and though they might banter about it over drinks in the lounge, it was high level, fun analysis. Not intimate.

Usually when a sub tried to engage her like this, she recognized it as a defensive measure, an attempt to get inside her. Mick was already there, though. Staring at the walls she'd painted, and what she'd put upon them.

Ros and the others accepted her sadism with genuine "my kink isn't your kink" tolerance. But they didn't ask her much about it, either, because it was well outside their comfort zone. She hadn't thought she wanted to talk about it, and maybe she didn't normally. But with him, it was different. She wanted to hear where his mind went next. He didn't disappoint.

"What if you had the chance to tour a gallery with an artist? A famous one. Ask them questions."

She stroked the bullet scars, but not like she stroked the cuts, bruises and welts she'd made. Those were marks she wanted to stay on him. She wished the bullet scars could disappear, could never have been there.

"I wouldn't want to do that. The person looking at the art...it's theirs in a different way. If I was the artist, I'd rather find out what meaning it gives to them. Rather than risk taking that away from them. Maybe the artist sees it as commercial crap he did for money. Or he was bored and it was something to do."

"Do you think that's why subs don't ask you what you see when you look at the marks you put on them?"

Her hand stilled, but as she remained silent, he kept going, his voice drifting and a little rough, going down a rocky slope in his head. "I'm betting when he goes home after a session with you, he twists himself around like a pretzel, to try and look. Or maybe he gets the light bulb idea to use two mirrors. When he sees what you've done to him, he frames it in terms of how it relates to him, his needs. How it makes him feel."

"That's typical. Expected."

"Yeah. It is. He's thinking, 'Did I please her, enough she'll be willing to give *me* that again?'" His fingers curved against the cross. "But does the selfish bastard wonder about you, and what made you choose *him* as your canvas? Does he feel fucking grateful for that, like he should? Does he hope he pleased you enough he'll have the opportunity to give *you* that gift again?"

She moved to the front, where she could see his face between the two upright pieces of the cross. "Enough," she said, far more gently than she usually spoke.

His gaze rose to hers as she put her hand on his face. It was haunted. "Enough," she repeated.

"You don't need to bind me," he said. "I won't move, no matter how much it hurts."

Her alpha preferences usually made that kind of assertion in the beginning. They saw this as a test of their abilities, a chance to prove their fortitude, what they were willing to take. Much like what he'd described, that was about them, not her. That arrogance was another enjoyable challenge, a wall to break down.

However, she heard no boast in the words, no arrogance in his suddenly flat expression. She answered in the same calm and rational way, even as it disturbed her, what it suggested was going on inside him.

"It's part of the creation. When you yank against the bonds, flex or quiver, the way your muscles move, the resistance, changes the welts, the shape of the bruises."

He thought it through. "Your strikes, my dance. The combination makes the art."

"They make the moment," she corrected. "Art is a bullshit term. It's a moment."

She buckled the left cuff over his wrist, keeping the forefinger claw out of the way. As she always did when she started to bind a man, holding him for her will and pleasure, she felt a nice charge in her lower belly.

But there was a deeper level to this. She'd said this was new terrain for them, and the mystery of it, the unexpected turns it had already taken, had removed any awareness of the world outside. She didn't know what time of day it was and didn't care. This space, and the man, was hers for as long as she wanted.

A stillness had gripped him. He was following her movements like she'd put her hand inside a cage where a savage creature hid in the shadows, waiting for his chance.

"Tell me what's going through your head as I do this," she instructed.

His mysterious eyes had gotten darker, the pupils expanding. The cords in his forearms stood out, his naked body vibrating. His cock was stiff, fully erect, fluid glistening on the tip. She thought about clasping and stroking it, but preferred to let him see her staring at it, make him long for her to do that. As he spoke, his breath teased her temple.

"I'm looking at all of you, taking you in on every level. Scent, taste, your sheer fucking energy, pressed all over me. I'm aware of your cunt, wanting it to be wet, wanting to fill it. I want to eat you, tear you to pieces, bathe in everything you are, take you inside me and keep you there. So I'm never without you, never alone in this horrible, fucking world."

As he spoke, he'd adjusted, thrusting his face forward so she was staring up at that beast, two pieces of rough-hewn cross the only barrier between them. She had one hand resting close enough to where he was cuffed that his fingers had latched onto her pinky. He was holding it uncomfortably tight, making the bones ache.

Some subs became far more dangerous when they were bound, as if the restraints gave terrible parts of themselves permission to come forth. She should step back and free herself.

She didn't move. "For some people, the only way to find love is through violence," she said in an even voice. "Like being born. Tearing apart and forever marking the person who carried us. So that someone a thousand years from now might look at a female skeleton and figure out she gave birth." Her fingers passed over the one at her throat.

"But they can't say she was a mother or not." Mick didn't blink. "Only the child can say that."

"Remind me to dig up my mother's bones and carve, 'Not a fucking mother' on them."

His lips curved, quick, grim. It made her think the dangerous moment had passed.

She wasn't often wrong.

She moved in front of him to cuff his right wrist. Instead, that hand shot between the V of the upper pieces and closed around her throat.

He yanked her to him, her left breast against the wood, pinching her nipple. His wolf's eyes were fierce.

"Kiss me, Mistress. Remind me I'm not a beast."

"Go fuck yourself, Mick."

His grip constricted, and blood pounded in her temple. Grabbing onto the cross to steady herself, she clamped her other hand over his tense wrist. Then she jammed the metal claw into the soft spot between two of his fingers.

The area was sensitive to mild amounts of pain, and she didn't make it mild. When a muscle flexed in his jaw, and a shudder went through him, taking the pain, pushing into it rather than pulling back, sensation rippled between her legs. As if a crop had touched her there.

She'd done that to herself before. If she had the urge and it wasn't the time or place to inflict it on someone else, she could get a mild charge from doing it to herself, visualizing when she'd next do it to a willing sub.

"You want to make someone afraid of you, go find one of your little doting subs."

The line between playing a game and getting lost in one's own fucked up head was a tangled helix. When her sister had breathed her last in Cyn's arms, Cyn had seen what she saw in Mick now. Contorted despair caused by a failure to live up to expectations, so profound that hell's punishments could never match how she could torment herself with it.

Cyn didn't have to know how he'd come to experience it to handle it. She wouldn't tolerate it in this space.

"Let me go, baby." Still assertive, despite the constricted airway, but she discarded her aggression. It wasn't needed.

What went through his eyes reminded her of cloud shadows passing over a desert landscape. Like a switch flipping, his fingers loosened and the look vanished. He didn't retreat. Didn't go behind a wall. He merely put the hand back where it needed to be so she could buckle the cuff.

As she did it, he went perfectly still again. The moment had passed, no need to analyze or discuss it. They understood each other without understanding a damn thing. And when she secured the second cuff, the most important battle was won.

He was hers.

When she moved to the corner table where she'd laid out her options before he arrived, those three words beat time in her head. Like that song he'd hummed when he took her to his uncle's car.

Gone, gone, gone.

The lyrics had stuck with her, despite the certainty she'd never see him again. She'd put it on her playlist, and had heard it tell her, over and over, that he would love her, long after she was gone. She was a practical person; she'd known it would be easy to idealize a ghost. But right now she latched onto the *Gone, gone, gone* part. That was where they were going, some place far beyond the world outside this space.

She pulled back the cloth that had concealed her options. Coiled single tail whip, cane, dragon tail, and tawse. An older Scottish sub had given her the last one, telling her the discipline tool had been used on him when he was a schoolboy. It hurt like hell, and enduring it had been a badge of honor among the boys.

Cyn had told Vera if that reincarnation crap she believed in was real, and a person could return as someone in the past, Cyn was petitioning to be a Scottish teacher back then.

She picked up the cane and paced toward Mick. She liked to leave patterns. She wondered if she could manage an M. For "Mine."

The desire unsettled her. She only wanted a man to be hers inside a session. During that time, she'd have a version of them no future girlfriend or wife would ever know. But the connection between her and Mick had existed long before now. It sort of freaked her out, but he hadn't raised any walls against her, so she wouldn't do that to him. They'd see where it took them.

She risked as much of herself in this space as her subs did. She wanted to hear them strangle on the grunts of pain, see their hands flex, bodies jerk, their eyelids squeeze against tears of rage and frustration as they fought through it, fought to keep pace with her. Keep it pure.

Give me something as good as what I'm giving you.

Make your marks on my mind the way I put mine on your body, so I can carry them into my week, my world.

So I don't give in to the clamoring urge to burn it all down. Or wrap my fingers around the throats of everything I love and try to swallow their air, feel what they feel. Take them inside so I'm never alone, so they can't leave me.

That was the fear that never went away, no matter how good life got, because the reminders of the dark spaces were always there.

Mick had dipped his head, catching her in his peripheral vision. For a heartbeat, it was as if they were the same person. He gave her words back to her.

"Let it go, baby."

It wasn't a permission. It was a confirmation that the space belonged to them both. The rest of the world and its judgments could go fuck itself.

Warm-ups were for subs who received a sexual charge as pain built from lower to higher levels. As a sadist, that didn't interest her.

She closed in and struck, that short snap of the wrist that delivered a small stroke but brought a sharp, concentrated slice of pain. It hit the bitable curve of his ass. Without any warning that it was about to happen, his flinch was immediate, his body tightening.

The impact rippled across his skin, the pain spreading out. That song in her head would set the tempo. The beats she counted out between strikes would make the subsequent ones hurt even more.

The man was battle-scarred and gorgeous, top to toe. No tattoos. Nothing to mar her canvas except her.

She brought the cane down again. And again. She was skilled enough to land the strikes where she wanted them, experienced enough to evaluate him without breaking the rhythm. She could multitask.

He'd braced his feet, fingers flexing in the cuffs, an invitation for more. She didn't require an invitation. By the time she was done, every sub knew how much pleasure she derived from beating the hell out of him.

They were there because they needed that knowledge, as much as they needed the pain itself.

Physical tools could break a man open, rouse his most violent impulses and difficult emotions. That was when the pain's impact would escalate. Having the soul stripped turned catharsis into real torture.

Though she aimed for that goal post, it was why she preferred the ones who would safeword before they went past it. She didn't want them crying, baring their souls to her, expecting her to put them back together.

She wanted a man who could take the fight. He might admit he was beaten, but just for this round. She wanted him to walk proud the next day, because he'd held onto his core, who he was, no matter what.

Just as she had.

What she wanted to see in their eyes was the knowledge of how far she'd taken them, what she'd seen and accepted, because the same existed in her woman's soul. They weren't alone.

She changed the rhythm, the spacing, and he started to move in reaction to the building pain. Writhing, jerking, grunting, cursing under his breath. Sweat built in the valleys formed by bunched muscles. When she stopped, red lines hashtagged his ass and upper back. She was quivering with her own reaction, palms creased with moisture.

She steadied herself before ambling around him, letting him see her. She tapped her palm with the cane like a disapproving schoolmistress.

Mick's fevered gaze told her he was still with her, but the haze was threatening at the edges. "More," he rasped.

"I'm not here to take orders from you," she said. "You need a reminder of that."

She returned to the table. Two filled gallon jugs were beneath it. After she put down the cane, she picked up one and came back to him. Without hesitation, she uncapped and upended it over his flesh. Harsh grunts tore from him as the saltwater bathed the raw cane marks. The sounds tickled her flesh like his tongue, his mouth. She wanted them on her.

She tossed the plastic jug to the side. It rolled across the concrete with a hollow series of taps. Circling to his front again, she put her hand up, showing the damp creases in her palm, his effect on her. "Taste my salt, Mick. Just like the salt I poured over your skin."

He was still twitching from the effects, but it didn't stop him from reaching for her, pushing against his bonds. His blue eyes transformed from that haze to sharp need in a blink, hungry for what she was offering. She closed her eyes as his tongue followed her lifeline. Goddamn, he was as precise and targeted as if he was licking her cunt. She had no doubt that was what he was imagining.

132

She braced herself against the cross with her other hand. It put it near his bound one, and he overlapped her fingers, holding on as he continued to tease her. She moved the hand away from his mouth to his hair, threading her fingers through the strands that had been neatly brushed. Not anymore. They fell forward over his wild eyes and bearded face, increasing the animal look of him. But as she stroked him, slow, easy, taking the moment, they changed.

She saw the despair come back. "More," he said, a rasp like a hiss.

She covered her uneasiness with an indifferent tone. "I don't care what you want. Remember? Telling me what you want just tells me what to deny you."

She'd had subs get really pissed at her in these moments, start cursing at her, calling her names. Their emotions unfettered from manners or rules.

Instead, that switch flipped behind Mick's eyes again. A resignation, acceptance. An unexpected spark of humor.

"You are a total bitch." A compliment.

He was pulling himself back together. How much would it take for him to safeword? The rational part of her, the responsible Domme she'd learned to be, thought sooner rather than later would be better. The part of her that was far less untamed and way more unpredictable hoped he wouldn't.

Ever.

"'If you do not teach me, I shall not learn.'" He licked his lips. She noted he'd bitten the bottom one, probably when she'd poured the saltwater over him. "That's a line from one of Samuel Beckett's poems. 1936," he added hoarsely. "He knew his shit, at least in that moment. That's when you usually know stuff. For just a moment. It stays if you hold onto it. Like I held onto you. You have to hold onto things. Or they're gone. Gone...gone...gone."

Had she been humming it? He met her gaze. "Teach me, Mistress. So I can learn."

She moved behind him, so he couldn't look at her and she could study him, this naked man bound to a cross marked with the blood and sweat of other men.

A million emotions were tumbling inside her.

Though most people focused on the end result of her sessions, the physical evidence of what she inflicted and how he absorbed it, the greatest energy expenditure was what went on in her head and how she monitored what was provoked in his, the man under her control. A vital effort to ensure she didn't kill him. Physically or mentally.

She'd learned a lot about herself in ten years. Learned to appreciate life and love, friendship and family. Learned to balance her darkness with those things.

She wasn't sure he had.

She was looking at a man who took too much and was asking for far more, wanting her to let that maelstrom have them both. If she ended up killing him, she had the disturbing thought he'd cross that threshold, turn around and give her a thumbs up and that mysterious smile. It would hold things about himself he'd kicked into a personal void until a session with her brought them back to the light.

No. Mick wouldn't do that to her. She stepped back from the drama. This was edge play. His behavior was a warning flag, yes, helping her identify treacherous areas for him. All subs had them. But once she was aware, it was under her control. He'd left her a tempting environment around those edges, and she didn't have to go that deep into his personal shit to play there. Even though the desire to do so was far stronger than it normally was.

Another warning flag.

He'd given himself to her just for now. This session. That was the most important boundary to remember.

Retrieving the single tail, she coiled it over and under her hands, several times. As the silence drew out, him waiting on her, she found her center.

She dropped the coil, shook it out, then threw the whip, snapping it over his back. The popper hit the most angry-looking hashtag. She wanted it to deliver a hefty sting, a bee stabbing a large bore needle into skin.

Since she was well-practiced with it, it did.

Mick jerked, head dropping forward. That ripple traveled from his shoulders down his back, over his buttocks, creating more delectable quivers. Ones that became rhythmic flexing as she started forcing that reaction with the whip. It was as if he was fucking a woman while she watched.

She could cut with the fall of the single tail. She thought of what she'd considered, cutting an M on his back. Like a Domme Zorro.

The black humor helped center her further. She adjusted her technique and landed the first cut. About an inch from where she intended, but if she needed to do a couple practice Ms, that wouldn't bother her.

Especially if she earned the reaction the first cut did. A grunt was wrested from him, his body bucking hard right after he made the sound, as if he was admonishing himself for the weakness. She increased her strikes, the targeting, so he couldn't stop the sounds of pain. She made sure she drew them out after every strike. A gift to her.

"Your pain belongs to me, Mick," she said.

She had a passable M, the four marks darker than the other practice ones. His fists were clenched, powerful thighs trembling. She wanted to leave teeth marks all over his ass.

Instead, she picked up the second full gallon jug and strolled in front of him. When he understood her intent, the tension in his jaw suggested maybe, for an instant, he thought of safewording. But he bit his lips instead. The bottom one was still bleeding.

"Stay still." Leaning in, she sucked on it, flicking her tongue over the cut. He closed his eyes, and another sound came from him, a muted one of such need she felt the pull of it in her own womb. He was still hard, though the flag's angle had gone down a few degrees.

She eyed him critically. "If your cock is fully hard after I pour this over your back, Mick, I will fuck you."

"Fuck my ass...or fuck me?"

"If either one pleases me, does it matter?"

His lips tugged in that rueful expression, an astonishing feat when he was shaking the way he was. But the pain she inflicted didn't do permanent harm, and if he sought this kind of session routinely, he knew it.

She had to know the difference if she wanted to keep her regulars in a condition to serve her. When this was done, she would instruct him on follow up care to ensure those cuts would heal fine. His muscles and joints would be sore tomorrow, mainly because of how he braced himself to take the mental and physical stress load, but maybe one of those little bird subs had a masseuse license. He could prevail upon her good will.

"Do what pleases you, Mistress."

"I always do."

She moved behind him. He steeled himself for it, getting ready. So instead of pouring the water on him, she leaned in and put her mouth on the M.

She traced the first line with her tongue, her lips. She'd made the strike closer to a welt than a cut, though she could taste the light smear of blood that had broken through. She moved to an area she hadn't struck with cane or whip, marking that skin with the suction of her mouth. When she adjusted and sank her teeth into the flesh around the center V of the M, he stiffened, hands curling in his bonds.

So far he'd avoided the involuntary digging that could result in splinters. Where his palms rested, the wood had been worn smooth by other sweaty and clutching fingers.

She'd drawn out splinters using her tweezers and a needle, while her bound sub breathed hard, head down, fighting the clash of sensations that came from inflicting pain for vastly different reasons.

Care versus cruelty. It was its own special mindfuck.

She drew back, uncapped the jug and poured it over his shoulder blades in a smooth arc. He jerked, a step-ahead reaction to the pain. His brain would tell him it was pain, and then recalibrate, an interesting reaction that rocked him forward on his toes and made his muscles quake from shoulders to calves.

The second jug didn't hold saltwater. It was a diluted salve, one from a local homeopath who also happened to be a high pain masochist. She was the wrong gender for Cyn's interests, but she understood aftercare needs. The ingredients aided in the healing, cleaning and protection of the wounds Cyn caused.

The first touch of it brought a wash of heat, followed by a rippling coolness, especially when she leaned in and blew on the track the fluid followed.

"Jesus," he muttered. When she looked at his profile, she saw his eyes were closed. He swallowed hard.

She rubbed the salve over his back with light fingertips. It would sting where she'd cut deeper. However, it was so much better than the saltwater, Sy had told her it was like the pleasure of her bite.

After she covered Mick from nape to ass with the oil, she took off all her clothes, not letting him see her, though his head came up at the sound of a zipper and rustling fabric. Retrieving a head mask from the table, she put it on him.

He tried to jerk away, but before he could dislodge it, she had it snugged down and zipped up the side. The nose area had a mesh panel for breathing. There were ear holes on the sides so he could hear. She could choose to open the mouth or eye slits, but she didn't right now.

His reaction to sensory deprivation was stronger than to the sting of the cane, cut of the whip or burn of saltwater. He went rigid for a full ten seconds as she stepped back, waiting.

137

Waiting for the muffled safeword to come, if this was a limit he couldn't tolerate.

He had no problem being bound, enduring high levels of pain, even with the threat of much worse on top of that. But everyone's "too much" was different. As different as the memories and experiences they carried within them, creating those hard limits.

That rigidity settled at last, one set of muscles at a time. She watched him breathe it out through flaring nostrils. And when she shifted to his front, his cock had performed as required. He was fully erect again. She expected he'd used the incentive she'd offered to counter his reaction to the mask.

She was naked, and she wasn't behind him.

Though she enjoyed a good strap-on fuck of a man with a muscular ass like his—especially if she used one of her special oils to make it burn like the fires of hell—she wanted him inside her. She'd liked how he'd filled her and wasn't in the mood to deny herself a repeat experience. She began to unbuckle his restraints, scraping her nails across cane and whip marks for the pleasure of it. "When you're free, turn around and put your back against the cross. Your arms behind you, gripping the middle part. No misbehaving. Not if you want inside my pussy."

His head turned in her direction. Even with the mask, the calm in his voice held menace. "You let me go, I could fuck you, with or without your say so."

She put her hand alongside his throat. "No, baby. You couldn't."

His jaw flexed and, though she couldn't see his eyes, she *felt* that odd despair from him again. Then it was gone. When she finished releasing the cuffs, he complied with her order. He winced as his tender skin came in contact with the wood, but he pressed himself harder against it by locking his hands together behind the narrow waist of the cross. The male mind could leap mountains for the promise of pussy.

Though the cynicism didn't ring true with Mick, she needed its reminder to give her breathing space. The intensity of what was ricocheting between them had her wanting to give him the clutch of her sex, not just for her own pleasure, but as proof of how pleased she was with him.

She put her hands on his shoulders, and abruptly his hands released and came back around to grasp her bare hips. The energy that thrummed through him reflected the impact of the flesh-to-flesh contact, the effort it took him to stop her, to stop himself from moving his hands anywhere else. He dipped his head in the general direction of his clothes.

A condom. She'd forgotten something she never forgot.

She shook it off and moved to the table. She'd left her own preferred brand there, and returned, tearing it open before she rolled it down his rigid length, giving him a few firm strokes that had his legs quivering as he restrained himself from thrusting into her touch. He could be well-behaved when he put his mind to it. When she wanted that.

"Unclasp your hands and lift them up to the cuffs. Hold onto them." When he did so, she put her hands on his shoulders, tightened her core muscles and climbed him, wrapping her legs around his hips.

To do that and keep herself there, her legs needed to be between his ass and the cross, wrapped over his hips. He adjusted outward for her without being told, to help her do that. As she fitted the head of his cock to her opening, she pressed her breasts against his chest and whispered into his ear.

"I'm fucking *you*. Stay perfectly still, or I stop."

She could hear the rasp of his breath, see the movement of his lips under the stretched fabric. Either prayer or curse.

She sank down on him, gripping his tightened biceps to lift herself and lower, lift and lower. God, he had a marvelous cock. It stretched, rubbed, pushed deep into her as she took more and more of it. She dropped her head back, eyes closing in pure bliss.

He'd proven better than every thought or fantasy she'd ever had about him. So far. She wouldn't build false hope for herself. But she could enjoy the hell out of this.

Her hands had moved up to his neck. His body was vibrating, at war with the urge to do what any male beast would, thrust into her heat and wetness. She rubbed her breasts against his chest, clasped his hips with tight thigh muscles. When she leaned back to slide up and down him at a different angle, her buttocks pressed against his upper thighs. All the things he wasn't allowed to touch.

When she straightened and pushed down on him again, that perfect angle, she convulsed, her climax driven like a charged rocket by his struggle to obey her, to serve entirely at her pleasure. The orgasm swept up through that joining point, her throaty cry echoing in the warehouse, bouncing against the silent floats, under the blank painted eyes of animals, monsters and voodoo queens.

She milked every last ounce out of the release. When she was done, energy churned within him, a tornado of pressure. She wanted the heat of it to scorch her. She bit his ear and put a thumb to his lips, pushing the zipper across the vinyl so he was free to speak.

"Want to come, baby?" she whispered.

She liked pushing a man to pure wild animal, everything gone except his awareness of that taut leash, her will. She wanted it to be the only thing that had any meaning in the universe, as he waited for her permission. And when she gave it, she wanted him to do what a wild animal did. Consume, tear, devour.

Somehow Mick was still there among all that. His breath rasped in and out, in and out. The words took effort to form, so much they were hard to make out, but she heard him. "That's up to you...Mistress."

He pressed his head against hers, a sudden move that reminded her of when he'd put his head against her stomach. What he needed from her went further than the spurting of his cock or a Mistress's control in a negotiated setting. He ached for something he didn't know how to ask for. Maybe he didn't even know the shape of it.

It created a similar reaction in her, but she'd choose the simplest route for it. For now.

"Come for me," she said. "Without moving."

Impossible, of course, but she gave him full marks for trying. He fought like a lion against the involuntary need to flex, thrust, jerk and buck as his cock spurted. A strangled moan told her the effort it took.

It made her do what she rarely did. Grant him mercy.

She began to rise and fall again, stroke him with her body, the clench of her sex, offering the friction she wouldn't allow him to seek for himself. It all came from her. She thought she heard a whispered *thank you, Mistress,* but she suspected it wasn't a thank you for giving him release.

Just the opposite.

It was for taking him all the way home with the leash still taut in her hand. Not letting it go.

When he was done, she slid to the ground. "Put your arms behind you again." Once he did, she moved away and donned her underwear, socks, boots, slacks and bra, letting him hear what she was going to deny him. Mostly. She left the shirt off, though she pulled her necklaces from the pocket where she'd tucked them and put them on again.

His lips tightened, but he remained still. Until she reached up to remove the mask. He jerked his head away, so violently he struck his cheek on the cross. He froze. Mumbled.

"Sorry."

He'd been almost equally resistant to her putting it on him, but she understood his reaction. "Don't want me to see your face, Mick? See what's there right now?"

"Yeah. Maybe."

So she removed it, as she was sure he expected after saying that. Running her hand through his rumpled hair, to kindly get rid of the hat-head feel, she then touched her fingertips to his jaw. He wouldn't let her lift his face, locking his neck and shoulder muscles against the pressure. He was staring at the ground off to her left, not even allowing himself a view of her breasts sitting on the demi-bra shelf.

"You're not looking for that," he said.

"Excuse me?"

"What's in my eyes. That's not what you want in a session. Like cleaning the snot or spit off my face. No reason for you to have to handle it." A tinge of humor threaded into his voice, like her curved needle stabbing into his skin, pulling the open edges of the wound together. "Remember? I can get myself to the ER while you have that congratulatory beer."

The words pierced her heart, and she rarely reacted well to deceptively softer forms of pain. "If you make me bend my knees so I can look up into your face, I swear to God I will cut a spiral around your dick with a razor blade and pour another gallon of saltwater on it. You won't be able to fuck a woman until Christmas. More importantly, you won't be able to fuck me again while you're here."

It was a whole body struggle, tension, uneven vibration, the drawing of an erratic breath, but at last he lifted his gaze.

Weariness, anguish, rage, bitterness. Pits in hell held more light.

"Oh, Mick." Tenderness wasn't part of her sessions, but he wasn't "one of her subs," the ones she held at arm's length even as she cared for and protected them. He was Mick. As significantly connected to her as Cissy had been.

But the Mistress in her saw the fear an indomitable man had, that she would make him pull the pin on the grenade of his subconscious. He was white-knuckling it now, afraid she'd broken him open such that he couldn't stop himself from doing it.

They'd gone deep enough for one day. Both of them. Time to ease back.

She returned to her table, picked up a towel and came back to wipe around his nose and mouth, gripping his hair when he tried to duck his head away. "Stop it," she chided. "Maybe I like cleaning up snot and saliva. How often have you served a Mistress, Mick?"

"A few times. I mostly do primal play."

"Oh." She quelled her disagreeable feelings about that, ignoring what it meant. But he'd picked up on her reaction, or wanted to assure her for his own reasons.

"We fight it out until we're both tired of it. Not like…I don't kneel once I win. She'll do some light bondage or impact play with me if that's what she likes. I've always kept it high level, easy. Nothing too intense."

It told her that normally he was a lot smarter about his needs. If he showed the signs he'd revealed to her, other clubs wouldn't be giving him the high marks Ros had talked about. They screamed danger to any experienced Mistress. To her and to him.

The reckless part of her was flattered. Which just meant they were the same kind of stupid. It also worried her, mostly for him. She tossed the towel to the side, stepped back and put her hands on her hips. "Relax your arms."

As he did, she said something she hadn't intended. "Do you have plans this evening?"

He eyed her, rubbing his wrists. The metal cuff marks from yesterday were still here, and the cross restraints had irritated them. "I have a late afternoon appointment, but I'm free after that. What did you have in mind? Scaling the spire of the St. Louis cathedral? Alligator wrestling in the bayou?"

Shit. He should have told her he'd had more work to do today. She might have gone easier…

What the fuck? She didn't do coddling. If the sub wasn't responsible enough to speak up and let her know his limits in a session to meet his outside responsibilities, that was his problem. Her reaction annoyed her enough she almost changed her mind, but then she didn't.

"Dinner. With friends."

Once a month, they met for a meal at Vera, Ros, Skye or Abby's house. Cyn brought wine and hors d'oeuvres, doing her part, because she told them her place wasn't set up for entertaining. Until Skye and Tiger had gotten together, she hadn't been the lone holdout on not offering a venue. Skye's warehouse loft had been more tech lab than social spot, with no dining room area, so they'd done their monthly dinners at Abby, Ros or Vera's place. But now that Tiger and Skye moved between her place and his, a spacious ranch property on the outskirts of New Orleans, they sometimes had the get-together there. Like tonight.

No one ever commented on Cyn not playing hostess. Even if something about that bugged her, she wasn't going to change it. Why she needed it to be that way went into the vault of things she didn't care to take apart.

Noting the quiver in his legs as he leaned against the cross, she pointed at a chair beside the table. "Sit."

"If you'll sit with me. I don't sit in the presence of a lady. Definitely not with a Mistress still standing."

"Unless she tells you to sit your ass down."

He moved to the chair and sat down. On the concrete floor next to it.

While watching him walk without a stitch of clothing was nicely distracting, his stiff movements told her he might need more than the salve to function tomorrow.

With an aggrieved sigh, she retrieved what was needed from her bag and perched on the chair before offering him the squat glass container. "Rub this where it hurts. If you don't, I'm kicking you out on the street."

His gaze slid down his body. "Naked?"

"It wouldn't be half as fun otherwise."

As he opened the jar, her hand fell on his back and stroked. Something she also didn't normally do, but she wanted to touch, so she was going to touch. His nostrils flared. "This is one of your tortures. What is it, dog shit?"

"It works. After the ointment soaks in, you can wash off the smell."

Dubiously, he dabbed his fingers in it, but once he put some on his thighs, she could tell the heat penetrated, and he applied it with more enthusiasm.

"So who's the dinner with?" The question was carefully casual, as if he sensed she'd made the offer with reservations.

"The team. Vera, Ros, Abby and Skye. Plus Lawrence, Tiger and Neil, so you won't be drowning in estrogen."

"I don't mind swimming in a pond of Dommes." He shot her an amused look. "It's slightly more dangerous than piranhas."

"Actually, humans can swim with piranhas, as long as the fish aren't hungry and the humans aren't bleeding. Just like sharks."

"I've never been around a Mistress who didn't have a voracious appetite. One in particular I know likes the taste of blood."

He was leveling out. Though it might be a shallow grave, his dark moments, whatever she'd seen during the session, were buried again. He put the ointment on his biceps and the round part of his broad shoulders, but he couldn't reach the center of his back. A place where abused muscles could knot like saltwater-soaked rope.

"Give me the jar."

"I can do it."

"Shut the fuck up and hand it over."

When he did and straightened, presenting his back to her, she suspected he might have been exaggerating the deficit in reach. She hid a smile. And slapped him upside the head.

Or would have, but he caught her wrist before it made contact. He gave her a return smile and put his mouth on her fingers.

145

While his mouth felt nice, she wasn't going to be denied her retribution. With the jar in her lap, she slapped his head with the other hand. He didn't take his lips from her palm or stop her this time, accepting the admonishment as his due.

"Let go of me and turn back around."

When he complied amiably, she eyed his back. "Ros has a three-legged cat, Freak. He can still contort himself just like any other cat and clean almost every inch of his body with his tongue. Humans got gypped."

"We got thumbs. It's always about the trade off."

She spread the pungent stuff over his shoulders and back. She wasn't pampering him. No woman would pass up the chance to stroke and knead his muscles and firm skin. She also wanted to feel the cane and whip marks she'd left on him, the M she'd created.

As she passed over other scars, the ones that didn't belong to her, she spoke again. "You've lived an interesting life, Mick."

"Everyone does, Mistress." His head was down, his gaze seemingly fixed on the concrete in front of his braced bare feet. "Even if most of it is spent in the same place, the mind can take you to hell and back. That's never about geography."

CHAPTER NINE

It had been a fucking interesting day all the way around.

A few hours after they went their separate ways at the warehouse, Mick thought about texting Cyn, telling her he couldn't come to dinner, and leaving it at that. He preferred not to lie to her. Instead, he found himself navigating the motorhome to Tiger's place on the fringes of the city, a property with marsh view and lots of acreage.

Not too bad for a man who'd had far better odds for being a corpse before he reached thirty. Or a permanent guest of the Louisiana correctional system.

Mick's research on the people closest to Cyn had produced insightful tidbits like that. He wondered if Tiger knew that Cyn and he had walked a similar path. Mick suspected he didn't. Cyn undoubtedly considered this group her chosen family, but there were doors she still hadn't opened to them. He understood not wanting to excavate what you'd killed and buried. Mick would be the last person to criticize her for that. If he threw those rocks, his glass house, about the size of a coffin, would shatter.

Tiger had lots of parking, and a fleet of vehicles were already there. Mick found a space for his that didn't block them, near Cyn's monster truck with the whip hanging in the gun rack. His back twitched, remembering the kiss of its cousin in the warehouse. She'd worked him over, but the ointment and salve had helped. Even if it hadn't, thanks to his eventful afternoon, that discomfort had been eclipsed. The way a toothache was forgotten when you slammed your hand in a door.

He'd *wanted* to feel the lingering pain of her marks, though. Losing that chance so soon kind of pissed him off. He didn't want to forget any single benefit of his time with her. Even the agony of that saltwater.

It had all been at her hand. At her pleasure.

147

He'd endure hell if it came attached to those three words. Mick sat behind the wheel, gazing sightlessly at the house, remembering her hands on his back, working the ointment in. Touching him. Just…touching him.

Hell, he needed to get his ass out of here. Out of New Orleans. Before he had to face the harrowing truth that the soul he'd thought he'd lost had been here all along. With her.

A bay window showed movement in the kitchen. Skye emerged from the side door, carrying a foil-covered tray. She saw him, damn it, and raised her hand.

Busted and stuck. Committed now.

She pointed toward the back and waved him on as she disappeared around the brick ranch house.

At least she didn't stick around to see him get out of the vehicle. He dry swallowed three more OTC painkillers to knock the edge off. It took a few tentative steps, and a fierce talking-to with his body before he could achieve a casual, sauntering gait and follow her path.

Cyn had seemed to want to see him in jeans, and mentioned this deal was casual, so he'd been able to balance his current state with her desires. He wore jeans without a belt, a T-shirt loose over them. Not sloppy; the clothes were comfortable but nice for presenting himself to her people.

He touched the side of Cyn's truck as he passed, his gaze scanning the other vehicles. Vera's Aston Martin, Ros and Skye's Mustangs. Skye drove a vintage blue one, Ros a more current model in red. Abby and Neil had come in his pickup. Tiger's motorcycle, a muscle Harley, was probably parked in the barn he saw near a dirt track.

Coming around the corner of the house, he saw a large gazebo, custom built with cedar. Roll-down screens kept out bugs, and it sheltered a nice outdoor furniture set and wet bar. A nearby concrete pad held grill, fire pit, and a cluster of Adirondack chairs. Tiger was busy at the grill, Lawrence and Neil keeping him company, lounging in the chairs, beers in hand. The women were under the gazebo, sitting companionably on cushioned chairs and love seats.

Cyn was in the same snug sleeveless top and boots, but she'd traded out her slacks for jeans with a saliva-producing fit. She also wore the skeleton necklace. It brought back powerful images from earlier in the day. Her arms were slim but strong. The way she'd climbed his body, lifting herself up and down on his cock with no aid, wanting him to act as if he was bound, had proven it. She'd carried herself to climax with no signs of flagging.

She glanced his way, but her brief wave toward the men was easy to translate. *Girl time right now. Go play with the boys.*

She still had a Jersey girl's frankness. The inner smile helped him keep moving the way he needed to, because even though she acted indifferent, he wasn't fooled. She was as hyperaware of him as he was of her.

The club, the straw bales, the warehouse, all of it had opened a fire of want. He expected it to burn hot long after he put New Orleans in his rearview mirror.

Stick that in the bucket of things he wasn't going to think about tonight if he could help it.

As Mick approached, Lawrence was already flipping up the top of a cooler. "What's your preference?" the former SEAL asked, reaching in to grab it.

Thank God, so Mick wouldn't have to bend over and dig one out himself. He glanced at the offerings. "Modelo with lime's good."

He thought the slow saunter, the casual slouch, was doing a good cover, but as Mick took the beer, Tiger held up his hand. "Don't sit down yet."

At Mick's curious look, the big biker strode away from the grill and ducked under the gazebo's screen curtain. As he plucked a couple throw cushions from an unoccupied chair, he tossed a comment to Cyn. She flipped him off, making the women chuckle. Cyn directed her next words toward Skye, probably about how rude her man was.

Tiger returned and dumped the two cushions in an open Adirondack chair, pointing Mick to it. His eyes twinkled. "You look like you could use the padding."

He'd decided to just stand, knowing the dangers of sitting in his current state, but his legs weren't cooperating.

"Thanks." Mortification seemed pointless, especially when the badass biker who'd provided the cushions was a submissive, and aware of Cyn's MO.

Mick gingerly lowered himself. Adirondacks were like the bucket seat of a sports car, which meant he wasn't sure how he'd get up without help, but he'd cross that bridge when he came to it.

"Thanks, man."

Cyn still didn't look his way, but from the light smile on her devilish lips, he expected she was aware of the exchange. If she and everyone else assumed his state had to do with their meet earlier in the day, that worked. He wished it was true himself.

"You gotta look to fellow subs for the soft stuff." Tiger pointed his spatula at Cyn. "Not getting it from that one."

Mick grunted. "I'm not looking for that from her."

Esteem, not tenderness. Yet she'd given him both, with equally devastating effects.

"Good thing." Tiger grunted. "She used to have Skye do her aftercare, for the subs that needed more of it."

"Were you one of them?" He didn't mean it offensively, though a simmering jealousy spurred the question. That reaction didn't surprise Mick, though he knew it had no justification.

"Only once or twice. She's not my kink. Not a criticism, man. I just don't need blood and pain in my life."

Mick made a *no problem* gesture. He got it. Every man here, including himself, had blood and pain in his life, either in his past, present or future. Yet they were all different.

150

Whereas Tiger had no desire to seek more out, Mick craved a bloodthirsty Mistress who served up agony like Paula Deen did a full Southern breakfast.

Tiger flipped the meat on the grill. One patty was on the corner, away from the others, and he removed it with a separate spatula, sliding it into a container. "Cyn's veggie burger," he explained, at Mick's curious glance. "She's vegan."

Add that to the list of questions he'd like to ask her. They hadn't really done a friendly "catch up" on the last ten years yet. Other things had taken precedence.

He noted the other men's positions. Neil's long legs were stretched out, ankles crossed, but he'd angled the chair so he could see Abby's every gesture, same as Lawrence with Ros. Men attentive to their women's needs.

When Mick had briefly met Abby at the club, he'd noted she rarely made full eye contact, though she would look to that person's left or right, pointedly enough to convey she was paying attention. Since he could recognize a Domme at fifty paces, he'd known right off it wasn't a submissive thing. His background search filled in the dismaying missing piece.

Her attention frequently touched on Neil—also a Dom, another surprise—as if he was a compass. He was still an active SEAL, which meant the TRA women provided a serious-ass support network during his deployments, for all the challenges her schizophrenia provided.

Anyone who hungered to see that kind of connection work, despite everything stacked against them, couldn't help but be affected by it.

Mick put the beer against his temple, cooling his skin. It steadied and reminded him to watch his body language. He was in the company of those with keen observational skills.

Case in point. He'd caught Cyn's attention. Her raised brow was likely the closest she came to "Are you okay?"

He tipped the beer her way. Then he realized her glass was empty. That was probably what the look was about. He really was off his game if he'd thought she was mothering him.

With an inner smile, he got to the edge of the chair and pushed himself to his feet. Fortunately for him, the chair was heavy-assed, solid wood, so he didn't topple it.

"Problem?" Lawrence asked.

"Just seeing if Cyn needs a refill."

He noted their speculative looks as he moved in her direction. Ducking under the screen curtain, he leaned over her shoulder where it pressed against the green striped cushions of the love seat, and slid his fingers along the curve. She sat next to Vera.

"Can I get you a drink, Mistress? Or anyone?"

He'd said he didn't mind swimming in a pool of Dommes, and he didn't, which was good, because he was fully pinned under their interested inspection. Only one had *his* focus, though.

Cyn slid her fingertips into his open collar, playing with his necklace, stroking his chest hair. It was better than aspirin. The pain throbbed, but it throbbed for her. "A Dr Pepper Cream Soda Zero. There should be a couple behind the wet bar."

"Because no one else here would want that crap," Skye's digital voice struck him as familiar, then he recognized Linda Hunt's voice.

"You like *NCIS: New Orleans?*" He sent an amused look her way.

"Yes. But *Silverado* particularly." Skye lifted her drink in a toast, still using Linda's voice. "'The world is what you make of it, friend. If it doesn't fit, you make alterations.'"

The chuckles were warm, and curiously, under their close regard, he felt enveloped by a protective female energy. Such a random sentimental thought suggested he might be a little loopy.

He retrieved the soda from the wet bar. None of the others needed drinks. When he returned to Cyn, he won another more-than-decent pain modifier, a brush of her hand over his, a brief nod of thanks.

As he came back to the grilling area, her attention followed him. He told himself she was staring at his ass, but the men's reaction corrected the notion.

"She's mother-henning you." Neil's at-rest demeanor matched a windless lake, so his ripple of surprise made an impact.

"What?"

"She's keeping tabs on you," Tiger clarified. "Either she's worried you have internal bleeding, or she's in an alien spaceship and that's not Cyn."

Mick shook his head at their grins and put the beer back to his temple. He didn't sit back down, not yet. The trickle of condensation reminded him of how she'd put her hand on his face at the maze. Cool and firm. Steadying.

She was responsible, watched after her subs, and followed the rules. He'd learned she'd had a few infractions early on at Progeny while she figured out the boundaries, but she hadn't had that problem in a while. Her sessions still got extra attention from DMs, because she tight-roped those lines rather than staying inside them.

Her decision to stay on those lines, instead of jumping over them, was about more than keeping her membership. Maybe they didn't know that, but he did.

She cared. She wouldn't offer to tend his hurts or God forbid, ask him outright if he was okay, the normal forms of "mother henning." But that didn't matter. The well was deep, but he could reach down into that darkness far enough to know what was there.

He tuned in to see the others looking at him. He didn't think he'd missed a question, but he needed to cover why he hadn't sat back down. "Point me toward the facilities?" he asked Tiger.

"Go in through the kitchen door. Guest bath is down the hall past the living room. Bring the vegetable kebobs when you come back out. They're on the counter."

"I can do that." He spoke with assurance.

He made it three steps in that direction.

Then his head swam, and his knees buckled. Before he could faceplant, somehow Cyn was there, ahead of anyone else. It proved his theory about care, though he wished he hadn't provided the testing ground.

"What the fucking hell? Mick…" She moved toward the ground with him, no real choice because he was a boneless sack of flour. *Shit.*

"I'm okay. It's all right. Should have eaten something." Having a fist pounded into his gut meant he'd thrown up what he'd eaten earlier, and he hadn't felt up to refueling. "Stop."

She ignored him. A Mistress like her could tell where a man was hurting from how he moved. She'd already pulled up his shirt. "Holy fuck. What…"

She was staring at the ugly red and blue bruising on his midriff. He tried to pull his shirt out of her hands, but she just smacked and shoved them away. It would have made him smile again, if he wasn't embarrassed as hell. Lawrence was kneeling on her other side, examining the injury. SEALs had medical training, to patch each other up in the field.

He carried some of that training himself. "My appointment and I had a disagreement. It's okay. He looks much worse."

Well, he would have, if he hadn't had two guys hold Mick while he punched him. He tried to get up and Cyn put a hand on his shoulder. "Stay down. You need a hospital, Mick."

Oh, hell no. "I'm good. Really. Not my first beating. As you well know."

The joke fell flat. In fact, it probably made her angrier. Most things did. He liked her anger, even as he liked when it

154

melted away in his hands, because she could give it to him and let it go. That was a gift.

"Mick."

Time to get his head out of the clouds and be a man. "Seriously, I'm fine." He met her gaze and squeezed her wrist to reinforce his resolve. "I'll be fine after I eat. Okay?"

Cyn looked at Lawrence, who was doing a gentle but still painful probe. He glanced at her, then at Mick, and back again. "If he knows his body well enough, he's probably right. Gut punches just hurt like hell and make you feel like throwing up."

"I need you to leave it at that," Mick told her when she set her jaw. "But if I'm making everyone uncomfortable, I can take mine to go." He looked at Tiger. "Smells too good to leave it behind."

Tiger stood behind Lawrence with Neil, both men studying him with hard eyes. Eyes that knew things weren't what they seemed. However, it was Tiger who reached down and offered him a hand up. "Already put out the place setting. Might as well stay."

"Appreciate it," Mick murmured, as he had to steady himself against the man's shoulder. "Though I expect that's not whose permission I need."

Tiger's expression said he had that part right, and his eyes remained watchful. An additional gut punch reminder of why Mick knew he could only be here a few days.

Ros and the other women were only a few steps behind Cyn, and her boss had a similar look in her ball-busting gaze. None of them were fools.

He needed to smooth this over, and not with bullshit. Mick squared off with them, though his attention remained on Cyn. Her expression told him nothing except she was pissed, but there was more to her silence. Which he hoped he could address, and then share a good meal with them. Even if he really did end up having to take most of his to go, because he couldn't hold down anything heavy right now.

"There are reasons I move around," he told her. All of them. "I'll only be here a few days."

When she said nothing, and her expression didn't alter, he nodded. "I'm sorry. I'll go."

"No, you won't," Cyn said abruptly. "You'll sit down and eat something. You'll take some aspirin, and put a heating pad and ice on your stomach." She stepped closer, laying her hand on his arm. "I feel like punching you myself."

"Anywhere but the gut would be considered a courtesy," he told her. "I had a handful of aspirin. I'm good on that."

The others had backed off, giving them a bubble of privacy. "Sorry," he added again.

"I'm not a fan of apologies. Especially when you're feeding me shit."

He gave her a level look. "I wouldn't do that to you. Just because I can't fill in details, doesn't make it a lie. Yesterday, when I saw you, the first thing I thought was 'Here's someone I don't have to pretend around. Someone who knows who I am, even if she doesn't know a damn thing about me.'"

He thought she understood what he was saying, because it won him a marginal amount of grace.

"Okay." She pivoted and moved toward the house. Skye had already headed that way, probably to get him the ice pack and heating pad. Which discomfited him, but short of being a rude ass and bailing, he was going to have to take the attention.

Tiger had gone that way too, but was coming back out of the kitchen with the kebobs. He stopped next to Mick and met his gaze, man-to-man. A different but no less uncomfortable attention.

"Will the trouble that gave you that beating follow you here?"

"If it would, I wouldn't have come," Mick promised. "Even if you cook the best steak I've ever eaten." His gaze

156

slid to Cyn, tracking her determined stride and set shoulders. "Or the company is everything I want to be around."

Sitting around a table and passing the food—while holding an ice pack Cyn had slapped against his belly—Mick mostly listened. Conversation included work, happenings in New Orleans, funny stories about marketing clients, Tiger's garage and being SEALs. Some anecdotes about scenes the Mistresses and subs had experienced were shared, plus thoughts about BDSM practices they'd seen, and the fellow lifestylers who did them.

It was the most normal meal Mick had enjoyed in a while. While it made the thought of leaving in a few days feel worse, he'd learned not to let stuff like that drag him down. He'd made the decisions he'd made for the right reasons, so he was at peace with that. It gave him room to focus on good moments, like this.

Cyn had chosen to sit next to him, which ridiculously made him feel like the boy chosen by the prettiest girl to dance. The table was an eight-seater, but they'd adjusted for his ninth chair. It required closer quarters, so her body brushed his. When she wasn't eating, her hand rested on his thigh, and she leaned against him, just a little.

Despite the earlier awkwardness, he'd been included in the conversation without reference to it. He suspected there was a subtle agreement that if anyone had the right to grill him for further details, it was Cyn.

He couldn't accommodate her on that, and hoped she'd let it go before it got ugly, but that was another reason he'd enjoy this while he could.

"We told him we'd be back for him," Neil was saying. "Just because he was standing on a sand bar in the middle of the ocean was no reason to panic."

Lawrence scoffed, his green eyes glinting with humor. "I'm sure it had nothing to do with you yelling, 'Hey, Tom? 'No man left behind' is a Marine thing, not a SEAL one.'"

Abby gave Neil a look of mock horror. Cyn was laughing with the others, and Mick was fascinated by the shape of her mouth, the light in her gaze, her grip on his thigh.

"So how long was he on the sand bar?" Ros asked.

"We got back before high tide." Neil shrugged. "Ninety minutes. He was stretched out taking a nap in the middle of the sandbar and had written *Fuck You* in the sand. When we pulled up, he said we could wait another goddamned ten minutes because he was in the middle of a good dream about a mermaid with…"

Neil stopped at Ros's amused expression, but Lawrence finished it. "High-capacity seashells."

"Figures," Cyn said. "A man faces death, and his final thoughts are about big tits."

"What else has greater cosmic meaning?" Tiger asked, fending off Skye's elbow with a grin.

"Where do you go after you leave here, Mick?" Vera took a bite of mustard potato salad.

"Texas. Three-day kink fest at a San Antonio club. The event isn't for a few weeks, but a face-to-face is good for identifying logistics and resources requiring more setup time."

All of which was true, but he would also be handling some other work in the area. "This is a damn good burger," he told Tiger. "The whole spread. You forget how much better food is when it's homemade."

He'd had a bite of Cyn's veggie burger too. She'd added traditional burger trappings, and it had been pretty good.

She'd eaten about half and was taking a break, sitting back and listening. Her hand had moved to his side under his untucked shirt, fingers resting just above the waistband of his jeans.

Putting his arm on the top of her chair, he slid his thumb over the point of bone at her nape. His other fingers were long enough to play with the bra strap under her scoop neckline. The contact drew her gaze to his face.

She must not step outside club lines much with her regular subs, because it seemed new to her, doing things he'd do to a woman that attracted him. Like on a date.

She wasn't shrugging him off, which was good. But she also had a more aggressive idea of what she wanted from a date. As her hand moved back to his thigh, she gripped it pretty high. Her smallest finger nestled against the give of his testicles. It wasn't a glass table, but he wasn't sure that would have stopped her.

The blatant hint of her desires had things humming between them. He'd dropped the ice pack beneath the chair. That and the heating pad that had preceded it, plus the continual flood of endorphins, were doing a good job on pain management.

Neil and Abby were across from him, and he noticed Abby looking at him, in that off-to-the-left way she had. "Do the demons talk to you?" she asked.

Other conversations paused. However, though Neil's gaze became more alert, he seemed relaxed and in sync with his wife. As Abby leaned forward, putting her elbows on the table, his long-fingered hand rested lightly on her back. Her attention remained on Mick.

The truth made the most sense. Cyn's gaze was on him as he responded. "Sometimes. Sometimes I'd do about anything in the world to get them to shut up."

Abby's hazel eyes flickered, their attention moving to his ear, his jaw. Slow, before she slid her gaze right onto his. So brief, and yet the piercing regard was effective as a bullet. Bullets only took seconds to hit their target. He thought of the times in history when people with mental illness were thought to be seers. There might be some truth to it.

"He's honest about his insides," Abby said to Cyn. "There's that, at least. Even if the numbers don't add up yet." She gave Mick a shrewd appraisal, head to waist. "And he's pretty, in a rough way. That's good. You need rough."

Cyn snorted. "What I need is dessert. Where's Ros's famous Snicker pie?"

"It's someone on the Internet's famous Snicker pie, modified for the vegan at the table, but I'm happy to copy it, since it only requires a few ingredients and two hours in the freezer," her boss responded. "Who's having a piece?"

She and Lawrence rose. While Ros pulled the pie out of the freezer, Lawrence found dessert plates. A few minutes later, nine slices were doled out, since no one was refusing dessert. A container of Cool Whip was passed around for topping. His kind of people.

When Ros put a piece in front of Cyn, Mick noted she rested a hand on his Mistress's shoulder, giving it a squeeze, before she also gave Mick a slice.

"It was good you could join us tonight, Mick," the TRA CEO said, but her blue eyes hadn't lost her earlier watchfulness. His ignominious collapse had raised questions he'd not answered, and there was no doubt, even at a table full of Dommes, that Ros was top of this pyramid.

"It's one of the nicest nights I've had in a while." He'd learned how to be mostly honest about what he was feeling, around people who led normal lives. Meaning those who didn't get beat up during business appointments.

She nodded and returned to her chair. Cyn didn't say anything, just pointed her fork at his pie and had a mouthful of her own.

Dessert and coffee took about an hour, the TRA women and their men relaxed around the table. Pushed back from it, arms stretched over the backs of adjacent chairs, and that wasn't all a boy-girl thing. Vera sat next to Skye, and often pushed her shoulder against the other woman's with fondness as the table erupted in laughter or comments over whatever banter or anecdote was being shared.

When Neil rose to grab more beers for him and Tiger—Lawrence and Mick having chosen coffee for their after-dinner beverage—Neil caught Lawrence in an affectionate head lock and planted a smacking kiss on the top of it before Lawrence broke the lock and elbowed him.

"You're so cute, Munch, I just have to squeeze you sometime."

"Get your hands off me, Twizzler. Or I'll ask my woman to beat you up."

Mick expected the nicknames came from their height differences. Neil was extra tall and lean, and Lawrence brawny but a few inches shorter.

Cyn wasn't a person who projected a willingness to be casually touched. But the women included her in their brief gestures of easy affection. From the earlier grip on her shoulder, Ros clearly had license to let that touch linger.

The Snicker pie was good. He'd look up the recipe. His small freezer could accommodate it, and it would be an easy way to remember this evening. He imagined himself miles away, sitting down with the full pie and a fork, thinking of the people here. As he ate the memory alone.

He had damn good reasons for being separate, not part of a family or community long term. If he was letting his head get messed up in those thoughts, it was time to go.

He waited until the others started to get up from the table. They were talking about adjourning to the fire pit. It gave him the opportunity to casually announce he had to take off and handle some things. It wasn't just because of his headspace. He did have shit to deal with before he could faceplant in his bed.

Before he departed, he helped carry some dishes back into the kitchen. Abby waved him off when he offered to do his part to wash, letting him know they'd deal with it later.

161

A s'mores plan was in process. Tiger was pulling some Hershey bars and marshmallows out of the pantry and holding them over Skye's head. She grabbed his belt to give herself jump leverage and snatched it. When he pulled her to him to kiss her mouth, the marshmallows were mashed between them. She put her hand in the pocket of his jeans to squeeze his ass as he smiled down at her.

Tiger lifted his head and gestured at Mick. "If it'll save you some dough, come back when you're done tonight and use our place as a camping spot. There's a nice place over by the bike track. You can see the sun come up over the marsh. I'll leave the kitchen door open in case you want to use our guest bath for a roomier shower."

The idea, particularly the isolation of the spot, had appeal. "I may take you up on that. Don't shoot me if I roll in after bedtime."

Tiger tapped the phone in his shirt pocket. "I've got cameras. I'll know it's you without leaving the bed."

Given the curvy, dark-eyed Domme with her hand on his ass, Mick didn't blame Tiger a bit for using the tech.

Cyn had been stacking dishes on the counter, but now she wiped her hands on a towel. "I'll walk you out."

"Good. It's a scary neighborhood, and I'm a little nervous."

"Shut up. Tell the nice people good night and thanks for putting up with you."

"Aw," Vera purred. "She said we were nice."

"I'm being polite," Cyn told her. "Doesn't mean I actually meant it."

Mick offered his farewells and thanks for the meal. As he bid Ros good night, he met her gaze. "Ma'am."

She nodded, but offered nothing more. He was used to bothering people, particularly those with radar for trouble. He didn't usually let it get to him, but it was a no-brainer why it did now. It couldn't be helped. He took his leave, holding the door for Cyn so she could precede him.

162

They walked toward the motorhome side by side, not touching, but that didn't matter. Every shift of their bodies as they matched pace brought a change in air currents he could feel against his skin. "I'm sorry I can't hang out longer. I would have liked sitting by the fire with you." He nudged her. "Maybe use the excuse to put an arm around you."

"It's New Orleans. It doesn't get really cold here, not like Jersey. We'll sweat our balls off for those s'mores." She sent him an arch look. "Even if it was cold, women don't get any colder than men do. You don't see women putting their arm around them or offering them their coat."

"Women do get colder, because they're thin-skinned," he told her. "Unless you're a vampire and happy being cold."

"It goes with my cold heart," she retorted.

He turned toward her, hooking the chain of her necklace over two fingers and cradling the skeleton in his palm, his knuckles over her beating heart. "There's nothing cold about you, baby. You've never brought a boy home to the family, have you? Is that why Ros gave me the mama bear eye?"

When he withdrew his touch, she studied him as if he was something she wasn't entirely certain how to manage. He knew the feeling.

"She's not old enough to be my mother."

"No, but she watches out for you. I'm glad you found a family."

She looked toward the house. Ros and Abby were visible through the kitchen window, talking, Ros pouring herself wine. Vera and Skye headed out the side, carrying the s'more makings, plus some Oreos. Lawrence and Neil were at the firepit, getting it going. Tiger trailed the women with a bottle of Jack and a couple shot glasses, probably for him and Neil. Lawrence seemed to prefer the low or non-alcohol beers. Probably because of his ex-wife, who'd been an alcoholic.

He'd done the background checks purely because he wanted to know the make of her family, even if he could only do it by cheating. If he'd known ahead of time he'd be

163

invited to this, he could have saved himself some effort. The women's strengths and personalities fit in ways that explained how they'd succeeded as business partners and evolved into the family unit. The men who'd bonded with each Mistress fit right into the tight weave.

Family figured shit out, so they could give one another what they needed. They loved through good, bad, and damned uncomfortable but necessary things.

Maybe seeing that up close and personal hurt more than usual because finding Cyn, being with her, told Mick that bond did exist for him somewhere. If he had time and what was needed to commit to it, to give her what she well-deserved. Which he didn't.

Cyn hadn't asked him to stay, he reminded himself. Or even invited him to come back. Everything about her said she shied away from that kind of thing.

All of that might be true, but he saw the potential in her eyes. It destroyed him to know he couldn't reach for it, convince her of the possibilities. He really needed to get out of New Orleans soon.

But not tonight.

She had her hand on his chest, was pushing him back so he leaned against his vehicle. He put his hands on her hips, sliding his fingers into the jeans pockets. Cyn's ass was made for snug denim.

"I'm betting they're watching us," she said.

"Why?"

"Because I haven't ever brought a boy home to the family," she confirmed. But she was done teasing. "You going to explain why someone beat you up?"

"No," he said. "It's something separate from the Progeny event, and it doesn't have anything to do with you. It's not something I want anywhere near you."

Her mouth went straight lined. "I don't need someone to protect me."

164

"You also don't need to be dragged into trouble that's not yours. You'd do anything for your family. I know you don't back down from a fight. I know you'll start one if it has to do with protecting one of them."

Though the pang the thought created was unexpected, he turned it into words. "I'm not family. When I leave, it's not likely we'll see one another again. This is closure, fulfilling the potential of what we felt that night, when we were too fucked in the head to know what to do with it."

Her eyes narrowed. "I was too fucked in the head. You were busy playing cop hero."

Yeah, he'd pissed her off. He moved his hands to her upper arms. "I'm calling it closure, not meaningless. I'm pretty sure these past couple days and whatever time you give me before I leave will be the most meaningful hours of my life for some time to come." *Maybe for always.*

"Even if it ends with you telling me to fuck myself and hit the road," he added. "But it doesn't change it. You may not need me to protect you from anything, but I'm going to, because I need to know you're in the world, and that you have this, instead of the future you would have had if you'd stayed in that cesspool of a town."

He'd hoped for a good night kiss, even a knee in the balls, if she put a sadist's true affection behind it, but he could read the room. He'd pretty much scuttled any of that by not telling her what she wanted to know.

Honesty could be a bitch. Literally.

She stepped back, out of his reach. "Good night, Mick."

When she marched toward the house, she had an iron rod in her back, but her hips still had that fuck-me swivel that could draw his eyes. He was just glad she was too mad to tell him he wasn't allowed to look.

Since his time looking at the real thing was short, he would   take   every   second   he   could   get.

CHAPTER TEN

No problem on the CNC session. We'll put something else in that time slot. Still hope to see you there.

It was the first text she'd received from him, the day after the get-together. She expected he'd waited her out, to see if she'd get past her anger. If she'd reach out first and at least let things go back to status quo.

Sure. Why should she care that he was beat like a piñata—by someone who wasn't her—before he came to dinner? Then tells her he wasn't going to reveal who did it, *and* that he wasn't her family.

With disgust, she decided to leave work an hour early and head for Roughnecks. She and Ros usually came to the boxing and MMA gym together, so Ros could spar with her as part of their workout. Cyn had improved the fighting skills of all four women, and Ros was a better-than-decent partner, sometimes taking the upper hand through patience and calculation. Cyn also sparred with more advanced members to maintain and improve her own level.

Recognizing her mood, she started with the punching bag. Controlled physical violence, focusing on her technique, usually helped calm her down if she was agitated. By the time Ros arrived, she should have burned off enough of it to make what was in her head more manageable.

The strategy would have worked, too. Except she wasn't good at overlooking an opportunity that seemed thrown in her path specifically to deal with her mood.

Roughnecks had a second level, which provided a running track, workout ropes, and bigger equipment. It was accessible via metal steps that clanged as people went up and down, entering and exiting the gray painted door at the top. It had a square window so no one slammed the door into someone else coming and going.

Even while working out with the bag, Cyn stayed cognizant of that foot traffic, because it was close to her.

166

Surviving the first twenty years of her life had depended upon awareness of her surroundings. Just like her fight skills, she never let that radar get rusty.

So she knew when a familiar person emerged from the second level. One that gave her a target far more appealing than the punching bag.

Matt Kensington.

Ros's friend, TRA's client, and the man who had bullshit outdated beliefs about fighting women, so he always declined Cyn's invitation to spar.

Today it wasn't going to be an invitation.

She was tired of being dodged, of people not letting her in and giving her the fight she wanted. No matter how irrational, selfish or fucked-up that was, that was where her head was. And she was going to act on it now.

When Matt reached the bottom of the steps, she met him there. The man looked like a hawk, with a curved nose and piercing brown eyes. He had a smooth block of a jaw and hands like hammers.

Matt preferred boxing, but he had trained with the MMA instructor on staff to expand his repertoire. He didn't have Cyn's skills, but he was a top-notch boxer with great footwork. On the north side of fifty, the man was still way fucking strong.

He wore a tank shirt and shorts, the shirt damp from the intensity of his workout. He used the big ropes upstairs and usually ran the track, then came down to get in the ring with a willing member or work the bag.

His workouts matched his business approach. His dad had been oil money, but since Matt had quadrupled the value of K&A and expanded its holdings to become a Fortune 500 company, no one could accuse him of living off his inheritance. He'd known suffering, losing his father in his teens, and his mother even younger.

He and his four-man team were a male mirror of the TRA executive board—all sexual Dominants. Savannah Tennyson

167

Kensington was Matt's wife and submissive, but also CEO of Tennyson Industries, a company that at times unapologetically competed with Matt's for business.

Matt was protective of his close-knit team and considered them family—another match for Ros's view of Abby, Cyn, Skye and Vera. He was also fiercely devoted to Savannah and their daughter, Angelica.

It irritated Cyn, made her angry with no desire to look at why. She knew she was in a bad space in her head today. Knew it, goddamn it. That was why she'd come early, without Ros. Not to work out with the punching bag, but because she didn't want anything to stand between her and the outlet she really craved.

Each time she thought of the text Mick had sent her, she was sucked down into what had brought her to the cemetery that night. Which was so far in the past it shouldn't affect her at all. But Mick showing up had changed that.

It was yesterday, it was today. It was still inside her.

"Cyn." Matt mopped sweat off his neck with a towel as he stepped off the stairs. He was over six feet, with shoulders as broad as Tiger's. Silver was threaded in his brown hair, and she liked that he didn't color it, didn't try to look younger than he was. No woman in her right mind would think he looked any less with it. Even in baggy workout shorts, he attracted female attention. In a suit, he was the definition of suit porn.

So was Mick, in the slacks and dress shirts he seemed to favor. He'd looked pretty damn good in jeans, too.

The bruising on his abdomen had been from fists. More than one set. He wouldn't let himself be taken down by a single opponent. No surprise to her there.

Goddamn men.

"We're sparring today," she told Matt.

Showing why he was good at business, as well as being a Master to a successful and complicated woman, Matt paused to assess. His evaluation covered Cyn's face, tone and body language.

She was good at those critiques herself, and recognized the impending courteous refusal. Even when she'd been more insistent in the past, enough that Matt's courtesy came with a touch of steel and Ros's rebuke to her later for pushing the issue, it had always been the same.

This time she wasn't putting up with that shit. She wanted to spar with the alpha dog in the room, and prove she had every right to be in the ring with him.

"This isn't about you fighting a woman," she snapped. "I want you to fight an opponent who wants the fight."

Needs the fight.

"No." Matt's brown eyes went cool. "Whoever you're wanting me to stand in for, I'm not him. Excuse me."

Patronizing son of a bitch. He stepped around her, and she stepped into him. The punch took him squarely on the jaw, her follow-through, footwork and control perfect. She hit him with the amount of force needed to prove she could hold her own.

It would also get her banned from Roughnecks if he didn't take it for the gauntlet it was.

That swirling, sick feeling in her stomach told her she was out of control, capable of anything. It had been a while since she'd felt that way, but it said she needed to back off, right the fuck now.

Mick's scar flashed through her mind. When she'd been miles away from him, trying to fall asleep in the car, she'd seen the glass cut him, again and again. She'd ended up in a ball, shaking with the truth. If his reflexes hadn't been as fast as they'd been, she would have opened up his throat. In a flash of fury, she would have committed murder.

No. She took a hard look at herself. This wasn't as far gone as that. Yes, it was on the edge, but she still had her hands on the reins. White-knuckled, but there. She pushed clients to an edge that could seemingly result in them telling

TRA to fuck off, yet instead they usually doubled their marketing budget estimate. They took the risk of the greater return her strategy would bring them, because they had faith in her direction.

She didn't doubt herself, she did the hard work, and she made it happen. Personally and professionally. She could dispense pain because she wasn't afraid to suffer.

Matt respected those qualities, she knew it. She was going to get the answer she wanted here. She refused to believe anything else.

The punch had prompted a few startled exclamations from those nearby. Even now, Grizzly, the ex-cop who ran the place, was probably headed her way, to handle whatever the hell this was. She planted her feet, waited as Matt straightened, rubbing his jaw.

She'd seen his flash of anger, the aggressor response that would have answered a strike with a strike, but he wasn't that kind of man. "Cyn. What the fuck?" he said quietly.

"You need to see me. I need you to *see me*. Not some person you refuse to fight because I'm a woman, because of some fucking antiquated idea of chivalry. You need to fight me because you see what I need and want. I'm not a goddamn brat sub."

She had the presence of mind to pitch that part low. Some of those here knew they were part of the BDSM scene, but others didn't. She wasn't outing Matt to those he might not want to have direct knowledge of that. Though from what she knew of him, that discretion had more to do with protecting his wife and her reputation in the corporate world than himself.

See? She had her head on straight. Mostly. Even if the rage boiling through her said if he refused her, she might punch him a second time.

"Matt, Cyn?" Grizzly had arrived. "We got a problem?"

Cyn's gaze didn't leave Matt's. She had no idea what was going on behind those raptor's eyes, but she'd seen Ros look at a challenge like he was doing. Silently, taking her time. Weighing variables.

Skye had told her that learning when to be silent, when to let people work through stuff, was as much a talent as knowing when to interject the right verbal push.

Verbal pushing was Cyn's thing, but it didn't mean she couldn't learn from Skye and others to improve her own wheelhouse of effective tactics. So she kept her mouth closed. With effort.

"No," Matt said at last. "Cyn and I are going to spar, if you have a ring available. I think that might be better than one of the marked floor spaces."

Cyn nodded as Grizzly looked her way. It ticked her off that he waited for one more from Matt to confirm this was legit, but whatever.

"Okay," the gym owner said. "Boxing or MMA gloves?"

"The lady's choice," Matt said, without a trace of irony or snark, but Cyn saw a glint in those dark eyes.

"MMA," Cyn said. *Motherfucker.* "Want to put some money on this?"

The CEO of K&A lifted a dark brow. "Think you can bet in my weight class?"

Oh yeah. He was goading her now. "A thousand," she said.

"If you win," he agreed. "If I win, I name my price after we're done."

She bared her teeth in a smile. "Long as you don't want me to suck your dick."

Matt blinked once. "While this defies all evidence to the contrary, your mouth's not big enough for that."

It took her right back to Mick when she hadn't known his name, and the taunt she'd thrown out that night.

"You don't have a big enough dick to get me on my knees."

"Does anyone?"

171

"Jesus," Grizzly muttered. "Ring Three. Let's get you gloved up."

MMA sparring gloves were less padded than boxing ones, but they still provided some measure of protection to the hands.

Cyn didn't usually wrap her hands for sparring matches, but she did for this one. Stan, one of the staff members, got in the ring to help her do that and pull the gloves snug over them. Grizzly did Matt's gloves, probably because he wanted to gather more info about what was happening. Again, annoying, but fine. She noticed Matt didn't have Grizzly wrap his hands first. A message he had no intention of hitting her hard enough to risk his hands.

She was going to change his mind about that.

Cyn tuned them out, keeping her eyes on Stan's progress and her focus on what lay ahead. She fought better on waves of aggression, because it was familiar ground to surf. She just had to keep it at the sweet spot, or the waves would surge to tidal wave size.

"Good afternoon. Have you lost your fucking mind?"

Ros had arrived. Her boss had made her way through the gathered members to grip the ropes and pull herself up. She was in her pristine workout leggings and sports bra. Her expensive workout shoes, teal with silver logo, perched her on the mat edge outside the ropes. Though her tone was pleasant, her blue eyes were shards of glass.

"No more than any other day." When Stan stepped back, Cyn tested the gloves in a quick set of warm up punches against his beefy palms. "Thanks, Stan."

"Sure enough. Kick ass, honey." He winked before he left the ring. Even those who'd seen her hit Matt were now viewing this as an impromptu sporting event.

Like seeing a Domme with extreme tastes, who only did private sessions, play publicly. The last time Cyn had done that—a favor for Vera—the session had gone well, but her interaction with the audience hadn't. She wondered how Progeny's management had responded when Mick informed them she was doing a public CNC session.

Except now Mick assumed she was backing out. *Asshole.* Management was probably happy to hear it, however.

"Cyn." Ros put a hand on her arm. Cyn's skin shuddered, rejecting the contact. A warning sign. Cyn made herself stay still, but she could tell Ros had felt it.

"It's okay," Cyn told her. "I'm okay. I just finally got him to agree to spar with me. Hey, if I get my ass kicked, then you can say I told you so."

"That's not my issue, and you know it."

Cyn shook her head and broke eye contact. "I'm in control. Leave it."

Ros wasn't buying it, but she didn't say anything else. She respected her women. Or maybe she trusted Matt not to kick the crap out of her accounts VP.

That wasn't going to happen. Because Cyn was going to win this. She was going to kick the crap out of *him*. She wasn't after balance, or purging, or whatever. She just wanted a fight that would be hard to win, so she could prove to herself she *could* win it. She could win the unwinnable.

She'd proven she could do that. No matter what other fights she'd lost, and who'd she'd lost during them.

"Bet on him if you want," she said shortly. Having no one who expected her to win made her fight all the harder. It always had.

Fuck you, fuck the world.

She'd forgotten how close that reaction could be, just waiting in the wings. But this was a reminder she could handle it, if and when and how it ever happened. She was going to shove away the sick, angry feeling, by fighting a man who lived his life on the top of the pyramid.

Sure.

"Cyn."

She had to tone down the hostility when she shot a look Ros's way, but her boss met it with a steady look. "Good luck. Watch your left. You still leave it open too much."

That was all, but it shifted Cyn's view the degrees she needed, easing that wrong feeling. She wasn't the same person she'd been when she believed it was me-against-the-world. And Ros wasn't the world. If she'd chosen to bet against Cyn, it *would* have felt bad. Like how Mick not telling her things about himself had made her feel.

Left out, separate. Not worthy of trust and respect.

Matt turned toward her, punching the gloves together. This was sparring, not a match, so no bell, no points system. They'd stop when they'd had enough.

Except when it came to fighting, she never had enough.

As they began to circle, calls of encouragement spouted from the audience, though there were no obvious preferences. The members liked a good fight, and since many of them practiced the same fight styles, this was a chance to learn from serious opponents.

She threw the first kick, and Matt blocked, the two of them twisting around one another and dancing back. For the next couple moments, that was the way it went, testing.

No surprise, Matt didn't throw any punches above the neck. Just like Mick. Damn men. But she expected that to change as they really got into it. When a fight became more intense, who the opponent was disappeared into counters, outcomes. Action, reaction. Competition took over, fighters digging into the arsenal of skills required to win.

Mixed martial arts had developed into a sport with protocols and rules to pull it away from its gladiator blood sport roots. At its heart, it was street fighting. Which was probably why it had appealed to her.

Warm up over. Cyn waded in, and the fight ramped up. As she danced, kicked and punched, she landed a few good shots, but fuck, Matt was astoundingly quick on his feet for such a big man. No wasted energy, and he used the split

174

seconds between exchanged blows to decide on the next one. He never stopped tracking her moves, learning to anticipate her. She'd studied his fighting style, but she realized this also wasn't the first time he'd studied hers.

Business rivals said it was "possible" for Matt Kensington to be surprised or outmaneuvered, but the person might never know it. He could move ahead of the mistake and calculate the best next steps, never letting emotion dilute his progress or cloud his end goal.

She went for a blitz attack. She had age, quickness, more MMA skills and better flexibility on her side, but they were narrow margins.

As she'd anticipated, the more they got into the fight, the more insular the world became. It pushed out everything. People shouting and cheering, Ros's hard-to-read expression, Grizzly's concerned one. It was just her and Matt in the clouds. Cyn was surfing the red haze, a fighter's fury locked with resolve, narrowing her world to one thing. Winning. Telling the world she would never be beaten, that no matter how it had broken her heart and torn her soul apart, she'd put them back together and they were better off that way.

Perfect stuff wasn't strong.

There. She'd found a split second that was all hers, and made contact under his guard. The kick hit his ribs, and she followed it with a hook to his jaw, the same spot she'd hit on the stairs. Pain flashed through his gaze, but it didn't slow his reaction. He caught her around the middle on the follow-through, lifted and brought her to the mat. The impact shuddered through her bones.

Yes, fight me. Goddamn you, fight me the way you would fight a man.

She snarled and struck at his face, bringing her knees up to shove him off. He blocked her and they rolled. For one superb moment, she was on top and landed another face punch before he flung her off. She rolled again, but he'd hit another gear.

175

The motherfucker had been holding back.

He brought her down to the mat once more. He'd been a wrestling champ in high school, because his mother wouldn't let him go out for football. Ros had told her that.

She hadn't had a helicopter mother. Just the thought incited the laughter demons shared in hell. Hopefully while they disemboweled her mother for the thousandth time, which would be half the number of times she deserved.

They'd abandoned any pretense at MMA fight forms. She gloried in it, a battle with no rules except keeping it…fair.

Winning a fair fight means you can respect your opponent when it's over.

She was back on her feet. When she waded in, she went for the side she'd kicked, a fast series of double punches.

Matt blocked, spun, twisted around. In hindsight, she realized he'd intended to ram her in the chest with his elbow to push her back.

But she ducked, thinking he was swinging for her face with the other hand. His elbow cracked her in the bridge of her nose, and the pain blinded her.

He'd followed through on the shove with the other hand. Normally she would have landed on her ass, turning it into a backwards roll to bring her to her feet. Instead, the pain in her nose took over everything so she landed flat on her back, her head bouncing off the mat.

"Fuck." She wheezed it, even as she tried to turn over and scramble to her feet. She couldn't do it, because she couldn't breathe.

"Goddamn it." Matt was down on one knee. He put his hands on her and she tried to shove him away, so she had room to get up and wade back into the fight.

"It's done. Fight's done, Cyn."

Ros's voice penetrated. Matt might have said it first, but it didn't register until it came from her boss, now bending over her. Grizzly was there, too. He'd probably brought Ros into the ring to break Cyn out of attack mode.

"I knew this was a mistake," Grizzly said.

"Not a mistake. It was a good fight."

Cyn was trying to take a normal breath and see past the pain obscuring her vision from her throbbing nose, but she heard that firm statement.

It came from Matt.

She squinted and turned her head gingerly to look at him. The emotions she saw prompted a shame she didn't want to address. But one of the things she felt from him was even more unexpected.

It was pride. In her.

A weird quake went through the crudely mended cracks in her heart and soul.

"Take a moment," he was telling her. "You got your wind knocked out of you."

"Ros," she wheezed.

"Right here, you crazy bitch." She had her hand on Cyn's shoulder, which was no longer flinching at her touch. It was done. The feelings that had driven her to do this were pacified. She was okay again. She was herself.

Cyn jerked as large hands descended on her face. "Hold still," Grizzly said mildly. "I need to make sure that cute little nose of yours ain't broke."

"You call anything about me 'cute' or 'little' again, yours will be broken."

"Won't be the first time," Grizzly said, unimpressed.

She was more breathless than wheezy now, an improvement. Air hunger sucked. His pressure around her nose incited a humiliating desire to whimper. She held it back with effort, and by closing her eyes before they watered and someone decided she was crying. If that happened, she'd have to kill everyone.

"Okay, I can't rule out a fracture, but if you've got one, it's not severe. Ice and avoiding being punched in the face for a while will heal it up. With anyone else, I'd say there's no danger of that, but you're you."

She would have rolled her eyes, but it hurt too much.

"I'll get you both ice packs and some ibuprofen. And do me a favor. Don't ever do this again." Grizzly ducked out of the ring and gave everyone a thumbs up. A short burst of applause and amiable calls penetrated her awareness, but Grizzly barked at everyone to get back to their workouts.

Cyn glanced at Ros as she rested on her heels next to her. "I'm ready for our match now. If you think you can keep up. You were dragging last time. Your live-in boytoy has made you soft."

Matt ran a hand over his face and glanced at Ros. "All I can say is she must be good at her job."

"I remind myself of that every day," Ros said. "Some days it requires more than once."

"You two are hilarious," Cyn said. "And I'm not good at my job. I'm fucking awesome."

Ros tugged her hair. "Yes, you are. You're still going to put an ice pack on your face, go home, swallow down some aspirin and spend your day resting. Or I'm firing you."

"You're just worried I'd *still* kick your ass today, proving my point."

Cyn was done lying on her back. She pushed up, ignoring that Ros helped support her on one side, Matt on the other, and she still swayed. They moved her to a stool someone had helpfully put in the ring.

She looked toward Matt. Fair was fair. "You won. This time. What are your terms?"

Ros's hand was at the small of her back, which was fine, but Matt's on her shoulder didn't feel as invasive as it should have. So Cyn twitched and he removed it.

"I'll get my stuff from my locker and meet you out front to discuss it," he said.

Probably a way to reinforce what Ros was practically demanding she do, go home and lie down. Since that throb in her nose was moving to the top of her skull, and her body said she was going to feel the effects bigtime when the adrenaline slipped away, Cyn might humor Ros and do that.

"All right," she told Matt. "I'll work out some more until you're ready."

His lips quirked at the obvious bullshit, but his eyes didn't smile. Once he rose and left the ring, he accepted handshakes and congratulations, but his shoulders were stiff, and he moved with purpose toward the locker room.

It irritated her. *She* was pleased he was being congratulated exactly as he would if he'd faced a better than decent opponent.

She'd fought well. Matt hadn't bested her on footwork or hand-to-hand skills. She'd missed some cues and let him grab her, giving him the advantage of brute strength. But she'd managed to break those holds, until his elbow made her see stars.

Howard Bluefield, a tank-sized boxer who worked out with Matt regularly, slapped him on the back as he passed. Tossing Cyn a venomous eye, he boomed out, "Well done, Kensington. Way to put the bitch back in her place."

Before she could open her mouth and tell Howard to go screw himself, Matt had turned and dropped him.

With one solid blow to the jaw.

Howard weighed about fifty pounds more than Matt, and had been a middleweight champ in his thirties. He could take a punch. Yet he staggered and fell onto his ass, with a stunned expression and glazed eyes.

Okay, it was still possible Matt had held back on her.

"She can hold her own against anyone here." Matt jerked his head toward Cyn. "Don't talk about her like that again."

Grizzly was back and standing at Matt's shoulder. He glared at Howard. "If you do, your ass will be out. I don't put up with that kind of shit. This ain't no espresso bar workout club. Our members earn the right to be here."

179

Howard rubbed his jaw and glared for form's sake, but he accepted Matt's hand to help him up. "Yeah, sorry. Got carried away." He glanced at Cyn. "Didn't mean nothing."

Cyn's nose was bleeding, she realized, but it didn't stop her from giving him a smile with crimson-stained teeth. She took the handful of tissues Ros gave her. "Fuck off, Howard. We all know you're an asshole."

Laughter swept those watching the byplay, easing the tension. Even Howard gave her a grudging smile, lifting one giant paw to throw off the comment.

But when Cyn's gaze moved to Matt, his attention was on the bloody tissues. Turning, he disappeared down the hall toward the men's locker room.

"Don't tell me I owe him an apology," she muttered to Ros as she used the ropes to pull herself to her feet. Ros steadied her. "I'm okay."

"Some days I doubt that." Ros stepped back with visible effort. "Is this about Mick?"

"No. And yes." Cyn scowled. "What the fuck does it matter?"

"Watch your tone with me. And tilt your head back."

Cyn made a face, but complied. As she gazed at the ceiling, Ros's hand was on hers, holding pressure against her nose. "If he matters, and he's done something to bug you, don't shut him down. Work through it with him."

Cyn made a noncommittal noise, but when the bleeding stopped, she exited the ring and sat down on the edge of it, tossing the tissues in a nearby waste can. Hell, the whole top of her face hurt, and the throb was starting to circle her head like a noisy carousel ride.

"He's not going to be here long. It doesn't matter."

Ros propped her hips next to her and crossed her arms. She tapped her manicured fingers against the inside of her elbow. "Yeah. Because something that happens over the course of a few days can't haunt you, crawl in your gut and get infected for the rest of your life."

Ros didn't know Cyn and Mick's history, but her aim was as irritatingly spot-on as always. "Where are you going with that?" Cyn retorted anyway.

"I don't have to go anywhere with it. You've heard me. But this is a different matter." Ros looked toward the locker room where Matt had disappeared. "Sometimes, Cyn, when you're working through your own shit, you don't look beyond it to understand where other people are, why they are the way they are, why they take the positions they do. You want to be respected, but respect is a two-way street."

Cyn frowned. "I work to earn respect."

"Yes, you do. But you also never leave the ring. And most of the things worth fighting for live outside it." Ros's gaze softened a fraction. "Your rage never goes away. You're successful, loved, respected. So why are you still fighting like you think none of those things are safe, that they'll disappear tomorrow?"

Cyn tensed, but Ros shook her head. "I'm not asking for the answer, and I never will. We're here if you ever want to let us in. But you've grown up a lot these past few years, and I expect you know the answer to the question."

Ros dabbed at Cyn's nose with a clean tissue. "A little smear left there. I got it."

As Cyn blinked, Ros balled up the tissue and tossed it. "Abby says schizophrenia can make a familiar face look like a monster. The worst part of an already awful illness is something in her head is determined to isolate her, pull her away from us. Your temper, your past, can do that, too."

Pained surprise swept through Cyn. Ros's neutral gaze shifted to rebuke. "The way Matt reacted to Howard wasn't just gallantry. Yes, you owe him an apology. He's your friend as much as he is mine."

Ros rose. "Think about that. Think about all of it. Including Mick."

Cyn had little patience for self-analysis, and definitely not if it persisted beyond the length of a coffee break. If the answer wasn't evident, she'd set it aside and work it out in her subconscious. Usually, the answer would come to her.

Which she guessed was what she was doing now. She sat on the curb outside the gym. The street didn't get many pedestrians, because a law office and a papered-over storefront rented out for a co-op art studio were the only other businesses. The intersecting street at the southern end was a popular thoroughfare, though, so she gazed in that direction, watching clumps of tourists, brisk locals, and slow-moving vehicle traffic. A distant clopping heralded the passing of a carriage, pulled by a dapple-gray horse.

She'd heard what Ros said, but the first thing she did when she sat down was review the fight in her head, all the ways she could have fought smarter.

While that evaluation would help her face her next opponent, she knew that wouldn't be Matt. Now her thoughts moved to what she knew of him, every conversation, the relationships he had with her, Ros and the rest of the team. She also thought of what she'd seen at the club when he was there with Savannah or his team.

Much as she hated to admit it, Ros was right. Once she set her own shit aside, it was clear as a stop sign why what she had done was wrong. *Well, fuck.*

She held the ice pack Grizzly had given her against her nose. Since she'd found the answer Ros had pointed her toward, she left it alone and turned her mind to Mick. Not what he'd done to piss her off, but how much she'd liked sharing dinner with him. Watching him laugh, leaning against him, being with him as a couple, just like Skye with Tiger, Lawrence with Ros. Neil with Abby.

Hell, maybe Matt had hit her harder than she thought, if she was having gushy thoughts. She wasn't the kind of woman who required a plus-one.

But life was more than requirements. Did she require Ros and the others? Maybe so, for some things. *Things that are worth the fight usually live outside the ring.*

Abby talked about seeing monsters conjured in her head. Cyn had seen the real thing, and she couldn't forget.

Because one of them was in her own mirror.

Ten years, and she still carried around the uneasy feeling that nothing meant anything. To a lot of people, life's impermanence was what gave meaning to the things that mattered. A lot of people were fucked up.

This wasn't helping. She needed to go. She'd send Matt a message to find out what he wanted.

Too late. Cyn opened eyes she hadn't realized she'd shut as Matt took a seat on the curb next to her. Gingerly. He, too, had an ice pack, which he was holding against his side, under his T-shirt. He'd put on jeans, and they looked almost as good on him as his suits.

"I notice Grizzly didn't check to see if your ribs were cracked."

"He did, in the locker room. And read me the riot act."

She narrowed her eyes. "He shouldn't have done that. I was the one who deserved the dressing down."

"Probably. But I was the one who knew better."

"Because you're older? And have a penis?"

His eyes glimmered with his normal humor, which she admitted was a relief to see. "Don't get angry," he said gravely, "but of the two of us, it's general knowledge that I have the more level head."

She thought of several arguments, then accepted the truth. "That's fair."

A bruise under his eye was swelling. She handed him the ice pack she'd been using, but he shook his head, gripped her hand and guided it back to her nose. An hour ago, she would have shaken him off, but her view was clearer now.

It bothered him to see what he'd done to her. Deeply.

183

She'd mocked his chivalry, as if he put on the trait like a Hugo Boss suit. Instead, it was his core.

She'd ducked, thinking he was going to hit her, but there was nothing in the world that would make Matt Kensington swing his fist at a woman's face.

She nudged his side. "You know, you hit like a girl. Maybe Savannah should do your fighting for you."

He rolled his eyes, but his expression eased. Then became more serious. "I'm going to ask you something that will piss you off, since most reasonable questions—and answers—seem to."

She lifted a shoulder. "Also fair."

His lips tugged in a half smile, since her answer cleverly could apply to either assumption. "Why do you see your father in me?" he asked.

If a car had sprung out of the pavement and run her over, it wouldn't have taken her off guard half as much. She almost bolted to her feet. Only locking every muscle prevented it. Anger predictably came in behind the shock, though she tried to keep it out of her rigid tone.

"I didn't have a father," she said. "Not one that stuck around, which was fine. I didn't need a daddy."

"Everyone needs a father, just as much as they need a mother," he said reasonably. "Even if, like you, they prove they can succeed without either one."

She stared at him. While not intentional, she knew her look was the kind that moved people out of her path at the club, and kept her staff on their toes. Matt excelled at that look himself, so no surprise, he didn't flinch or blink.

She wasn't that hard to figure out. Not in a world that harped on broken home clichés. Maybe hers had a different twist, but the basics were the same. She could be mad, but the unavoidable realization she'd disrespected the man, a fellow Dom, and a friend, made her offer an honest reply.

"I don't see him in you." She could have left it there, but other words came forth, tied to the sentence. Like pulling a chain of clothespins off of a sub's tender flesh.

She knew what the pain she inflicted felt like. Because she always did it to herself first.

"I have no idea who my mother fucked to come up with me." She paused, staring at the newsprint covering the windows of the art studio across the street. Why wouldn't they want natural light? "You're what I once pretended he would have been, if he'd showed up and rescued me. But he didn't, and then I got pissed that I would ever let myself wait to be rescued."

The ache in her throat startled her, but she couldn't seem to shut herself up before she offered the last of it. "What makes me mad is knowing you would have. You're proof of what he could have been, if he'd only cared enough."

When she felt him shift, she recoiled. "Don't touch me. And don't look at me. Please." She forced out the unfamiliar word, hoping it would shock him enough to comply.

He mostly respected the request. She realized they were sitting close enough her shoulder pressed against his biceps.

"As a futile nod to my vanity, I'll deny I'm old enough to be your father's age."

She bit her lip against a smile, because the smile hurt. "You're not vain. Arrogant as hell, yes, but not vain."

She still didn't look at him. She hadn't asked him not to talk, and maybe she should have, but when he continued, his voice was easy and quiet.

"When Angelica reaches your age, I hope I haven't failed her in any significant way, so she won't feel the pain you carry. It won't be for lack of trying, I know that. But I think if your father had been a better one, what he would have said is it's time to drain the poison. Let it go."

The direction of his voice, a word or two drifting her way, then altering course, suggested he almost looked toward her, then stopped, respecting her request. "You are a strong and beautiful woman, Cyn. Despite the challenges you've faced, you fought past them, worked hard, and proved your value. To yourself and the people who matter. Those who call you friend or family. Or Mistress."

He uncrossed his ankles and bent his knees, bracing his feet against the pavement. "Is someone in the running for the last one? Beyond the occasional session?"

"Why would you say that?" Startled, she glanced toward him. He met her gaze again. The brown eyes were thoughtful.

"Because you're always taunting me, trying to provoke me into the ring. Usually it's more amiable. This felt driven by someone who's gotten under your skin."

"Which means it has to be about sex and a guy?"

The corner of his lip tipped up. "Are you saying it isn't?"

She scoffed. "Nice try. I'm a better poker player than that."

"You're excellent." He linked his hands over his knees. "Lucas wants another poker night so he can recoup his money. Ben just wants to ban women from attending."

"Typical." She chuckled. "Your CFO wants to balance his bank account, and your lawyer prefers scorched earth."

"Having team members with different approaches can be good for a company." Matt nudged her. "If they're the right mesh. As Ros well knows. Back to our subject. If, hypothetically, someone has gotten under your skin, I can threaten him for you. Beat him up. I'll consider it dress rehearsal for when Angelica starts dating."

"Thanks," she said dryly. "But I prefer to reserve the pleasure of beating him up or threatening him myself."

"I figured. Bring ice packs for him." He lapsed into companionable silence. Another carriage went by at the end of the street, this one with a white horse. There were flowers woven into the harness. "You know what you said, about a sub bratting? It's not that different, what a submissive or a Dom is seeking. Trust. Even if it exists only in that session.

But sometimes we stumble on a trust that reaches soul deep, and well outside the club doors. It's incredibly rare."

The words rippled across her nerves, creating an uneasiness that competed with the throb in her head, but she kept her tone indifferent. "Are you going somewhere with this?"

"When we think we've found it, it destroys our world, tears it apart. We have to rebuild it with a whole new view of what the world can be." Matt stretched his long legs out in front of him again and propped an elbow on his gym bag. "If we've seen how fucked up the world is, it's harder. We have to rebuild without thinking about it too much."

"Not thinking about things too much is one of my strong points," she noted. "In case you hadn't noticed."

Matt's brown eyes twinkled. "I like you a great deal, Cyn. You're the TRA woman I'd try to poach first, if I didn't respect Ros so much. And if I didn't know the synergy of your team is as vital to TRA's success as my team's is to ours."

Fortunately ignoring her flustered shock, he pushed onward. "Whoever he is, the man who put you in this headspace? If you're considering a longer investment, you'll need to give yourself some time and breathing room to believe in it. And to let him earn it."

She wasn't some neophyte Domme needing a mentor, but she recognized a friend's advice. She just wasn't used to it coming from outside the TRA group. It helped her feel better, there was no denying it. She also realized she didn't want to be mad at Mick anymore. She took out her phone.

CNC is still on, unless your earlier text was you pussying out. Let me know if I need to find another sub for it.

She followed it with five cat emojis. With arched backs and fuzzed-up tails.

As Matt put the ice pack on the curb and tested his jaw, Cyn gave him a critical look. "I better not hear you were mugged. I want Savannah to know you were beat up by a girl."

"I was beat *upon* by a girl. And you should want me to tell her I was mugged. The most protective women in the world are submissives. You know this. You spar with Marcie."

Marcie was married to Ben. When he and Marcie hooked up, she'd been it for him. Marcie took everything he needed to give out, and received what she needed from him in return.

Out of the handful of female fighters at Roughnecks, Ben's fierce submissive provided Cyn the most consistent challenge in the sparring ring. Some smartass had added a score chart on the gym's leader board, *M vs C*, with chalk marks to show the accumulation of victories on either side. They'd suspended the workouts—at least until Marcie was no longer pregnant.

"You're only up by one on her," Matt followed the train of thought. "My money is on her to pull ahead by year end."

"Hope you didn't bet a lot. Having that baby is going to give her different priorities."

"It sure will. Being a mother will make her determined to improve her fighting skills. So she can kick ass to protect those who matter."

While talking with Matt about Mick as a "hypothetical" relationship was unstable but okay ground, this terrain was quicksand. Cyn pushed herself up. "I've got to go."

"All right." As he rose with her, shouldering his gym bag, Matt gave her face another assessing look. "Ros is right. Go home for a nap and more painkillers."

"Same to you." She started to move away, then remembered. She wasn't a welcher. "So what do I owe you? You won the bet."

"A weekend of babysitting," he said, with an easy smile. "About four months after the baby is born, the team is planning on taking Ben and Marcie for a weekend getaway. You can bring Vera or Skye□—"

There were things that could steal her breath even faster than being knocked flat on her back. As she tried to reinflate her lungs, her mind scrambled to do damage control, react like any normal human being would to an entirely reasonable request. She didn't have panic attacks. She wouldn't allow it.

She rallied enough to give him a brittle laugh. "I'm *so* not a kid person. How about that thousand? I know you always give your winnings to charity, so I'll send it wherever you want. But Vera or Skye would love to do the babysitting thing, and either one of them can solo it with no problem. Or Skye will bring Tiger. Angelica would probably love sitting on his motorcycle with him. Like a big iron horse. Kids love animals. Didn't I hear you took her to the Audubon zoo not long ago?"

Shut the fuck up. You're babbling. If she could hear her desperation, so could Matt.

A frown flitted across his brow. She didn't want him to say another word. No matter what he said next, she might vomit up information she didn't want to give.

Baby formula, hidden under her sweatshirt. A policewoman's grip on her arm, yanking it back to cuff her. The formula falling onto the pavement, rolling away.

Oh God...

"Email me where you want the money to be sent. I've got to go. See you at Progeny. Or here."

When she bolted for her truck, she half expected Matt to try to stop her, because he was that assertive, an overly protective kind of male, and only an idiot would miss how freaked out she was.

He didn't, though. He respected her space, which she appreciated, because by the time she reached her truck in the alley parking space, she was weighed down by feelings so heavy she could barely pull herself into the seat. She slammed the door and turned over the engine. Before she put it in drive, she raised her gaze to the mirror, locked it on the braided whip in her gun rack. A reminder of who she was.

You proved your value. Damn straight she had.

To the people who matter. Not so much.

Her phone buzzed and she glanced down at the screen. Mick had answered her on the CNC thing.

Glad to hear it. I'm yours, Mistress. See you then.

The snarled mess of her feelings met the tangle of how she felt about him. She really was going to throw up.

She shoved open the door, leaned out and left her breakfast in the gutter. She was close enough to Bourbon Street no one would be surprised to find it. Still, she used a bottle of water to wash it mostly into the drain.

See, she'd grown. Become more civilized. She swished some water in her mouth and spat into the gutter, then closed the door, leaned back in the seat and took a breath.

Yes. All right. It would all be okay. She needed to cut Mick out of the past and paste him firmly in the present.

Ladies-in-Charge would be the perfect way to do that.

CHAPTER ELEVEN

Much like Roughnecks, Progeny always offered Cyn the chance to spill off energy that could push to an unhelpful pressure point in her daily life. An event night was something even more special. And a night dedicated to Dommes? That was like a carnival's promises, delivered to all senses. Inhaling cotton candy, kettle corn, the cool freshness of ice cream and snow cones. Hearing a soft rush of voices, seeing lights sparkling in the darkness. Feeling heat touching the skin, excitement prickling the insides.

When she lived in Jersey, she'd picked up extra cash working the shooting gallery booth at a traveling carnival. The troupe had set up in an abandoned strip mall parking lot for several weekends one fall.

She'd shadowed the intriguingly polite carnival mechanic, a skinny twenty-two year old with soulful eyes and a shy heart. He'd taught her how to repair the rides. He tested them all after closing every night to see if they needed tweaking. She rode the Ferris wheel with him, the wind blowing in her face, the stars much different when seen high in the sky. His shoulder had pressed against hers, and he'd smelled like popcorn, cigarettes and peppermint.

He'd asked to kiss her. She said no. Then kissed him.

At Progeny, the olfactory input might be different, but it was no less engaging. The aroma was musky cologne, fragrant perfumes. That first glow of perspiration, a dew that spoke of sex and need. Leather, wood, fire, oil. Candles with exotic scents like bergamot, sandalwood and cinnamon.

Mick's army of volunteers had been male and female submissives who knew what pleased their Mistresses. He'd also pulled in key insights from select Dommes. Still, no one except he and a few of the submissives had known what the final outcome would look like, which made seeing it for the first time worth a long look.

In Cyn's case, that included an absurd spurt of pride.

My man did this.

Blackmore's raucous Renaissance Faire pub song, "All For One" was blasting in the foyer. *We'll drink together, not alone...* Studded leather straps curtained the club archway. Two of them were wrapped around the lifted wrists of a blindfolded male sub, feet planted shoulder width apart. He had dark hair, shaved at the sides and nape, tousled on top, giving him a boyish look.

A gold and black brocade corset defined his lean and muscular upper torso, the contours from wider chest and shoulders to straight, slim hips, the shallow dip of the back. The loops of the shoestring style lacings rested on his buttocks, the rise and shape of them also made more prominent by the snug hold of the corset.

His black slacks had a loving hold on that ass, the cuffs brushing perfectly polished brogues. The calligraphy sign over him was an invitation.

Touch me however you desire, Mistresses. Feel the possibilities of the evening. A footnote at the bottom added, *Lace your own male sub in a handmade corset at the Vendor Market.*

Cyn wondered if Skye could get Tiger into one. Maybe if it was in leather, and had skull and flame patches.

Vera appeared at her shoulder. "How can you doubt there's a Goddess, when you see something that sweet?"

She wore a skirt suit in a rich mango color, with a vanilla-colored blouse. The skirt showed off her stockinged legs and the jacket had ruffles over her backside. Flourishes of pale orange adorned her white high heels.

"You look like an ice cream cone," Cyn noted.

"Something a male will want to lick, all the way to the cream center. If I give him permission to do so."

"Got that right." Cyn shot her a grin. "You go left, I'll go right."

Cyn put her hand above the sub's right knee as Vera did the same on the left. Whereas Vera caressed her way up his thigh in silky spirals, Cyn dug her nails into the thin slacks and went straight up. They moved in sync, though, so that when they reached the crease between thigh and testicles, giving them a passing fondle, their fingertips brushed.

Cyn was sure he wore a condom under the pants for the erection he was exhibiting. Depending on what each Mistress chose to do to him, he might spew a few times this evening. He was well-trained, not thrusting rudely into their touch. Cyn knew his Mistress, and suspected Grania had ensured good behavior by threatening him with a chastity cage, which would prevent him from having an erection at all. A Dungeon Monitor was nearby, keeping a protective eye on him.

If Cyn had donned her metal claws, she could have left the slacks in tatters. But Grania had dressed him, and only she had the right to shred his clothing.

Cyn thought of lacing Mick into a corset, then cutting each string with her claws, slowly loosening the garment and bringing it down until she could bite his nipples with those metal tips.

That might be a good way to start their CNC scene, to get them both into it.

She was already fantasizing, and she'd barely left the foyer. She didn't know if that was a good sign or a warning, that some things were too good to be true.

As she and Vera moved past the bound sub, they didn't neglect the rear view. Their hands slid down to the shallow valley of his back, playing with the loops of the lacing before indulging a cupping of his tight backside. They exchanged a wicked Domme smile, infused with pure delight. Cyn felt like she could smell popcorn and peppermint, feel the firmness of the mechanic's lips. He'd been her first real kiss.

"There's an opening ceremony on the dance floor stage in fifteen minutes," Vera said.

"It's probably already wall to wall."

"Ros is saving us a high top." Vera gave Cyn's face a critical look. "The nose is swollen, but in this light and with your makeup, no one will notice without a close look."

"You sound surprised. I know how to do makeup."

"I just figured you'd enhance the bruising to look scarier."

"I'm plenty scary without help. Don't I look like it?"

Cyn had chosen her black slacks over booted heels, but tonight her sleeveless shirt choice was a transparent black fabric with silver thread running in straight lines to the hem. The front and back of the shirt were held in place with a clear elastic band that connected them at the rib cage on either side and tightened the bodice. Under the glittering fabric, her curves and nipples were shadowed but evident.

At Vera's raised brow, Cyn shrugged. "I'm in the mood to be extra bitchy tonight."

"Goddess help him."

The next thing they encountered was the dessert table. Chocolate truffles, cupcakes, cookies, a chocolate fountain with fresh fruits and shortbread. Nearby was an open bar. A two-drink maximum on alcohol kept play safe and event costs reasonable, but there were limitless sparkling waters, sodas, fruit juices, and even coffee and tea, the latter making Vera happy.

"I swear you were stolen from a British nursery and shipped to the U.S."

"I've always wanted to have a British accent. Skye put one into my digital voice. It sounds good. Maybe I should cultivate one."

"If you sound like Mary Poppins when you lecture me on proper work behavior, I'll get horny."

"When are you not?" Vera gestured to one end of the table. "I think someone was thinking of you."

Cyn saw a vegan section, with more cupcakes, cookies and candies. She was going to scoff at Vera and remind her she wasn't the only vegan, but then she saw what Vera was

194

pointing at. A selection of all the vegan desserts had been set on a cake stand and covered with the glass dome. Someone had painted on the glass, bold, swirling black and silver letters, with a toss of glitter to draw attention to it.

Mistress Cyn's Only.

Vera was chuckling, and had that look that women got when a man did something stupidly romantic.

Cyn was mortified. And pleased. She retrieved one of the cupcakes and a napkin, while Vera helped herself to a couple cookies from elsewhere on the table. Then they headed onward.

More subs like Grania's were scattered about the main floor, suspended on webs threaded onto large rings. An automatic motor rotated them, the metal catching the light. The rotation was very slow. A Mistress could put her hand out, keep it still, and her fingertips or palm would slide over soft skin, an erect cock or taut nipple, a wet cunt.

All of the subs on display were up for auction. The highest bid would win their service for the remainder of the night. Like most of Progeny's special event fundraisers, the proceeds would go to charity, like a local domestic violence or homeless shelter, or one of NOLA's several animal welfare organizations. Tonight the funds were earmarked to combat human trafficking. Since the legit BDSM world often got lumped in with criminal behavior, it was an issue the membership felt strongly about.

Submission and service were willing choices, always.

Cyn stopped beside Vera at the table with literature about the organization. A jar for additional donations was half full.

The spot was manned by a husky male sub with a thick beard. He looked like a pirate crewman or a Renaissance busker in his linen shirt, red sash and dark pants. His collar's tag said "Property of Edwina." Pewter rings on his fingers had skulls and Harley Davidson logos, and his black bandana was printed with more white skulls. Amiable chocolate brown eyes with thick lashes were saved from being too pretty by a two-inch scar on his cheek.

Because Progeny did reciprocity with other clubs, many here tonight were visitors. Cyn didn't know Edwina or her sub, but Vera gave him a familiar nod.

He beamed at her. "I've already emptied the jar twice," he said. "Everyone's being especially generous."

"That's wonderful." Vera looked at a brochure. "I assume the charity was verified, Theo?"

"Yes, ma'am. Absolutely."

Cyn put a couple twenties in the jar. "Have you seen Mick?"

"Not in the last fifteen minutes, but he's here somewhere." That quick smile again. "He's been on site since sun up. Because he's doing a session tonight, he's making sure everything's square and everyone knows their job before he turns it over to Jillie. She's his second."

"Sounds like he'll need a nap before that session," Vera observed, flicking Cyn an amused glance.

Theo nodded vigorously. "That's no lie. He's signed up to do a CNC session with Mistress Cyn, and everyone here says she's a ball-busting bitch."

Cyn leaned in, bracing her fingers on the table. Theo's gaze slid to her, then his face flooded with color.

"Would you say that's a respectful thing to say about a Mistress, Theo?" she asked silkily. "To her face?"

"Oh shit. Uh, no ma'am. No, Mistress. My apologies. To both of you." He surged to his feet and hit the table with his knee, almost toppling it. Vera steadied it, pressing her lips against a smile as he managed a clumsy bow.

"He's a good boy," she told Cyn. "Stop fucking with him. You love being called a ball-busting bitch."

"I prefer ball-*removing* bitch." Cyn gave Theo a critical, searing look, then put her uneaten cupcake in front of him. "You're doing a good job. Just watch your manners. You're swimming with sharks tonight, and your flesh looks mighty tender."

"Yes, ma'am."

As Cyn moved on, Vera sent Theo a wink before joining her. He let out a relieved breath. He also added a prayer for Mick. And thought nametags for future events might be a good addition to the suggestion box.

Mistress Cyn looked like she didn't weigh more than a buck ten, but those eyes were pure black hole gravity.

Cyn found Mick up on the main stage. Spiral, one of Progeny's staff subs, was handling the warm-up before the kickoff while Mick stood in the wings. He was talking to another volunteer helping to man the curtain.

Spiral, who also did stand-up comedy and community theater, had his audience laughing, whistling and tossing out suggestive proposals. Cyn paid little attention to him. Her gaze stayed on Mick.

Was it normal to feel this way after not seeing someone for less than a full day? She'd done without him for ten years, for fuck's sake.

Vera had joined Ros and Skye at a high top. Abby was the only one absent tonight. Bigger events with unpredictable variables caused her problems. Some god deserved a habanero enema for inflicting this on their friend. However, Abby genuinely seemed to welcome the stories they'd bring her about things she couldn't do. Most days, she'd made her peace with it. Neil was a big part of the reason for that.

Case in point, he was taking her out on his boat tonight for a cruise in the bayou. Cyn didn't know how anyone could enjoy anything that involved alligators, snakes, spiders and mosquitoes the size of planes, but it worked for Abby, especially with Neil at the helm of the boat.

Cyn hung back at the mezzanine, since the elevated position offered a better view of Mick. Him being in the wings made sense. He didn't strike her as a person who sought the spotlight, or would even enjoy it, though he didn't seem afraid of public speaking. Afraid of anything at all, really. He was like a dead calm expanse of ocean, the water still as glass, everything beneath hidden.

Was the mystery part of the appeal? Maybe. But it was a lot of different things.

He looked good, in the kind of outfit he always wore, the slacks and dress shirt in that fabric that clung to his muscles, enhanced by his braced stance, arms crossed over his chest. Her skeleton cross rested in the open neck, a dull gleam. So far, she'd never seen him without it. A message that affected her far more deeply than it should.

No matter how strange the event planner role had seemed to her, he was good at this. But she'd noted his skillset rested in his network of resources and recognizing and guiding the talents of people around him, people who had the enthusiasm and interest to bring the brainstormed vision to life.

She wasn't even sure if he liked events with big crowds.

Nothing about the man made sense. Yet as she looked at him, what was on her mind weren't unanswered questions. It was his scent, his hair against her fingers, his body under her hands, the thrust of his cock inside her. How he moved against the clamp of her legs and arms, the feel of his breath on her neck, the way he shuddered when she bit him, struck him. Gave him pain.

The look in his eyes, wanting more, more, more. Not begging. Demanding, needing, like he needed water, food, salvation, a baptism in pain to escape whatever was going on below that calm surface.

He was scanning the audience. The lights started to come down, getting ready for the kickoff, but before they went black, he found her. Their eyes met, and then the darkness swallowed her.

She couldn't have planned that one better.

Spiral took center stage, his voice dropping to a loud whisper through the mic. "It's getting close to go-time, esteemed Mistresses. Alphonse is showering, but he knows he only has fifteen minutes to get clean and dressed before he has to head this way, to be here with us tonight. To meet his Mistress and be everything she desires. But we're just voyeurs, so be quiet now, like little birds on the wire, so he doesn't know we're watching..."

Laughter rippled through the room. As the stair lights engaged, Cyn moved to join the others. Ros nudged her drink to her, her preferred Dr Pepper. The club tended to keep member favorites in stock, but she wondered if Mick had set some of those aside for her as well.

The curtain rose, accompanied by a collective inhale of delight. A portable shower had been set up, screened by a curtain with a clear top half and an opaque gray bottom. Water from the shower head visibly streaked the transparent part. Sink, vanity and mirror were arranged around the shower, as if they were looking into Alphonse's bathroom. A standing wardrobe, presumably holding Alphonse's clothes for the night, stood a few feet away.

At the moment, he wore nothing at all.

He was already wet, his dark hair slicked down. It was long enough to reach his shoulders. A dragon tattoo was on his back, the spread wings over his shoulder blades, the tail following his spine. The curtain obscured where it stopped, but Cyn was guessing it would be curled over one buttock.

It was a female dragon, with lashes and feminine mouth and shape. Her talons looked as if they were dug into his skin. He was soaping himself. Thoroughly. After their initial expressions of delight at the tableau, Mistresses called out complaints about the curtain's concealment, though their tones of mirth said they were enjoying the titillation.

As if responding to the feedback, a female pit bull trotted ponderously onto the stage. Looking neither left nor right, she grabbed the edge of the curtain and brought it down with one easy tug. To the accompaniment of thunderous cheers and foot stomping, she carried it away like a fluttering banner and disappeared into the opposite wing.

The dragon's tail *was* curled over his buttock, with a barbed tip that, like the talons, looked like it was pricking the skin, several drops of blood inked over the taut curve.

Alphonse, acting as if he'd heard none of the commentary, turned around. Not enough to reveal his cock, but hinting at it behind the length of a carefully posed muscular thigh. The Mistresses groaned and hooted.

"Rotgut, you little minx. Bring that back."

He sighed when the dog didn't reappear and shrugged. He turned away again and finished his shower with lots of flexing—ass, shoulders, and thighs. Plus more taunting half-turns that had the women straining their eyes to catch a glimpse of what he was concealing.

Alphonse shut off the water, leaned out and snagged a towel off a standing wooden rack. "Thank fuck she didn't get the towel," he grumbled. Before he used it, he shook his head like Rotgut might have done, then stepped out of the shower and turned toward the audience, finally revealing his cock. The very satisfying length and girth, plus the one-word tattoo above the base, caused another round of cheers.

Hers.

The twinkle in his eyes and curve of his lips gave the right nod of acknowledgement to the crowd, but he stayed in character. He slowly wrapped the towel around his waist, seemingly oblivious to the boos as he positioned himself in front of the mirror and ran his fingers through his hair. He smoothed his hands over his ass, well defined by the grip of the towel. The muscles along his back shifted, his shoulders twitching as he used a razor to touch up his clean jaw.

Laughter burst out as Rotgut reappeared and moved into stalk mode, her front legs down as she crept up behind the seemingly oblivious Alphonse. When she delicately took the hem of the towel in her teeth, the audience erupted with yells of encouragement.

"Tear it off, Rotgut. You go, girl!"

Cyn laughed as Alphonse pivoted with a protest. He and Rotgut proceeded to have a tug-of-war that Rotgut, despite her excellent training, seemed to enjoy thoroughly. When she won, she dashed joyously off stage, the towel in her mouth.

"Damn dog." Alphonse sighed, putting his hands on his hips, a very nice effect. With another shrug, he turned toward the wardrobe.

Then he started getting dressed.

Alphonse took his time with the reverse strip tease, pulling on black boxer briefs and cupping himself through them to adjust, turning to make sure the fit was good on his ass. After that came slacks, a zipping and fastening, another substantial adjustment where he cupped balls and cock, checked out his backside. When he donned a cotton tank, he did it facing the audience before turning his back to shrug into the dress shirt, another equally appealing view.

The tie was next. He wrapped it around his wrists, holding it up to the mirror to see how it looked, then put his mouth to it. It was easy to imagine the brief but lingering kiss as an homage to the absent Mistress he hoped would be binding him later.

The one whose ink was over his cock.

A hum rippled through the crowd, a reaction Cyn knew was shared by her and the women at her table. They all understood it, both Domme and sub, even from different angles. Had Mick kissed the skeleton cross tonight with the same thought as Alphonse?

After the tie was on, he donned socks and dress shoes. Checked the mirror and brushed his hair. The front already drying and feathering over his brow.

Final piece. The suit coat. After he shrugged into it, he turned to the audience, sliding an easy hand into his trouser pocket, the coat panel folding over one hip. "So," he said. "Will I please her tonight?"

That about brought the house down.

With a rakish grin, Alphonse did a spin and walked toward the back of the stage, a sexy stroll, before he exited stage left.

The thunderous applause continued as the lights rose. Spiral returned to center stage and gestured to the performers to come out and take an additional bow. Alphonse emerged with Rotgut and her pet parent slash trainer, a Vietnamese woman with a full bloom of streaked silver and black hair twisted up on her head. She wore a gold silk shirt with a chain belt over a white skirt embroidered with a gold dragon. Matching embroidered slippers had gold ribbons crisscrossed up her calves.

To equally enthusiastic cheers, Rotgut caught a treat out of the air. With a wicked grin, the trainer tossed one to Alphonse, which he snagged in a hand and then dropped to one knee before her. As he rose, the woman teasingly petted him through the fly of the suit, mouthing, "very good boy," to a lot of laughter.

Alphonse kissed her other hand, and gave Rotgut a fond stroke. After they departed the stage, Spiral saluted the audience with a look of barely suppressed anticipation, his face wreathed in a smile.

"Enjoy the night, ladies. You've earned it."

The night, with all its possibilities, had begun.

Mick was no longer in the wings. Cyn did a loop of the main traffic areas. Later tonight he'd be under her command alone, but if she had the chance to watch him work, she wouldn't mind.

Though she hadn't corrected what she'd told him that first night, that what he did with his dick was his own business, she bet he'd followed her initial desires, keeping his hand off himself. Suffering for her.

Ros, Vera and Skye were browsing at the Vendor Market, set up near the club's rear bar area. Lawrence and Tiger were there, too. They leaned against a high top, not far from where the women were shopping.

Amused, Cyn noted they had a table card, the words written in Ros's recognizable black script.

Taken. Move on, bitches.

"Taken" was double underlined.

When she reached Ros and raised a questioning brow toward the men, her boss made a face. "A lot of guest Dommes are here tonight. Tiger and Lawrence could barely take a swallow of their drinks before one was checking to see if they were available for play."

"That's why you abandon subtlety. Put big ass collars on them, preferably with interior spikes so they remember not to look at anyone but you two. Some of these Dommes have no modesty. Asses in skin-tight latex, boobs hanging out."

"Uh-huh." Ros's gaze swept her transparent top.

"That's different. In this lighting, a man has to work to confirm what he thinks he's seeing, and then I can catch him at it and punish him."

Just as she suspected, Skye was considering corset options for Tiger, and had found one with a trio of skulls embroidered on it. As she held it up for them to see, Cyn offered an approving nod. "You put that on him," she called to her friend, "he'll hold onto the number two spot in my spank bank."

"As long as he's not number one," Skye signed back. "That's for me alone."

"Greedy bitch. You get the real thing." Cyn tossed a lascivious look at the man in question. In his hip-cocked stance, his jeans molded his lower body in their usual mouthwatering way. A Harley Davidson logoed vest was all

203

he wore up top. As Skye brandished the corset at him, he had a dubious but willing expression.

Ros zeroed in on the important part of Cyn's statement. "Who's holding your number one spot?"

"Why Lawrence, of course. He gets me all creamy and dreamy, every night." Cyn chuckled as Ros made a claw gesture toward her. Then her boss took a closer look.

"Does the nose still hurt?"

"No more than expected. Vera said I covered it well."

"You did." Ros paused, as if she might say more, but only linked her arm with Cyn's and bumped her hip. A sign she was forgiven for tangling with Matt. Not that she'd asked for forgiveness, but it was nice to know. Matt and Ros had likely talked since then, and Matt had let her know they were good.

Which rankled a little, since Cyn had assured Ros they were, but Matt *was* Ros's friend, and Ros hadn't been privy to their talk on the curb. Cyn knew he'd respect her privacy on what she hadn't been able to keep herself from saying.

She was still wondering how the dad stuff had boiled up and why she'd just blurted it out like that. But no matter the wrench he'd thrown into it with the insane babysitting idea, she'd leveled out since and felt surprisingly okay about the whole thing. Personal growth. She could tick that box for the year.

As Ros moved away from her to do her own looking, Cyn scanned the growing number of people wandering through the vendor area and elsewhere. The planned public sessions would start in eighteen minutes. The schedule displayed on the screens throughout the club indicated six stations, each session at them scheduled for thirty to fifty-five minutes. As she left the Market, she passed one of them. Chairs had been set up in a crescent before a foot-high platform, like a small theater. Those who preferred to watch on the move could stand behind the seating area.

The first set of sessions would include wax play, cock-and-ball torture, rope suspension, forced orgasm, strap-ons and mind fuck interrogation. There would be four rotations throughout the night, for a total of twenty-four scenes. A lot of people were going to miss their bedtime.

She was at ten o'clock. CNC. *Consensual non-consent, Mistress Cyn and Mick.* It would be well attended, because people who didn't do edge play were still intrigued by it. Like climbing the rock wall at the gym, and then watching ESPN televise climbers scaling a cliff with nothing but their hands and a rope harness attached to the crevices along the way. The thrill could be viewed from a safe seat.

It would also be well attended because of Mick. The mysterious and hot event planner, popping up on the schedule to do a CNC scene with one of the club's biggest sadists? That was a not-to-be-missed.

She didn't give a shit. During a scene, she didn't pay attention to anything except what was going on between her and her sub. Which was why she preferred private play. Someone making a random comment, sneezing, or letting their phone go off while she was in the zone didn't make her happy.

That had happened during her last public session. Someone's phone had started playing "Let It Go." Who the fuck had that as a ring tone?

Cyn had been doing a scene with a public play preference sub who had a hard time voicing his safe word when he needed to do so. It was a favor for Vera, who believed Cyn had the skillset to resolve the problem. He was already on probation for lack of self-care, having let one-too-many Mistresses push him too far before they realized he'd gotten himself into a bad place.

Vera claimed Cyn was as soft-hearted as she was, just in a different way. That was bullshit, but Cyn would do any favor her clan asked of her, because it was always important, not just shit they were dumping on her. They would do the same for her.

Cyn had enough experience to recognize when he was getting too close to that line, as long as she could keep herself focused on every minute change in his physical and mental state. Then the goddamn phone went off.

She didn't immediately react. She pushed him to the point where she needed him, then put her hand on his shoulder and leaned in. "A Mistress wants a sub who knows how to care for himself, for her," she murmured. "So she can play with him again. If you don't safeword when you should, I will be very angry with you. Do you want me displeased?"

"No, Mistress. No. I just don't know if I can..."

"Yes, you can. Because if you don't, I'm going to rip your fucking throat out with my teeth. When you lose control of your bowels, it will get on my shoes. Do you want my shoes to get dirty?"

"No, Mistress." She saw the whites of his eyes as they rolled in her direction. She gripped his hair, yanked his head back and sank her teeth into the flesh around his windpipe. She had a very strong jaw, and through pain and stress, she'd pushed him into the grip of the mindfuck. He believed she meant it.

The usual desire rose, to cut through, find blood. She held onto it, her fingers tightening on his neck below her grip. He was bucking, trying unsuccessfully to dislodge her. His breath started to rasp and he choked. Her teeth cut through, and the metallic taste of blood touched her tongue.

"Abraham Lincoln," he gasped out. "Abraham Lincoln."

It took effort to rein in the roaring urge to follow through, to clear the red haze in her vision, but that was good. He'd remember those three extra-long seconds of terror, when he thought she wasn't going to stop. So next time he was in a session with a Mistress, he'd safeword right when he should.

Regaining control, steadying herself, she let go of his throat, but dropped her hand to his cock, gripping and stroking.

"You don't want me to stop doing this, do you, Branch?"

"No…no Mistress. Oh, fuck…" He bit his lips, pressed his forehead to the webbing he was restrained against. It was quivering with his body. But he remembered his manners and asked.

"May I…"

"Not yet."

She stripped off the condom on one upward stroke, letting it fall between his feet. In the same motion, she pivoted and closed in on her audience, specifically the fan of Disney earworms.

Cyn plucked the phone from her beringed hand— emeralds and gold, with streaked hair to match. Ignoring the woman's startled protest, she came back to Branch. Wrapping her arm around his hip to reclaim his cock, she brought the phone around the other side as she leaned against him. He'd take the full-body contact as reward and reassurance.

She'd been swift enough he'd barely lost any momentum, so as she pumped the stiff shaft, he was ready to blow. "Now, Branch. Come."

She kept the screen against the meatus, and felt the fountain of semen baptize phone and fingers. She was fine with that and worked him thoroughly. When he was all done, she put her palm on his back. "Well done. Don't forget this lesson. It's important."

"No, Mistress. I won't. I promise." He was near tears. During the session, through pain and interrogation, she'd stripped him down to *why* he couldn't safeword. He'd be vulnerable to subdrop, but that was where Vera came in.

As her friend entered the circle and took over the aftercare, Cyn turned away and tossed the sticky, drenched phone to the slack-jawed woman. She caught it against the lustrous green silk she wore over ample breasts. The dry cleaner was going to have a hell of a time getting that out.

"Try silent mode next time," Cyn suggested.

Returning to the present, Cyn remembered the taste of Branch's throat, his life force beating like a hapless bird against her. She had no patience for that kind of weakness, the inability to protect himself, but she'd gotten the job done. He'd had no problems since, and discovered a self-confidence Vera said he wouldn't have found without her.

Fine. She'd done it because Vera had asked. She wasn't a therapy Mistress.

She'd found Mick. He was talking to several Mistresses, reservedly accepting compliments over the kickoff while answering questions. He held up a subtle finger to a stressed-out Jillie, who'd appeared at his elbow, likely looking for direction on some problem.

Cyn wanted to mess up his nice clothes, pull away the shirt to put her hands on his wide shoulders, explore heated skin down to his waist and the muscular, resilient ass. His dark hair was brushed and gleaming, curling at the collar, the thicker strands swept back from his high forehead. Even dressed up and all civilized acting, he conveyed a dangerous physicality that would be hers to goad tonight. She wished it was ten o'clock already, but anticipation brought its own rewards.

He was giving her real memories to add to the endless fantasies she'd had about him. She wanted to give him the same. He knew how to walk through fire with her, craving the burn as much as she desired to add fuel to the flame.

When he courteously extricated himself from the Dommes, Cyn leaned against a pillar, watching him.

Jillie had her hair in a ponytail and wore sparkly white leggings and a pink corset. A dainty kitten collar was wrapped around her throat, pointed felt ears perched in her hair. Dillard's sub, also his wife. They enjoyed mostly psychological power exchange, and the girl liked being publicly spanked. They'd been together four years. Dillard was fifteen years older, and they were a good match.

Despite the little girl appearance, Jillie could handle truckloads of responsibility. She was also an accomplished freelance photographer and graphic artist. She'd done some layout work for TRA, contracted by Skye.

After Mick explained what he wanted and she nodded, about to dash off, he stopped her with a hand on her shoulder. He rubbed her collarbone with his thumb, offering what Cyn suspected was a gentle admonition to take a breath and enjoy the night. Not to take it too seriously. Jillie managed a smile, the breath, and calmed down. Then she scurried away.

When he turned, Cyn waited, watching his gaze pass over his surroundings. On the first round, he was cataloging how things were going, and if anything needed his attention. On the second, he was looking for someone. When he paused on Vera, chatting up a sub, and did a more thorough search around her, Cyn knew he was looking for her.

She enjoyed the feeling, but still she waited. People moved all around her, but as soon as Mick's attention passed over where she was, his gaze threaded through the interference and located her.

She had her arms crossed and one booted foot hooked over the other as she leaned against the column. She'd left her hair loose, softly curled around her face. There was a hint of sunrise color in her wet crimson lipstick. Though her eyes needed little enhancement, she'd added liner to make them more piercing.

His gaze slid over her face, then down. He paused, confirming that yes, he was looking at the hint of her nipples through the sparkling fabric. His lips tugged wryly at the tease, then finished the sweep to her boots and came back to her face.

His eyes narrowed. With surprise, she realized he'd detected the swelling around her nose she'd concealed with the makeup. As he moved her way, she thought if he came at anyone with that hooded gaze and warrior purpose to his stride, whoever he was pissed at would know they were in trouble and needed to run.

She liked that about him.

When he reached her, she rested a hand on his chest. She played with the cross, caressing the scar with her fingers. She was aware of curious glances, people marking the intimacy between them.

Yeah, he's mine. Go away.

"I think you like knowing I carry your mark." Mick chose a different angle to echo what was in her mind.

"Almost as much as you do," she said.

He didn't deny it, placing his palm against the pillar by her head, leaning in to create a space like a room with a *keep out* sign. He gently traced the damage around her nose. "So who do I need to kill?" Those dangerous eyes said he wasn't kidding.

"Protective men give me such a tingle." Despite her cynical tone, his response actually did, and the touch on her face was one she welcomed.

The fascination of the watching members had increased. She never allowed a sub to touch her without express permission, and even then, it didn't happen often.

She ignored them, shut it all out. Everything but him. "You can stand down. I got this from a sparring partner, and he's been icing his ribs ever since. He's a business associate, and Ros's friend."

"Not your friend?"

"He is. Just not a close one." That was a kneejerk response. She'd reevaluated that since her discussion with Matt. But she changed the subject. "You ready for tonight?"

"I made sure my health insurance premium was paid."

"A sensible idea." She gestured to the busy activity around them. "You did a good job. Everyone is pleased."

"I had a good team." He shrugged. "Recruiting from the inside knowledge and resources a club already has makes it far easier."

She cocked her head, ready to tease him. "Sounds a little like cheating."

"It's still work. But I expect you do the same thing with clients." He twisted one of her curls around his finger and watched it drift back into a loose coil against her cheek. "No one knows their wants and needs as well as the business itself. Sometimes you just have to get them to look at those needs and wants in new ways."

"Careful. I might hire you to work for me."

"I like the idea of working for you. But not pushing papers or making phone calls. I just want to seduce you."

Mick delivered the line with such intense sincerity that, instead of making her want to laugh in his face, a strange tremor went through her.

"I am going to make you hurt tonight," she said decisively.

His lips split in a sensual smile. She moved her hand to his mouth, stroking the softness of his beard. He didn't move from his braced position. Without being told, he knew she liked to touch without distraction.

Just like he'd proven he knew when she wanted to be touched before she even said so.

"Seduction is a vague term," she noted. "Seduction of the body, the mind, or the soul?"

"You left one out."

She gave him a warning look, just as she pushed the twinge in that particular organ away. "Did you tell Jillie you were pleased with her, so she'd run off and do your bidding?"

"I'm a smart slave driver that way. More carrot than stick."

"I've seen your carrot. That works."

He gave her a direct look. "She hasn't. Nor has any other woman here."

"I wasn't implying otherwise. But outside our sessions, I have no claim on you. You can marinate your vegetables wherever you want."

His gaze didn't warm. "Bullshit, Mistress. You can fuck with me a lot of ways, but that's not one of them."

She leaned her shoulder against the column, dipping her head toward his hand. His fingertips slid against her forehead, capturing another curl.

"Have you fucked with yourself, Mick? Or did you decide your dick was all mine?"

"I didn't have to make that decision. You did. And I honored it. Even as I've thought of nothing but you. I didn't know it was possible to have that many hard-ons daily after puberty."

Her lips curved. "Has it been difficult? Did you suffer?"

"I've been planning an event for three hundred demanding women and just as many hopeful submissives." He met her eyes. "Yeah, I've thought about stepping in front of a truck to get some relief. But then I would have missed my session with you."

She trailed her fingers over his cheeks, stroked his beard again. "I do have one criticism. A proper event planner would help the vendors show off their wares by wearing them himself."

"It would be difficult to focus wearing a vibrating butt plug or sparkly banana catcher. And the erotic oils get messy."

"No one else could focus if you were slicked down in oil. And I'll laugh at you if you wear a banana catcher. They make a man's package jiggle in a very non-sexy way."

"Women look far better jiggling than men. No argument." He studied her. "This isn't idle banter. What are you wanting, and should I be scared to ask?"

"Nothing scares you. I want you to wear a corset. I want to put it on you. Do you have the time right now?"

Surprise crossed his features. He looked toward the Vendor Market, then his gaze brushed over one of the screens that showed the current time.

"Spiral and Jillie can cover for me a little while." His expression was hard to read. "Though a few more little birds might flutter up to ask me questions."

"I know how to scare birds away. Particularly those more than capable of using their brains to make a decision."

"You know how to scare dragons away, woman."

He straightened and offered her an arm, a courtly gesture she didn't expect. Any more than she supposed he anticipated her taking it, slipping her fingers into the crook of his elbow, her fingers whispering over his firm biceps.

They headed for the vendor area.

CHAPTER TWELVE

Corset sellers had visited the club before, but their target clientele had been women. This one was dedicated to the male demographic. A tall man made up of angles and little body fat, he wore one of his own creations, striped gold and red, with gold ribbon lacing. He'd put it over a silk shirt and brown slacks. A man who knew how to use his own assets to market his product and skills, the outfit suited him. His long-fingered hands had created every garment he sold. His scene name was Tailor.

As he helped dress submissives according to their Mistresses' preferences, he offered instructional insights in a crisp British accent that might have been as affected as the one Vera was contemplating, but it never slipped.

"A corset for a woman emphasizes the hourglass shape. With men, it's the V-shape, from the shoulders to the waist, smoothing the stomach and chest, a blend of waistcoat and corset."

He adjusted a lace, touching the nape of the young man he was dressing. The Tailor gave the watching Mistress a knowing smile as the submissive blushed under his obviously Dominant touch. "They're always a delight when they're this sweet."

"Sweet is overrated," Cyn muttered to Mick. His lips pressed against a smile as he threaded a finger through the belt loop of her slacks and tugged.

"Men have worn corsets throughout history," the Tailor continued, for the gathering of potential customers and those who liked watching the fittings. "In the 1800s, a Frenchman said, 'The secret lies in the thinness and narrowness of the waist. Catechize your tailor about this … Insist, order, menace … Shoulders large, the skirts of the coat ample and flowing, the waist strangled.'" The Tailor winked. "That's my rule."

"Insist, order and menace," Mick murmured. "Now I understand why this appealed to you."

She stuck her tongue out at him, an impulsive gesture that made his eyes sparkle. When the Tailor finished with his current client, she raised a hand to catch his attention.

"How may I assist, Mistress?"

She dipped her head toward Mick. "What would you suggest?"

Tailor ran a critical eye over her subject. With his arms crossed, Mick appeared relaxed, though the expression in his eyes had changed since they'd moved away from her. What was in them had the Tailor looking a little uneasy.

Mick had that effect if he didn't put any warmth in his gaze, or if he went silent. But the Tailor showed he had a spine, and wasn't unused to more intimidating personalities. Especially garbing male submissives in a BDSM club environment.

"This one."

He'd taken into account what she was wearing as well, pulling a corset of silver and black brocade off the rack. It had silver hooks and black laces. Sleek and sexy, and sure to enhance the hero vs. villain mystery of the man who wore it.

"I'd like to put it on him," Cyn said.

"Of course. That's part of the pleasure. I recommend he remove the belt, so it will lie more smoothly over his waistband."

Cyn stopped Mick as he put his hand to his belt. "I'll do it."

"Yeah, because if he removes the belt himself, half the female subs watching will pass out."

Laughter rippled through the gathered voyeurs. The ones who were female subs didn't deny the assessment.

Vera had called out the comment. She and Ros were at the table Lawrence and Tiger had shared earlier. Tiger was gone, probably watching the public sessions with Skye, since the first round had started. Vera and Ros had the two seats

215

and Lawrence stood beside Ros. His hand was braced on her chair back, thumb stroking her below her shoulder blade as he watched the goings on with his usual impassive expression that most couldn't read.

Cyn knew it conveyed total attention to whatever his Mistress wanted, and his readiness to get between her and any threat. Though he'd learned to tone that down in known environments, a former Navy SEAL was never off duty.

Since Ros had one elegant leg bent to brace her foot on the chair rung, the other crossed over her knee, Cyn's attention was caught by her high heels. Tonight's selection was exceptionally spectacular.

The back stem of the shoe was a shirtless kneeling male, bearing the weight of wearer's heel on his back. A draped silver chain connected the collar around his throat to the cuffs on his uplifted wrists. Another attached to the back of the collar and ran to the strap around Ros's ankle, like a leash binding him to his Mistress.

Where *did* the woman find these things? Cyn put her hands to Mick's waist to unbuckle the belt and strip it off. She noted the muscle tension beneath her touch, and coiled the belt around her knuckles, feeling his heat through it, before she moved the couple steps needed to lay the belt in front of Vera. "Could you hold onto that for me?"

"My pleasure."

"No sniffing or rubbing it on you."

"You are no fun at all."

Sy wandered up to stand at Vera's side. He nodded to Cyn in a friendly manner. But when she came back to Mick, she noted Sy's presence had introduced a different attitude to his stance. And that unsettling look in his eyes? It had increased. Exponentially.

Cyn reached up and touched his face. "Are you under the impression we aren't completely alone?" she asked.

Mick's gaze came to hers. As they held, and she showed him what she wanted, how she felt, the fire kindling there

216

changed target and purpose. "Not a soul here but us, Mistress."

While watching her do something like this, it would be normal for Sy to fantasize about the next session they might share. She suspected that was the root of Mick's adverse reaction. He wasn't the kind of rooster who liked to share his yard.

His possessiveness didn't surprise her. Her reaction to it did. Cyn didn't find it tedious or annoying, like she did whenever a sub tried to make more of their sessions than was there for her.

As she mused on that, the Tailor was taking Mick's measurements. He disappeared behind a curtain, returning with the proper size of the silver and black design. He unwrapped it from the clear plastic that protected it and loosened the laces before handing her the garment.

"Shirt off or on?"

She graciously considered the demands on Mick tonight and decided accordingly. "On."

"Slide it onto his shoulders and flatten the shirt as much as possible before you start hooking it," the Tailor said.

Mick's gaze met hers as she threaded the garment onto his arms and had him shrug into it. She spread her hands over his chest, smoothing the fabric over the man beneath. Stepping closer, she reached behind him to do the same down his back. As she did, she brought her body fully against his, thigh to chest, experiencing heat and hard male.

His chuckle was a puff of air against her temple. "Keep doing that, and it's not the belt that's going to be the problem."

"If your dick gets in the way, I'll tuck it under the corset. Tie it down as tight as I can." She made sure she rubbed herself against him before she stepped back. His look was the same one he'd had before he hunted her down in the straw bales. A patient predator. Waiting.

The Tailor was standing close enough to hear the exchange, though as a gentleman, he affected deafness until Cyn addressed him directly. "If you have lace or fabric scrap, you should expand your offerings to include cock corsets. Laced sheaths that match the corset or complement its colors. That's a way to make sure it doesn't go to waste."

"Indeed, madame." His eyes gleamed. "I'll consider it."

"Free marketing advice from Thomas Rose Associates," she told him. "If you ever want to expand your operations, think of us here in New Orleans. We have a country-wide client base."

Ros chuckled. When Cyn winked at her, her boss lifted her glass. Then Cyn's attention came back to the only thing she wanted occupying it.

"Hook the front fasteners," the Tailor said, "and move to the back to tighten the laces."

Cyn fastened the silver hooks with deft fingers, though she took her time with the sensation of binding Mick. The Tailor checked in with his assistant as she did, but by the time she was almost done, he was back at her side. What she was doing with Mick was attracting an audience, so the Tailor was more than happy to promote the theater.

Cyn did the last hook, resting her fingers on him as she tipped her head up. The blue eyes were fixed on her like he never wanted to look anywhere else. No woman was immune to that. Even a hardass like her.

"I'll enjoy cutting you out of this, giving you back your ability to draw a deep breath. But not too soon, so you better learn to breathe shallow."

"I don't breathe around you at all, Mistress."

She curved her fingers against the brocade. Lifting up on her toes, she brushed her mouth against the corner of his, then stepped behind him.

As she studied the lacings, the Tailor reminded her and their viewers of the process. "The upper part of the rabbit ears, here in the middle, tightens the top, the lower part tightens the bottom. You can pull and adjust as you go. When it's as tight as you wish, tie the ears together to hold it all in place."

He gave her a knowing smile. "Seeing your sub react to the adjustments is pure foreplay. The journey brings as much pleasure as the end result. The reason for wearing a corset goes far beyond fashion."

Cyn gripped the rabbit ears. She'd worn a corset before. It wasn't her usual preference, as she had more interest in imposing restriction than experiencing it herself, but her familiarity meant she could give Tailor a nod, tacit permission to move off and help his other customers, leaving the rest between her and Mick.

Mick was waiting to see what she would do and how she would do it. She pulled on the ears evenly and watched the upper and lower sections close in on his body, around his chest and just below his waist. She pulled on the shirt at the bottom, smoothing it out further. Discomfort from a wrinkled shirt wasn't the kind of pain she wanted him to experience.

As she tightened and adjusted, the garment closed around him, emphasizing and embellishing his shape as the Tailor had said, the triangle of broad chest, the slim waist and flare of hips. The rise of the buttocks became a far more prominent visual target. Nice. Really fucking nice. The corset accentuated the masculine form, tempting touch, taste and teeth.

She smoothed her palm over all of it, moving to his ass and fondling, running her fingers over the seam, the creases between buttocks and thighs.

She lifted on her toes and spoke against his nape, giving him a small bite. "Take a deep breath, and brace yourself."

When he did, she did the final pull. Countering it with the planting of his feet as she'd required helped her make it as tight as she wished. His quiet grunt told her he felt it. She tied off the ears and came back to his front to look at the overall effect.

Wow. The silver and black with the blue shirt and slacks made him into total eye candy. She didn't want to devour him. She needed to.

The Tailor appeared at her elbow with a sales book, offering it to her with a pen. "If you write down your club account number, the charge will be put there."

The corset was well worth the cost. She wrote her number down, adding a generous tip. He murmured his thanks, then handed her a small bag. "An extra set of laces. To replace the ones you'll cut."

He'd heard that part of her conversation. His solicitousness, his attention, how he handled his customers, made him an excellent shopkeeper, but those qualities also made her want to test a theory. She met his eyes with a direct message in her own.

After a few beats, color stained his high cheekbones. He smoothly shifted into a downward gaze and a subtle dip of his head, telling her what she needed to know.

With the right Dominant, he was a switch.

"You should have tea with my friend after you finish for the night." She tilted her head toward Vera, watching them with interest. "You might enjoy one another's company."

"More valuable advice." The Tailor gave her a small smile. "Thank you, Mistress."

Cyn returned her attention to Mick. Putting her hand on his chest, she looked up into his face. It had become oddly pensive. "How does that feel?"

"Does it matter?"

Her short nails could pull out a chest hair. She had plenty to choose from in the open collar of his shirt, so by the time he'd blinked, she'd taken one. He winced.

"I don't respond well to being answered with a question," she said. "It's a deflection."

The pensiveness disappeared. What she saw instead invited her into flame-licking heat. "It feels like the first step toward our session. Where I won't be able to do a damn thing to stop whatever you want to do to me."

If she had any doubt how he felt about that, leaning against him told her. As he spoke, his erection convulsed, substantial as a brick. She rubbed against it again. "You're right about that. But it's not ten o'clock yet, and I have things to do. So I'll see you then."

She began to move past him, but stopped shoulder to shoulder, facing in opposite directions. Ros and Vera were checking him out with undisguised appreciation, either because of the corset or the noticeable hard-on. Lawrence looked a little annoyed, but accepting. Ros was devoted to him alone, and the stimulation here would drive the creativity of her demands from him later.

"Mick?"

"Yeah?"

"Tonight, keep your hands to yourself. Don't let me see them on any more of your little subs."

His head turned toward her, but she didn't look his way. "Or it'll go worse for me later tonight?" he asked.

"Yes. Because there won't be a session at all."

It was a new feeling for her. The session was the session; everything outside of it wasn't her concern. It was why Sy could watch her do this with no issues. But it had bothered Mick, seeing him there. Something similar drove her now, thinking of how Mick had touched Jillie. How easily he touched and stroked the submissives, protected them. He didn't want to top them, but they fulfilled a need. Tonight she'd deny him anything he needed that wasn't her.

She didn't normally care when she was being a selfish bitch, but she was irritated with herself. As she began to stride away, Mick grasped her arm. She turned on him, but before she could snarl, he touched her face, met her eyes. "Understood, Mistress."

Deeper things in his gaze made her demand okay, though she had the uneasy feeling she'd stepped hip deep into a trap she'd set for herself.

As she moved away, his grip slipped free, but with enough lingering pressure to tell her he'd been tempted to hold onto her.

She didn't rejoin the others. Instead she visited the stations, where the first scheduled sessions were in progress. Skye and Tiger were at the rope one, Skye watching a Domme suspend a male submissive roughly Tiger's size. Skye's loft apartment had steel ceiling beams.

There were plenty of things Cyn intended to see, absorb and experience, to put her in the right state of mind by ten o'clock. But first she needed time to herself.

When she stepped onto one of the smaller back patios, she was alone. The bigger patios in front were more popular. She heard the faint sounds of the city, as well as a boat horn going off, nighttime traffic on the nearby river.

She wasn't afraid of change, of facing challenges. But those challenges had never penetrated the areas inside her she protected and kept locked down.

You left one vital organ out…

Babysitting…

Doing a CNC event could take her down roads she no longer traveled. She'd known that. But she'd told herself it would be fine.

It *would* be fine. Because not only was she a different person than she'd been when she'd been on those roads, Mick was an experienced player who knew this world, the boundaries and rules.

"Okay, I'm where I can talk. What the fuck were you thinking?"

She turned at the sound of Mick's voice. He'd stepped out of another patio access and had his phone to his ear. He moved to the railing, facing the groomed vegetation as he listened. He was turned away from her, muffling parts of his responses, but she assumed he was handling a logistical issue elsewhere in the club. Until his reaction changed.

"When?" His shoulders tightened, then slumped, before they became rigid again. He dropped his hand to the rail, his grip a white-knuckle clamp. She drew closer. Not to invade his privacy or eavesdrop, but to be there.

"Yeah. I'm thinking. Shut the hell up."

When someone screwed up at TRA badly enough they were fired by day's end, Ros's voice held that tone. Well, an echo of it. The cold threat in Mick's voice implied a different form of termination. One that didn't involve an HR exit interview with Vera or signing a final paycheck.

Abruptly, he put the phone to his chest, his chin down, head tilted to his right shoulder. A hard quiver ran through him. Even without knowing the cause, she recognized the emotions vibrating from him. The silent scream version, the kind of pain you couldn't give a voice, because once you started, you wouldn't stop.

Time ticked, the bushes rustling from a zephyr's touch. His fingers tightened impossibly more. If the railing hadn't been painted iron, it would have shown the impression of his grip.

She'd moved forward two more silent steps when he let out a long, shuddering breath. She stopped as he drew in a new one. It reinflated his posture, straightening his back, his shoulders, his head. One muscle at a time, like a meditative exercise where he was ticking off sections of a body he was repossessing, pulling everything back under his control.

"Okay," he said into the phone, his voice flat. "I'll deal with it. Don't do a fucking thing until you hear from me. I'll figure it out the way I usually do."

The response pulled a harsh chuckle from him. "Yeah, you sure as hell will owe me. Put a tighter leash on those morons so they don't do something that stupid again. Set them up with a game station or something."

He clicked off and pocketed the phone. As he braced his hands on the rail and tipped his head back to the sky, the door opened, letting a trio of subs, two male, one female, onto the patio. They were enthusiastically discussing a fireplay scene they'd watched.

"Girlfriend, I want to do it, but I'm so scared of fire."

"That's why you should do it. So you can see it's nothing to be afraid of. It's like being licked with a really hot tongue."

Giggles greeted this insight. Mick stayed in place, his back to them. The draped branches of several small trees in the landscaping on the other side of the rail shadowed him, but it was only a matter of minutes before he'd be recognized.

He would rise to the occasion, she knew, but those kinds of wells could go bone dry if pulled on too often, and emotional dehydration resulted in crazy behavior. Like getting beat up before dinner. Or challenging a friend and client to a no-holds-barred fight.

Cyn moved to stand beside him, her advance drawing the threesome's attention. They followed her track to Mick's side, but the glance she shot them quelled any thoughts of approaching the event planner. After a pause, they returned to their conversation.

There were perks to being scary.

Mick had stiffened at her appearance, but when she didn't say anything, merely standing and gazing at the sky with him, he returned to doing the same. The weight of his thoughts was palpable as he tried to work through them, so she gave him the room to do it.

The three subs headed back inside. There was a ten-minute break between station change outs, and that break was close to ending.

"You know, some people think a sexual sadist at my level has no finesse, not like other Masters and Mistresses." Cyn leaned her elbows on the rail. Her hip bumped his thigh as she bent forward. "That I'm all about dishing out pain and I don't watch the nuances, my sub's emotional state."

"That's bullshit." Mick grunted, still staring at the sky. "You have to pay closer attention. With your reputation, subs want to bottom with you because they're fucked up. They don't want you to stop."

He spoke neutrally, no judgment. But the edge behind the observation was a blade, ready to cut any flesh that got close enough.

"But they do stop," she said mildly. "Because they know their limits. It isn't about their threshold for physical pain. It's about their respect for me. And for themselves. Plus what experiencing the pain, the release from it, brings to their lives outside those sessions."

"What is that?" He pushed back from the rail, his gaze dark ice. "Forgiveness, absolution? Catharsis from whatever fuck-up they've committed? Or is it as simple as that's what makes you wet and gets their rocks off?"

Excessive self-analysis was the most toxic and destructive form of sadomasochism. She didn't have to understand why she liked to inflict pain, or got more sexually aroused by it than any other type of sex play. She also didn't have to analyze her past. She just had to do her job for TRA well, stay within the lines at the club, and not agonize over the things she was or wasn't.

"We're not doing this tonight," she said.

When she straightened and turned to leave, Mick grabbed her wrist. His half turn from the rail put him at a balance disadvantage. She shoved him, and his weight worked against him. Before he could recover, she'd reversed the grip on his wrist, twisting his hand inward and back, a painful pressure point that made the recipient aware of how easy it would be for her to break bone.

He bent into it, body against the railing, but his attention didn't get corralled by the pain or derailed by the potential

225

for damage. His other hand shot out, and he gripped her throat. Just like he had at the warehouse.

She could break his wrist. He could choke her into a faint. They went still, two gunslingers with their weapons held at ready, waiting to see who would blink first.

She sneered and put more pressure on the wrist. The pain had to be rocketing through his arm and shoulder, but he responded like a masochist. He absorbed it, used it to fuel his own violent reaction. His grip constricted. She went for a different tactic, even though her voice was a little strained.

"When did you become a monster, Mick? Did you really just stop being a cop, or did they kick your fucked-up ass out?"

She knew how deeply the whip would cut before she threw it. His fingers trembled and fell away from her throat. She released him as he stepped back, bumping into the rail as if he'd forgotten it was even there.

Her brow creased as he turned away. She watched the flex of his shoulders, the loosening. He was pulling it back together again, just like he had on the phone.

How many times did a person get knocked down and get up? It wasn't a clever riddle. The answer was as many times as was needed, or until they couldn't do it anymore. Some people were smarter about that limit than others. Others would keep trying, even if their legs were cut off.

Whatever this was, she knew her decision was the right one. She started to move away from him again. She'd let Jillie know the agenda had changed.

"Don't. Don't cancel it." Mick lifted his head, stared at her. "Give me a fight I can win."

"You won't win a fight with me."

"I will if it gives you something that works for you. Something that gives you pleasure."

She moved back to him and touched his face. "No. It feels wrong, Mick."

"Then let's figure out how to make it feel right again. Because up until a few moments ago, it did." He pressed his face into her palm, as if drawing steadiness from her touch. Aligning pulse rates. Heartbeats.

She studied him. "You won't tell me what that call was about."

"No. But I'm all right. Just got some unexpected news. Which I'm used to, so I don't know why I call it unexpected. Unpredictability is how I live my life." His smile was ghastly. "Though sometimes it's a good thing. It's what brought me here, to you."

"You're too messed up tonight, Mick."

"No. I'm no more messed up than usual. You can depend on me. Let me give you this, follow through on it."

The desire to have him bound, waiting on her will and pleasures, was a strong tide that had been rising ever since she'd agreed to do it. But she wasn't the girl she'd been. She didn't give in to her impulses as readily.

Mick lifted his hand and closed it over her wrist. Firm but not painful. She wasn't fooled now. It could all be an act. It *was* an act.

"No," she said.

His mouth tightened, but his phone buzzed with a text. When he glanced at it, the curtain came down, all those emotions vanishing. She was looking at his impassive, hard-to-read expression, coated by genial professionalism. "The screens in the front area are grayed out."

Her gaze stayed fixed upon him. "Find Skye if the tech person can't troubleshoot it. There's nothing computer-related she can't fix."

"Thanks. I will." His frustration was still there, but it was tempered by a rueful smile. "A functioning alcoholic operates better with some alcohol in his system, Cyn. I'm always fucked up, and that's how I operate best. Don't let it disqualify me from doing this with you. I'll be at the station at ten. I hope you will be, but I respect your decision on it."

He strode away, moving back into the club with his usual assurance, projecting laid-back, easy authority.

Fuck.

Cyn rubbed the top of her nose, a habit when she was mulling an irritating problem. The minor explosion of pain reminded her why she couldn't do that right now. She bit back another curse.

What she'd done with Matt had been fucked up. But sometimes those kinds of steps had to happen for shit to resolve itself. However, Matt wasn't a sub dependent on her control and judgment.

On the flip side, she'd had ten years to know who she was, what she wanted, and how to get it. She demanded more from a sub than he thought he had to give. She introduced him to that undiscovered country, while leaving him wanting more. She stayed in control.

For many of them, it was a way to deal with stresses in their own lives. It wasn't the first time she'd peeled away all defenses during a session. Maybe when Mick found how deep she could go, and how much he could trust her with what she found there, he'd trust her with more of it. Doing a session tonight could help him feel better.

Or fuck him up worse.

She'd told Matt she wasn't known for thinking things through. If her gut said *let's do this*, she'd fling herself into that abyss.

She was standing on the edge of Mick's darkness, and her heart—that neglected vital organ—was telling her to make the leap. Because there were times BDSM play wasn't about play at all, but what was needed to save a soul. Save a life.

Overly dramatic? No doubt.

Screw it. She was going to do this.

CHAPTER THIRTEEN

Cyn wasn't into excessive navel gazing, but as the clock ticked toward ten o'clock, her thoughts took her deep into her identity as a Domme. She thought about the things she'd found in that role, things she knew how to control.

What she could ask of herself was limitless. If she pushed herself until she broke, that was her choice, no guilt about it. Even after she broke, she could keep asking, telling herself to get up, refusing to shatter. If she ever couldn't be put back together, it was because she was dead.

Mick had a lot of that to him as well. But something about it wasn't working. And he wouldn't share enough with her for her to know how to fix it.

Not that he'd asked her for that, goddamn it.

Mick tempted her to be kind. Softness could expand like a giant marshmallow and smother you. She'd stick with pain. Mick needed that.

Give me a fight I can win.

He liked the fight. He needed the pain. She needed to inflict it. Leave it there.

There was a reason the offerings tonight were being called public sessions, not demos. They were intended to allow the Domme and sub to focus fully on one another, their audience merely fortunate voyeurs.

Cyn had taken it a step further. Since she didn't believe in time limits, she'd chosen a location that no one else had. If she went over fifty-five minutes, she wouldn't be fucking with anyone else's schedule.

The Pit was twenty feet in diameter, with a two-foot-tall black wall around it, like a circus ring. A silver chain border was painted on it. Inside the ring, the floor was a sleek epoxy in swirled gray, white and black, sloping toward a center drain.

As she stood outside the Pit, watching the staff anchor the metal cross, her body was tight as a drum. She'd already set out her tools on a table they'd provided and covered them. The act, the drama, mystery and anticipation of it, was for an audience of one. Her sub.

Someone entered her personal space, standing at her elbow. Vera. Her friend didn't say anything. She just stood with her, watching.

Cyn put in her earbuds and switched her phone to the album she wanted.

The first track was "Where the Devil Don't Go," by Elle King. Closing her eyes, she let her body ease into the rhythm. It would be followed by "Exs and Ohs." The roughness of Elle's voice, the assertiveness, the raspy edge, took Cyn's head where it needed to be.

She let the anticipation of having him under her control build. Along her skin, in her mind, against the inside of her eyelids, she absorbed his imagined reaction to what she would do to him. On her tongue, it was a taste she would savor, with every bite she took out of him. Literally and figuratively.

As the music filled her head, she banished the audience from her awareness. It was better that way.

Watching a hardcore sadist and a hardcore masochist go at it was unsettling. Potential triggers for viewers could cloud their recognition of the usual power exchange dynamics. Those dynamics *were* there, if a person set aside their personal shit to see them. Progeny had members who couldn't do that, but they also couldn't seem to make themselves not watch when it was going on.

She didn't apologize for her preferences or justify them. She didn't do cuddly aftercare for her subs *or* her audience.

The staff member in charge of setup looked her way quizzically. Everything was in place, so Cyn nodded. He was done.

She didn't speak to Vera when she left her to step inside the circle, but she didn't need to. Vera retreated to the seat Ros had saved her.

Once Cyn occupied the space, no one else would come into it without her permission. The only exception would be Olivia, the DM assigned to the station.

She'd requested Olivia, because Cyn respected her. With her experience level, and because of the type of Domme she was, Olivia could stay detached and critically evaluate what was happening in an edge scene. Cyn had used her as a spotter for her private sessions when she'd been trying more extreme things, where having a second set of eyes made practical sense.

Ros and the others respected Cyn's needs and desires as a Domme, but they weren't sadists. Watching her more experimental or extreme sessions was tough for them. They didn't have to witness it.

Olivia was tall, a big-boned woman with bisque-colored skin, a shaved head and light brown eyes. She was seventy-one, but bore few lines on her don't-fuck-with-me face. Her club clan included seven submissives under her protection and several Masters and Mistresses she'd mentored in her forty-two years as a Mistress herself.

Some members had club "families" or "clans," in their account profile. Dominants, submissives or switches they deferred to, who knew their preferences and triggers. Who they played with, or to whom they could go for help and mentorship. Cyn didn't put that info in her profile, but no one doubted who hers were. They were in the audience now.

Ros and Vera were at one of the rear tables, pushed back against the mezzanine railing. Lawrence stood to Ros's right. Most subs would find a similar spot or sit on the floor in front, leaving the assembled rows of chairs for the Mistresses. As fast as they were filling up, Cyn knew there wouldn't be any left.

Skye had chosen to stay on the mezzanine, above and to the right of Lawrence. She sat on a two-seat table, one foot braced on the railing, the other propped between Tiger's spread knees as he sat in the chair next to her, his arm loosely around her hips.

Her friends enjoyed a high intensity scene as much as anyone, but that wasn't why they were here. When she met Ros's gaze, she knew they were a reminder of who Cyn was to them. Who they were to her. Who she was to herself.

They had her back. They knew her. And they'd known she'd needed that reminder for this scene, before she realized it herself.

Moving to the table, Cyn picked up a bottle of water, cracking it open and taking a drink. When she lowered the bottle, Mick stood outside the Pit, watching her.

Magnetism was the only way to describe how drawn she was to him, and him to her. It had been there from the first, and it was even stronger now. Call that whatever anyone wanted to; she couldn't explain it, but she sure as hell wasn't going to deny it. Or deny herself.

Sexual tension had taken a hit on the patio, but the chance she could have called this off and hadn't, had twisted itself into the mix, bringing it back up again. She wanted him at her mercy, but had no intention of giving him any.

Give me a fight I can win.

You won't win this fight.

In this mode, her instincts were heightened. He wanted to be here, wanted to give her more, but he was going to try and hold part of himself back.

Too late, motherfucker. When you get into the ring with me, nothing's off limits.

"It'll be fine," she murmured, to no one in particular. "I've got you."

Anticipation overflowed. While yes, she mostly shut out awareness of her audience, the energy of their expectations enhanced her own. They weren't sure what they were going to see, but knew it was going to be intense.

She gestured to him to come over the wall and join her.

He was evaluating her body language, same as she was doing to him. They circled one another, two cats prowling. It reminded her of the straw maze primal play. A faint smile touched his face, as if he was remembering it, too.

No wrestling tonight. She came to a stop. So did he. She crooked a finger at him to bring him closer as she stopped her music player.

"What scares you, Mick? Tell me."

The scene wouldn't officially begin until she gave Olivia that cue. Regardless, the seating area outside the Pit quieted down, people straining to hear the exchange.

His blue eyes held hers. "You don't give a shit what scares me, Mistress. You want to know what hurts. What will hurt me the most."

The jagged edge was there, like the glass she'd cut him with. Yeah, he was ready for a fight. Some of the most volatile ones happened with only words, a look. A touch.

"Pain can be enhanced by fear," she noted. "Salt and pepper to my food, adding to its flavor."

"You don't need my help to do your job."

She tilted her head toward the cross. Not a St. Andrew's X. This was like the kind they wore. Bolts welded to the arms were attachment points for restraints.

He'd picked up on the symbolism, his gaze moving to the only jewelry she wore tonight, her skeleton necklace. "Going to keep me on it until I'm nothing but bones?"

"If that was a concern, you shouldn't have entered the circle. Stand before the cross, facing it. Put your hands on the horizontal piece, arms out."

A tip of his head and he headed that way. His insolent swagger had the crowd murmuring, exchanging amused or perplexed looks, eagerness building.

The challenge was intended to goad her. It did. He was saying he could stay ahead of her.

Keep telling yourself that.

She affected disinterest in the attitude as she moved to the table and removed the covering over her tools. Several knives were there, plus some of the items she'd had at the warehouse and other options she hadn't.

Her hand moved over her favorite strap-on. The front panel was studded with quarter-inch spikes. As she shoved the phallus into a man's ass, they would puncture his buttocks, forming a grid of small wounds.

She likely wouldn't fuck him in front of an audience, but the table was within his view to drive his reaction. She let the creative process kick in, considering each item's impact upon Mick, how his body, mind and deeper levels would respond to them.

Seeing a man waiting for her, fully dressed, ready to be bound, raised the heat. It was almost time to ring the bell and let the fight begin.

He was humming. "Gone, Gone, Gone" again. His hands rested along the cross's horizontal piece as she'd ordered, arms stretched out straight, fingers gripping the top edge. He had his feet aligned on either side of the anchored bottom post, about a foot between them.

With a half smile, she fished out her ear buds and put them in his ears, tucking her phone in the top of the corset, against his flat pectoral, caressing him there. She backed it up to "Where the Devil Won't Go" and adjusted the volume down. He could hear the song, but he could also hear Cyn.

His blue eyes met hers. Elle would be telling him about drowning in fire, and how Lucifer was going to be the path to freedom.

He didn't smile. She leaned in, mouthing, "Don't move," and bit his bottom lip, teasing it with her tongue before letting go.

Moving to her table, she picked up a knife. The blade was so sharp it could go into human skin like room temperature butter. As she came back, she issued her second command.

"Don't move," she repeated.

She put the blade against his nape, her hand on the back of the corset, a steadying safeguard. When his rib cage lifted with his breath, it created a red line that swelled with tiny drops of blood.

"Man's got to breathe, Mistress," he murmured. Causing another small scratch, forming two parts of a triangle.

"You said you didn't breathe around me. And you breathe if I tell you to breathe, Mick."

His constrained chuckle created a star, lopsided as if it had been scribbled by a child. More tiny drops of blood.

She took the knife away and leaned in to lick and nip. She held off on the pleasure of a deeper bite. She'd wait until he had more exposed skin.

Moving closer, she put the heel of her free hand against the front of his slacks, rubbing his cock. The playlist was on "Ex's and Oh's." Perfect. He thought he could taunt her, but she could kick sand right back at him.

"I like having a stress toy. Maybe I'll have you come to my office and stand with your dick on my desk all day. I'll squeeze and play, trace those pulsing veins with my letter opener. When someone comes to the door, I'll have you tuck that big cock in the top drawer of my desk. I'll push it closed a millimeter at a time, until you tell me you need me to stop."

Her eyes half closed. "Look at you, getting even bigger against my hand. You like pain and threats, Mick."

"I like your hand, Mistress. Your cunt. Your mouth."

"I like yours. Open up."

In the time it took to issue the order, she'd moved to stand in front of him and had the tip of the knife there. As he complied, she slid the blade in, holding the flat of it on his tongue. "Did you just imply my mouth was made to serve your dick?" she asked pleasantly.

His flashing eyes held hers, and he sealed his lips over the blade. If she twisted it a fraction when she pulled it free, she would slice into his tongue or lips.

The steadiness and swiftness of the hand holding the weapon would determine how severe the cut would be. She enjoyed her knife play, how sensitive the skin was to a sharpened blade.

Holding his gaze, she pulled it out, smooth and easy, but a deliberate minor degree away from level. He didn't flinch, but the knife was so sharp he wouldn't feel the cut during execution. Blood welled, two drops, one on the bottom left, one on the top right.

She rose on her toes and tasted that, too. Then she took the earbuds and her phone from him to walk them back to the table.

When she returned, she put the knife to the first X of the lacing. The ties separated. She followed the track down. "Take off the corset, then put your hands back up on the cross."

When he did, he twisted enough to hand it to her, rather than letting the garment drop to the ground. Their fingers brushed. His mouth was a straight line, his eyes focused on her in that "you're the only thing I see" way. Not artifice. She was literally the only thing in his world right now.

She took the corset back to the table. "Put your arms back up, Mick," she reminded him.

His shirt creased over his shoulders as he complied. She gestured toward two staff members, waiting for her cue outside the circle. "I was going to bind you myself, but you haven't proven yourself worth that attention."

He hadn't been expecting that. He'd assumed she'd do it herself, indulge that intimacy.

"I've been soft enough with you today," she told him, coming back to flick his nape with her nails. His shoulders tightened, his jaw flexing. When she stepped away, he stared forward at the cross's vertical beam.

The staff members, Greenman and Janus, were strong and tall, on par with him physically. She handed Greenman a set of manacles for Mick's ankles and Janus two pairs of handcuffs. Fast to put on and uncomfortable. Metal cuffs dug into wrist bones when a sub pulled against them.

Janus clicked one bracelet of the first set of handcuffs on Mick's right wrist, looped the chain over the cross's horizontal bar, and clicked the empty cuff through the bolt. The arrangement held his wrist securely against the cross. He did the same to his left wrist.

Greenman fastened one of the ankle manacles to Mick's leg, threaded the short connecting chain behind the anchored bottom of the cross and attached the other. Mick could keep his feet braced a few inches on either side of it, but no further than that. The more stress she put on him, the more he'd have to rely on the cross and the pull against his bindings to maintain his balance. When she removed his socks and shoes, the manacles would put the same uncomfortable pressure against his ankle bones as the cuffs would against his wrists.

Mick held still, but her man didn't like being touched by men. At all. When they were done and exited the ring, she moved in again and put a hand on his shoulder. It was just them again.

"You won't turn your head to look at me anymore, not unless I say I want you to do that. You don't deserve to look at your Mistress until you've served her pleasure. Do you?"

Her touch had brought a slight easing to his shoulders, but the attitude was still there, evidenced by his next words.

"Whatever you say, Mistress."

She didn't mind being challenged when it was real, not theater. She was pushing him with a lot of subtle messages, drawing the dark side to the top.

"Answer me like that again, and you'll be gagged with a nice big butt plug that tastes like motor oil and makes your jaw ache. Then I'll stick it in your ass."

Before she could take the idea further, a loud question from the audience reminded her of what she'd forgotten.

She hadn't officially started the session.

"What do you do if she goes too far?"

Cyn pivoted toward the Mistress who'd posed that question to Olivia. She was clad in Valentine heart red latex and black thigh high boots, a good look for her, though her fashion sense didn't improve Cyn's reaction toward her.

She reminded herself she'd agreed to do this publicly. So her response, spoken before Olivia could answer, was mild. For her.

"Olivia is one of the most experienced DMs at Progeny," Cyn said. "She also knows my play style. If she has a concern, she'll step in and pause the session to evaluate the situation. However, if you're already uncomfortable, I suggest you go find the puppy play area so you can hug one of those subs. Find your safe space."

You fucking pussy.

She didn't say that, but it was as clear as if she had. Though Vera gave her a warning shake of her head, Ros was biting back a rueful half smile.

The Mistress subsided sullenly. Olivia sent Cyn a patient but firm, "you know you were supposed to let me answer the question" look. Cyn responded with a *my bad* shrug.

"This is a public session, not a demo," Olivia followed up with the Mistress and the rest of the audience. "If you have a mild or moderate concern or question, it should wait for the end. If you feel it can't wait, signal my assistant."

She pointed to one of her subs, a tall, slim black girl several feet away, wearing denim short shorts, black tights and a white tank top, nothing under it. "Rae will meet you at the bar to hear your question. If she can't answer it, she'll bring it back to me. However, keep in mind my first priority is focusing on the scene and helping Mistress Cyn keep her sub safe."

Olivia paused, scanning the audience and gauging response, including the red latex Mistress. "A consensual non-consent scene is difficult for some people to watch," she continued. "If you are one of those people, I recommend you quietly exit and go to one of the other stations."

Olivia sent Cyn a pointed look, a reminder of the other step needed before the official start. Cyn shifted to Mick's profile, drawing his attention. She affected a formal tone, causing his lips to twitch. He obviously knew this wasn't her jam.

"You understand this is a consensual non-consent session. You've agreed to it, and acknowledge if you use your safeword, it's only for a medical emergency. You further understand it will be up to me to determine if it is a true medical emergency, corroborated by the DM. If it's not, the session will continue. Do you understand?"

"I do."

"What is that safeword?"

Mick pressed his forehead against the metal. His shoulder muscles tightened, as if he were struggling with his response. "Cissy."

Outwardly, she didn't react. Inside, she froze. Was he serious? She expected him to try to throw her off her game. She didn't expect him to be cruel.

His flat tone gave her no clue to his intent, so she pushed her reaction aside and treated it the way the audience would. "Sissy. A good choice if you pussy out before a true medical emergency."

"Cissy," he said. "C-I-S-S-Y."

He didn't lift his head to look at her. She pursed her lips and stood there several long seconds, until Olivia prompted her.

"Cyn?"

Cyn nodded, a short jerk of movement.

"The session is beginning," the DM announced. "While the request for quiet applies to many scenes, it's particularly important for CNC. No distractions for Domme or sub from here forward."

239

Cyn moved to the table and regrouped. It was just her and a sub wanting to be subjected to whatever she demanded of him. She could let everything else go. This was the one place where everything made sense. In giving him pain, she channeled her own.

Yes, there was a danger in that, because that abyss had no bottom. But that was why she made sure her subs could use their safeword.

He might be fucking with her, but Mick knew this world. He was a goddamn kink event planner. He was also a strong-willed, complicated man.

Let me be your demon.

Demons were called while inside a circle, and if nothing was allowed to break through the boundary, they stayed locked in it. Everything outside of it blurred.

Picking up a box cutter, she approached Mick from behind. "Hope this was expensive," she commented. "And your favorite."

She'd slept in his black shirt the other night. She wasn't giving it back.

Grasping the collar of the blue shirt, she shredded it with several slices. When she pushed the fabric away, scraps draped over his raised arms, club air movement making them flutter. While she'd mostly avoided skin contact, she'd sliced a thin trail between two bullet scars.

She was more precise with his slacks, a straight cut from the waist to the ankle of each leg. As she pulled the garment from his body, she revealed dark red jersey boxers. As she cut those off, she let the razor tip punch through and dig into the meat of his buttock. He tensed, hands clenching above the cuffs, but otherwise he didn't move.

As she kicked the ruined clothes aside, he stood before her naked, except for the fluttering shirt and his footwear. "Get rid of the shoes and socks."

It was awkward, since he couldn't move his feet more than a few inches from the post. The concentrated twitches of

240

buttock and torso muscles were absorbing to watch. Though she'd mentally noise-cancelled the audience, Cyn expected they would appreciate that, too.

When he finished, she used her boot to shove those into the pile of ruined clothes, getting all of it out of her way. She put her hand on the back of his neck. "Turn your cheek toward the cross."

When he did, she cupped his skull and leaned into the contact. "Keep your head turned like this. Nowhere to hide."

His eyes sparked, his mouth tight. "Good."

"I suggest you not push me, Mick."

"You don't suggest anything, Mistress. You fucking tell me."

He'd had an issue earlier in the night. It would be part of this, no way to get around it, but it wasn't the first session she'd done with a sub in a pissy mood. Usually she enjoyed getting what she wanted out of him and, as a side benefit for him, it dealt with the mood.

She found herself wanting to give Mick that solace, but it would only happen if she focused on what she wanted. The worst thing she could do to him was make him feel she'd put his needs before her own.

He wanted the selfish bitch. Needed her, to cut him open and drain the poison. It was an impossible-to-explain give and take, a dotted line between narcissism and generosity. Impenetrable indifference and heartfelt care.

Cyn donned black latex gloves and chose an ointment. When she returned to him, she paused.

She wasn't an elaborate scene planner. She followed her inclinations, her compulsions, feeding off his reactions and her own desires. Even so, what she did now was something she rarely did. She asked for additional confirmation. "Tell me you're okay, Mick. You want to stop this, we do it now. I'm not your mommy. I'm not going to ask again."

With his cheek to the cross, she saw the faint, derisive smile. She couldn't see his eyes because he'd closed them.

"I'm fine, Mistress. You're so sweet to ask."

She didn't move. As the moments ticked, his eyes finally opened. Message received. Nothing was happening until he stopped fucking with her.

His expression was unreadable, but his voice held genuine regret, painful courtesy. The energy coming off of him had the pressure of a brick wall. "I apologize, Mistress. Yes, I'm okay. I'm ready for whatever you want."

Don't cancel it. On the patio, he'd forgotten himself—or who she was—enough to ask her for what he wanted. Or maybe not. What was between them lived outside her normal session play dynamics. He'd spoken to Cyn as much as her Mistress self, and revealed his needs.

Yes, something was off, but her knowledge of him gave her confidence to see where this would go. If he was starting in a bad place, she could take him to a better one.

After dropping generous dollops of the ointment on his shoulders, she began to rub it into his flesh. Back, upper thighs, then his ass. She pushed her fingers into the crevice, working it into his rectum.

When she finished, she stripped off the gloves, tossing them into a trash can beneath the table. She fitted two claw rings onto her forefingers. Words were etched on the decorative bases over her knuckles. *Blood* on the right. *Pain* on the left.

Positioning herself behind him, Cyn ran them down the inside of his spread legs. While she used all her nails, those two led the way, biting into skin. Not enough to break it yet, but they left a red mark.

"Sometimes I do a session with nothing but these," she told him. Moving past the thighs, drawing circles. "They can drag. Puncture or slice. On a man's back, front, his balls or cock. The palms of his hands, or the backs of his knees." She moved over that area and he twitched. It was ticklish as well as uncomfortable. "The soles of his feet."

She'd reached his ankle and raked the claw over his right arch. Another red line. "Men expect a woman's touch to be soft. Even when it's rough, they don't expect it to be as painful as what a man could do to them. Though men like you know better."

So did she. A woman could shred the soul inside the body, leave it standing like a hollowed-out tree.

She was used to ghosts haunting her when she did sessions. She let them stay and watch, proving they couldn't touch her.

She retrieved her dragon tail, threading the triangle of fabric through her knuckles as she paced around him. She took her time, letting the ointment's effect kick in. He twitched as the places where she'd raked the claw began to tingle, like a foot waking from sleep. Which anyone knew was uncomfortable, especially if movement was restricted.

He still bore marks from their warehouse session. Those weren't a problem. Though he was moving well enough tonight—the man could take a beating—his abdomen and ribs would still be tender. She'd keep her focus on his ass, back and thighs.

She snapped the dragon tail between his shoulder blades and the air whistled through his clenched teeth. The dragon tail hurt on a normal day. The flesh-sensitizing ointment made it hurt even more.

During the pause to ensure subsequent strikes would have more impact, she gave him another order. "Turn your head back toward the cross now. Put your forehead on it."

It removed concerns about hitting him in the face with the whip. Her next blow struck high on his shoulder. Then the middle of his back. Lower, across the buttocks. To the shoulder again, followed by the thigh. Back to the shoulders. No pattern, no way to anticipate. Increasing helplessness. Mindfuckery was also important to the escalation. Pain and suffering flooded in, breaking down his mind, taking him over completely. Making it all hers.

He jerked with the strikes. His ointment-stimulated skin had to be screaming. He ground his forehead against the cross.

She changed out the dragon tail for the cane and went back to work on his upper thighs and ass, his back. She used wrapping and tipping among the concentrated blows. Caning was an art where the smaller the target area, the more sting it had. Occasionally she brought it up between his legs, batting it against his testicles.

He was sweating, skin shuddering. She lashed the rod through the air before several of her strikes, the whipping sound making his muscles tense involuntarily before the actual blow landed.

He was grunting and yanking against his bonds, pushing himself into each blow. She paused. She usually took a break around this point, though she didn't broadcast it that way. She'd get a drink of water and survey her handiwork. She'd maybe give her sub some water, and stroke his throat with her claws. Command him to hold still as she drew one slowly down his chest toward his nipple, watch the blood well forth and put her mouth to it. Let him see the crimson smear on her lips.

That pause, a breather, often allowed a sub to endure even more when she renewed her attack. A glance toward Olivia confirmed all was good with her, but before Cyn could move toward her water bottle, Mick spoke.

"You're being soft on me, Mistress."

He was staring at the cross. Having the syllables bounce off the metal made them hollow. Cyn put her hand on one of the hashmarks she'd created. The tipping she'd done should bring up some nice welts. Her right claw pressed into the hashmark. "Pardon me?"

He gritted his teeth, but he wasn't done digging his own grave. "Maybe it doesn't hurt you as much anymore. So you don't have to make it hurt as bad. Maybe you don't know what darkness is, what it takes from you."

He turned his head and locked gazes with her. That thing that made people uneasy around him when he didn't wear the event planner façade was there. Naked, unmasked.

"You're just like the rest, pretending something wounded you when it was never more than a superficial scratch. You got in the car and drove away, after all. Didn't you?"

She'd wanted to crack him open, and here he was. The savage animal. The coldness in his eyes made his mild tone all the more eerie. She didn't scare, but it raised the hair on the back of her neck.

"Are you a bitch or not?" he asked, emotionless. "Can you *really* make me suffer?"

He was bleeding, sweating, shaking. She knew the signs. His pain level was easily at an eight or nine. Yet he didn't want a break. He wanted more.

That night in the cemetery, he'd yielded to her rage. If he'd become aggressive, kicked her ass, cuffed her and put her in the car, she'd be dead or in prison now.

Faith in that memory, the one moment when someone had been fully in her corner, had driven her forward. When he reappeared in her life, the strength of that bond, the way it felt, had confirmed it hadn't been an ephemeral thing, belonging to only that moment.

He was shitting on that sacred memory, doing his best to make her doubt it. She didn't, but even if he hadn't understood the depths of her darkness then, he did now. Sometime during the past ten years it had found and taken him. And now he'd opened that yawning abyss wide, a darkness far too tempting to them both. Everything they needed was there, a complete immersion in pain. Whether giving or receiving, they'd bathe in blood that was their own.

She took two steps back. He tilted his head, tracking the movement like a predator. The challenge was all over him, as evident as a shouted taunt across a battlefield.

245

Take us there, goddamn you. I should have let that happen that night, let it end there, for both of us, because we were better off. We were better fucking off...

The earlier thought had been a fleeting thing. Now the truth was before her. If he'd displayed this behavior in another venue, he would have been blacklisted. It was her. The walls that contained what he carried had crumbled. The tortured soul mocking her wanted the punishments of hell on this side of the ground. He could find that with her, because he knew a lot of her truths. She'd opened that door to him the night she'd cut him, and it had never closed.

Her nature, if fully unleashed, was more than willing to accommodate a self-annihilating masochist. She didn't dream of heaven after death. She dreamed of Hell, where she could inflict punishment on every unredeemed soul through eternity.

She'd been blindsided, and it felt like a betrayal. She was suddenly very alone in this circle, and it hadn't started that way. She shared the space with someone who understood. Well enough he shouldn't have done this.

But just because it seemed like someone knew your soul, who you were, didn't mean they did. It only meant they knew their own soul and it had aligned with yours for a little while, so you both mistook it for a bond. A connection. Until the paths diverged, and you realized you'd never known one another at all.

She'd accepted that truth a long time ago. She just hadn't wanted to believe it about him, because what she felt for him was stronger than anything she'd ever felt toward a man.

Yes. No. Stop. Think. He's not in control. You are.

She stared at him, but she was remembering his metamorphosis on the patio. When he'd looked hit by a truck, then, like a freaking cyborg, he'd reset all the broken parts, restored the pleasant party planner façade.

But that look in his eyes…he couldn't fully banish it. Just dress it up with smiles, charm, sexual charisma.

246

She'd wanted to tear him down and open him up tonight, and she had. It was her particular skill. Usually when she found the most vulnerable corner of a sub's soul, she quietly closed the door and moved away. She wanted him to *offer* it to her, but she didn't take it once he did. She'd never wanted to establish a trust that deep, and accept everything that went with it.

Could she close that door after he'd made it so personal? Her mind turned it over. She breathed. She thought. She considered.

Then she picked up the knife she'd used to cut the corset.

No one moment solved everything, but the sparring with Matt had reminded her of something vital. As did the presence of Ros and the others in the distant audience.

She knew who she was. She knew who she'd been. And she knew who Mick was. Even if he had lost himself.

She knew what he was really seeking. And needing.

Back in Jersey, he'd germinated the seeds of her present self. She'd found a place to plant and nourish the traits she valued. She'd pruned back the ones that wouldn't serve her, even as they'd always be part of her.

So here she was. Mature and grown up. At last.

She advanced on the cross. Considered her actions as she looked at the canvas of his back. Among the scars already there and the newer marks she'd put upon him, it was time to add to the picture.

Wherever they went from here, he would remember it as belonging to this pivotal moment, another significant fork in the road they traveled.

"You never should have done this," she said quietly. "You can't make me doubt you. Or myself. How dare you even fucking try."

She was faintly aware of the gasps as her arm came up, the blade sweeping in front of her.

She cut him from shoulder blade to hip, then went the other way, creating an X where the two lines crossed dead center between shoulder blades and the small of his back.

The blood spilled out, like from a brush loaded up with too much red paint and slapped against a wall. As before, the sharpness of the blade, the swiftness of her strike, meant pain came in the aftermath. His spine went concave, head snapping back, his breath a harsh gasp. When he looked her way, his gaze was drowning in fire, like Elle said in the song.

Yet aching for more. Demanding it. Screaming for it.

"No," she said softly. "No, Mick."

He'd made her care. He'd used her for this, to take her to this place. She wasn't sure she could forgive him for that.

She stepped back.

The Mistress with her too-loud question was at the bar with Rae. No surprise there. The audience probably wondered if she was out of control, but just the opposite was true. She'd never felt so calm.

Cyn moved to the edge of the Pit, knowing a touch-base with Olivia was warranted. She could tell nothing from the DM's flat expression, but before either woman could speak, Mick did. "Leave her alone."

Mick leaned heavily against the cross, and his voice was hoarse, but those dangerous eyes were flashing at Olivia as if he thought she was ready to go after Cyn. "I didn't safeword. Don't. I wanted this. Leave her the fuck alone. It's not that deep."

He was shuddering. The ointment's effect would last for some time, in his rectum, in the abraded skin, everywhere she'd marked, but especially in those two cuts.

Cyn turned back to Olivia. "He's correct. I didn't cut past the skin layers, so he won't require stitches, and he has no problem with scars. But I can stitch them up if that's what he wants."

Though the idea of doing it, like she had that night in the cemetery, didn't appeal to her. Intimate déjà vu wasn't something she wanted to experience right now.

"Would you like me to address the Mistress's concerns?" Cyn asked. Even to her own ears, her tone was eerily polite.

"No." Olivia's eyes flickered with mild alarm. "I'll handle that. Is the scene over?"

Mick hadn't used a safeword, but that was a sub's safety net. If a Mistress knew it needed to be called before then, because the sub needed it, she needed it, or she just wanted to call it done, that was what happened.

"It's done. You can talk to Mick, make sure he's okay. That'll probably make the audience feel better."

Olivia agreed. She entered the circle. As she did, Cyn's attention moved to Ros. Her boss's blue eyes were troubled, but she gave Cyn a slight nod. Vera had already reached the spot Olivia had vacated. "What do you need?"

Cyn couldn't tell how Vera felt about what she'd seen, but if she had enough faith in Cyn's judgment to ask her that, rather than anything else, Cyn knew they were good.

"I need one or two of the club's volunteer med techs to help dress his back. Preferably female subs."

Vera disappeared on that errand. Mick's face was turned away from Olivia. The DM offered Cyn a negative gesture. He wasn't willing to be verbal with her. "Do you want the cuffs off?" the older Mistress asked.

Cyn nodded and put the key in her palm. The audience was rising, spreading out, talking among themselves. While there were some uncomfortable looks, most were used to stretching their minds to accommodate things that weren't their kink, as long as the boundaries were observed.

The utter containment Cyn exercised now, Olivia's discussion with her, the quiet talk she'd attempted to have with Mick, seemed to satisfy almost everyone. Even the tight-lipped Mistress.

249

"Cyn." Ros's sharp word snapped Cyn's attention back to the cross. Janus had stepped back into the Pit, probably to offer Olivia his help to remove the cuffs.

There was a reason Cyn had requested female sub techs.

Mick snarled like a wolf and lunged against the chains. Though he couldn't get anywhere, the force made the cross creak alarmingly. That, and the violence of the act, was enough to have the man wisely stepping way the hell back.

"Piss off," Mick spat. "She hasn't told me it's done. *No.*"

Cyn retrieved the key from Olivia. "I've got this," she told her, low.

Olivia nodded and had Janus join her outside the Pit's perimeter. Mick watched him retreat. Rabid animals looked calmer. His lip had broken open again, the cut from her knife earlier. All he needed was foaming saliva.

Cyn moved into his field of vision, blocking out the others, and met eyes that held the flatness of death in the wildness of the storm.

"It's over." Cyn put her hand on his face and gave him a no-nonsense, behave and settle down look. "I should have followed my instincts. That call fucked you up."

She couldn't deal with how she was feeling right now as a woman. But she could be a Mistress. He was a sub whose care was her responsibility.

He's mine to care for.

His ass is mine to kick.

"Her," Mick said, turning his head toward Olivia. "Just her. I'm sorry. Sorry."

Olivia's brow creased. "It's all right. You don't need to☐—"

"The apology is for me, Olivia."

Mick's limbs were locked, holding him up. Otherwise Cyn was certain he'd be hanging from his bonds like a tortured prisoner in a dark cell, all his strength taken from him, mentally and physically. Knowing he'd fucked up would be a far greater agony than anything she'd done.

She thought they might be sharing the same body. It was the only explanation for why everything hurt at the moment. Especially in places hardest to heal.

Olivia spoke to Janus and sent him away, though Cyn expected the DM would remain until aftercare reached the point she could confirm her presence wasn't needed. Which wasn't yet, because Cyn hadn't taken off his cuffs. Or the manacles.

"Want my help to get him down?" Vera was back. Cyn saw the requested two female sub med techs on the opposite side of the Pit, on the wall. Vera had likely put them there until things calmed down.

"Thanks." Cyn drew her over to the table and lowered her voice. "You don't have to stay. You and the others should go to the VIP lounge. Show's over."

"I'm going to pretend you didn't say that. I'm staying. At least until I stop feeling like I witnessed a crime and did nothing."

That stung. But Vera's next words told Cyn she'd misunderstood. "I'm sorry he hurt you like that."

Now she understood the look in Ros's eyes, in Vera and Skye's tight-lipped expressions. It wasn't about her; it was for her. They were experienced Mistresses, enough to recognize what had happened, even if they didn't get the full scope.

"He knows me, Vera. He knows me, down to my soul. So he pushed me, thinking he could get me to really hurt him."

Vera's hand gripped hers, a brief squeeze. "Then he doesn't know you as well as he thought. Because you didn't, and you wouldn't. We all know it. He knew who you were. He doesn't necessarily know what you've become. And the same goes for him. Would the man you knew have pushed you like this?"

"No. But he does know me, Vera. He still knows me."

"Then he needs you now. He needs his Mistress. He's cut wide open," Vera added, low. "And I'm not talking about what you did with your knife."

Cyn didn't disagree. Somewhere below her anger at him was anger at herself. Even subs who knew how to protect themselves could slip or stumble. Especially if she was pushing hard on their boundaries, the door to those dark places.

She'd considered that could happen to him, but she hadn't anticipated the full effect. She'd mired herself in assumptions about their past and ignored the impact of the things she didn't know about his life.

She should have anticipated, should have watched out for him. At any level, a power exchange could morph, evolve. Disintegrate a person's walls until they stood, raw and vulnerable, even more than the day they were born. Leaving them shivering, no protection.

Fuck that. He had protection.

"Enough." Abruptly, she advanced on the handful of watchers lingering outside the Pit. "Move along. This scene is no longer public. Take your asses elsewhere."

Most scattered, understanding. The loud-mouthed Mistress was still there, looking like she was taking it in her head to be offended, insist that since it was on the public floor, Cyn didn't have the right to insist on privacy.

"I can introduce your teeth to my boot if you need clarification."

"Are you threatening me?" Her eyes, enhanced with contacts in the same Valentine red, narrowed, her matching long nails curving.

I don't do girl fights, sweetie. I'll break off those nails and feed them to you.

"Go run to management. But leave this fucking area."

She tried to stare Cyn down, but Cyn knew the signs of someone who'd never been in a fight that actually turned physical. Whereas Cyn's first gang fight had been when she was twelve. She'd used a brick to smash the knife-wielding hand of a girl about to stab a fellow member.

The Mistress stomped away on her high-heeled boots while muttering. Softly.

Cyn turned at a scraping noise. Olivia had apparently dispatched Janus on an errand. He and Greenman were returning with freestanding panels. They were setting them up along the outside of the Pit to shield the area from passing eyes.

Ros had risen from her seat. Tiger had come down from the mezzanine. When he reached the railing on the other side, Skye put her hands on his shoulders, his at her waist as he lifted her to the floor. Lawrence was beside Ros.

Cyn moved outside the panels, where she could still see Mick but speak to her friends. The key pressed into her clutched palm.

"Thanks for being here."

Ros nodded. "If you need me, I'll be in the lounge. Unless there's something you need now."

"No, Vera is enough. Thanks. Just…thanks."

Abruptly Cyn pivoted, disappearing behind the panels.

Vera and Ros exchanged a significant look with Skye. Then Vera told them what Cyn had said, about Mick knowing her soul.

"She's not usually the romantic of the group," Lawrence commented.

"She's not. Cyn's soul is not a pretty place." Vera's expression was troubled. "If he sees it without flinching, accepts it, my guess is his own is a mirror. What we saw tonight confirms it."

Ros met Vera's gaze, more than one significant thing in the silent communication. Skye nodded at their look, on the same page. But for right now, only one thing mattered. "Stay with her," Ros said to Vera.

"Count on it."

"Tiger and I will hang here," Skye signed. "She might need help with him."

Vera noted the two med-tech subs had moved back as the panels were set up. Before they'd been set in place, though, their concerned eyes had been fixed upon Mick. Their eagerness to help was obvious, but so were other things.

His bound position, even in his current shape, gave admiring eyes time to study his naked form. Vera thought it might be wise for them to keep both their emotions and ogling toned down. Cyn's mood seemed exceptionally... territorial.

She caught their attention with a "wait here one more minute" gesture, before she stepped inside the space with Cyn.

When Cyn noted Vera's reappearance, she was at the table, wetting a clean cloth with a jug of distilled water. As Vera approached, Cyn cast a critical look at Mick, slumped against the cross.

"If Tiger's still here, bring him in. Mick is solid muscle, and he's going to drop when those cuffs are taken off, no matter what he thinks."

Vera headed back out while Cyn approached the subject of their discussion. When she touched the damp cloth to the edge of one of the cuts, the blood leached into it like red dye. Mick stiffened, but she put her other hand on his shoulder.

"I'm here," she said.

The tension eased. A lot of things were happening here, but they'd deal with it later. Right now, she'd do what she rarely did. Aftercare. Because no matter how much she wanted to kick his ass, she refused to let anyone else do it.

Olivia had brought a chair inside the panels and sat unobtrusively a few feet away. Though it indicated she thought her oversight was still needed, that was fine with Cyn, as long as she didn't interrupt.

Vera returned with Tiger. Skye was with him, but moved to stand with Olivia. Tiger took in the close-up of Mick's back, but his expression remained neutral. "When you take off the cuffs, I assume you want him on that mat you've rolled out over there. Face down, or are we still going for maximum pain?"

Tiger knew his Mistresses. Though she couldn't feel any amusement herself, she appreciated the dry male humor.

"Session's over," she repeated. "Just be ready to take him to the ground. His knees aren't going to hold him." She bent to remove the ankle manacles.

"Fuck they will," Mick muttered. Even phasing in and out, he had picked up on the exchange.

She unlocked the cuff on Mick's right wrist, and was in enough of a mood to drag her arm against his sensitive back as she reached across it to unlock the other. After she pulled the other cuff free with a rough yank, she rammed her knee into the back of his. He folded like a house of cards, into Tiger's ready grip.

She'd barely pushed, knowing it wouldn't take much. The way Tiger's biceps bunched told her how much of his weight he was holding, despite Mick's belligerent, "I can walk."

When Tiger turned him onto his stomach on the mat, he made a quelling noise to Mick, equal parts reassurance and warning. "Easy. Don't get crazy on me, man."

Mick blinked. Something clicked, drawing him out of his head. "Just don't grab my ass," he said distinctly.

Another smile crossed Tiger's face. The relief that came with it was mirrored on Vera's. Cyn didn't know what her own face showed. Mick's voice was tired, but the edginess was draining away fast. Perhaps it was the removal of the bonds, a physical reinforcement that the scene was over. Telling him it was time to pull his shit back together.

"It's a nice ass, but it's the wrong gender," Tiger said. "So it's safe from me."

As he'd been lowered to the mat, Mick winced at the effect on his battered body, but made no protest. Tiger put a brief hand on his shoulder, then straightened.

Cyn's attention moved to the base of the cross, where dripped blood had created what looked like a smeared dance pattern. She turned to Skye and communicated by sign, not wanting Mick to be privy to the conversation.

"He'll need help getting to his vehicle when I'm done. I'm going home after I take care of him. I don't want to talk about this tonight."

"Understood," Skye responded. "We'll wait outside the screens. Let us know when you're ready."

Translating the exchange and anticipating her next move, Vera had called in the two subs. Cyn passed them her first aid kit, though she saw one of the girls had the club's kit as well. "Cleaning and dressing with pressure bandages," she told them. "Last chance, Mick. Do you want stitches?"

She didn't have to draw his attention. His gaze had remained on her ever since he'd hit the floor.

He shook his head.

"Then close your eyes," she said. "I'm not dealing with your shit right now."

He looked ready to argue, but let out a sigh and closed his eyes. As the women followed her direction, she noted his fists were still clenched, and it wasn't because it hurt, though she knew it did. She squatted at his side and straightened the fingers there, tapping them.

"You fucked up. It's not the end of the world."

His fingers twitched in response, but remained pressed to the epoxy floor.

Her world would go back to what it was in a couple days. She'd eventually remember what had been good about this session, until it wasn't.

His world would go back to what it was, too.

Pushing her feelings about that away, she glanced at Vera, who was kneeling next to the sub on his other side.

256

"Don't you say a word to him," Cyn said. "A kind word from a Mistress right now will break him."

Vera pressed her lips together, but stayed silent.

Cyn moved away. Deliberately, she picked up her phone, put the earbuds back in and leaned her hips against the table as she watched over him.

"America's Sweetheart" started up. Elle sang about a woman who was the exact opposite of the title. Cold-hearted, foul-mouthed. Fuck anyone who thought she should be anything but what she was. That cap-it-all line "you love me anyway" was the heart twister. Cyn ignored what it made her feel.

Under her eagle eye, she noted the women didn't linger over their care, but they were thorough. The cuts would break open and bleed again if he insisted on doing anything more than getting prone, but the antibiotic ointment they applied, the bandages they taped in overlapping layers over the two long cuts, would keep it clean and healing. The wound depth was far less than what she'd inflicted on him years ago, the cuts much neater. The thin scars they formed would fade in time, only noticeable to the one who bore them, or the one who'd inflicted them.

Mick's eyes had opened again, but he stared into space. It wasn't subspace or subdrop. He was in a world both far distant from this, and totally encapsulated in the here and now, but only with her. She didn't think he'd remember anyone else's presence. Which meant he needed more supervision to ensure he was all right.

She shouldn't care, but she did. When the women rose and nodded to her, she pulled off the ear buds and took a knee beside him. Vera had brought Tiger and Skye back in.

Cyn put her hand on Mick's head, stroked his hair.

"I'm gone in a couple days," he mumbled, eyes still focused somewhere else.

"Good." She slid a finger over a strip of medical tape. It covered a bullet scar. "This will hurt when it comes off."

His lip curled. At last, his eyes lifted to hers. "I wouldn't expect anything else."

She took her hand away. "You should have told me."

"What?"

"That you were fucked up like this."

A weird smile tilted his mouth, a glimmer of his usual self. "I   was   pretty   sure   you   always   knew."

CHAPTER FOURTEEN

She rose and moved away from him. Mick watched her pack up her stuff. He was hurting in a lot of ways, the least of which were physical. He could tell she knew it. That made him feel worse.

"Vera'll make sure you're steady and all there."

Mick had heard his Mistress admonish her friend not to cosset or cuddle, an obvious effort for Vera. But Mistresses like Vera did aftercare. A sadist did injury treatment. Though the knife cut might have been enthusiastic, he'd deserved it. Everything Cyn had done to his body would heal. What he'd done to her, to both of them? That was a different matter.

She came back, planting her booted feet by his head. He had the urge to pillow his head on one of them, put his mouth against her ankle. He might get his teeth kicked in for his trouble, so he let it be a drifting, fond fantasy, an attempt to counter the sick feeling in him that shouldn't have been part of this.

A lot of things shouldn't have been part of this.

"Jillie says they have the event covered," Vera said. "Tiger and Skye can get him to his vehicle."

"Good. Thanks." Cyn had fished in his ruined slacks for his keys, and tossed them now to Tiger. "He keeps shirts in the closet, jeans and other stuff under the bed."

"Cyn." He started to struggle up, but the world flipped off its axis and rolled away like a marble, him hanging onto it. Vera's hand was on his shoulder, Tiger's on the other side, holding him. "Goddamn it…"

Cyn was gone, striding through the opening between the panels. Her shoulders didn't even twitch.

As he continued to try to get up, Tiger gave him a less gentle shove to keep him on his ass and draw his attention. "She's not in the mood, man."

"I fucked up. I need□—"

259

"Obviously." Skye used Alan Rickman's precise, sardonic tone. "If you know anything about Cyn, you'll give her some space right now."

"But who does…" He paused, fighting to find the right words in a brain turned to soup. "Sometimes Mistresses need aftercare, too."

A smile touched Vera's expression, balancing the troubled look. "Yes, sometimes they do. Ros is meeting her in the parking lot. She'll make sure she's okay."

That was good. But once his head was on straight, he was going after her as well. It was his job to make sure she was okay. Especially when he was the only one who could fix what he'd done.

He'd felt like shit plenty of times. This went beyond that. If he couldn't make amends, he wasn't sure if he could face tomorrow. Was this part of the problem of not being a defined sub or Dom? If he'd thought of himself as a submissive, he'd have bowed to her wisdom on abandoning the session, rather than steamrolling her with the need for the fight.

Whether Dom, sub or switch, a person had the power to hurt and destroy someone else. God, he was a fucking asshole. He'd totally lost sight of what he should have done. What he should be. Maybe what he was, with her.

He had to fix it.

Skye went to the motorhome to retrieve clothes for him while Tiger stayed at his side. When she returned, she had one of his T-shirts and sweatpants. Comfortable stuff.

Once he could get to his feet and seemed reasonably in his right mind, Skye and Tiger accompanied him to the parking lot, ignoring his insistence that he was fine. Vera followed behind, typing on her phone. Probably giving Ros an update, and checking on Cyn's status. Mick didn't see either woman in the parking lot, and Cyn's truck was gone.

Tiger stuck close, which Mick admitted was useful, since he was having trouble navigating a straight line. When he went up the steps of the motorhome, he felt the light pressure of a female hand on his back to head off the possibility of him toppling backward.

Face planting in his bed seemed almost as appealing as sex. Almost.

He sank down at the table instead, bracing an elbow on the surface. "I've got it from here. Thanks."

Skye and Vera looked dubious, but they were Mistresses. As his gaze moved to Tiger and held, Mick hoped he was telegraphing what he needed.

Tiger slid his hand along Skye's neck and shoulder, thumb caressing her collarbone. "If you want to go watch a couple more sessions, I'll hang with him a bit, keep him from doing anything stupid."

Her dark eyes came Mick's way. She used an appealing female voice with a Southern accent. "Take some aspirin and get some rest. You're going to feel like shit tomorrow."

He felt like shit right now.

"Those who administer and take pain the way Cyn and you do have an intimate relationship with it, at all levels."

That came from Vera. She was looking at him with that penetrating look all good Mistresses had. A lot of good subs, too. Like the biker who stood silently listening.

"She's never told any of us the full story of what brought her here, but we've never doubted it was a terrible one. If you're dragging her backwards on that road, you're not someone who needs to be in her life, no matter how much I feel for who you are and what kind of pain you're handling."

Mick blinked. Direct, and another punch in the face, but honest. "So you patched my hurt to expedite me getting my ass back on the road."

Her eyes, pale silver like water, didn't waver. "We handled aftercare, because Cyn asked us to do it. Take that as it's meant. Good night, Mick."

Tiger moved out of the way so the women could exit the vehicle. As Mick gazed moodily at the floor, he was aware of Skye signing something to Tiger before she rose on her toes. His arm went around her to give her the extra lift. The kiss was tinged with regret, probably because dealing with Mick was going to delay enjoyment of some Ladies-in-Charge inspired sex.

Great. Now he was a cockblocker, too.

Would Tiger feel any better knowing Mick was suffering some of the same frustration? His mind had no problem running the erotic stuff side by side with his emotional turmoil. Recalling every whistling sound of the cane before it struck, the prick of those claws, even the cut of the knife, sent electrical current straight to his cock. Mick wanted nothing more than to have Cyn straddle and ride him to climax as his body throbbed and bled for her.

She could wear those claws, reach back to rake them over his balls, or press the pointed end between them, that ultra-sensitive spot. She'd command him to hold still, absorb everything she wanted him to take, including the sweet clasp of her wet cunt, sliding along his length.

Tiger sat down on the couch across from him. His long legs reached across the aisle, his booted feet crossed at the ankles. Stretching an arm out along the couch, he surveyed his surroundings with interested eyes.

If he had to have company, Mick was good with a strong alpha who understood the craving to submit sexually to a woman. He liked that Tiger was quiet, too, not saying much until he gestured with his hands.

When Mick blinked, a half-smile crossed Tiger's face. "Sorry. Skye and I have been signing most of the night because of the club noise. I said this is a sweet setup. We do a good bit of camping and have been thinking about getting an RV. Nothing too big. I have too much capital sunk into my garage to take on a monthly payment for one this size, but a fifteen-footer might be nice."

262

"There's a good used market for them. Plenty in decent condition, and with your mechanic skills, you could keep it in running shape."

"Yeah." Tiger leaned forward, his forearms on his spread, denim clad legs, large hands clasped loosely between his knees. "You're into some bad shit, man. I know the stink of it. The club vetted you, but passing a background check is nothing more than the price of covering your tracks."

Mick gauged the man's intent. "Hope you saved up your energy tonight. It takes effort to beat a confession out of a pain junkie masochist."

Tiger didn't smile. "Not the best time to make a joke. If me, Lawrence and Neil believe you're a danger to Cyn, to any of our women, no one will find your body. And don't give me another round of the 'none of it will touch her' bullshit. Because I know how that goes."

Yeah. He did, too. Which was why he kept clinging so grimly to his resolve to leave New Orleans when he'd planned to. Not one moment later.

Or sooner, guilt whispered.

"If you feel that way, why did you invite me to stay on your property?"

Tiger grimaced. "Because of what doesn't fit with the stink. You're crazy in love with her, and it's killing you, because of what has hold of you. That conflict hit too close to home tonight, and turned that session into a shitshow."

He wasn't sure if hearing it out loud made him feel better or worse, so he stayed silent. Tiger sat back again. "So why did you really want me to stay behind with you?"

"I need a favor, though I know I've done nothing to deserve any. I need to borrow a vehicle. I'll bring it back to you before I wrestle this old girl to a campground."

"Don't like our place?"

Mick had enjoyed the tranquility of the spot. The idea of doing it again appealed, given how worked up he was inside.

But even so… "I'm usually good at picking up signals. I thought I was receiving a stay-the-fuck-away one from you."

"We'd rather have you where we can keep an eye on you until you leave town. Your head's screwed up on the signal issue." Tiger shot him a frank look. "Which is why you should stay away from Cyn right now."

"I need to see her, and it needs to be tonight," Mick said bluntly. "I could Uber it, but since she's likely to kick me out after I say what I need to say, I'd rather not wait on her curb for one to come back and get me."

"The vehicle I can handle, but I don't have her address. Skye's never been to her place. None of them have."

At Mick's disbelieving expression, Tiger lifted a shoulder. "They're Dommes. They understand why certain boundaries matter, and when to cross them. They've never needed to cross that one."

"Okay. Will you still loan me a vehicle?"

"Going to try to get her to tell you where she lives?" Tiger's expression said how likely that attempt was to succeed.

Mick made himself meet the other man's gaze. "I know where she lives."

He'd known within a few hours of running into her again. The same way he'd known about Lawrence's alcoholic ex, Tiger's criminal background, and a lot of other details about the TRA women and the men in their lives.

Yeah, certain boundaries mattered, but crossing this one was the least of his crimes. He hadn't gone to Cyn's home, but he'd memorized the address.

Showing he understood what the reveal meant, Tiger's gaze hardened, but Mick didn't let his falter. He knew he had to give the man more of himself on it, though.

He'd never allowed himself to entertain any thoughts of his and Cyn's reunion beyond this week, but he'd sure as hell spent time piecing together ways to keep her in his sights.

"Once I leave, I thought I could call up satellite captures of her place. Or if I came close to New Orleans again, I'd use my drone to catch her sitting on the balcony of what's probably a posh townhome, having her favorite drink."

He was betting Jack or Jim. Maybe he'd see her comings and goings, heading out to Progeny for a session with some lucky prick like Sy. Wearing those sleek outfits she looked so good in.

"I'd probably be pathetic enough to zoom in on her porch deliveries. Specialty foods, new clothes. Subscription boxes from Inquisition-Reenactors.com."

Tiger's lips twitched, but there was no humor in his eyes. Nor in Mick's.

"Vera's right," Mick said. "I know what she came from. Keeping her and the life she's built here safe means more to me than breathing. If I thought I was going to screw that up, I'd dig my own grave so you, Neil and Lawrence could put me in it."

Tiger's large, booted feet rocked back and forth. The fingers resting along the top of the couch twitched. Mick could well imagine that hand holding a gun. Or choking the life out of someone who threatened his beautiful Mistress or the people they called family. He could respect that.

"I have a truck you can borrow," the biker said at last.

☒

After Mick changed into a black button down and jeans, more appropriate wear to meet a Mistress, Tiger drove him and the motorhome to his business, Roseland Garage. He had a small Toyota pickup there, an old one but it ran well. He'd take Mick's motorhome back to his and Skye's place. Mick would bring the truck back there.

Skye followed them in her Mustang, telling Mick that Tiger had brought her in on the plan. Mick wasn't dumb enough to assume her assistance was an endorsement, but when they reached Tiger's garage and Tiger handed Mick the keys to the Toyota, her parting words weren't as discouraging as he'd feared. Hearing them in James Earl Jones's deep voice didn't hurt, either.

"Be truthful. More truthful than you've ever been in your life. And don't let her get hold of anything sharp."

"So expose my belly, but don't let her slice it open."

Tiger's lips tugged in a near smile. "Every sub's SOP with a pissed-off Mistress."

"Except Cyn won't waste time on a symbolic evisceration," Skye added helpfully.

Mick got into the truck—stiffly enough that Tiger felt a sympathetic wince. The guy might be messed up, but Tiger liked him, no reason to deny it. As Mick turned over the engine and moved to exit the parking lot, Tiger glanced at Skye, seeing the same struggle in her expression. He slid his arm around her waist and she leaned against him. "Should we follow him?" he asked.

She shook her head, signed, "They've known each other a long time. If this goes back to the beginning, that's where they have to resolve it. That's what Vera says. They can't do that with us there."

"I'm more concerned about what happens if they don't resolve it. Like if we're going to need Clorox, a lot of shop rags and an alibi for her."

His beautiful Mistress's lips curved, but then her gaze shadowed. "Ros said Cyn didn't want to talk, but she was all right when she left her.

"What do you think?"

Skye glanced up at him. Despite the serious turn the night had taken, anticipation gripped him at the shift in her eyes. All that sexual fuel intake tonight hadn't vanished—it had merely been held in the tank. Proving it, she hopped into his ready arms, clasping her legs around his hips. As he leaned back against her Mustang, her tempting breasts rested with heavy promise on his chest. Since she had one hand curled around the back of his neck, fingers stroking his hair, she propped her phone on his shoulder and typed with swift fingers. The voice was the Southern one, modulated to a sexy purr.

"I think we better make the most of the time we have. Before that Clorox and alibi is needed."

Mick hadn't yet done that satellite check. The townhome he'd suggested was merely a venue that fit Cyn. So would a trendy loft like Skye's. He figured she'd go with a rental, versus the permanence and upkeep of home ownership.

When it came to profiling people, anticipating who they were, what they wanted, what they would do according to the situation, his skills were exceptional. Well above average.

He'd been dead wrong on this.

Cynbad Marigold owned a twenty-two hundred square foot single family residence. One with three bedrooms and two full baths, according to the development sign at the landscaped entranceway, since the developer was still selling lots.

It was one of the post-Katrina suburban neighborhoods surrounding the city's core, like extra ruffles on New Orleans' skirt. The house had vinyl siding, architectural shingles, and a blue door with a silver knocker. Crepe myrtle trees were in front, along with pots of geraniums—fucking geraniums—on her brick stoop. He saw a glider rocker and side table on the porch, as if she liked to sit out at night and wave to her neighbors as they went by, walking dogs, jogging, or coming in from work.

He walked toward the front door, but as he did, he heard a rhythmic *clang* and *chunk*. It was coming from behind her six-foot-tall privacy fence, which screened the rear yard.

Few lights were on in the houses near her, and nobody was taking their dog out before bedtime. But suburbs always had eyes. If someone was suspicious enough to call the cops at this late hour, Cyn wouldn't let them haul him off. Maybe.

He went around the side and slid open the gate latch. Hopefully she didn't have a dog half as scary as she could be, though he was prepared to run.

No dog greeted him, but if the house had been a shock, the backyard put him on his ass.

Cynbad Morgan liked flowers. Lots and lots of flowers.

Not the kind symmetrically arranged by a well-paid landscaping company, either. These were planted by homeowner hands, creating spaces that reflected personal preference. A greenhouse attached to her garden shed provided a controlled environment for more exotic-looking things. Like orchids. Over a dozen of them, the blooms offering a range of delicate to bold colors.

The shed and greenhouse foundations were bordered by black-eyed Susans and pinkish-white guara. The lightest wind moved the tiny flowers of the latter, a heavy weight on long, slender stems. Along the vinyl fence were dense stretches of plump zinnias, in various colors.

She'd decided to start a new bed of something, because she was in the center of the yard, ferociously hoeing, chopping up grass like she was cutting up a body for compost. No need to guess who she was imagining.

As he stepped through the gate, he saw a crouching gargoyle to his right. It squatted on a concrete post, its wings spread. A morning glory vine with nighttime furled purple blooms climbed his wings and muscular shoulders. At the foot of the post, a trio of concrete bunnies, each small enough to sit in his palm, grouped around a solar light shaped like a frog.

She also liked lawn art.

He moved toward her. He wasn't trying to be quiet, but he couldn't think of what to say, and the lush grass muffled his footsteps. He stopped several feet from her, just as she straightened, pulling in a shuddering breath that yanked at his own heartstrings.

She'd changed clothes, and was wearing a faded pair of jeans with dirty sneakers. The shirt was a heavy cotton tank, bearing a logo from a garden shop, flowers spilling out of a wheelbarrow.

Her shoulders were so fine-boned. Nothing suggested her extraordinary ability to carry as much as she did on them. Then there was the heart shape of her ass. He wanted to rest his head on it. Sleep there. Kiss it, bite it, hold and squeeze it.

The ache the thoughts caused was just one more pain to bear. "Did Cissy like flowers?" he asked.

She spun, the hoe whipping around in a lethal swing. He ducked and back pedaled, barely escaping having his skull cleaved in two. She registered his identity, though her grip on the lawn tool remained as tenacious as a Scottish warrior's on his claymore.

"What the *fuck*, Mick?"

"Sorry, I didn't mean to startle you."

She recovered fast, though her brown eyes remained hot. She at least lowered the hoe, the business end on the turned earth. "Did Vera tell you how to find me?"

"No. Tiger said none of them knew where you lived."

"Vera knows. She just doesn't put it in the files." The eyes narrowed further. "So if she didn't…"

"That's not what's important. I□—"

She shook her head. "I didn't give you permission to be here. Leave."

"You're right." He held up his hands. "But I have to apologize."

"You already did that. I want you gone." She threw down the tool and advanced, her fists clenched. "I will put a bullet in your ass if you don't get off my property. This is my place. Mine."

If she'd gone to these lengths to keep the people closest to her from seeing where she lived, she had big reasons for that. He didn't want to disrespect her, but he'd be gone in less than two days. He had to fix this.

Tiger was right, that the stink could get on the people you cared about, but it wasn't merely the life-threatening stuff that could damage them. He planted his feet, met her stare for stare. She didn't respect weakness, and he'd handled more explosive situations than this.

"You can do that. But I'm going to say what I need to say. I owe you an explanation. I wasn't expecting...what happened tonight. I've never let that out, never thought anyone could open that door..."

"So it's my fault?"

"No, damn it. Will you... Can you listen? Then I'll go."

She stalked over to a patio chair. Chimes hung on shepherd's hooks nearby. More little solar lights, on sticks. After he'd pulled up, he'd thought maybe she was housesitting for someone on an extended world cruise, but he'd checked. The house was in her name. Cynbad JoEllen Marigold.

Yet as he looked around him, he realized it made sense. "Is this what you and Cissy talked about having one day?"

Her expression didn't alter. "You're on a clock, Mick. Get to it."

He took a seat in the other chair, even though she hadn't invited him to do so. He had to pretend this was civilized.

Maybe that was what their surroundings were about, too.

He knew how to be direct. His life had depended on that ability, plenty of times. Also on his ability to lie so no one would doubt him, which meant he had to believe what he was saying even more than they did. It was an important habit for his job, a destructive one for real life.

Fortunately, as difficult as honesty was, he'd never wanted to give someone the truth so much. So it might not be smooth or pretty, but he was going to do it.

"Three days before you and I met, I was part of a raid. A human trafficking ring. But they found out we were coming, and killed the twelve girls they had, ages eight to fifteen."

270

Her mouth tightened, but she said nothing. Life's horrors weren't a news bulletin for her. "While I was manning the barricade," he continued, "I heard a task force guy say if they'd had more accurate information, if the confidential informants didn't so often double cross them, get killed or too scared to help, or flat out disappear, they'd have better chances of getting in before things like that happened."

They'd had to help zip the corpses into bags, lift them onto the gurneys. He remembered how beautiful one girl's eyes had been, even glazed in death. They'd been the kind of eyes a boy would remember long after his first kiss with her.

"Before that night, I was already on a downward spiral," he admitted. "Drinking too much after work, feeling like we were pissing against the wind. Too much to fix, not helping enough, seen as the enemy most of the time. Hands tied because of politics and the wrong kinds of decision makers."

He drew a breath. "I was drawing away from the other cops, not able to hold onto that connection. That night, handling those bodies, I knew I wasn't where I should be."

She still didn't look pleased with him, her body rigid with the offense of him invading her space, but she was listening. She'd sat back and crossed her legs.

"How I went outside the boundaries that night we met was a decisive moment. I'm not saying that's the way it should always be done, everyone going rogue and doing their own thing. But I just knew…my head was built to help a different way."

He clasped his hands between his spread knees. The shirt she wore had holes and carried soil stains from past gardening work, as well as fresh earth she'd stirred up with her chopping. He wanted to pluck it off her gently, feel her warmth beneath the cotton. He curled his hands against his knees.

"I thought about it for a while. Made some contacts through people I knew. Finally sat down with a guy who had my kind of thinking. He was already involved in a loose network. They just lacked someone willing to do what it took."

He met her dark gaze. "Someone who craves pain that never ends is already wired to keep his head and operate under levels of mental duress most can't. Go figure, right? What they needed wasn't someone to save the ones already in it. They wanted to get at the information needed to nail the major players and dismantle networks. They needed someone to run the long game, get in deep, be part of the system, seem like the same soulless bastard as anyone else. Take what he learned and funnel it to the right agencies. Logistics, operations, resource caches. When the key important people who could be flipped would be most vulnerable to being taken down."

He took a breath. "If the current trafficked victims are freed or helped by that, good. But no matter what's happening to them, even if right in front of my face, that's not my job. I have to be a part of the machinery facilitating it, keeping it oiled and running, with money, with buyers, whatever's needed to maintain my cover."

He had to stop and stare at her feet for a minute. It had been a long time since he'd had to put it into words, a job description straight out of Hell's HR department. "My handler told me I was perfect for it. I don't have any family left. My parents died when I was young, and my grandmother raised me after that. She died a few years before this went down. No siblings, and I've had trouble keeping close friends."

He lifted his gaze. "My grandmother said I always had a reserve to me, a watchfulness that made people uncomfortable. She wasn't mean. She was worried about my isolation. I never felt much desire to fix it. Over time, I realized it connects to a dark place inside me. The other cops sensed it; they couldn't pin it down, but I don't think they were sorry to see me go, even though they had my back while I was one of them. Anyhow, that identity, everything about my background, was scrubbed and restructured."

The story had her full attention, though she still didn't look happy with him. "So what does someone find when they dig into your background?"

"If they go deep enough, they'll find what was created to give me entry into trafficking circles. I was suspected of being a dirty cop, and when I quit, it was just ahead of them looking for an official reason to fire me.

"I'd been drifting on the edges of the BDSM scene before you and I met. My handler suggested I use kink event planning as my job cover. Privacy is everything in that world. I had his help and contacts to keep anyone from going beyond a simple membership vetting to find that fake record. Being accepted by clubs and organizations that use my legitimate services is a cover that works on the illegal side. Right or wrong, plenty of people assume BDSM is a cover or bridge to criminal sexual behavior."

He grimaced. "Deep cover experience taught me how to become the friendly guy my grandmother encouraged me to be. The event coordinator. I already told you how I do what I do. I don't have to be the Martha Stewart of party planning to be good at it."

"You're very good at it." The implication in her tone was clear. *Even if you're shit at other things.*

He took that as his due, the kick he needed to get into the rougher stuff. Mick leaned forward again, laced his fingers, unlaced them. The skeleton pendant dangled in open air, the chain twitching against his neck.

"This next part, I'm just going to get it out. It's the only honest way to explain what happened tonight."

He kept his gaze on her hands, her thighs, the way she sat. He thought about her body, how it felt against him. How it felt, just to be in her presence. Close enough to touch, even if touch wasn't permitted. It helped, to hold onto that.

273

"Here's a typical night at my other job. I'm sitting with a group of guys, drinking an aged Scotch and comparing it to Kentucky bourbon. Twenty feet away, a teenager who's never had sex before is being raped by a billionaire who paid for the privilege. He wants to take the kid's virginity in front of an indifferent audience. Once that's over and the bill's paid, he'll take her home to be his live-in sex slave. I'll never see her again. Never know what happened to her, because my focus isn't on some end buyer piece of shit, but the men I'm drinking with. They supplied the kid, and connect to much bigger players who control the funnel of 'product.'"

He moved his attention to the ratty sneakers. They looked like something from a dollar store. She didn't wear any socks with them. She had dirt on her ankles. He thought about washing that off for her. Gentle hands, fragrant soap. Warm water.

"The fucking wasn't just about exhibitionism. It was also business. He didn't want to get home and find out she wasn't a virgin. Like checking everything's in the bag at McDonald's before you leave the drive thru."

He could feel the weight of her gaze increasing, evidence of an emotional reaction, but he still didn't look up.

"I've given advice on where to bury a tobacco farm worker so she wouldn't be found or connected to the people who disposed of her. A pregnant woman. She dropped in the field, probably from heat, malnutrition, dehydration. She was close enough to full term her fellow workers tried to get her baby out, but the cord wrapped around his neck, like a damn suicide in the womb.

"All forty-four of them—now forty-two—were kept in a barn when they weren't working. No air conditioning, with old soup pots for toilets. They won't run, because if they do, their family members back home will be killed in the most horrible ways possible. So they work until they drop."

"Mick." Her feet shifted. He shook his head, sitting back. Scraping his chair out of range. *Let me get it done.*

274

"If I was a cop, or officially associated with any agency, I couldn't stand by when I witness or learn about crimes of that magnitude. Outside any official capacity, sponsored by concerned citizens with endless pots of money, I'm like a CI. I'm deep in the system, a problem solver, with the connections and experience to make things happen. That cover comes from eight built-from-the-ground-up years of verifiable history and reputation among them. I'm considered the go-to in certain situations, a man who can put the right people together, get things done."

Mick rose and paced to the end of the patio, circled back, sat down again. "The call I took earlier tonight had to do with a crew that runs a small but way too damn busy distribution hub in Texas. I've been working a plan to get a higher up in their organization to meet a major buyer there. The information I can collect at that meeting might eventually shut down that artery, capture him and a shitload of the main players in their network."

Cyn's hands were laced in her lap. He wondered if she ever wore rings. "There are over sixty people at that location right now," he continued. "Various ages, some slotted for domestic or farm labor. But twenty-seven are girls, ages twelve to sixteen, premium age for the sex trade. Something happened while they were being 'seasoned' by the onsite handlers, and two of them died a few days ago. Local law enforcement stumbled on the bodies earlier tonight."

He remembered the fear in Salazar's voice. "The call was the onsite man in charge. He was afraid it was going to get back to the higher up, or the major buyer he's coming to meet. He wanted my help to make sure that didn't happen."

Which had meant placing the right calls to point local law enforcement toward another culprit, equally as guilty. Just not of that particular set of murders. Criminal activity at the border gave him a grab bag of options.

Mick took a slow, even breath. Let it out. "I had to tear him a new one for not telling me about the girls sooner. Not because it's a goddamn tragedy, but because his carelessness jeopardizes future business transactions. Letting his men get carried away with the girls wastes assets."

He rose again. This time he made a wider circle, stopping at the earth she'd turned. He nudged it with his toe, watching it crumble at the pressure. "If I get the intel I want, feed it to the right people and they do their job, it might severely damage or even destroy a pipeline that currently traffics hundreds of people. But those girls will still be dead. I won't know what happens to the others. The agencies might be able to track where they are and get them back to their families. They might help them stay here, if that's a better situation, but it gets more complicated for the ones who've been forced into doing criminal activity before they reach them."

He turned to look at her. "Hundreds against two. Sounds like a way to sleep at night, doesn't it?"

"No. It doesn't."

"No, it doesn't. Every one of them has eaten a part of my soul, Cyn. I'm pretty sure there's not much of it left."

Against the gravity of what he was telling her, what had happened earlier tonight shouldn't really matter. He'd fucked up, she'd handled it, two people fumbling their way around in a relationship. Life would go on, for both of them. Unlike those girls.

But somehow resolving it mattered just as much to him. To his sanity. Maybe because of how many things he couldn't fix.

"The smarter traffickers, they force you into a corner where you have to do something illegal, something a cop or agent isn't allowed to do, even undercover. After eight years, I've earned my place in their world, so these days I can usually refuse without casting suspicion on myself. 'I don't partake of the merchandise, mix business with pleasure.' That kind of thing."

"But you couldn't always do that," she said quietly.

"No. One of the most common ruses to get women here for the sex trade is they're promised a job in the States, or a modeling gig. Young girls are young girls."

Except not all of them were the same. He remembered how she'd been that long ago night. Already far too cynical to fall for such a trick. When had she lost that innocence?

"When they get here, they're taken prisoner. Some are broken in by having multiple handlers rape them. Or they're strung out on drugs, their minds fucked with in a bunch of ways, so they think they have no options. Early on, when I didn't have the bonafides I have now, I was put into the 'go ahead and test the merchandise' scenario. A friendly invite that was neither friendly nor an invitation."

He'd avoided her gaze earlier so he could get certain parts of the story out. Now he wouldn't allow himself to look away. He would face her judgment, see every emotion she revealed. Disgust, revulsion. Rejection.

She didn't show him anything. Just waited for him to say what he was sure she knew was coming.

"They had a view window to determine how the 'merchandise' was adapting, how ready the girl was to be put to work. It was also to make sure no one damaged her, impacting her value." A method he'd told Salazar to employ going forward, if he wanted to stay alive. "Prepping the girls sometimes involved deliberately hurting them, but you and I both know the difference between pain and damage."

When she blinked, he nodded. "Ironic, right? I know the body's capacity for pain. Withstanding it, surviving it."

He sat down in front of her again. He almost reached for the persona he used with traffickers, to speak more nonchalantly, businesslike, as if discussing the sale of hammers or fruit pies, but he wouldn't give himself that out. Not tonight and not with her.

"I was as gentle as I could be. Nothing about it consensual, but I made it clear I could make it not so awful. During that testing period, I had to do it three more times, different girls. One was nearly comatose from the drugs they'd given her, like I was fucking a corpse. The other two were so grateful for my 'kindness,' it told me exactly how infrequently they experienced that."

His tone became flatter. "I don't drink anymore, beyond a beer here or there to be social, or in situations where I'm playing the part. Never to excess. The only thing I steep myself in is dungeon play with Mistresses, and I never let that get out of hand. Just a quick fix to ease what's inside me. Until you and I crossed paths."

He'd come back to his point. Almost full circle. He tried to keep his voice even. "I should have walked away when I saw you. Left it at a polite hello. Or blown you off, been an asshole. I consider every variable like that, in every situation, how best to handle things. I stand outside of it like I'm fucking God, determining which button to press. But I met your eyes, and…fucking hell, none of that came into play."

She had a brittle look in her eyes, and it was becoming something else. He wasn't sure he could bear to see what that something was. So he'd finish it up and go.

"After all this time…you were someone who knew me before. Who could see me, who I am. I didn't know how much I'd missed that. And I didn't know, until you opened me up, how much I wanted a Mistress who could rip out my insides the way you do. I've been in control with Mistresses, always. I let myself not be in control with you…and as a result I hurt you."

He shook his head. "I've done a lot worse things deliberately than what I did to you inadvertently, but it was like the last part of me that *I* trusted vanished with *your* trust. I'm so sorry for that. All the things I wish I could have changed these past few years, obviously, that one can't top the list, but if I could only choose something about me, for me? That sure as hell would be number one."

He let himself reach out and brush his fingertips over her clasped hands. One final touch. "The last truly honest

278

moment I've spent happened when we first met. Until tonight, when I couldn't stop myself from unleashing it all on you. Call it bullshit if you want, but don't call it a lie. Because I sure as hell know the difference between that and the truth."

Cyn had kept her reactions locked down, but inside her mind was whirling. As he rose heavily, she was thinking about the math problem he'd presented. Nine hundred versus two.

Sacrifice the present for the hope of the future.

Mick glanced around the backyard. "Sure is pretty here. I'm really glad you got this for yourself. You deserved it."

All the various emotions she'd seen cross his countenance during his explanation disappeared, reabsorbed by his steady look, his firm tone. "It goes without saying, I've just put my life in your hands, and the lives of a lot of other people. But I trust you to keep that secret. I'll be leaving after I finish up some things at Progeny. If you hold off coming back until then, you won't see me again."

He took off the necklace and laid it on the table beside her. "You keep this. It belongs to the guy I once was. The one you could count on."

He crossed the yard, headed for the gate. He moved with wooden purpose, projecting an unmistakable message.

It's okay. I don't need or want anything from you.

What she felt from him was very different.

He'd travel on to another place, another event, while he kept working his real job. She couldn't say if it was right or wrong. Whether the ends justified the means was the moral dilemma for anyone doing what he was doing.

She'd had a session with an undercover cop. His need for pain had been astronomical, too, to let it all go. In the aftermath, what she'd pieced together about him was, no matter how fuzzy the lines were, because he was operating legally as an undercover cop, he had some boundaries to cling to, lines he didn't have to make the decision to cross.

"There are times we feel hampered by that," he'd told her. "But crossing the line, becoming the monster, means the bad guys win again. You have to keep telling yourself that and believing it, or you can't do it anymore. Even when you believe, it takes its toll. Undercover isn't a long-term career choice, and I'm about at the end of my stint. Either you get out, or get taken out."

She'd had a couple more sessions with him, and then he hadn't come again. About six months later, the club had circulated an obituary notice. John Compton, police officer, killed in the line of duty. Looking at his official picture, in his uniform, his steady eyes, strong jaw, she knew what had drawn her to him was her memory of another cop she couldn't forget.

Mick *had* chosen to cross that line, become the monster to stop the monsters. Yes, he'd said he had something in him that made him suited to the job, but she remembered that darkness from the cemetery. It had called to her own. It wasn't something awful or evil.

She'd lived in darkness, but had stopped short of becoming it. He'd linked his identity to it, woven the two together in an astonishing and unsettling way. She didn't know what that made him now, but she was sure of one thing. The monster lived in him because he'd invited it in, but he wasn't the monster.

"Stop."

It wasn't a request.

He had his hand on the latch, and she could see him fighting the desire to obey her, versus the compulsion to keep going, because the latter was best for her.

He didn't get to make that choice. She was the Dominant here.

She crossed the grass to him. When she reached him, she put her hand on his arm. It quivered hard under her hand.

What had he called her, a frayed wire? That's what he felt like.

She steadied herself against him as she removed her sneakers to bury her toes in the thick grass. This time of night, it was cool.

"You asked me if this is what Cissy and I imagined. It was a place as far away as the moon to us. So yes."

His blue eyes, clouded with side-by-side uncertainty and grim purpose, were what a ghost's would look like, a haunted spirit that would never find rest. He wasn't hiding behind the façade anymore. She preferred that, even as it made her want to give him things she shouldn't.

"Do you know how to weed a flower bed?"

A tired smile crossed his face. "I've never done it."

She pointed to the one closest to them. "Pull out what's not a flower. Pull gently so you don't disturb the roots of the flowers. Grab one of the buckets stacked up by the shed and put the weeds in it. Dump them in my compost container. Don't talk to me for a while. You don't have my permission to leave."

She had picked up the necklace from the table, and now she put it around his neck. She gazed into his troubled, strong face. "You also don't have my permission to give that back."

"Cyn."

"Shut up." She nodded toward the buckets. "Weed. No talking until I say you can."

He stared down at her. "I never told you I was a sub."

Her hands tightened upon him. "I know what you are with me."

281

CHAPTER FIFTEEN

As she pivoted like a soldier and marched toward her bed of turned earth, Mick thought about what he'd considered at the club. Dom, sub, switch, top, bottom. He'd had to put on a lot of hats, and refused to identify with any, make it personally his. Such temptations were the enemy, keeping him from doing his job the way it needed to be done, so he'd avoided them in his personal life to reinforce the message in his professional one.

But there were lines that represented pretty damn important things. Loyalty, commitment.

"Cyn… Mistress?"

She turned toward him. He did what he'd done only for her, at least in this way, with this significance. He dropped to one knee, and this time faced the reason he'd done it. The real reason.

"I'm a submissive."

"Is this like an AA meeting? Hello, my name is Mick and I'm a sub?"

He didn't crack a smile. "I need to belong to a Mistress. I need to feel like I'm hers, like…"

"Like you're seen." The barb dropped from her voice, leaving something more painful and necessary.

He cleared his throat. In for a penny, in for a pound. "Yeah. But I don't just want a Mistress. I want you."

She didn't pretend to mistake his meaning. She lost a full shade of color, which could have amused him if the moment hadn't held such gravity. "Mick, as of a few days ago, I've never even been in a formal relationship outside of Progeny. I'm not ready⬜—"

"Yeah, you are. Everything I've seen and felt the past few days says you are."

She narrowed her gaze. "A good submissive doesn't interrupt his Mistress."

"I didn't say I was a good submissive. Just that I am one."

She gave him an exasperated look. "What does that even mean, a relationship with you? You said you had to leave."

He saw the brief flare of hope in her eyes, that maybe his declaration had changed that. It was quickly replaced with self-directed horror that he'd made her consider the relationship question at all.

He loved that flare, even as it tore up what was left of his heart to douse its light.

"I do have to leave. Doesn't change what I'm saying."

He rose. He was in his own skin, being himself, riding a strength of purpose that for the first time in a long while felt clean. "It isn't about setting up house, or making you commit to me. It's me committing to you. The only place I've ever felt like was home. You think that sounds stupid as shit, creating a home out of the memories of a girl I spent an hour with a decade ago. But when you live the way I do, having the chance to spend a few more days with a woman who understands me…that's a lifetime, Cyn. I'll take that lifetime, if you'll give it to me."

She gazed at him a long moment. "I want you," she said slowly, "to shut up and weed. I mean it."

His lips curved. "Yes, ma'am."

Cyn watched him find a bucket, then move to the bed she'd indicated needed weeding. He knelt on the ground and started fishing among the flowers. The solar lights and night sky didn't offer much light for that kind of work, so she picked up a flashlight and brought it to him. She dropped it by his side, along with a foam garden mat, printed with cheerful daisies. "Use that for your knees."

She returned to the bed she'd been breaking up with the hoe. But by the time she arrived, he was at her side, picking up the hoe before she could. "Without seeming too sexist, seems this is a better job for a man with no gardening experience, while the weeding is for delicate, skilled hands. I know some Mistresses look for reasons to punish their subs, but you don't really want me to mangle your flowers, do you?"

Sensible. Cyn pointed to the ground. She'd marked the bed size she wanted with plastic stakes, a five by three rectangle. "Chop this area up, about six inches down. Go easy. Don't break open those cuts on your back. I'm not in the mood to dress them again."

He grunted assent and got to it. She moved to the flower bed, ostensibly to weed, but mostly she watched him. He moved carefully, respecting his body's need to recuperate, but his strength was evident in how easily he turned the earth. She'd have a new bed in no time. She'd have to think about what to do with him for the rest of the night.

Normally, that would be a no brainer, but a lot had happened. Plus, when he finished the task, she could tell he was flagging. Even though he was too good at covering it, it was difficult for a man to hide his physical or mental state from her. His body had had enough.

"What's next?" he asked.

She pointed to a hammock strung between two maple oaks. It was tied low on the trunks, far enough off the ground to clear it when weighed down by an occupant, but not much higher. She liked trailing her fingers over the grass, and having the cluster of zinnias behind it nodding over her with their bright colors.

"I'm okay," he said. "I can keep helping."

"Go lie down. Don't argue."

He made a face, but moved in that direction. Getting into a hammock that low to the ground took obvious effort, but once settled on his side, his arm tucked under his head, she could tell his body gave a sigh of relief, sinking deeper into the cradle of the ropes.

For a while, the quiet was broken only by night creatures and the thumps and rustles as she tossed weeds into the bucket. She assumed he'd drifted off to sleep, but when she sat back on her heels, he spoke through the gloom, his voice a calm stroke along tonight's overworked nerves.

"I get the house and yard, how they connect to Cissy. But what about the gardening? You really get into it."

She dumped the bucket in the compost, turning it several times with the crank so the contents would smother the weeds and break them down into nutrients. Then she turned the bucket over and sat on it facing him, bare feet braced, knees spread.

"I don't sleep much. When I first got the place, I'd stay up, paint walls, walk around the backyard. Then one day Vera brought me a flat of flowers at the office. There'd been a sale at the garden store. I brought them out here. Planted them with the help of a big spoon from my kitchen, using a tea pitcher as a watering can. That night I slept better than I had in a while. Don't know why. I just did."

She shrugged. "So I started doing more of it. Got some garden tools. Put up the hammock. Used that mosquito netting tied up over it to keep the bugs away when I slept out here. I'd fall asleep listening to crickets and looking at the flowers."

Watching them dance and whisper with the wind, like a bunch of giggling girls. Like sisters.

His fingers were curled in the rope above his head, his shirt open at his throat, revealing the gleam of the skeleton against curling dark hair and warm skin. One knee was up, rocking back and forth, denim stretching and creasing.

Though Mick wasn't unaware of his looks or magnetism, he wasn't consciously drawing attention to his long and powerful body, the potential of it. Though the jeans and black button-down he wore looked *very* good on him.

She'd had to cut the session short. No release for either of them. A CNC scene often wasn't about the climax, but right now was a different matter, in her garden, with his body within touching distance.

"How about the vegan thing?" he asked. "Why did you choose that?

"Because I prefer it." Her way of saying none of your damn business. There'd been enough painful revelations for one night.

"So you never eat meat."

"Only human. But my freezer is low on it right now."

He grunted. "Now I know why you want me to lie here. You want me to go to sleep so you can cut up my body and restock it."

"Why would I wait until you were asleep to kill you? It's far more satisfying to make you watch."

He chuckled. Cyn rose to take her weeding tools to another bed. While she was doing it, she was thinking. She glanced his way. His eyelids were half closed.

"Mick?"

They opened fully. "Yeah?"

"That darkness in you could have made you become just what the fake records say you are, but it didn't. Because there's something else in there, too."

His expression said he wasn't sure he agreed with that, but he responded a different way. "Same goes. That Mistress was out of line tonight. You knew what you were doing."

"It's not a bad thing for people to make sure everyone is okay. It was her approach that rubbed me the wrong way."

"Yeah. Management was leery about you doing the public CNC. They know some people can't handle extreme play, and you aren't the type to do audience handholding. But they think pretty highly of how you conduct your scenes and ensure your submissives are safe."

Hearing that surprised her. But sometimes she jumped to conclusions on what people thought about her. *They think I'm trash. They think I go too far. Fuck them.*

"It's a way of controlling the relationship," Vera had told her. Once or twice. "Reject them before they can do it to you." She'd rolled her eyes, both times, when Cyn told her to fuck off.

"I handled an event in San Francisco a couple years back," he mused. "During my off time, I did a scene with a sadist Domme who... She was creative. I had trouble walking for a couple days afterward. But at the end of her sessions, she cries. Cries over how she hurt me, cries over whatever makes her need and want that so much. It's part of her process.

"I held her, kind of a weird reverse aftercare, but it worked for both of us, not just because I like to care for a woman, but because I know that feeling. Wondering why you are what you are, why the pain not only turns me on but makes me want more and more and more."

His words floated across the lawn between them. Their meaning and her understanding of them made her feel quiet and restive at once.

"The crying is a catharsis, a reset," he continued. "She feels okay with all of it, okay with who she is. No regrets. Maybe for some of us, it needs to be painful and deep to find that. It just takes us a while to figure out how and what level."

"Without ending up on the wrong side of the prison bars."

"Yeah." His lips tugged. "Though since some subs like to sleep in a cage, that might not be the punishment society thinks it is."

"I think a cage under a Domme's bed is a far cry from supermax prison." Still, thinking of the scar he bore beneath the necklace, she grimaced. "You got lucky that night, in the cemetery. I could have killed you."

"Maybe. But it wouldn't have been your intent. And I'm betting you would have put your hands on my gushing neck, held pressure and figured out how to dial 911 with your toes to get me help."

When she sniffed and made an indifferent noise, his lips curved. "Do you have a cage under your bed?"

"Why would I give a sub something cushy like that when I have a perfectly good and very cold bathroom floor?"

Another chuckle. She liked the masculine sound of it, the way it vibrated in the night air. "Ever been camping?" he asked.

"In nature?" She didn't conceal the note of horror.

He laughed. "You like gardening."

"Yes. *Controlled* nature. Flower beds, individual plants who are blissfully not overly talkative. No woods, itchy plants or hidden things that slither or crawl."

He raised a brow. "You survived one of the scariest neighborhoods in Jersey."

"Dense nature is mysterious and weird. Violent people are easy to understand."

"How about staying at a nice campground in a motorhome, with brick-and-mortar bathrooms and showers?"

She gave him a suspicious look. "That's not a casual question."

"Nope. After I leave New Orleans, I have a couple days before the San Antonio thing. My other job...I have a few days on that as well. When that happens, I find a quiet campground and take the down time. You should come with me. You can catch a flight back to Louisiana."

"You just pointed out our reunion had a definite end point. Why are you trying to prolong it?"

Even though the night shadowed his features, she could feel the weight of his regard. "You're asking a question you know the answer to. Just like I know why you're putting me off. You want me to stay, but I can't. You're still pissed at me, because I fucked up and abused your trust. You don't want to risk your heart on more. All that's fair. But will you think about it anyway?"

288

She'd seen him raw and vulnerable tonight, but with the calm evaluation and that direct gaze, he was reminding her the capable, in charge, level-headed male wasn't an act.

He also knew her kinder moments weren't her preferred gear. Which she proved with an icy nod. "I'll think about it, before I say no and tell you to fuck off."

His mouth tightened. But his response was light. "Okay. But consider the benefits. You'd have a dedicated sex slave. I'd make all the food, handle all the travel details, and pay for your plane ticket home."

"I can pay for my own ticket. The rest doesn't sound unappealing. Except the whole camp thing."

"You've seen my motorhome. I'd let you have the big bed. I'll stay on the couch or the table bed. Unless you want company."

"I like having a lot of room. Is the couch bed cramped? Particularly for a big man?"

"Oh yeah. I'd be eating my knees."

She pursed her lips. "Well, there is that."

She knelt and began to weed again. He didn't say anything more. She was so attuned to him she knew when the eyes that rested upon her closed. She glanced over her shoulder to confirm he'd drifted into a doze. He'd turned further on his side, probably because the ropes were irritating his back, and had his arms crossed, elbow pushed into the hammock, hands hooked under his arm pits.

She was done for the night. After stacking her tools by the shed, she turned to study him and consider her options.

She could drape the netting around the hammock and leave him sleeping there. He'd understand. He had no invitation to come inside her house, and he'd leave when he woke. She'd glanced through the gate crack and seen the pickup truck. A Tiger loan, she was sure.

Instead, she drew close and dropped to her heels. She threaded her fingers through the hair over his brow.

She thought back to the warehouse, how he'd leaned forward, and put his forehead on her stomach. Sighed so deeply.

Now she understood. He'd waited so long to belong to someone who understood him, who had a chance of understanding him. He'd said that to her in a couple ways, but words didn't mean much to her. They became meaningful and made an impression when the actions fit.

Ten years ago, he'd given her something to have faith in. Since then, he'd possibly lost his own.

She understood how fucked up the human mind could be, especially when trying to survive the world. Add in the full-blown attempt to make it better, and he bore the curse of guilt and self-doubt, paired with balls-to-the-walls courage to forge forward.

She hadn't been the grown-up when they'd met. Now she was, and when their paths had crossed again, that deep sigh part of him had known she was who he needed.

The child part of her had felt hurt and betrayed by him tonight. The woman, the Mistress, had rallied and patched him up. Both parts of her had retreated here to think it over, and grieve the lost memory.

But she didn't have to grieve it. He was the man she thought he was. He'd just stumbled, been emotionally raw before the scene in a way he hadn't expected, and that had taken over in the way that anyone who did intense sessions knew was a danger. It was how vulnerable they were to each other that had made it go wrong, but that wasn't necessarily an end to things. It might be the gateway to the true beginning.

She could send him away, but she would be damning his soul. She knew it. When he said, "I want someone who knows me," he'd meant someone who could handle his darkness, accept it. Want it. Love it.

Love him.

He hadn't said those words to her, probably because he knew that might scare her off. She didn't know if she was capable of love. But he thought she was. He'd likely call it a fierce, battle goddess's love, but she didn't call that love. She called it loyalty. Trust. A willingness to be around another person without wanting to choke the shit out of them. Most of the time.

The night when he'd said he didn't classify himself as Dom, sub or switch, she'd known he was wrong. He'd acknowledged it himself tonight. But when he'd said he wanted her specifically, that wasn't about being Dom, sub, switch or vanilla.

It was not the first time in her life a man had claimed to love her. But it was the first time in her life she thought she might love *him*.

He wasn't sleeping heavily. His eyes lifted without any disorientation, any sense that he didn't know where he was or who he was with.

"I'm going inside," she said. "Come with me."

Mick noted she tracked how he was doing when he rose from the hammock. He was stiff, but moving okay. A masochist tended to recuperate from a beating like a conditioned athlete from a hard workout.

He'd noted her lingering look, approval of the jeans and shirt. He was relieved she was back in a headspace where she wanted to notice that. Though he wasn't in great shape for more tonight, if she wanted anything from him, he'd make sure he provided it.

She laid her gardening gloves on a shelf on the screen porch and wiped her feet on a mat. Then she paused at the door, her back to him. He stopped behind her.

Mick gazed at the crown of her head, the tense set of the shoulders. As she continued to stand there, he leaned in, his chest brushing her shoulder blades. Closing his hand on the doorknob, he turned it, fingers tenting against the panel to push it inward.

The aroma of cookies wafted out, mixed with vanilla, baked in a house with an underlying clean and welcoming scent. He'd detected hints of that fragrance in her clothes and on her skin. "Nice," he noted.

Her shoulder lifted, her chin jutting to the right. "One of those plug-in air things."

"I'm familiar. What's it called, in case I want to make my motorhome nicer for my female camping companion?"

"None of your damn business." Prickly and defensive.

He made a guess. "Grandma's Cottage?"

"I will go in, lock the door, and leave you out here like a stray dog."

He tried to nudge her over the threshold, and wasn't surprised when he took an elbow to the ribs, but she kept the strike wide of where he'd been pummeled a couple days ago. He took that as another encouraging sign and didn't withdraw, instead increasing the pressure of his body against hers. And braced a hand against the doorframe as she planted her feet and pushed back. "You wouldn't treat a stray dog like that," he pointed out. "Only a sub."

"True." With a put-upon sigh, she relented, stepping in fully, and bestowed a dour look upon him. "Come in. As long as you're not a vampire."

He stepped inside. They were in a laundry room, and the plug-in resided in an outlet there, beside the entry to the kitchen. On a rack were rubber garden clogs and waterproof boots. A black rain jacket hung on a peg. Next to it was a riding crop with a red loop on the end and a red braided handle. The way she closed her hand on it before moving into the kitchen seemed like a coming-home ritual.

Her kitchen was clean and functional, but elaborate cooking wasn't her thing. She had a coffee pot, a toaster, and a microwave over the oven. No other appliances.

"I'm going to get changed. Look around as much as you like." At his surprised look, she shrugged. "You've seen the worst of it."

He assumed she meant his discovery that she lived like June Cleaver. If June liked tying Ward up and subjecting him to astronomical levels of pain.

She'd disappeared down a hallway. He heard her walking up stairs to the second level, though her feet didn't make much noise, suggesting they were carpeted.

He moved into the living room. A cozy sofa and easy chair arrangement greeted him, along with a widescreen television between two built-in bookcases. Not holding many books, but the left side one had movies. Older Hallmark Hall of Fame films, plus romantic comedies and dramas. Stories with happy endings, or at least a hopeful message. She also owned series and movies that were the polar opposite. *Dexter*, *Criminal Minds*, and true crime stuff. They were filed in a pattern. Two happily-ever-afters, followed by a darker title. All the way to *Zombieland*, with Woody Harrelson.

"Hunh." The shelves on the other side of the TV held memorabilia. Two marketing awards were separated by a doll who looked like a marriage between a Day of the Dead decoration and a Tim Burton film character. Her white face was accented with black to look like a skull. Flowers had been hand painted over the cheekbones and jaw. His lips curved in a smile. It was Cyn. Wild, curly brown hair, lean body, dark, dangerous eyes. Probably something a client had custom designed and gifted her after she and TRA propelled their business into the next tax bracket.

The marketing awards were local stuff, but impressive. *Best Marketing Manager,* offered by a New Orleans business magazine. The other was for TRA as a company, *Best NOLA Start-Up.*

The room colors were bold but not too much. Furniture was trendy-looking yet comfortable. She chose for herself, simple but stylish. Much the way she dressed.

Down the hallway, he found a guest bedroom, and a room next to it with a closed door. She'd indicated nothing was off limits, but he assumed that was within the constraints of courtesy—don't dig under beds or into the back of closets. However, he did try the knob. When the door opened, something hanging off the back gave him some resistance, thumping lightly against the panels.

He'd found her home dungeon, a discovery that gave him mixed feelings. Anticipation about the possibilities he saw, as well as less excited feelings about what she'd done here—and who with.

He'd checked into Sy, and found he was a decent musician and long-time New Orleans resident. He'd had a couple arrests, bar brawls. At Progeny, he was well thought of, and Cyn clearly considered him a friend. The way he'd acted tonight, watching her put Mick in a corset, hadn't given off any possessive vibes.

Those had all come from Mick. Stupid, but he couldn't deny it. Cyn had looked thoughtful when she picked up on it, but not displeased.

The St. Andrew's Cross and spanking bench, the gold standard of home BDSM equipment in a limited space, were sturdy and anchored. On the wall were four framed photographs, blown up to 18x24 size, and a center painting, slightly larger.

He recognized the photos right off. They were pictures of her "canvases," men's backs, buttocks and thighs. The different flesh tones were layered with cuts, welts, red lines and bruising.

Would she have asked to take a picture of him, if they'd finished tonight the way she'd intended?

The center painting was a mix of the same tones, colors and slashes, perhaps inspired by the others, but this was abstract art, not a specific person.

He moved his attention onward. A table next to a wooden wardrobe held a sous vide tank. He wondered why it wasn't in the kitchen. He also wondered why it was turned on.

A U-shaped copper tube rested in the water. The two prongs, about ten inches long, plugged into a rubber handle like a bicycle grip. The lip was hooked over the side. The length and cock-sized width of the U's rounded end suggested a lot of unthinkable things.

From the rising temperature of the water, available via a print display attached to the tank sensor, she had to have switched it on before she went to change.

He put that distracting thought to the side to see what had thumped against the back of the door. Almost thirty different weapons for impact play. *Christ.* Slotted paddles, slappers, tawse, spatula, rulers—both metal and wooden—switch, cane. The wardrobe next to the sous vide table probably held other supplies, plus her longer whips, lubricants and whatever else she chose to pack into her go bag for Progeny. Including the always present first aid kit.

Did she still have the original paramedic go bag, tucked away somewhere?

Another of those plug-in things was in here, but the scent hinted at leather and sand, silk and heated flesh.

It was probably called Fifty Shades of Grandma.

He imagined her expression if he suggested it, and the chuckle, though it didn't get past his throat, didn't feel bad. He needed that. Compared to what his roughest days or nights had been, it was strange to feel so raw over what had happened in the past few hours, but he kept his core emotions locked down, which semi-protected them. Tonight had required that he strip and put them out there. For her.

An old-fashioned wooden classroom chair with attached desk was in the center of the room. Did she sit there to look at her sub, bound on the cross or bench? Absorb his energy and admire her work, what she'd done to him?

"This room doesn't fit the rest of the house, does it?"

He turned to find her leaning in the doorway. She'd changed into a black tank, soft and clingy, no bra beneath. It was the first time he'd seen her in a skirt. The knit fabric stopped above the knee, showing off her legs. He suspected it shaped and clung to her firm ass.

Feet still bare, but clean now. He wanted to press his lips to the arch, the painted toes, rest his mouth against the ankle he'd thought about washing for her. He'd kneel in front of her as she ran her fingernails along his back, dug into the marks she'd left on him. He'd prove how much he wanted to keep letting her hurt him.

He dipped his head toward the sous vide. Bubbles had started to gather and stream around the pipe. "Do I want to know?"

"That's not the right question. What's the right question, Mick?"

He pressed his lips together. "No questions at all."

"Fucking right." She moved past him, letting her fingers drift along the back of the door, pausing on the slapper. "This one has metal threaded through it. One of my subs said it was the most painful thing he'd ever experienced. I took that as a personal challenge, next time we had a session. You have that dangerous look again, Mick. You're wondering how many I've had in here."

"Not my business."

"No, it's not. None."

From the significant pause, he realized she wasn't reinforcing her right not to tell him. She'd answered his question with that one word.

None.

She nodded toward the chair. "I use that to sit and think. I come up with ideas for sessions at Progeny. No one comes here. No one sees where I live."

"Is this where you tell me I don't get to leave now that I have? And it's not a garden bed but my own grave you had me dig in the backyard?"

Amusement glimmered in her dark eyes. "If that was true, I would have had you dig it much deeper."

He thought about being laid to rest here, where her fingers could sift through the soil his flesh and bones enriched, helping her flowers grow. His peace with the idea, bordering on yearning, unsettled him, and he pushed it away. Her eyes tracked him too closely for that kind of thought.

For a long time, in his mind, she'd remained a scared, angry kid, with the seeds of the Mistress she was going to be there to intrigue and haunt him. Nothing he'd envisioned himself ever getting the chance to experience.

The scared kid was gone. She was a Mistress. Her volatility was a sincere, crazy, wild part of her, but so were her advanced perception skills, the decisions she made. The man who thought her unpredictable nature took the place of rational thinking missed how complicated her mind was. The two worked hand in hand.

"So why haven't you played with anyone here?"

"It doesn't fit the rest of the house, the whole picture."

"Of course it does. It's all you. It fits together, if anyone looks deeper."

Her phone buzzed. A continuous vibration, so a call, not a text. Her expression was thoughtful, a reaction to his words, as she pulled it out of her waistband and connected. Her eyes filled with fondness, lazy humor. "Why are you calling me? Lawrence should have given you three orgasms by now, before you deigned to fuck him into a post-coital coma."

She rolled her eyes and moved to the chair to sit down. "Okay, four. Whatever, you boastful bitch."

Mick followed her movement as she adjusted her knees outward, the skirt climbing her thighs. Her nipples jutted against the tank's clingy fabric. One bare foot brushed the base of the chair. She propped the other on the edge of the seat, knee bent, her elbow on the small desk as she held the phone in that hand. Some of her brown curls had fallen over one eye, so she studied him through that curtain. The lamplight gave her gaze a demonic reddish cast most subs probably told themselves was contacts.

Cyn dipped her chin downward. An unmistakable order.

"He's here with me," she said. "No, I don't want company. He wants to be buried in my backyard. Do you think I should grant his request?"

As she asked that, he dropped to one knee in front of her. She grasped his hair, tugging his face to her thigh. She bent to bite his ear, pricking it with her canines before she let it go and brushed her mouth over his cheek.

The chair had rocked and scraped across the floor from the collision of their two bodies. Unlike the cross and bench, it wasn't anchored. He slid his hands along her thighs to the back slats and wrapped his hands around the wood, so he could make sure it didn't topple with her in it.

"No, we're fine. Seriously. I've just told him to eat my pussy, so this call isn't lasting long. He has a clever mouth, and he knows what to do with it."

The command had his fingers constricting on the chair, knuckles pressing against the curves of her buttocks. As he put his mouth on her inner thigh, he could smell her arousal. It stiffened his cock, rigid need gripping his lower body.

He took his time, though. She was right. He did know how to use his mouth, but it had never been as important to use it in a way to please a woman as it was right now.

To please this specific woman, which meant a certain learning curve. A man who didn't slow down for that curve could fuck up, spin out and crash.

And hell, the trip was worth hitting the brakes.

She felt the same. When she put her hand back in his hair, wrapped and pulled, hard, she wasn't pulling him closer. She wasn't going to let him do this without reminding him she had every right to hurt him while he did.

Her skirt pushed against his forehead as he worked into that heated, dark area. When he reached her labia, he used all parts of his mouth to learn their texture, softness and taste. He played his lips and tongue over her clit, and she braced her foot on his back. She didn't put the sole on the bandages, but on a group of welts left by the cane. As she pushed down, rubbed her heel against them, the pain went right to his cock.

She couldn't have paid him a greater compliment, believing in his ability to endure whatever she did to him while he gave her pleasure.

He covered her with his mouth, sucking, nibbling and stroking with more focused intent. Thrust. Flick. Tease.

Her voice was getting a satisfying strained note. He wasn't following much of the conversation anymore. That wasn't his job. He did catch the last part, though.

"Go fuck Lawrence some more if you're getting hot. That's why his ass is there. To serve yours."

The phone dropped the few inches to the floor. She found his clenched hand and gripped it, another anchor and connection. "Fuck me with that beautiful mouth, Mick. Let me feel your teeth."

He did, not too much, not until she said so. "Harder. Bite my clit."

He did and a gasp broke from her throat, a raw noise. She pulled harder on his hair, lifted her foot from his back, then brought her heel back down, a thump against tender skin. She kept doing it, moving against his mouth with her clit clamped in his teeth, his tongue playing over the succulent flesh. She wrapped her leg around his back, her other hand coming to his neck, fingers digging into his nape.

She'd donned one of her claws. He had no idea when she'd put it on, but the rough sound that came from his throat was gratitude. She raked it across the back of his neck, and then dug it into his shoulder as she started to climax. The cry of pleasure that broke from her, uncontrolled, a free fall with her in his hands, in his care, was a sound he'd hold onto forever, and strive to hear again and again. Any time during the short time they had that she'd allow it, and he'd fight for those chances.

He kept his weight back against the chair's pull, his hands sure and firm, even if his arms trembled with the effort. His cock could have knocked a baseball out of a stadium.

She worked herself against his mouth well after she was done, testing his resolve, his ability to hold position. The skirt folds didn't allow him the gorgeous view of her upper body rolling over those waves, but he could imagine.

It was probably ten minutes before she stopped, moving the foot to his chest to push him back. She sat up and adjusted her skirt. Her nipples, still prominent, made his mouth hunger to suck.

"Stand up and take off the shirt. Let me see you."

He obeyed, and her lip curled, a sign of appetite, as she moved her eyes over his shoulders and chest, down his abdomen until she stopped and studied his size, straining against denim. "Unbutton the top and push down the zipper. Slow."

His strangled cock revealed itself, pressing against cotton. "Lawrence owes you a beer," she said mildly. "I think his Mistress is going to use him until dawn."

"Lucky Lawrence."

"Would you say that about yourself, if I did the same? No matter what I choose to do to you?"

"I think you know the answer to that, Mistress."

"I do. But your reasons are suspect, Mick. You lost my trust tonight."

"Then I've put myself in hell, Mistress. Without you. Maybe you'll give me a chance to find my way back."

Her eyes rose to hold his. "I don't want to hurt you."

What she meant would take this conversation to a different plane. He didn't want to go there.

"That may be the cruelest thing you've ever said to me." But he didn't smile, because it wasn't a joke.

A long moment passed in silence before she spoke again. "Turn around facing the door, your back to me, and take off everything. I want nothing hidden."

When he complied, he heard the creak as she left the wooden chair. As she stood behind him, he kept his hands half curled at his sides. A pulsing ache in his chest tried to affect him, deflate him lower down. He wouldn't let it.

She started to remove the bandages. With the medical tape designed to feel like it was removing skin, she chose both uncomfortable options. Quick rips and slow pulls. He gritted his teeth and held still.

She disposed of the medical waste in a trashcan behind him. He stared at the wall. There were several mirrors in here, but when she'd told him to face the back of the door and its instruments of torture, she'd made sure he couldn't look for her reflection without turning his head. He knew better than to try that.

Relief pushed the ache back up, away from his cock, as she brushed her fingertips on the top right part of the X. She followed it all the way down. Then did the left side, with a brief pause over the place where his heart was trying to thud through his chest. He spoke between beats.

"A lot of people don't realize you know how to be in control and out of control at the same time. Do they?"

She kept outlining the cut with her fingertips. That was the hand wearing the claw, so he knew she'd eventually use it. Hoped she would.

"No. Sometimes I'm not sure of it, either. Do you know what stopped me from going deeper with the knife?"

Knowing he'd disappointed, hurt and angered her had been a far worse wound. One that needed the kind of stitches he had no right to ask for. But that was his answer to the question, not hers.

"You would have been okay with that," she said, answering for him.

"And you deny subs what they want," he finished.

"Yes. It's my wants and their needs."

"What about your needs?"

He sucked in a breath as the claw pressed into the cut. Blood trickled, telling him she'd opened that seam. "My wants and needs don't have to be separate, Mick. That's the kind of Mistress I am."

She put her hand on his arm to turn him around. He lifted a hand to her face, and she caught his wrist in her grip, her claw pressed on the pulsing artery there.

He stilled, staring down at her. Her kissable, bitable mouth, her dark eyes and wild curls framing her face. He could turn this into a primal play fight, here and now. The temptation rose, making his erect cock twitch, and he leaned into her, telegraphing it, even as he kept his arm motionless in her grip.

"No," she said. "I want something else right now."

The short battle of wills was mostly on his side, him getting his will to listen to hers. But when he had it contained, she knew. She let him go and walked to the table, propping her hips next to the bubbling tank.

"The sous vide maintains a constant temperature. It's how it ensures that it doesn't overcook food while cooking it all the way through."

"I'm familiar."

"Have you ever used one?"

He shook his head. "Not a lot of room for big appliances in the motorhome, but I've seen it done."

She glanced at the temperature gauge. "Burn play is intensely painful, but can be done this way without lasting harm, if you know what you're doing. You're good at staying still when you're in pain, Mick. I wonder how good."

He was starting to get an idea of where this was going.

The look in her eyes intensified, seeing further inside him. When she spoke, the words echoed up from that well.

"I want to kiss you while you're screaming, Mick. I want you to scream into my mouth, give me all that pain I'm causing you. It will make me wet, and I will take you to my bed and ride you until I've had all the pleasure I want from you tonight. You'll get pleasure if I say you do."

He managed to lick dry lips. "All right."

A corner of her mouth twitched. "Were you under the impression I was asking your permission?"

"No, Mistress. Far as I'm concerned, CNC is status quo for us."

She blinked, then gestured to the spanking bench. "Kneel behind it, facing me. Arms stretched out to either side on the bench."

That would put his hindquarters facing the wall, which suggested she wasn't going to fuck him with the pipe, thank God. But she could also be luring him into a false sense of security.

She read his mind pretty well. "I've seen Mistresses adjust the temp accordingly to fuck their subs with this technique. Or make them suck on it like a dick. I'm not interested in that. And it's not your fear I want, either. I assume you already know that about me."

He did. It was part of why they fit. Tiger had said he had enough blood and pain in his life. Mick had enough fear in his.

When he knelt on the cushioned step on the wall side of the bench, she ran a strap behind his bent knees and cinched it down. She did the same to his arms, using straps at shoulder, elbow and wrist. He could curve his back like a cat, but he couldn't lift his arms, which gave his head a limited range of motion. He could look in either direction, or prop his jaw on the bench.

303

When she stepped back, she removed her shirt, revealing the darker flesh of her nipples, the crinkled points against paler curves. She hooked a thumb in the waistband of the skirt, showing her hip bone as she cocked her stance like a man did when he put a thumb in his jeans pocket or behind a belt.

She ran her hand over his hair, a deceptively gentle stroke. She was sinking deeper into that miasma she created, where the desire to give pain was taking over everything else. His whole being yearned toward her.

She went to her wardrobe and retrieved a bit gag.

"Hard to kiss you with that, Mistress."

"I'll be kissing *you*, Mick. You'll be screaming."

She fitted it into his mouth, pushing it past his teeth which initially clenched, resisting. Pushing a practiced finger into the hinge of his jaw, she wrenched it open to shove in the bit. Then she slapped his face. "Behave."

An aggressive response rocketed through him. A few minutes ago, it would have triggered that wrestling match he'd wanted. Now he twitched against his bonds, testing them. Webbed nylon in good condition was a bitch to break.

She returned to the sous vide tank, ostensibly ignoring him, except the hip action said otherwise. The mesmerizing movement of her bare back and shoulders, her slim neck, was an unconscious bonus.

"You're so beautiful." His heart turned over like a bingo ball in a cage. Or a rock falling off a cliff, seeing the ground coming, but if she was there...okay. Just, okay.

She put her chin to the bare shoulder, a brief acknowledgment, her lashes brushing her cheek. Then she grasped the rubber handle attached to the pipe and lifted it free of the water. The glistening copper dripped, reminding him of her slickness when he'd fed on her pussy.

She made an adjustment to the controls before she moved his way. The tube uncoiled behind her. It was a closed system, water flowing into one end of the U-shaped pipe and going out the other, back to the tank, to maintain the constant temperature.

"Remember, no matter how much it hurts, it's not going to burn you enough to require medical care. I promise you that. Tell me you understand."

"I understand." He could manfully assert he would be fine, that he didn't care, but the brain's survival instinct could put a lot of pressure on a man's resolve. Offering that key piece of knowledge would placate it enough to help him serve her desires.

"Good." She stood before him. A total bitch, a tough woman, a badass. Yet her breasts were small and sweet, her bone structure so delicate, the nip of her waist calling to the grip of his hands. He wanted to cherish, devour and fight her, all at once.

She laid the pipe on his shoulder and biceps. He'd steeled himself to immobility, ready to resist the instinct to jerk away, but it felt…warm. Not too bad. If she put it against the places she'd beat upon earlier, it'd soothe like a heating pad.

He was smart enough not to be deceived, though he savored what she did as she waited. She stroked his hair again with her free hand. No pulling this time. She leaned her hip against his arm, letting him feel fabric and warm skin.

Then the heat started to change. To increase. Exponentially.

CHAPTER SIXTEEN

Cyn knew the moment the sensation moved from heat to burn, and watched his muscles tighten against the very strong desire to pull away. Only to find he couldn't. The straps wouldn't let him. That awareness would combine with the pain, adding fight-or-flight adrenaline.

He wasn't a runner. The initial flinching turned into an embrace of the pain, him pushing against it, lips curled back against his teeth, daring it to make him reject his Mistress's desire.

Her body was damp, tight as a cable, quivering.

The shudder through his body became more tectonic, and the first gasp escaped his lips. His teeth clamped down on the bit. Though he'd tried to reject it, she'd been warned some subs could bite down on their tongues during this. He'd already proven there was a reason for her to protect his tongue. She would be using it again before long.

She didn't move the pipe, holding it as the brain became convinced she was burning him to the bone, his skin on fire. She saw the knowledge in his eyes, he knew that wasn't happening, but the pain…

Oh, how it felt to watch the pain, feel it channel out of her and into him, sharing it like the same closed system that was keeping the water hot.

He groaned, body rocking what little it was allowed. She leaned forward and started playing her mouth over his. Teasing little licks around the bit, a nip of the top lip, then the bottom. She wanted his mouth free, but she wasn't risking his tongue. Or him biting her and drawing blood.

That was her job.

As the groan became a curse, then a cry, she absorbed the heat of that erratic breath, the sound into herself, and fed on it. "It hurts so much, baby," she breathed against him. "I love how much it hurts you. I want to fuck you one day while doing this."

The hoarse scream erupted against her lips and tongue, the moistness of her mouth. And still she held the pipe in place. He wouldn't plead, wouldn't tell her to stop. She knew he wouldn't, which was why this worked, because the darkness couldn't have her, couldn't take her past what his body could physically endure.

People could be broken by mindfucks, which was why she'd told him upfront he wasn't being catastrophically burned, even as it felt exactly like he was. If she fucked with his head, it would be for different reasons. Not that. As she'd told him, this was about pain, not fear.

At last she lifted the copper tube, noting the U-shaped angry red mark on his flesh before she threaded the pipe beneath the bench and laid it against his upper abdomen, a diagonal line a few inches over his cock.

His eyes snapped up to her. He hadn't realized she'd do it again, in a different place. "I might do this all night," she told him.

That *was* a mind fuck, a card she played at the right time, because now he broke her heart, drawing her in, winning her over completely. The wildness in his eyes, the curl in his lips, the mix of *oh fucking hell* and *oh God* and *whatever she wants, that's what I want*, came together in one delicious storm in his expression.

She cupped the back of his head, made a calculated choice and unlatched the bit, letting it drop away. He knew what to expect now. He might bite his own tongue, but not enough to impede what could serve her. She was equally certain he'd use his formidable will to override any reaction that would damage her mouth, lips or tongue.

She kissed him as he groaned, snarled, cursed and then screamed again when the heat reached that searing level. As she stroked his hair, she kept telling him, against his lips, "Give me what I want, Mick."

He was nodding, accepting the pain, fighting his mind, giving it all to her. When she once again lifted it, she stood up and laid the pipe on his back, on the inside of his right shoulder blade, parallel to the X mark. As she did, she bent close enough to bring her nipple to his mouth.

"Kiss it," she whispered. "Gently."

He obeyed, dialing back his frenzied reaction. The teasing tickle of his lips was marked by a strained tremble that sent a thrill through her. She kissed the crown of his head, telling him he belonged to her. She had him.

She was his Mistress.

She brought him once again to where he lost the battle to roar out from the pain, then she lifted the pipe away. This time she dropped it into the metal bucket she'd put next to the bench. She unbuckled the strap holding his legs, and moved to his side. Putting her other arm around him, she freed the straps holding him to the bench one-handed, preparing to control his slump away from it.

Instead he half-lunged at her. His knees hit the floor as he wrapped one arm around her hips, the other around her back. He bit her breast and the skin over her rib, like Adam paying homage to the part of him that had been given to Eve, connecting them forever. He licked it, kissed her, held her in arms so strong the grip hurt.

His teeth left marks on her breast, his fingers bruising her flesh. But she could handle pain as well as he could. There was a reason they mashed up the terms like a celebrity couple. *Sadomasochist.*

"Baby, it's all right. Level out. You're a little crazy. Don't make me regret freeing you. You're a guest in my home. Don't be impolite."

That stream of quiet nonsense was intended to bring him back to himself. She was still digesting what he'd told her about his life, but one thing was clear. He'd developed a phenomenal degree of self-control to neutralize his reactions to the horrible things he saw.

On the flip side, extremes in a secure BDSM session could unlock things he didn't trust himself to let loose in any other part of his life. He'd proven that in the Pit, but this time she was more prepared for it.

Unfortunately, he didn't know that.

Mick shoved away from her, backpedaled to the wall and hit it hard. The wall shuddered, the tools on the back of the door vibrating.

"Don't come close. Don't."

He was naked, shaking, but he didn't look diminished. He was a savage animal. She could have kept him bound until he leveled out. Maybe she'd let more tender feelings interfere with her decision-making. A problem she didn't normally have.

But her gut told her she'd made the right call. Just like it told her what to do now. Picking up the copper tube, she put it across her breasts, just over her nipples. Felt that welcoming initial heat, felt it growing into something else.

He still had his head down, caught in a world of his own. But she could be patient. Patient enough that when he at last raised his head, she had dropped to one knee, because the pain was too much to stand. Her lip had curled back, teeth clenched against making a sound.

"Christ." Mick launched himself from the wall. He hit the spanking bench with his shoulder, making him stumble, but he reached her and knocked the pipe out of her hands.

"What the fuck…" He had her on her ass next to him, leaning against the bench while his gaze darted between her and the pipe, looking at it like it was a poisonous snake.

She put a hand on his, a reassurance, as she reached over, retrieved it by the handle and dropped it into the bucket before it could burn her floor. Then his hands were on her, touching the red lines across the top of her breasts.

He put his mouth there, light, gentle. She let him do it as she rested her other hand where she'd first put the pipe against his shoulder. Stroking lightly.

"Goddamn, Mistress." Mick showed her those tormented eyes. "Why did you do that?"

309

"To remind you of who you are. To bring you back to the here and now. With me. It worked." She peered at him. "Want a beer?"

He dropped his head to her shoulder, a different kind of quiver going through him. One caused by a desperate chuckle. His mouth rested against her breast again. "That's your aftercare for this? Burn yourself and offer me a beer?"

"Hey, remember what I told you. If you miss your mother, you've got yourself the wrong Mistress."

He sighed. "Have you ever done that before?"

"First time on someone else. I test everything on myself first. Practice."

"You said you've never had anyone here. Have you thought about it? Doing stuff like this here, in this room?"

She put her hand on his face, making him meet her gaze before she responded. "Extensively."

She hadn't allowed herself to indulge softer things like this with subs. She'd been concerned it would make her less cruel, and she needed to be cruel. Yet she'd never been as aroused, as mentally involved in a session, as she was when those two reactions tangled with him.

She didn't have to worry about Mick deciding she was too cruel or too kind. She could explore this feeling in the shielded safety of her home with him, the first person she'd allowed here that was friend or family.

"Want to see something silly?" she asked.

Before he could answer, she stretched out a leg to hook the student desk with her bare foot and drag it over. He stopped her, instead bringing it over with his stronger grip and longer arm. She pointed out the carving on the inside curve of the chair's arm, tracing the block letters with her fingertips. M.I.C.K.

"Did you do that?" he asked.

"No. I'm not that sentimental. But it's why I bought it from a secondhand shop. Where do you think that Mick is now?"

He met her gaze. "Nowhere as good as where this one is."

She told Mick he could sleep in her bed, as long as he stayed on his side. "I'm not a Care Bear or a kitchen utensil," she told him. "I don't cuddle or spoon."

He thought that first part might not be true. He was a little too manly to call it cuddling, but the way she'd stroked his hair and kept her arm around him after the scene suggested otherwise.

He followed her upstairs, vision full of her slim back, the movement of her waist and hips, the flex of her calves as she padded up the steps ahead of him. She'd kept on her skirt, but had told him he wasn't wearing clothes until she said so.

When they reached her bedroom, his beloved sadist pointed him toward a cushioned chair and began to change for bed like he wasn't even there. She pulled off the skirt and took pajama bottoms and a gray tank out her dresser.

Normal stuff a woman would wear, not intended to be sexy. But he got to see her head-to-toe naked. She had a sleek pelt of trimmed brown pubic hair. All those slender limbs, honed muscle, small curves. Her ass wasn't big, but the heart shape of it begged to be cradled by his hands. At least in his own mind.

She disappeared into the bathroom. When she re-opened the door and stood at the mirror, she brushed out her hair, tied the curls back with a crimson ribbon, and went to the bed.

"Do whatever you need to do, then come take the left side. Do I need to text Tiger and tell him you're alive? Or, more importantly, that his truck is fine, and we'll get it back to him tomorrow?"

"I can do that. In fact…I need to go get my phone from my jeans downstairs. It's important that I have it with me."

He wasn't anticipating anything, but predictability wasn't a given. Ever. The spurt of resentment and mild anxiety over remembering what his priorities had to be was normal. He wouldn't let those reactions get the upper hand. Dwelling too much on how the revelations that had brought him here would take him from her in a very short time would interfere with the minutes he had with her.

And yes, even if he had a couple days, he would measure it in single, precious minutes.

He saw the recognition of some of that in her eyes before she nodded and turned away from him. "Do what you need to do." She turned off the light.

It wasn't a rejection. Not exactly. They'd gone a lot of new places tonight, both of them, and she didn't do reassurances or empty platitudes. She was going to sleep, and no matter how intertwined they'd been only a half hour before—hell, it was like their souls had been wrapped around one another—that was then, and this was now.

He went downstairs, retrieved his phone, and checked it. Nothing new. His efforts earlier in the evening had worked. Everything was still on schedule. Salazar had calmed down.

Mick had mostly stopped giving any energy to revulsion over what passed as operational considerations in his world. But tonight had left him a little raw. Raw enough to have to take a beat now. He closed his fingers over the phone, tattooed it against his thigh. After a few steadying breaths, he headed back up the stairs, two at a time.

She had her life, he had his. They were self-contained people. Even when, like this, all the heaven and hell each person carried inside had to break loose and make itself known.

He took a quick shower, letting the cool water slide over the burns, soothing him further. She hadn't told him he had to clean up before bed, but he was a good guest.

After he dried off, he finger-combed his hair. Then he switched off the lamp.

312

Ambient light from the window showed him where she lay in the giant bed. She looked small, his Mistress with a galaxy-sized personality. When she'd put that pipe against her breasts, all he could think about was getting to her, getting it away, even though she was doing it to herself.

I test everything on myself first. Practice.

She was right about him and his "little bird" subs. It was a natural thing, that instinctual desire to protect a woman. But what he felt toward Cyn, the strength of the past, the reality of the present, who he was, who he had to be... There wasn't anything in the world he wouldn't do to protect her.

There were three pillows across the bed. She'd said to stay on his side, and a side was where a pillow was, so it was reasonable he could take the middle one. Right? As he inched over, and took in more details, his brow creased. She lay on her back, sleeping with her arms tight over herself, like a bat in a cave, wings wrapped across the body. Her breath was even. She'd gone to sleep that fast. Maybe. Or maybe she was setting him up, and if he reached out...

But he did it anyway. Slowly, moving his hand until it covered one of those clenched hands. A light tug, just a continual easy pressure, and her hand shifted, slowly letting their fingers intertwine.

Her head turned in his direction. "Just us here, Cyn," he said. "Us here, the world outside."

She rotated in his direction, even more slowly. She waited to see what he wanted, and he let her know. Another tug, bringing her closer. Then she was in his arms, sliding hers around his back, against all those marks she'd put on him. Her head pressed on his chest, under his neck, and they were holding one another.

He hadn't cried in a long time, and he wasn't going to do it now. But if one tear slid down his nose and landed against that oddly girlish ribbon, leaving a salt-drop stain, that was okay. The universe wouldn't out him.

Cyn woke before dawn, after two reasonably good hours of sleep. Sliding out of the bed, she stretched and moved to the window, looking down at her garden below. She noted the even rectangle Mick had tilled for her, the splashes of color in her flower beds, though a far darker hue at this hour.

A couple times during the session, she'd noted his gaze latch onto the painting flanked by her "canvases." When she'd mounted the photographs, she'd wanted an appropriate centerpiece. She'd bought an actual stretched white canvas and paints, and when she got home, she went right to it, unable to wait. She put down the rapid slashes and strikes of paint the way she threw her whip, batted with the cane or switch, struck with the tawse. Then she'd laid a broad diagonal slash over all of it, like the scar she'd left across his chest.

Now he had an X on his back as well. She might add that to the painting.

In the corner of that painting was a roughly sketched black skeleton, arched back as if crying to the heavens, bony fingers reaching for what seemed so close, yet out of reach.

That was how it felt for people like them. They never forgot what they saw or endured. True happiness would never be theirs. Maybe it wasn't anyone's, because the pain and loneliness, the suffering, was part of the air all living things had to breathe.

But moments could belong to each of them, like a rosary, the beads counted upon to find meaning and joy.

She turned to look at him. He slept mostly on top of the linens, a sheet snagged around one thigh, across his hip bone. He had a healthy erection happening, which made her loins twinge. She might go over and ride him awake.

She turned her gaze back to the window. She didn't really seek out sex like that. Usually it was part of a session, a give and take of power, Mistress and sub. She could go that way with him in her bed, but she wasn't sure that was what she wanted right now. What she wanted was a little alarming.

A shift and rustle. In the corner of her gaze, she noted him lifting his head, figuring out where she was. He sat up and slid out of the bed, disappearing into the bathroom. When he returned, he came and stood behind her. She imagined him looming there, strong and silent. Maybe rubbing sleep out of his eyes, rumpling his hair with a large hand.

"When was the last time you took a deep breath, Mick?" Her voice stayed low, respecting the darkness.

"When was the last time you did?"

She closed her eyes, drew it in. What did Vera talk about, breathing through the chakras? Her chakras needed a sander, because her breath hung up on each one, pulling, tearing things loose that made it hard for her to complete the act. But she managed it.

"Just now."

"How did it go?"

She decided not to answer that. Or ask him if he'd tried it, and how it had gone for him. Instead, she looked at her greenhouse, at her orchids behind the murky panes, and posed an easier question. Easier for her, at least.

"Can you guess how I want to be touched, Mick? Right now?"

His hands came around her, one cupping her throat, tipping her chin to his shoulder, while the other slid down her front, finding his way under the tank to press against flesh.

"I don't need to guess with you, Mistress."

He slid his palm lower, beneath the pajama bottoms to her mound, over her clit and labia, taking full possession of her pussy, with a massaging, demanding touch.

It wasn't the too-fast groping of a teen looking for the only parts that interested him. It was the skilled touch of a man, reading her voice, her body, understanding who she was. He found her wetness, collected it on his fingers and

315

pushed into her. His mouth came to her ear, breath on her neck. Cool mint. He'd brushed his teeth before he'd come to her. A considerate lover, even as his fingers and his grip on her throat said something far more demanding.

"Right now, this is how you want to be touched," he said in that wolf-like rumble that teased the nerve endings at the base of her spine. "You want it fast, a hard push. You make your subs wait until they feel like they're going to die, but when you're ready, you're damn well not going to wait."

He pushed the bottoms down, circled her waist with one strong arm and lifted her out of them. He used the other hand against her thigh and mound to bring her hips back. Her hand landed on the glass as he drove into her wet heat. Fast enough for her to feel the stretch, but not so fast he hurt her. Not in the wrong way.

"Oh…"

"Fucking love to hear your moans, Mistress. Keep doing it." He adjusted so his hand could cover her breast, fondle and squeeze, rocket more sensation through her. "I'll push you as hard as you want."

"Harder. Faster."

He responded with that spine-tingling chuckle. "Anything you want, honey." His lower hand had moved to their joining point, and he was playing with her clit, over the stretched labia. The climax clawed up from her center, out into her throat, taking her moan to a raw scream.

She arched back against him, her feet hooked over the back of his knees as he held her against the window frame, showing her just how strong and skilled he really was, how untamed he could be.

"Mistress…"

"Don't ask. Just come with me."

Those words could mean so many things. To both of them, but he took it literally, coming inside her. The window creaked alarmingly, and with a huff of breath between climax and rough laughter, he shifted them to the nearby cushioned chair, so she had her knees on the seat, her hands gripping the back as he groaned out his finish, working himself deep inside her.

When they slowed and caught their breath, he was holding her just as securely. Which was good, because her legs might buckle if she tried to use them. He slid out of her, but lifted her off her feet, carried her to the bed and laid her down on it.

It was an unusual occurrence for her, letting someone else hold her up. She was in control, but she was letting him...take care of her.

He wasn't done pleasing her. He'd removed the condom he'd used—the same subtle act of consideration as the minty breath—and disposed of it. When he came back to bed, he dropped several more on the night table. Not presumption, but preparation.

"That was one way you like to be touched," he said. "This is another."

He dropped to one knee and put his hand next to her leg. "May I kiss your foot, Mistress?"

She nodded and closed her eyes as he did it, response rippling all the way up her leg. "And here?" He put his hand on her shin.

"Yes."

Another lovely wave of sensation, through a body still vibrating from climax. He worked his way up, asking each time. He lingered in places that weren't the obvious spots. Just over the knee, high on the thigh, her hip bone. Each became an erogenous zone because it was his mouth, his fingers, upon that expanse of skin.

By the time he reached her mouth, her whole body was...trembling. He paused, leaning over her. She saw all the wounds of the earlier part of the night in his eyes, no longer bleeding. It was hard to tell if they were healing or if they'd just delayed infection.

She'd take what they could get.

317

"Mistress, may I kiss your mouth? Drown there? Stay there forever?"

Her lips curved, even as they quivered from the intensity of his gaze upon them. "Until I get hungry for breakfast. How are you at making eggs?"

"Better than hens."

She wrapped her arms around his shoulders and brought him to her chuckling mouth, the laughter melting into heat. He just kissed her. Kissed her and kissed her, until their bodies were pressed close again, and her legs opened to him, welcoming him back inside.

"You like to be touched endless ways, Mistress," he whispered against her mouth. He paused above her in the dark, lodged inside her, their hands holding onto one another. "Hard, soft, all at your pleasure. When you want it, however you want it, that's the main thing. You feel the difference when a man is doing it that way, instead of any other."

She'd never had sex with a man on top. It didn't feel like a prison, not suffocating. Not with Mick. She didn't feel out of control. Far from it. As she held him, and they both shuddered through another orgasm, it felt like another first.

He felt like a man who belonged to her. Who had been created for her. An entirely dangerous and deranged thought.

But she was no stranger to those states of mind.

When Cyn woke for the second time, it was full daylight and she smelled breakfast cooking. She wasn't a deep sleeper, but not only had Mick made it out of bed without waking her, he'd had enough time to make a meal.

The last thing she'd remembered was his arms around her. It hadn't been a bad thing.

When she brushed her teeth and hair, she noticed she was missing her hair ribbon. She'd been half-awake when he'd untied and slid it away. He'd nuzzled her curls as they slipped down around her face. Going back to the bed, she

318

found the ribbon under his pillow. His own scent touched her nose as she re-adjusted the pillow.

She'd never woken in the morning with a man in her bed. Well, she still hadn't, since he was downstairs. If it ever happened again, she'd tell him he'd damn well better keep his ass in it until she woke up and *told* him to go make her breakfast. She wouldn't have minded starting her day riding a big, thick morning erection, no matter that she'd had it inside her only a couple hours ago.

She didn't see herself getting tired of fucking Mick anytime soon.

She tied the ribbon back in place, washed her face, did moisturizer, decided to forget about makeup for now and went down the hall in her tank and loosely-tied pajama pants. On her landing was a painting of a New Orleans street scene, musicians playing saxophone and drums while a woman in a white dress danced, her blonde hair sweeping around her as she laughed.

Cyn touched it as she usually did, then headed downstairs. It was a sunny day, and the front living room windows drenched the stairs and foyer in sunshine.

She paused at the opening to the kitchen, because the view was worth taking a moment. Or ten.

A lot of people wished for a "stop" button, to absorb a view as long as they wished before it changed. A Mistress had that button. She just had to tell her sub to stay in the pose she wanted. Cyn's problem was she wanted to see Mick in all sorts of positions and states of dress. She was too impatient to stay on just one.

"A true masochist," she commented. "A man who will cook with hot oil while naked."

Mick looked her way. His dark hair was tousled over his forehead, his blue eyes gleaming. "My Mistress said no clothes until she said so. You may get a letter from the HOA. Your dog-walking neighbor looked a little startled when I brought in your morning paper."

319

"If I thought you were serious, I'd beat you with that spatula." She crossed her arms over her chest.

"See, my day's already full of promising things." His gaze passed over the ribbon in her hair, the push of her nipples against thin cloth, the exposed hip bones above the drawstring of the pants. "You make girl slumber party wear look pretty damn good. Ever thought about reverse Daddy Dom?"

"What? That is not a real thing."

"Everything has the potential to be a real thing. It just has to cross someone's mind." He grinned. "It's Daddy Dom, only he's not the Dom. She's a little girl in charge of her Daddy, making him do stuff for her."

At her look, he hummed a 38 Special song, bringing to mind the lyrics. A man so caught up in his woman, "his little girl," that he'd get down on his knees for her.

She came across the kitchen, no longer willing to deny herself the right to touch him. "Keep cooking," she told him. After a quick inspection to ensure all the bruising, cuts and welts were healing properly, she pressed herself against his battered back side.

When she reached around him to work his cock in her hand, he huffed out a chuckle. "You're going to mess up your breakfast."

"Not if my sex slave knows what his first job is, and it has nothing to do with what his dick wants."

"Understood, Mistress." She felt the tightening of his muscles as he focused on cooking while she was doing her best to distract him. Firm strokes, cupping his balls, teasing his thighs with her nails. She'd left her claws on the night table. An oversight, but she had other options.

He was scrambling the vegan egg mix he'd found in a carton in the fridge. He'd added some of her counter spices and chopped up tomatoes and peppers to add to the mix. Toast with muscadine jelly waited on a plate on the non-hot part of the stove. He must have planned to bring her breakfast in bed. Once he added the vegetables and slid the finished omelet onto the plate, she had a command for him.

"Make the oil splatter, Mick."

"Not while your hand is around my cock."

She withdrew it, placing her palm against his back. Laid her cheek over it, already knowing he'd want to make sure her face was protected.

He picked up the oil and tipped it to drizzle more in the still hot skillet. When she heard the sizzle and sharp pops, he stiffened, drawing a breath in between his teeth.

"Where?" she murmured.

"Chest, stomach. Cock." He let the breath out. "Just a couple drops."

"Good." Her hand came back around to reclaim him. She put her mouth on the dual column of red-tinged skin inside his shoulder blade, where she'd put the copper tube.

"God." He tipped his head back, fingers gripping the oven handle. "Do you ever give yourself pain, for you? Not the testing thing for your subs."

She paused. "Why would you ask that?"

"Because certain sadists will use themselves if they don't have someone else to hurt when the urge comes upon them. You strike me as that kind."

A dicey area, but she wouldn't deny it. Giving him one last caress, she moved to the coffee maker, putting in her preferred K-cup.

"Sometimes. But I have good access to subs these days, so it's mostly to help me know what they're experiencing. Before we have a session, I ask them their one to ten pain threshold, but I also ask them what produced a ten or a one, because it's different for everyone. Last year, we had a guest member with a nerve disorder. Almost any contact play was a ten for him."

He'd specifically wanted her, having heard about her reputation. "A feather along his skin felt the way a Wartenberg wheel would feel to someone else."

321

As she slid into a seat at the kitchen island, Mick brought the plate to her. He'd added a small bowl of applesauce with a sprinkling of cinnamon to the arrangement. "So what was he looking for?" he asked.

"Someone without empathy. Someone who would push his limits and wouldn't stop until he safeworded."

He frowned. "You have empathy. You're all empathy. You feel and want the pain, too."

"His words, not mine. I don't care if they have the wrong impression of me. What matters is if they interest me, and he did. We had a good session. He blacked out. When he woke, it was because he was in the arms of the sweetest little kitten sub we have. She was stroking him with a feather."

Mick's lips twisted. "Woman, you are diabolical."

"No argument there." She looked down at the food. He'd made himself comfortable in her kitchen, and she didn't mind. "Have someplace to be today, Mick?"

"I need to check in with Progeny on Monday to finish up, but my Sunday is yours."

"Good." She paused. "You were planning to leave soon after that?"

"Yeah. But I can carve out an extra day, if you've changed your mind about going camping with me."

"We'll see." She didn't want to think about what it would mean if she agreed to go. Or how it would feel if she told him good-bye.

"I meant what I said, Cyn." He braced his hands on the island. "About committing to you, even if I'm not here."

She drew back. "Don't say that. You can't promise something like that."

"Why not?"

"Because you said it yourself. We might not see one another again for months, or years." Or never again. The unspoken words raked her insides, so she shoved some additional hard truth at him. "There'd be no point in you making such a promise to me. I'm not set up to trust that kind of oath."

"Exactly," he said. "You've never had anyone dedicate themselves wholly to you, wanting to be bound to you in every conceivable way. I've wanted that since we met. Ten years proves that has nothing to do with how many miles are between us."

She shoved away the inexplicable panic his words caused. "Why is this so important, Mick? Why?"

His eyes fixed on her in that way a man's did when what he was saying was pulled from a core as solid and unshakable as anything could be.

"My dad cheated. All he had to do was walk out the door, and his dick was on the prowl. I was the kid who got to sit on the sidelines and watch, like every other kid who's had to go through that. People hear about your parent's infidelity and say this incredibly stupid thing: 'It has nothing to do with you.'"

His expression went cold. "Really? They came together out of love, made a promise to love one another, had a kid born out of that love, but when they betray that love, it has nothing to do with the kid? It has nothing to do with him when it breaks his mother's heart, her confidence, her self-worth? Yeah. Having a parent whose family isn't enough for them to keep their legs closed or dick in their pants, it sure as fuck involves the kid."

He took a steadying breath. "You didn't ask for that commitment from me. I get that. But when I say I'll be faithful, you can count on it. Even if we never see one another again. Knowing you accept that from me, it will bring me a kind of peace. A balance, when it doesn't exist anywhere else."

She knew he didn't mean those instances when he might be 'tested.' That didn't count, because those were bites out of his soul. She stared at him as the second hand of her kitchen clock ticked. God help her, he meant it. God help her, she believed him. And understood why he was asking her to accept it. It was about how he wanted to serve her. His Mistress.

"All   right,"   she   said.

CHAPTER SEVENTEEN

As she pulled into work on Monday, Cyn tried to remember the last time she'd had a sexual workout that left *her* sore.

She slid out of the truck. Two aspirin were staying on top of it. She didn't do much more than coffee in the morning on workdays, but Mick's presence had inspired her to bake muffins. She wasn't much on cooking, but she liked to bake. They'd split one as they'd shared coffee.

Coffee was his preferred workday breakfast, too.

He'd made good vegan eggs. *Better than hens.* His sense of humor was sideways, not full on.

She was still letting him go. Holding onto people didn't bring anything but pain, and he had a busy life, same as her. But going camping with him, having him for a few more days? That idea was growing on her.

Just because it happened far more rarely to her—maybe never—she wasn't immune to that besotted euphoria that happened when two people clicked. Noticing bird song, silly smile on your face. All that shit.

It would hurt when he left, but an intimate relationship with pain meant she didn't armor herself against its inevitable arrival. It would only suck the energy out of this.

Speaking of sucking. Last night she'd bound him spread eagle on her bed and edged him for two hours. Sucking on him, biting him everywhere. Riding him, denying him an orgasm by wrapping a strap barbed like a vampire glove around his balls and the base of his cock. The tiny needles had dug into his substantial erection, which never flagged.

When she freed his hands, just to see what he would do, he gripped her hips and gave her his strength so she could push herself down on him even more forcefully. It proved how much he loved seeing his Mistress get off on hurting him, losing herself in that pleasure.

She climaxed all over him, straddled his face and made him clean her with his mouth, then removed the strap and lay in his arms, letting him suffer another thirty minutes while she played with his cock, rolled his balls in her grip. Then she whispered in his ear.

"Come inside me, Mick. Gentleman's choice on position."

His chuckle was a chain pulled to the capacity of its links. "No gentleman here, baby." In a heartbeat, he'd turned her and was on top, gazing down at her with those intense blue eyes. Just enough time for the condom before he thrust inside her. She let her moans tell him how pleased she was with the power of his thrusts. She watched him groan through his own climax.

Afterward, she had him lie upon her, cradled between her thighs, as she trailed her metal claws up and down his back, slow and easy, dragging the sharp tips lightly over the sensitive areas.

"Like a feather," he'd muttered against her throat. Put his teeth on her throat and fell asleep that way.

Coming back to the present, she smiled, putting down the container holding the rest of the muffins so she could lift her arms to the sky. A full body stretch. She touched her toes, finishing the move to get the kinks out. When she strolled into the kitchen, Bastion waited with her coffee, his full mouth pursed.

"My, my. Is Sadists R Us having a half-price sale?"

"I'm just looking forward to increasing our bottom line today, for the benefit of TRA and my beloved boss, Rosalinda Thomas."

"I'm calling an ambulance."

She put the muffins on the counter. "Made from scratch."

"You *baked* for him?" Bastion's dark eyes shone. "When you unchain him from your basement, can we put him in mine?"

She laughed. Picking up her coffee, she headed for the back staircase. "Meeting in twenty and I'm running late."

"You're never late."

"I am today."

"Do me a favor and don't let your department see this side of you. They thrive on your meanness. They believe you shack up with Satan and dine on children."

"Don't worry. Terrifying them with my usual management style will only add to my good mood."

She paused. She hadn't told Mick yes or no, drawing out the anticipation, but that was that, and work was work. "Do me a favor and clear my calendar? I'm going to be out of the office for the rest of the week."

Bastion put a hand to his brow. "Catch me, I'm feeling faint."

"I'm not worried. The floor will catch you."

Her good mood lasted until she reached the top floor. Vera was standing in the doorway to Ros's office. When she turned in Cyn's direction, the worried set of her mouth had Cyn ducking into her office only for the time it took to put her coffee on the nearest flat surface. She hurried their way. "Abby?"

The other woman's gaze cleared, as if that hadn't been on her radar, which eased the tightness in Cyn's belly. "She's fine," Vera said. "She had a late start, but she'll be here for the staff meeting."

"Okay. So what's up?" Cyn peered into Ros's office. "Please don't tell me Matt had internal bleeding and ended up at the hospital. Though I admit it would make me feel marginally better about him kicking my ass."

Humor vanished at Ros's expression. Cyn saw anger, concern, and regret. A worry even deeper than Vera's. "You're sure this isn't about Abby? Where's Skye?"

"She's in a design meeting with her people. Come in and sit down, Cyn."

That one sentence told her that this was about Cyn. Was the anger and regret about her, too? Perplexed, Cyn came in and sat. To push down her automatic defensiveness, her readiness for a fight, she reminded herself of their friendship, how much they'd been through. But that mental assurance only went so far, so her tone had an edge.

"What's going on?"

Ros was doing that back-and-forth thing she did with her pen, a seesaw over her knuckles, the pen's front and back tapping the top of the desk. "About a week ago, I reached out to a contact to do more digging on Mick."

Cyn sat up straighter. "You did what?"

"Before your hackles rise, keep in mind I'll always do what I think is necessary to protect my family."

"I'm not going to do anything to harm this family," Cyn said, stung.

Ros leaned forward, her blue eyes shards of glass. "How many years will it take, Cyn, before you know you're *one* of that family? One of the people I will do anything to protect?"

It brought her up short, but she knew the answer. Ros did, too. *Why are you still fighting like you think none of those things are safe, that they'll disappear tomorrow?*

Because it had been Cyn's experience that, as soon as someone else's life mattered more than her own, Fate took them away from her. Either physically, or by revealing a side to them that killed her love and loyalty as effectively as death itself.

Cyn met Ros's stare and went with the only answer she could face right now, without knowing what was going on. "Why didn't you tell me you were going to check into him?"

Ros's gaze shifted to Vera's, then came back. "I wasn't looking for your permission, because I didn't need that. But I intended to share what I found with you, whether innocuous or not. If you wish to hear it. That's your choice."

Ros had her hand tented on a folder on her desk. Mick had told her what he was into. She didn't need to see it. But what if what was in there was something he'd left out? A lie of omission, or because he wasn't ready to share it. If it was the latter, hearing about it would be a breach of privacy. If the former…

As Cyn stared at the folder, she expected a whole nonverbal conversation was happening around her. But she understood that. Cyn finally looked up at her boss. Perfect makeup, hair curled close to her finely made shoulders. Pen set aside and fingers interlaced on the desk.

"Okay."

Ros opened the folder and spread the information out. Cyn saw photos, plus reports on official-looking agency letterheads. The picture on top was a surveillance photo from a restaurant. Mick was having dinner with three men, and he was smiling, toasting the man to his right. Ros tapped the man with her manicured nail.

"He was convicted of human trafficking two years ago, a few months after this picture was taken. He's part of an organization that convinces women in other countries there's work here. They bring them in, take away their passports, brutalize them and put them to work in the underground sex trade."

Cyn picked up the photo and gazed at it as Ros continued, watching her closely. "Law enforcement groups have noted Mick's connection to the human trafficking trade. Though they have no concrete proof of his direct involvement in criminal acts, they've deduced he's a logistics person for the distributors. A problem solver."

Vera touched another of the reports. "They have secondhand reports that he's ensured human cargo gets over the borders in Mexico and Canada, as well as through other access points. He meets routinely with traffickers all along the distribution chain."

Anger flashed through Ros's gaze. "It explains why he's good at event planning, juggling details and adapting to last minute crises. A BDSM event is nothing next to this."

Cyn fanned out the other photos. More of the same, Mick rubbing elbows with different suspects, from high placed players to middlemen, based on the captioning and support data. He didn't stand out. Same well-dressed, understated look, professional and pleasant demeanor. Just businessmen meeting and networking. *Casual business attire just works better for most things I do.*

No one would suspect what they were doing, which was the whole point.

She remembered Mick's terrible story, about sipping drinks while a billionaire raped a teenage virgin.

"Cyn." Vera had sat down in Ros's other guest chair, her proximity a sign of support, probably for her and Ros both. "This has got to be devastating to hear. We're so sorry."

"Except for Tiger's instincts for criminal behavior, nothing about Mick supported this." Ros set her jaw. "We liked him, Cyn. We liked him for you. Skye wants to have him skinned alive."

"I'm sure Tiger can arrange that," Cyn said absently. "With Lawrence and Neil for backup. Neil is particularly good with a knife." She picked up another report, one from New Jersey PD. She saw his rookie picture, the young cop earnest and serious. He looked only a couple years younger than when they'd first met. Staring into his eyes sent a jolt through her, past and present gripping her in a short bout of paralysis.

"He was originally a police officer in New Jersey," Ros said, summarizing the material for Cyn. "Though he officially resigned, he was suspected of being dirty. Taking money, making the contacts that led him where he is now."

Vera gestured to the information. "Nothing can be pinned on him. He's been pulled in several times, and they've tried to flip him. He insists he's a club party planner. No amount of threats can rattle him."

"He's an extreme masochist," Ros scoffed. "Of course threats don't work."

Cyn rose and moved to the wide panel of windows, gazing out at the branches of the live oaks. Tiny ferns grew in a line along one, and a squirrel was scampering among them.

So cute. That was the usual reaction to seeing a squirrel. She thought about the things Mick had told her, under the duress of a session or simply while holding onto her.

"Have you ever thought about a squirrel's life?" she mused. "The daily struggle to feed herself, not be hit by cars, eaten by a cat or hawk. Relocating every time her places to forage and nest are cleared to build houses. And when she bears young, she has to keep them safe from countless predators."

She watched the squirrel bounce forward to meet another squirrel.

"Most people we know can't imagine what that's like, what it does to you to be on guard all the time. You can find pleasure in life, in a good meal, in a warm place to sleep that's reasonably safe, but you never count on it lasting."

Proving her point, the two squirrels chased each other around the tree. They found time to play. Live. Because ten minutes from now, it might all change.

She thought of Mick sleeping in her backyard hammock, how he'd opened his eyes when she touched him. She'd read his gaze without him saying a word. *You're my home, because you might accept. Accept what no one else can. Or maybe should.*

Over the few years she'd been working for TRA, Ros's confidence in her judgment had been tested, because their business approaches were very different. Just like their styles of sexual Dominance. But what formed them, the foundations, were similar enough to help them…accept.

A lot of what she was about to say wasn't going to make much sense, but their world was permeated with that, wasn't it? Needs and cravings most people didn't understand or acknowledge. As a result, understanding wasn't always the primary goal. Acceptance was enough.

Acceptance was a gift beyond measure.

She turned and met Ros's gaze. When they'd crossed paths, Cyn had been struggling to feed herself. Ros had never treated her as if she was superior, though. She'd recognized her as an equal, a fellow Mistress. And Cyn had grown into that expectation. She honored that bond now.

"I understand that squirrel's life. Everything I get, for however long I get it, is a gift. I find what I'm looking for in the men who meet me in a world of pain, stay with me there until we both can draw an easy breath and face the world again. You gave me that, when you introduced me to that world. But it was Mick who planted the seed, a long time ago. He was the first man to drop to his knees for me."

Even if, at the time, it was an emotional submission rather than a physical one.

"I need you to believe in my judgment on this."

Cyn could see her boss weighing all of it. Vera was digesting it as well, and when she and Ros at last met gazes, they had an accord. "All right," Ros said. "Then we do."

Cyn let out a breath she hadn't realized she'd been holding. But now she had another choice to make. Mick said his life and the lives of others were in her hands. She'd still be respecting that, because she knew she could trust these women with the information.

Cyn moved to the door and closed it. Returning to the guest chair, she sat down and tapped the photos. "This is a cover. A really deep cover. Whoever dug this up for you, you can't tell them that. Mick is leaving in a few days, and he won't be back."

She cleared her throat over the words. "If your contact asks you about it, tell them that I sent him on his way, thanks to their info."

Vera looked at the scattered documents. "I do trust you, Cyn, but this…wow. How long has he been doing this?"

Too long, I think.

"About eight years. The cop part is true, though not the dirty part. Ten years ago, Mick saved my life. Not in some dramatic way, like pulling me out of a burning building, but he pulled me out of the natural disaster of my life. Gave me the means to get out."

Her finger was passing back and forth over Mick in the photo. Noticing Vera's bemused glance, she stopped.

"I know you wonder why I've never told you everything about my past. It's not about trust. It's about things it took me a really long time to pack up and put away, and once I got them there, all I want is to see the dust accumulating on them. No need to look at what's in them anymore."

Even if what was in those containers was toxic waste that still affected her heart and soul. But that was why she balanced that waste with what she valued in her life now.

"You asked when I'm going to realize I'm part of this family." She met Ros's gaze again. "Probably never. My history, what's in those packed suitcases, makes that nearly impossible for me. But your trust means everything. And I trust you two, Skye and Abby, more than I've ever trusted anyone in my life. Except him...and my sister."

She filled in the blank, because anticipating the question was like waiting for a fired gun. "She died a long time ago."

Vera's eyes darkened in sympathy and Ros's mouth tightened, but showing their awareness of Cyn's current state, neither pursued that further. Instead, Vera put the contents back in the folder and slid it to Ros. "So he's not a villain. He's a hero."

"He doesn't see himself that way." Cyn straightened. "Remember when I said not to be kind to him, because it would break him? To do what he does, he has to be like the other monsters."

What was in the file, what he'd told her, said he'd accomplished that, enough that he had accepted he *was* one.

Accept could be a double-edged sword.

Cyn saw the import of her words sink in. "That was why Tiger picked up the bad guy vibe from him. For Mick to do his job, do good, he has to allow a lot of bad to happen in front of him. Has to participate in that bad."

Her gaze shifted back to Vera. "Don't ever call him a hero where he can hear you. It would tear him up inside."

They understood. When a sub carrying a lot of pain was opened up, experienced Dommes knew coddling wasn't always the right way to handle it.

"Are you okay with it ending in a couple days?" Ros said.

"It's the way it has to be."

Vera's concerned look toward Ros made Cyn's brow furrow. "What? Why?"

Ros laced her fingers on the desk. "You're not going to like hearing it."

"Since when does that stop you from saying any damn thing to me?"

Ros's lips twitched. "True enough. Let me say all of it, though, before you react as I expect you will."

Cyn sat back, crossed her legs, straightened her back and folded her hands on her knee. "I've grown as a person these past few days," she informed Ros. "Let me have it."

Ros's amused expression settled into a more serious mien. "Over the past several years, Abby, Skye and I have each committed our lives to a man we wanted. All three of them brought a common thread. Each changed our view, irrevocably, of what we wanted. Of who we weren't willing to live without.

"Each man seems to understand the things we want, the care we need, in ways we don't." Ros's lips tilted ruefully. "Though he won't be hearing me admit it, that includes Lawrence."

Vera gave Cyn a significant look. Cyn looked between them, then understanding dawned. "Oh, hell no. You are way off base."

"If that's the case, why do you look as if you were thinking of someone who makes you feel just that way?"

"I was thinking of Bastion," Cyn retorted. "He knows just how I like my coffee, which is as intuitive as I need a man to be. Mick and I crossed paths again all of a couple days ago."

"It took Lawrence and me only a few days more than that. Though Abby and Skye had Neil and Tiger in their lives longer, when they turned their eyes in that direction, the connection happened almost immediately."

"We're not going down this road." Cyn wagged a pointed finger at them. "What you're talking about is a fucking romance novel fantasy, and I don't waste time on that shit. If Lawrence has given you things you didn't even know you wanted and needed, that's great for you. But, no offense, if I haven't taken the time to figure out what I want and need from a man, I sure as fuck am not going to inflict myself on him as a Domme."

"So is he what you need?"

Her declaration was intended to shut them down, but she should have known better. Ros excelled at inserting full stop questions into her pricklier observations. Not denying her assertion, but giving her a different perspective. Even so, she was way off base on this one.

"When it comes to a man, I don't think of what I need and want beyond the time it takes to cut him from the herd and find how compatible my wants are with his needs," she informed them.

"So you don't think about what you need?" Vera asked.

"If I want it, that's what I go after. The whole point of working my ass off is I no longer have to focus on needs. They're covered."

She rose. "My project managers are probably getting a carb coma from the baked goods Bastion brought for them. Are we good here?"

Ros and Vera nodded, but exchanged another look. This time, Cyn decided to ignore it. "Good. After today, I'll be out of the office for the rest of the week. Mick is taking me camping before he gets back to his life. I'll fly back to NOLA. Bastion will make the travel arrangements. I'll have my cell."

Vera's brow reached her hairline. "Camping?"

"In his motorhome. No crapping in the woods or anything ridiculous like that."

Cyn moved to the door, but when she reached it, she paused. She owed them more.

"I'm all right," she said. "I appreciate you being my friends and family. Protecting me, and Mick."

When she let her gaze move to the folder, Ros anticipated her question. "My contact told me to destroy the information. We'll say nothing, Cyn."

"Thank you." Her phone buzzed. It was Bastion's heads up that the client had arrived. "Shit. Gotta go."

Ros opened the folder to look at the top photo. Mick's disturbingly genuine smile, as he shared drinks with a lowlife responsible for untold amounts of suffering. "Another reason I believe her is how much I want to. I like him."

"We all do. That's been another commonality as well, hasn't it?" Vera observed thoughtfully. "Each man, even before it's settled between him and the woman in question, feels like he's destined to be part of our family. When he leaves, it's going to affect her profoundly. She's already bracing herself."

"She knows we know that." Ros sighed and stabbed her pen into her desk organizer, creating another tiny hole. Bastion replaced it about once every three months. "But that isn't what we need to worry about. The two of them aren't going to be done after that trip."

"How do you know that?"

"You're asking me questions you know the answer to."

Vera grimaced. "I was hoping you might have a different opinion."

Ros shook her head. "He's the one for her, Vera. I feel it. So do Skye and Abby. Even Tiger, Neil and Lawrence see it, which is why they haven't run him out of town on a rail."

Vera glanced at the folder. "There's no happy end to the life he's living. Tiger barely got out of his family's MC in time. But he wasn't an undercover agent, trying to save people's lives. This is a calling, not a job. How do you walk away from work like Mick is doing?"

You don't. The response lay between them, unspoken but weighing heavily on their hearts.

"Cyn already knows that, too." Ros dumped the information into her shredder and hit the on button, grinding it into confetti.

When Dale had instructed her to do that, his reasons had been chilling. *"You don't want this data connected to you. These people have a long reach."*

"I'm glad I didn't have children," Ros grumbled. "You all give me enough sleepless nights."

Vera reached over the desk and patted her hand. "My money is on Cyn to figure this out. She conducts scenes like an interrogator. Or a treasure hunter. She gets as up close and personal with a man's soul as his chosen god. Or goddess."

"Don't let her hear you say that." Ros gave her a tight smile. "She reacts to the spiritual stuff the same way she does to 'romance novel bullshit.'"

"We've always believed what's in her past is better left undisturbed, until she wanted to share it. But we've also never seen her with a man who seemed like it would really hurt her to let him go. That could open up a lot of things."

"Like an earthquake." Ros tapped her pen again. "Figures the man she finally wants to keep is the one she can't without endangering herself or others. She knows that, too, which gives her all the more reason to let him go. Damn it, she deserves a shot at it, just like the rest of us."

Vera pursed her lips. "If we're right about who they are to one another, we're overlooking the important part. If he's been doing this that long, then he needs her, too. Badly."

Ros nodded. Cyn's love expressed itself by protecting, providing. Not by leaning on anyone herself. But that didn't matter. "So we be there for her, because she'll never ask. And whether she realizes it or not, she's reached the limit of what she's prepared to lose. Let's be ready to back her up, however she needs it."

CHAPTER EIGHTEEN

She was in a motorhome at a godawful early hour of the morning, heading for Texas.

Instead of the comforting sights of cheek-to-jowl buildings or mobs of people headed to work via trolley, car or on foot, she was on a rural highway where farms, marshland and dense stretches of forest surrounded the road. She smelled cow manure and nature instead of beignets from Royal Street or the pungent morning-after filth of Bourbon.

She'd lost her mind.

She felt mildly better when they passed through small towns. Skye had mentioned such places when she took motorcycle trips with Tiger. She often left her Harley at home, preferring to ride on the back of his, resting her hands on his waist, pressing close to him, her legs on either side of his hips as they leaned into turns together.

Cyn understood the appeal of that part, just not the locale. However, as Mick navigated through the narrow streets of a town's postage-stamp-sized "downtown," she noticed a woman sitting at a card table outside of Mindy's Kitchen Diner. The black woman wore a faux leopard stole, her hair in a fuzzy top knot. Thick-rimmed glasses reflected the early morning light and obscured her eyes.

The sign attached to the table with masking tape announced she did tarot readings. The letters had been hand drawn with markers, surrounded with doodles of flowers.

Houses lined the main street, flanking businesses like Mindy's. One single-level clapboard house was a storm away from falling down, with rotted porch boards and a roof covered with a blue tarp. Nearly twenty sets of chimes swung from the eaves of the lopsided porch.

I'm here, the owner seemed to be saying. *And who I am is more than you think.*

Cyn thought of where she'd grown up. Her neighborhood, the apartment. Her mother, who'd been exactly what anyone would have thought she was. Or worse.

Her mother had never hung up a chime, or anything symbolically like it, in her life.

Cyn lowered her window. Tentatively, she put her hand out, letting the breeze pass through her fingers. She rested her other hand on her hair to keep it out of her face. When she glanced toward Mick, he was watching her. He gave her a light smile, then returned his gaze to the road.

He liked looking at her. Of course he did. She was a good-looking woman with the kind of body that attracted male attention. But that wasn't why he was looking at her like that. Which was why it flustered her. Absurdly so.

She'd never acted like a crush-infected teenage girl. Even at that age. She wasn't starting now. "So where are we staying tonight?"

"I reserved a spot at an RV park. If you're up for it, there's a festival happening about twenty minutes away from it. We should be able to spend the afternoon there, grab a late lunch, then head for the campground."

"I'm not much a festival person."

"You've never done a New Orleans' Mardi Gras?"

"Of course I've done Mardi Gras. That's different. You're talking about a small-town's version of a festival, with funnel cakes, a rickety Ferris wheel and Jack and Diane walking around with their hands in the pockets of each other's jeans."

"Versus flashing your tits for beads and drinking so much you vomit in the gutter."

"I have done neither of those things at Mardi Gras."

"How about the rest of your ladies?"

"Ros has us sign NDAs to prevent that kind of information from getting out."

He grinned. "This festival is for exotic flower enthusiasts. Specifically orchid nerds."

"And you just happened to be surfing the national schedule for orchid-related events?"

"I had to make sure I had additional ammunition to convince you to come with me," he said, "so I did a little research about what was happening in the area."

She studied him. "You're lying to me, Mick. Why?"

He put his eyes back on the road. "Some things, I can't tell you the reasons. There are people I have to protect."

"You're meeting a contact there."

He didn't confirm or deny. "I already had it on my radar as a stop. After seeing your greenhouse, it seemed to fit together pretty well."

Apparently realizing how that sounded, he lifted a hand. "It wasn't why I asked you to come with me. I wanted as much time with you as I could get."

Before he "really" had to leave her. Hearing him acknowledge it rattled the ton of rocks she'd piled on top of her own feelings about it. When he glanced her way again, she wondered if her eyes had the same look as his. Resignation mixed with a fierce desire to have what little they could grab together.

"I would never take you somewhere you'd be in danger," he told her. "But if that was a possibility, I'd make sure you had all the information you needed, so you wouldn't be going into it blind. Yes, it's a contact, but that's all I can say."

A faint smile crossed his face. "His interest in orchids is the real deal. He's also big into roses."

Cyn settled back. "Don't lie to me again, Mick. About anything. Big or small. If you can't tell me, just say you can't tell me. I'll respect that." Or try to.

"Yes, ma'am. You look sexy as hell, by the way."

She'd chosen belted boot cut jeans and a short-sleeved gray shirt with a loosely laced V-neckline. The words *Rock and Roll* printed on the shirt were surrounded by red roses. Her square-heeled boots had a strap and silver buckle at the ankle. One leg was bent, knee leaning against the door, her

341

elbow braced on the window as she looked over at him, still holding her hair back from her cheek and mouth. "No picture taking."

"I keep my pictures here." He tapped his forehead.

"None on your phone?"

"Not of people."

So no one could piece together his movements or real identity. Or hurt people he cared about.

"In this line of work, you have to stay two or three steps ahead of the bad guys," he said, confirming her thoughts.

"So there's nowhere in the world you store a photo album with pictures of your parents? Old report cards or a teddy bear from when you were a kid?"

"No," he said seriously. "I burned it all or gave it away. Everything I own is in this camper."

"So what's with the Precious Moments collection?"

"I visited the chapel once, when I was passing through Missouri. Those half dozen pieces...they're just innocent, feel-good stuff. It's the *Untouchables* movie line. 'Some part of the world still cares what color the kitchen is.' It's a reminder, why I do what I do. Call it a meditation focus. They ground me when I get a little uneven."

He nodded at the glove compartment. "Closest thing I have to a photo album is in there, if you want to take a look."

She found a sizeable stack of postcards. As she put them in her lap and flipped through them, she saw they were from all over. No personalization, no handwriting on the backs.

"When I first started doing this, I thought about figuring out where you'd landed," he said. "I was going to send them to you as I made my way back and forth across the country, into Mexico, Canada, South America. My handler told me that was a really bad idea. But I kept buying them, putting them there."

He lifted a shoulder at her look. "A lot of nights, when I'm eating dinner and don't feel like TV, I take those out and flip through them. Imagine you in each one of them."

342

He said such things so casually. She made herself match the tone, even if the confession rocked her.

"How long have you been doing that?"

"Since I had about a dozen of them. I'd had a particularly bad day. I was in a hotel room that night—this was before I bought the motorhome. I put them on my chest, held them there. Then I started to look at each one and picture you there, and the kind of stuff we might have done together."

That half smile returned. "The good news is now I don't have to feel like a perv, having those kinds of thoughts about someone who still looked like a teenager in my head."

Every moment they spent together was going to make parting more difficult. But...fuck it. She unfastened her seatbelt, crossed the space between them, and put herself in his lap.

"This is unsafe," he said. But he shifted his legs so she could settle deeper into his lap and put her head against his neck, her arms around his shoulders. She propped her chin on one and gazed into the back of the camper.

"You aren't usually the affectionate type, Mistress." A rough note was in his voice.

She wasn't. But she wanted to touch him, often and a lot. And she could, because he belonged to her. At least for now.

She stayed in that position for a half hour, just resting upon him without saying much as the miles passed under the wheels. When he told her they were close to the festival town, she went back to her seat. They cruised down Main Street, passing under a banner that proclaimed *Welcome Orchid Lovers. Eighth Small Town Orchid Enthusiast Festival.*

"STOEF," she noted.

"Yeah. The people who organize it call themselves Stoeffers." He winked at her. "It moves around. Whoever wins top prize for their orchid gets host town location for the next festival. So this is home to last year's winner. It's become more popular with each one. Which, given how niche this is, means a few hundred people instead of a few dozen."

"There's no way you know this off the top of your head," she decided. "You've met your contact at one of these before."

"The moving around is a plus, and he really likes his damn flowers. Like someone else I know."

She arched a brow. "Is he married? Good looking?"

"Solidly married and looks like a mud puddle. Oh, and he's at least a hundred years old."

"I like older men." She gave him a look. "Perv."

He pointed a warning finger at her, though his lips tightened against the laugh. "I'm not that much older than you, woman."

Mick pulled into a parking area, a field adjacent to the local high school, the setting for this year's festival. He opened his window to pay the parking fee in cash. An elderly man in a bill cap, wearing jeans and a festival T-shirt, stepped up to take the bills. "Where you folks hail from?"

"New Orleans," Mick answered.

"My wife loves it up there. Have to take another trip that way soon." The man gestured toward the football, baseball and soccer fields, populated by tents and other event structures. "There's a raffle benefitting the local hospital, if you want to buy some tickets when you go through the front gate. There's also a general plant sale under the big tent."

Cyn leaned over Mick. "Any Monkey Faces?"

The man beamed at her. "They're always popular. Get yourself over to the sale early, you might be able to snag yourself one, but some of the growers are here too. You can place an order if they don't have any with them."

He sent them toward large vehicle parking. Once Mick found a spot, he switched off the ignition and glanced her way. "Monkey Faces?"

"They look like them," she informed him. "I have one that's white, but I'd like a brown one, too."

344

He preceded her down the steps, giving her a hand to the ground before he locked up. "You never stop surprising me."

Thinking of the postcards, she decided the feeling was mutual. She shifted behind him and, with a quick squeeze of his shoulder for warning, she hopped up onto his back for a piggy-back ride. When he grasped her legs and gave her a heft, she wrapped her arms around his chest and bit his ear.

The easy places for her to explore were pain and darkness. Playing in the light, being flirtatious, was new, but she was willing to risk it with him.

"For a woman with your muscle tone, you're surprisingly light," he commented.

Or he was particularly strong. "I have hollow bones," she informed him.

"Ah, like a turkey vulture. That makes sense."

She pulled his hair. He didn't stop her, and carried her with amiable ease, his hands sure on the crooks of her knees. She didn't feel the need to get down until they reached the first tents. There were trucks for food and drink vendors, and portable restrooms. On a music stage, people tested equipment for the local entertainment lineup, starting in the next hour. Comments drifting their way suggested there would be dancing.

Because it was early, most of the current attendees were dedicated enthusiasts who wanted to beat the crowds to the vendor offerings and have ample chance to talk to the growers showcasing their efforts.

Maybe she qualified as one of those, because she fell into conversation with the woman operating the first booth they passed. She lived in Mississippi, so she could speak to breeding and care of the flowers in a hot and humid climate.

Mindful of the parking attendant's warning, Cyn moved on before too long, though she intended to come back. She headed for the big tent sale area and was delighted to find a Monkey Face orchid in a speckled brown color. The stamen, which looked like a snout, was a rusty red. The grower had put it in a crimson pot, the gold sticker of his nursery on it.

The tent staff agreed to keep it until she was ready to pick it up, and she returned to her explorations. For the next hour, she discussed soil amendments, light requirements, and the common and unique efforts others followed to help the unusual flowers thrive. While breeding wasn't her passion, hearing how new orchids were created or known varieties enhanced intrigued her.

Mick had different reasons for being here. But though there were benches and picnic tables, as well as groupings of folding chairs for people-watching and listening to music, he seemed content to stick with her. He followed the conversations, saying little, but he didn't seem bored or impatient; just the opposite.

She wasn't usually oblivious to the reason for a man's behavior, but a vendor had to clue her in. As she handed over a card so Cyn could order from her selection of fertilizers, the woman murmured, "He hardly takes his eyes off of you. I'd hold onto that with both hands."

Cyn offered her a wicked smile. "Good advice. He's definitely the two-handed size."

The vendor's startled look was followed by an appreciative chuckle and conspiratorial wink. She also offered Cyn a complimentary bag of allium bulbs.

When Cyn stepped away, Mick had brought her a Dr Pepper. One of the beverage vendors had a fountain drink set up and added her preferred cream soda flavor, just like a drugstore. As they continued to wander, they shared it.

Orchid growing attracted a range of personalities, which made it even more suitable for Mick's purposes. No one really stood out as not belonging. Even Mick looked like the patient boyfriend, indulging his girlfriend's more learned interest.

However, when she sat down for a short presentation on winter care for orchids, he excused himself with a brief squeeze of her shoulder and a quiet word, telling her he'd be back.

She followed him in her peripheral vision, noting he was sauntering casually toward a specific booth. Once there, he stood next to a man talking to the grower. A few moments later they walked off, as if he and Mick were together, and Mick had caught up to him.

He'd told her he couldn't tell her much, which meant she shouldn't pry. Even so, she'd marked broad shoulders, dark hair threaded with silver, khaki slacks and a navy-blue shirt. Clothes of good quality, and he projected the carriage and confidence of a man with money, a trait she'd learned to identify early in car sales.

She returned her attention to the workshop, but her mind wasn't on it. Mick had assured her there was no danger here, but he hadn't said whether this contact was someone like him, or the people in the photos. Human traffickers could have hobbies. She didn't like having him out of her sight.

The workshop concluded a very long fifteen minutes later. As she rose from her chair, thinking she might "casually" go find his ass, she saw him returning.

Mick handed her an origami flower shaped like the Monkey Face she'd bought, even down to the white and red colors. "A woman was making these," he told her.

She twirled it. His face told her nothing, but she felt tension from him, as he processed whatever information he'd gained.

Though it wasn't in her nature to be agreeable when she was out of sorts, adding to his concerns would help nothing. She linked an arm in his. "I'd like to see the booths on the south side, then I'll be ready for lunch. How about you?"

His expression cleared, as if he'd been braced to deal with attitude. He knew her well. "Yeah. There's a good place in town. They have vegan dishes. Even vegan desserts, if you want to indulge yourself. I *did* research that."

"How I like to indulge myself? Or vegan options?"

"The latter. I'm figuring out the other as I go."

She chuckled and walked with him toward the south side booths. Once there, she pointed him toward a bench built around a giant live oak. A nearby sign said, "Whittler's Bench, 1957." It was currently occupied by a man doing just that, carefully carving on a piece of wood.

"Take a moment to work through whatever's going on in your head. No need for you to stand attendance on me while I talk about the same stuff you've already heard six times."

"I'm fine."

"Yes, you are. Go sit. Work the problem." She placed a hand on his chest and looked up at him. "It matters to me, that you're prepared for whatever comes after I leave. I don't want to hear something happened to you and wonder if it's because I distracted you. That would piss me off."

He put his hand over hers. "Two things. First, I do my best problem solving under duress. So maybe you'll figure out ways to help me with that, later tonight."

"I'm not known for being intentionally helpful in those circumstances."

"It's a side benefit." But he stepped back, willing to follow her direction, even if gratifyingly reluctant to leave her side.

"Mick. You said two things."

He shook his head. "I shouldn't have said that."

"But tell me anyway."

He sighed. "If something happens to me, you'll never know, Mistress."

"You don't think anyone would come looking for you?" The idea made her impossibly angry, though she did her best to keep her voice even.

"I know it. Because that's the way it has to be." He met her gaze. "If they send people in to look for me, it blows my cover and the op I had in motion, which might have a chance of being seen through."

Detecting her reaction, he closed the space between them again, and touched her face. The firmness to it wasn't submissive. This was the pure alpha, who could take the reins if needed, even if it wasn't his preference with a Domme like her.

"I know you'd look for me, Cyn. I'm telling you no. You understand why I don't carry pictures in my phone. Don't risk people for my life. I gave up that choice a long time ago. Don't give me something to carry on my soul, eat away at it, the way worrying about you in my world would do. And don't let that get into your head and ruin what you have."

"And what's that?" she asked tightly.

His look reminded her of the commitment he'd made to her, but his lips curved wryly. "This beautiful day at a flower festival."

She pointed to the bench. "Fine. Sit."

He complied, but only after giving her hand another squeeze. A hard one. He sat down on the bench, legs braced, arms crossed over his chest as he leaned back against the tree. The man whittling asked him something, and Mick responded with a short answer and friendly smile. The man grunted and went back to his whittling.

If the elder had stories to tell, as his appearance suggested, he'd be telling them to Mick before she came back. When he wanted to turn it on, Mick had that quietness that encouraged people to offer him what was in their heads.

She found herself reluctant to move away, but made herself do it. The next grower she visited had made the drive from Oregon. After examining his samples and asking him questions, she went to peruse his plants for sale he'd set on several nearby tables, carefully protected from the Texas sun with a sail shade.

A few moments later, she noted she wasn't alone. Raising her head to look across the table, she met the gaze of the man Mick had been speaking to earlier.

He had the same stamp of attractiveness Matt Kensington had. Rugged authority and a palpable aura of charisma matched eyes that could penetrate steel. The shade of brown, infused with the filtered golden sunlight, was almost amber. They reminded her of a tiger's.

The stillness in them was also like Mick's. Was that watchful quality something people in the intelligence and undercover worlds had to cultivate?

Mick didn't have the usual triggers, which was why it was hard to recognize his strong submission needs until the right stimuli brought them forth. This man didn't suffer from the same issue. His orientation operated on a level impossible to miss, particularly by those who had it themselves.

He was a sexual Dominant. Which meant he likely understood things about Mick that she did, though she knew their connection had never been sexual. Mick's cock was responsive to women only. This man projected the same solid hetero vibes.

He had another kind of vibe, too, and if she was right about it, she was moderately less wary about being this close to him. *This* was his handler, which meant he was on the same side as Mick. Hopefully on Mick's side, period.

Maybe she was about to find that out, because there was no way this was a chance meeting. However, in case she was wrong, she purposefully continued toward the next group of plants, a display-only selection of orchids, protected behind plexiglass. After several seconds, the man moved with her, ambling to the other side of the table.

His attention wasn't as singularly occupied as hers was, because when he examined what was before him, his gaze brightened as if he'd found treasure. "Come see this." Genuine excitement was in his voice, as rich and masculine as spiced brandy.

They were within a stone's throw of passing festival goers, and the grower and his assistant were keeping an eye on their area. Probably to facilitate a sale if someone had a question or interest. Or to ensure no one tried to reach over the clear barriers to touch the display flowers.

In short, if she was wrong, she was reasonably safe.

Said every murder victim before they ended up dead.

Still, since she was rarely if never in a cautious mood, she came around the table and stood next to him. When she followed his gaze through the plexiglass, she drew in a breath, sharing the same amazement he'd expressed. "Shit. How did he manage to grow that here?"

"With a lot of care. Maybe an ironic deal with the devil."

It was an Angel orchid. Usually grown terrestrially only, it was very difficult to pot, but somehow this grower had managed it. The Angel orchid's native world was India. She wondered how it felt, being so far from home.

The petals looked like the wings of angel. Inside those petals was the cowled face, as well as what looked like a woman's breasts. Oversized, but that might increase its appeal for a male enthusiast. Like this one.

This is the real deal for him, she recalled Mick's words. The man had a cleft in his chin, and the fingers resting on the edge of the table were strong and capable. His ass was as rock solid as Dale Rousseau's, a retired Navy SEAL Master Chief who was close friends with Ros, and had once led Neil and Lawrence's team.

Also the likely source of intel on Mick.

"Have you ever seen one of these in real life?" the man asked.

As two hobbyists, the two of them could certainly interact without incurring suspicion. She shook her head. "You?"

"Once or twice, in India on business. I wonder what he'll take to part with it."

"I'm betting he won't. I wouldn't. Unless I was sure you'd take very good care of it, value it like he has."

Those amber eyes met hers. "Perhaps. Do you know what they say about water and orchids?"

"You never overwater them."

"Yes. That keeps it simple. But it's more than that." The man backed up a step and propped his hips against a stack of wood pallets. The shirt pulled across his shoulders as he crossed his arms over his chest. "You don't put it on a rote watering schedule. You pay attention to what affects the flower, what kind of light, humidity or potting mix works best for it. Even the air movement is important. Every detail, every nuance matters, and it can change from day to day. Those details fit with another passion in our lives."

He'd crossed his ankles, and because she was her, she noted what the movement outlined in the groin area was more than capable of stretching a sub's eager lips. But his words drew her attention back to the amber eyes.

"When you're inflicting pain on him, you're watching every reaction, aren't you? Everything that's going on inside him. I'm not a sadist, not to that level, but that kind of attention?" He nodded. "That's what nourishes us. Isn't it?"

CHAPTER NINETEEN

She held his gaze for a couple beats. Rather than replying, she moved toward a bench placed at the rear of the tent. A conversation there wouldn't be overheard, and behind it was a gravel service road the festival vehicles had used for setup. The grower's truck was pulled to the side, parked behind the bench.

The Angel orchid lover might just wander on, and that would be the end of it. But he came to sit down next to her. The man moved as good as he looked. He had that in common with Matt as well. And Mick.

"I don't know your name," she said.

He extended a hand. "Tyler Winterman."

It gave her pause, not just because he offered it so easily, but it was familiar. The reason eluded her, but she shook his hand, like business associates. He had a warm palm and strong grip.

"Cynbad Marigold. Though you know that, I bet. Why did you tell me your name?"

"He wanted me to tell you, and give you a number to call. If ever you need to know his status, you can use it to reach out to me. I'm a safe contact."

"He wanted to make sure I don't go looking for him in the wrong places, and if I get worried about his whereabouts, he knows nothing would keep me from doing that."

Tyler lifted a shoulder. "Submissives know their Dominants, as we know them. It's a closed circle. My sub is a switch, a formidable Mistress in her own right. My angel."

The weight he put into those two words, the endearment, told her why he was interested in purchasing the flower. "To get anything past her takes a great deal of subterfuge," he added. "I've laid my heart at her feet. The effort of hiding something from someone I love so much is too difficult. Eventually, it's just unimaginable."

"His whole life is subterfuge."

"He excels at it," Tyler agreed. "I don't give out that kind of praise lightly. He's learned how to twist lies and truth together so well no one can tell the difference. Except him. He never confuses the two, the most remarkable thing of all. His conscience would be a lighter burden if he did."

Tyler stretched an arm out on the bench behind her, not as a come-on, just something a big man did to get more comfortable. He also had a quality that made the gesture a protective reassurance. An offering, if she was willing to trust it.

Buddy, you're barking up the wrong tree for trust.

But he was giving her information. She didn't know what Mick had told Tyler it was okay to say, but she was going to find out, with the question most important to her.

"Everyone has a breaking point. So, Dom to Domme. How close is he to breaking?"

Tyler's mouth tightened to a firm line. The acknowledgement stabbed her like one of her own knives. In the heart, the gut. Scraping her throat raw, making it hard to speak for a few moments. Tyler filled in the silence.

"First, you're asking me a question I suspect you already know the answer to. You're looking for reinforcement from the informed perspective I possess. Second, I'll expand on it, if you give me an honest answer to a question of my own."

"My lack of tact, otherwise known as my honesty, is legendary."

His lips twitched, but his eyes kept that piercing look. "Are you his Mistress? You understand what I'm asking."

She did. She could conduct a thousand sessions at Progeny, have a million orgasms, but he was the first man who'd coaxed her heart into the equation and kept it, making it his and no one else's.

She hadn't told him that. But he knew. The bastard knew her, just as she'd told Vera. However that had happened, it was simple truth. Same as the answer to Tyler's question.

"Yes."

"Good. He's needed that, for a very long time."

Tyler took out his phone and made an adjustment on it. "Blocks listening equipment," he told her. "The risk here is minimal, but I prefer to stay vigilant."

"I'll watch your back." Cyn gestured over his left shoulder, past the front of the parked truck. She could see anyone approaching from that direction, something Tyler couldn't do unless he could owlishly turn his head a hundred and eighty degrees.

She received an approving look, but Tyler got right to it. "Shutting down trafficking operations involves a number of agencies, informants, and a hell of a lot of work and frustration. For an undercover operative, it requires steel nerves and an armored conscience buried deeper than three stacked graves. Mick is one of the best I've worked with."

"I thought you didn't work for an official agency."

Tyler shook his head. "Not anymore. I did for many years, before I went to the private sector. I maintained the contacts and resources that allow Mick's work to bear fruit, without being actively engaged myself, connected in ways that can come back to my life and family. It's why you and I can have this conversation, though your discretion is important. Your life and mine have intersecting points, in the BDSM world and business. Ros and I have met in both."

Cyn blinked, surprised. "She doesn't know…"

"No. There are always guesses about my background, but even those who know more about that believe I'm fully retired. And for all intents and purposes, I am. But what I can put to use for active people, I do. This is one part I can still play, that I desire to play."

Tyler rested his ankle on his opposite knee, his hand draped loosely on his calf. "Over the past eight years, Mick's work has been vital to identifying important vulnerabilities. That intel has shut down trafficking routes, resulted in the arrests of key operatives and the seizing of their funding sources. On top of that, he's done it without blowing his cover, and saved countless future victims."

Tyler paused. "Those results require tremendous patience, and a sizeable investment of time and energy. They require people who can play the long game. He's had to watch people suffer and die, because his job wasn't saving them. It was making sure it couldn't be done to others."

"He told me."

"Yes." Tyler looked toward the orchids. "But I'm sure you know there's no way to fully understand it. We can do what ifs. What if you learned a plane is going to go down because of a terrorist. Three hundred people will die. Men, women, children. Mothers, fathers, sons, daughters. People with plans, lives, who laugh, cry, and who are loved by countless people on the ground. Every one of whom would beg you to save the plane and curse you to hell, want you dead, for doing nothing when you had the means to stop it."

The words surrounded her as the ghosts of those people would. "But in this hypothetical situation, if you do stop it, you lose access to the terrorist's funding source, a network supporting a dozen more plots, some even worse. Do you let the plane go down?"

He shook his head. "No official agency can stand up to that kind of scrutiny. Nor should they. But it's required of confidential informants and free agents like Mick. The depth of his cover has brought us that level of intel, at those kinds of costs."

He paused, his eyes moving to lock with hers. "To this day, he will ask if an op accomplished what was intended, but he won't let me tell him the details of who has been saved, what specific horrors have been prevented."

"Because there are types of pain even a masochist can't bear," Cyn said, remembering what she'd told Vera about calling Mick a hero.

Tyler's expression shadowed. "He says no ends will ever justify the means, not to those whose suffering he had to disregard or exacerbate with his actions. He says if I want to incapacitate him, fuck with his head, I should tell him he's done a good job. So I bite my tongue. I don't add to his load. We're fighting a hydra. Every one of them we shut down, others crop up, because trading on human misery for sex and labor has been going on since well before biblical times."

She rolled that over in her mind. "So what's the answer to my question, Tyler? How close is he to breaking?"

From his earlier expression, she knew his response, but it still hit her hard to hear it aloud.

"It's time for him to come out. He's at that point all deep undercovers reach. He's starting to cannibalize himself to keep going. Statistically, his odds of getting his cover blown are also getting higher, no matter how damn good he is."

"Why don't you pull him out?"

"It's not my call. It's his. Neither of us is officially working under government authority. If I told him I wouldn't back him anymore, he'd just keep doing it, doing what he can. So I will back him as long as he refuses to quit."

"But you've told him it's time."

"In several different ways." Tyler's flat expression reminded her of Mick, cloaking deeper and darker things. "He'll either figure it out, or become a casualty. An unknown hero, only remembered by the angels."

"And me. Who's nothing like an angel."

"There are all kinds of angels. I think he needs someone like you in his corner." Tyler's faint smile returned. "He could do a hell of a job advising, heading up a task force, letting fresher minds and souls wade into the shit. I've told him that, too. So far, deaf ears."

Tyler rose and pulled out his wallet, removing a business card. The conversation was about to be over.

When Cyn took it, she started. "I *knew* your name sounded familiar."

She was a little disgusted with herself for not immediately recognizing it. However, what that name was associated with in the business and BDSM world hadn't been a ready fit for an undercover handler at an orchid festival in Small Town Texas.

A lot like imagining a cop in a New Jersey cemetery as a kink event planner in New Orleans.

Tyler Winterman. Old Georgia wealth, co-owner of several BDSM clubs and executive producer of erotic films. Hell, Skye had done the visual tech for a recent NOLA charity function where one had been previewed.

"The best cover is a highly visible one," Tyler told her. "Especially when it's my actual job, a field I entered after I left government employ. It was that thought which made us decide to nudge Mick toward event planning, to pay for his gas and lavish lifestyle." Tyler's gaze glinted. "It was a pleasure, Cyn."

As she accepted that parting handclasp, she had one last question. "How do you know he needs someone like me?"

"He's never chosen a Mistress to keep." Tyler's intent look would have woken a dead woman's libido. "And you appreciate orchids."

×

When she returned to Mick, he was still at the Whittler's Bench. His arms were crossed over his chest, eyes closed, while the man talked to him. He nodded every once in a while, making a comment or two.

As she approached, his eyes opened fully. He said something to the man, shook his hand and came toward her. His expression showed obvious pleasure at her reappearance. Nothing else. No awareness of what she'd been doing, who she'd been talking to. Damn, he was good.

"I'm ready for lunch," she told him.

For the rest of the day, it was as if that interlude with Tyler, that part of Mick's life, didn't exist. She honored his obvious desire for that, and enjoyed the unfettered pleasure of it herself, but what Mick had *not* asked Tyler to discuss with her stayed in her mind.

It's time for him to get out.

The RV park was a nice place, as he'd told her, with vending machines, bath houses and a pool. After they set up at a campsite on a perimeter spot and shared a light dinner, Mick suggested lighting their fire pit. Despite the warmer daytime temps, evenings could get chilly.

He'd put out two camp chairs side by side. They enjoyed the fire and looked up at the stars. He'd brought her a beer and had his legs stretched out, head tipped to the side as they talked about a lot of things.

She told him about her arrival in New Orleans in the battered Cadillac. He shared things he'd seen on his travels. Out of the way locales with interesting characters, like the man beside him on the Whittler's Bench.

"When I was in tobacco country a couple years back, a guy I met had a fully functional Henry Ford car in his shed. Took me for a ride. Everyone has a story. You figure out their story, you figure out a way to connect, a way to get in. Just like anything else."

After taking a sip of his own beer, he glanced her way. "When you're handling a new sub, it's that way, isn't it? Finding the way inside them, figuring out what makes them tick. Faster, slower. What will make the ticking stop altogether."

His fingers shifted, laced with hers. From the weight in his regard, she knew he'd purposefully given her an opening, if she wanted to talk about things.

"When you told me what you really do, I had the sickest feeling inside," she admitted.

His eyes darkened. "It's pretty awful stuff. I'm sorry. I dumped it on you."

"You wanted me to understand what happened during the CNC. That wasn't what made me sick to my stomach."

She let go of him and drew her feet up on the chair, linking her hands over her knees. It was a defensive posture, but she'd decided what she was going to do. She just needed to find the courage, the shovel, to dig it out.

"You okay?"

"Yeah. But don't touch me." She wasn't looking his way, but she'd felt him straighten, about to reach out, reacting to the strain in her voice.

She tried to control the churning in her gut. *Stop delaying before you puke. Get it the fuck out.*

The power of suggestion could be a bitch. She bolted out of the chair and barely reached the bushes before she lost most of the dinner they'd shared. Well, shit. She'd have preferred not to taste the recycled version.

He was behind her. "Don't touch me while I tell you this." A plea this time, not a command. She despised the panic she heard in her own voice. "Promise me."

"I promise. But I want to hold you."

She shook her head, and he didn't press it. "You want to come inside? Lie down?"

"I can't do it in there. Don't want to." This story needed room. Needed the heat of the fire, the darkness. She didn't want to fill an enclosed space with it. "Let's go sit back by the fire. I can tell you now."

"Do you need to?" His voice held concern. Care. "If it's for me, I don't need anything bad enough to put you through this."

She wiped her mouth with a trembling hand. "Some sadist you'd make."

"Never claimed to be one." He stayed close as she returned to her chair. Though he respected her desire not to be touched, he brought her a damp towel to wipe her face and a fresh bottle of water to rinse her mouth. He sat down next to her. "I liked when you were sitting in my lap while I was driving. Lap's here if you want it."

"Cradle your Mistress? Is that the reverse Daddy Dom thing you were talking about?"

"Just an offer to hold you, Mistress. The way a woman needs and sometimes wants to be held."

She rubbed her hand over her face. Stared into the flames. She let the visual take up everything so her stomach wouldn't heave again. Or heave as much.

Why she was doing this, what track she was planning on following tonight with him, this was an important part of it. Holding onto that purpose helped.

"My mother would have babies and sell them." She said it flatly. Just got it out there. "To the highest bidder."

Mick went still, but she kept going. "Maybe it was a rich couple who couldn't adopt the normal way. Maybe they gave my half-sibling a pampered life. I'd tell myself that. Even knowing it was far more likely to be someone who wanted to groom the baby from birth for some horrible, twisted need. The buyers in that market pay even more, if you have the right trafficker to find them. She did. I met him. He wasn't anything a desperate rich couple wanting to be parents would have touched with a mile long pole."

"So you see," she said in a painfully offhand way, "my mother was doing what you fight against. And me and my sister Cissy helped her."

She needed him to listen, to witness. Not to comfort, and fortunately, she was with a man who understood that. *Don't touch me when I talk about this, because every drop of glue I've used on myself will disappear. I'll break into a million pieces.*

"My sister was born with brain issues and an underdeveloped arm, so my mother couldn't get a premium price for her. She was seven years older than me, and when I came along, my mother had learned the benefit of having live-in child labor. Cleaning, running to the corner store. Helping to take care of a pregnant woman, and the baby, for the short time we had it after it was born."

She took another breath. "Cissy wasn't stupid. She actually liked fixing things. If there was something wrong in the apartment, she could figure it out. Or when I was little, she'd fish broken toys out of dumpsters and put them back together for me."

I fixed it, she'd announce. Every time. It was their inside joke, a comforting little ritual between them. *I fixed it.*

Cyn closed her trembling hands into fists. "I was supposed to be another sale, but my sister got attached. Like a doll or favorite pet. For whatever reason, my mom said, 'Fine, we can keep this one. For now. She'll earn her way when she's old enough.'"

Mick stayed silent, like the forest around them. Maybe that was why he liked places like this. No judgment, no words. Just the peace and detachment nature had.

"She changed her mind about that when I was three. The trafficker had a buyer interested in someone my age. I don't remember it clearly, but Cissy told me I bit him when he came to look at me, hard enough to draw blood. Cissy also threw a fit, which she almost never did. She was so gentle. So docile."

Cyn paused. Her nails were biting into her palms.

"Cyn."

She shook her head and continued. "Cissy doubled her efforts to teach me how to be useful. Things like cleaning the house, brushing my mother's hair, doing her toenails. If you've ever been pregnant, you know what a bitch that is."

A ghastly attempt at sarcasm. *Goddamn it, hold it together.* "Me and Cissy ran the household, let her sit on her ass and be pregnant. We would care for the babies together when they came, until they weren't there."

"You had one arrest on your record. The baby formula."

"Yeah. We didn't have friends. No one from the outside came into our crap apartment. When I first went to school— she didn't let Cissy do that, since special needs kids require too much parent interaction—Mom had figured out how to keep me from drawing attention. She said if I brought the school to our door, they'd put me in a dark hole. After I got too old for boogeyman stories, she said social services would take me and Cissy away from each other and I'd never see her again. Classic prisoner conditioning. Once you get bars and locks embedded in the mind, you can leave the cell doors open wide. Monsters seem to be born with the skillset. Like there's a class on it."

"Yeah." His voice was tight.

"She'd disguise her pregnancies so nobody in the building knew. She just looked fat. A midwife who got a cut would deliver the babies, until Cissy was old enough to learn how to do it. Saved Mom the extra money."

Cyn had taken off her boots and socks, and adjusted one foot so it pressed against the heated concrete around the firepit. It was way too hot, but she wanted to hold it there, feel the burn reach the bone.

Mick slid out of the chair to kneel in front of her, gripping her ankle and drawing her foot away. He put it on his thigh, his hands on the arms of her chair, bracketing her. "No," he said.

"You aren't the only one who craves pain."

"I know. But that's why you have me. To channel yours so you don't take it too far."

What was in her chest grew so uncomfortable she thought she might stop breathing. But she needed to get this out. So she closed her eyes and sat back, her arms folded over herself. She put both feet on his thighs, curling her toes into denim. He'd worn jeans today. The man looked really good in them.

"I grew up with the looks Cissy didn't have. When I was twelve, Mom said she wouldn't send me away, but I had to earn my keep. Cissy begged, pleaded." Cyn paused. "I told her it was okay. That she didn't need to protect me. That it was inevitable, and at least we could stay together."

She pressed her lips together. "She asked me what inevitable meant. I told her that something couldn't be changed, no matter how much we wished otherwise."

She thought of that picture on her landing, the blonde dancing with the street musicians. Whenever memories of Cissy were too painful, that was where she went in her mind. She held that picture now, to keep the other from coming into her head. It wouldn't work when she had to say it, but it helped her get out what had happened before then.

"The man my mom whored me out to did take my virginity, but he wasn't brutal about it. When Mom was pleased and got a good payday, she'd give Cissy an extra share, and we could get some things for ourselves. I thought about that, during. Forty-eight hours later, I did something I've wished all my life I'd done forty-eight hours earlier."

Mick had heard it all before, same kinds of stories, all different kinds of people. But hearing it come from her lips, he thought the rage he contained might break the universe.

He'd known her life was rough. He'd remembered the gang tattoo, her wild animal fear, and lack of trust. He hadn't imagined this.

When he'd first reached for her, that recoil, the genuine fear he might try to give her physical comfort, had nearly torn him from the frame.

Whatever she'd done to be who she was now, whatever clay she'd come from that had made her bite a pedophile at age three, hard enough to make him look elsewhere, couldn't accept comfort in such a way. So he did it in a way she could. He stayed on his knees in front of her, listening. Keeping between her and the fire pit. He had his hand over the foot she'd tried to burn. A light touch, but there.

Tentatively, she put her palm on his shoulder. Her fingers curled in to grip his shirt, an anchor he thought.

"When I got home, I was excited," she said.

"He'd paid me a $100 tip, telling me my mother didn't need to know about it. Gave me a wink, our secret, and said he hoped to spend time with me again. I didn't think about any of that. All I could think as I took the bus home was that Cissy and I could go shopping. Mom was off somewhere. Don't know where."

Her gaze moved past his shoulder to stare into the fire. "I ran up the stairs. Cissy was in the bathroom, and I banged on the door. 'Let's go shopping.' She didn't answer."

Her grip was so tight the fabric pulled at the collar. Her nails dug into the scar she'd put upon him. He didn't move. He took her pain, just as he said he would.

"She'd run herself a bath, sat down in it in all her clothes, and killed herself. She was done. She wrote 'Sorry' on the mirror. 'I can't fix it.'"

He saw something waver damn close to breaking in her expression. It almost made him ignore her demand for space, then she pulled it together, and got that hard, brittle look he remembered too well.

"She'd reached her limit. But I had, too. When Mom came home, and after we handled Cissy being picked up, I told her I'd remove the dick of the next person who touched me without my say-so. She gave me a day to grieve, to see if I'd come to my senses. When I didn't, she said I had to bring in money, or I could get out. So I got out."

She took a steadying breath. "Sold my body a few times, on my own terms, then found the underground fight world." A feral smile touched her mouth. "I got beat up pretty bad the first few times, thinking I knew about fighting. Fingernails and biting were my fallbacks when I didn't know anything else. But I learned how to move, use my brain along with my fists and feet, and started winning."

She brought her attention back to him, easier with this part, which told him the worst was over. It wasn't much comfort. "I worked odd jobs, some legal, some not, whatever was needed. I was too mad to have a plan. I ate at soup kitchens, took showers at the Y. Tried the gang route, but thank fuck I was smart enough to realize that was a dead end, soon enough to get out. My mom had an abruption a few years later, and died. The baby with her. You know the rest."

Leaning forward, she touched the skeleton necklace against his skin. "Cissy always wanted to go to New Orleans. She had a Pete the Cat storybook, and liked the picture of him sitting on the lamp at Jackson Square. So when I got into the Cadillac, where to go was an easy decision."

"I can't believe that old beater made it that far."

"She had a tough heart." Cyn's fondness for the car was obvious. "Reached the city limits before the engine started wheezing. I pulled into the nearest garage, which was attached to a used car dealership. While they were determining the estimate of what I couldn't afford, I started talking to someone who was looking for a car. I gave them good advice and steered them to the right vehicle. The owner was watching me. He said I had a knack for sales, and before the conversation was over, I had a job. He gave me a piece of that commission, enough to rent a room, and I went from there."

Some of that broody expression returned. "You asked me why I was vegan. People don't think about the cow, herded up a chute, waiting to be stunned and killed, then hoisted up by her legs. They do things to keep her calm, you know, unaware of what's happening. Because it can affect the meat." Her lip curled. "But before that, she was eating in a pasture, hanging out with other cows. She didn't know that she was always just meat. All our siblings who were sold for whatever sick fuck's purpose? We were just meat. That's all we were."

Cyn's expression grew murderous. "I heard Mom say once, 'If a person is raised a certain way, they don't know any better, don't want or need anything more. Like saying a bird in a cage doesn't know it's meant to fly. Fuck her and fuck that. Whatever created us doesn't take that away. We can find it again if we get the chance, see the path, follow it. I found it. I did."

"Yeah. You sure did." He anticipated her, shifting out of her way as she pushed out of the chair to pace to the other side of the fire pit. It was mostly embers now. She stopped abruptly and looked up at the sky. Her hands had remained clenched through most of the story. He wanted to open her fingers, massage her palms. Press his mouth there in comfort.

She wasn't ready for that, but he rose and came to her side. Not touching, but close. Standing at her back.

"Cissy was so upset that night, before I went. I got impatient with her. 'Whatever, some guy is going to stick his dick in my hole. I'm not going to let it touch me in here.'" Cyn beat on her chest. "Because of the hundred bucks and that wink, I almost felt benevolent toward him."

She shook her head. "Pissed me off so bad with myself that two days after she killed herself, I found him, jumped him with a bat and whaled on him. No idea if he lived or not, and don't really give a shit, honestly. He was a piece of shit paying a mother for her twelve-year-old's virginity, so you know, him being gentle and polite doesn't really balance that out."

Cyn was coming back to herself, enough to hear the New Jersey street kid emerging in her voice. It was always there, ready to be called. Ready to infiltrate her dreams.

She took a beat, recalled her surroundings. Where and when she was. "I think about Cissy every day," she said slowly. "I talk to her sometimes, too. She was my older sister, but as I got older, I took care of her just as much as she took care of me. Still…"

Her voice got a little unsteady, but she didn't try to stop that. With Mick, it was okay. "I know she thought of herself as my mother. And she was, in all the ways that mattered."

She turned to face him, so he'd know she was pulling herself together. Enough to turn that feeling in the direction she'd intended all along. Toward him.

"What you said earlier, about me not knowing if something happens to you. And not wanting me to try to find you. I understand you're protecting me. And how pointless it would be of me to try, who I could endanger, beyond myself, if I did."

She fixed a fierce gaze on him. "But one thing you better carry with you, Mick, is that you matter to me. You are bonded to me. So if it's possible, you damn well show up at my door again. Whether it's in a year or ten years. When you can be present in my life, be present. I respect the vow you made me, but truly? I don't care who you've been with in the meantime, whoever gives you what you need to get through. In the world you and I have been in, sex can be an act of kindness, a respite when you need it most. But your heart and soul, those are mine and mine alone. Right?"

"Yes." His face had taken on that expressionless look, the one that those at the club found unsettling. But she understood it better now. It meant he was feeling things strong enough he had to use that look to hold it together.

"So come back to them when you're ready. But no matter how often you come or go, they stay with me."

A ripple disturbed that flatness. He looked down at his hands and nodded. Cyn put her hand on his arm and he covered it, squeezing, but then he eased back. She wasn't the only one who had a hard time being touched when exposing raw wounds.

"Mick, do you ever think about stopping?" She kept her voice neutral.

"I did at one time. Not anymore. There's this point you reach...the way I'm embedded takes years to accomplish. So who loses if I stop? How long will it take someone else to reach the level I have? I told you they haunt me, Cyn. What will they do to me if I'm no longer doing what I do?"

His gaze showed the ghosts. "I'm destroying myself with this. Tyler sees it, same as I do, and he's been a good friend. But so what? I'm not some suit working a dead-end job, or a soccer mom not self-actualizing, or whatever buzzword psychotherapy bullshit you can slap on it. People's lives are on the line."

His jaw hardened. "I don't give a shit about self-care. There are things in your life where that just can't matter. Where you find the strength to go on based solely on why you're doing it. Not because you remember to take ten minutes of 'me' time, or whatever narcissistic bullshit someone wants to call it. 'Well, gee, Mick, I really want you to take care of yourself, so don't worry about me.'

"That second girl I had to fuck? She was pulled out of a rice field, her whole world now drug addiction and servicing men in a ten-by-ten room. But hey, the most important thing is I get to live *my* best life. Right?"

She wanted to argue with him. But she didn't. Instead, as absurd a comparison as it was, she thought of what Ros said about TRA's clients. What did they need? What information would help them understand why a marketing strategy would or wouldn't work for their business to succeed?

"The wear is showing, Mick. If they tried to force you to have sex with a kidnapped girl now, could you do it?"

His face told her the answer. "Glad to hear it," she said softly. "Because when they cut pieces off your soul, you have to hide them somewhere, to remember who you are, or at least give them a proper burial. The alternative is you hand them away and become soulless." She gave him a penetrating look. "Which do you think you've done?"

His harsh laugh startled her. "I hid the pieces with the person I never expected to see again."

Emotion obscured everything for one erratic breath, a hard triple thump of her heart. She gripped his shirt front. "You've lost too much of your soul, even if it is in someone else's keeping."

"Your keeping," he corrected her.

"You're going to slip up, get killed. Maybe get others killed at the same time."

That had an impact, as she knew it would. Pointing out a client's vulnerabilities. "So here's the question. What do you need to keep doing it, staying smart, sharp and never losing sight of the goal? That you're doing it to save future people, so they don't end up where that girl did."

When the problem was difficult, she didn't ask easy questions, not in session, not in her professional life. Not to her friends or family. "Tell me what you need, Mick. Your Mistress requires an answer."

"I need a home to go to." His gaze latched onto her like the cuffs she put on his wrists. Not as a restraint, but as an unbreakable bond. "I need to know I can always go home."

She weighed that against what Tyler had told her. Looked for the balance. "So you've told me what you need. You know the next question."

His eyes sparked. "What do you need, Mistress?"

"I need you to always come home. I need to not lose you."

As his arms enclosed her, she put her cheek against his forehead, her arms wrapped around his shoulders. "All right," she said. "Take me to bed, Mick. Give me pleasure. Work your ass off for me. Earn your right to be home."

A shudder went through him. "You got it, Mistress."

CHAPTER TWENTY

She led the way into the motorhome. Feeling him so close behind her, she knew something different was called for. She wasn't yet sure what, but it was part of the challenge, letting her intuition craft their direction, while the man submitting to her control provided creative inspiration.

"You remember the night I asked when you last took a deep breath?" She turned to face him.

"Yeah."

"You didn't answer."

"I watched you do it. It didn't seem to go so well."

"Let's do it now. Together."

He gave her a reluctant nod, and they tried it. It went the way it had for her the first time, a lot of weird catches, as if too much was in the way. She thought he found it the same, so she moved closer and laid her hand on his chest. His hand rose and laid upon hers, stroking her fingers. His head was down, thoughtful. "Again," she murmured. "Eyes closed. Both of us."

It was easier. As if they were clearing the path, widening it through that joined touch. Another breath. Drawing it in, pulling it up, her fingers tightening on his chest, his hand constricting over hers.

"Again," she whispered.

Twice more. The last time, there was a different note to his, a rasp. His fingers convulsed. He let her go and stepped back. "Works better when you're hitting me with something. I never forget how to breathe then."

Light filtered in through the high windows, sketching the planes of his face, the set of his eyes. Her intuition got a big spike, in a very surprising direction. So surprising she hit the pause button and thought, *Really?* at whatever was pushing it.

Yeah, really, came back, loud and clear. *But you'd better tie him down, because he's going to fight you like hell.*

They'd been to extreme places together, at least from the perspective of people in their world who didn't travel down those roads. But the two of them didn't necessarily need those extremes, not in this moment. Maybe just the opposite. What they needed was the knowledge there wasn't a "too much" for them. In either direction.

Demons weren't driven away by darkness, were they?

Like that prison rape scene, with him as guard and her as prisoner, taking control, what she was considering was something she'd imagined. Something flirting around the edges of her central fantasies, because when it became more than that, she'd shied away from it, not trusting why it held such allure. Its appeal freaked her out some.

But a session with a sub was like a scavenger hunt, and she'd learned the first image that hit her at the starting line was usually the right clue. However, she agreed with her subconscious on how he might react to it.

"Bring me two sets of handcuffs, Mick."

During the drive, she'd considered her options in the limited space. So as he retrieved her club bag from where it had been stowed, she was already changing the height on the table, raising it.

She took the cuffs from him before she stepped out of reach. "Take off your shirt, and put your chest on the table, hips to the edge."

After he pulled off the shirt and laid his upper torso on the table, she noted he could manage it with a slight bend of his knees. It was why she'd adjusted the table to the height she had. That position would get uncomfortable over time, but not too much for the period she intended him to be in it.

She clicked a cuff over one of his wrists and pulled his arm out to the edge of the table. She let the free cuff dangle and did the same to the other arm on the opposite side. He had his cheek against the surface, his eyes tracking her movements. She scraped her nails over his back, watching the muscles respond, his shoulders flex. He shifted his legs, drawing attention to his delightful ass, but she held off on her desire to fondle, for now.

Pulling a coil of rope from her bag, she ran one end through the empty cuff on the left side of the table. Going to one knee and ducking under, she pulled the rope over to the other dangling cuff and drew it through until the bright orange band she used to tell her when she'd reached the mid-point of the rope was centered.

When she drew out the slack, the chain clanked against the table as she pulled his arms out further. She knotted the rope, then tossed the two ends on the seat cushion. Emerging, she retrieved those ends. As she did so, he perused the stretch of her upper torso, the curve of her ass.

"I should blindfold you," she said.

"You're mean."

"Thank you, Captain Obvious."

A smile touched his lips, though his gaze remained steady upon her. Intense. He'd be expecting where she'd take this. He'd be wrong. Anticipation was building inside her as she crossed the rope ends over his nape and shoulders, taking them through the cuffs, which made their hold on his wrists tighter, having to share that space with the rope. She brought it over his lower back and waist. One more loop under the table to hold down his hips, bind his thighs, and she slid what remained between them, back to that first knot under the table.

As she cinched it, it brought the rope against his denim-covered testicles, enough pressure and separation to get his attention. She put her hand there to confirm it, petting and pinching the firm sac. She heard the chain rattle again, felt the quiver of his inner thigh muscles against her wrist.

The table's support pole was more than sturdy enough to hold him. Even a man as strong as Mick wouldn't get it to budge if he yanked against it, though he could probably rip the tabletop loose. The way she'd bound him, it would be difficult to get the leverage, but she wouldn't discount the possibility. The man was strong.

But he would only do that if he felt that threatened, or wanted to take the fight to that level.

"During the time we've been apart, I've been becoming the Mistress you really need. Which means ignoring what you want."

He didn't need physical pain, not right now. He needed something far worse, more excruciating. Thinking about how much more gave her gut a hard kick. She wouldn't want to face what she was about to do to him.

Except she was going to. With Mick, nothing felt separate. Not what she did to him, not what he experienced and gave back to her.

Putting her hand in the center of his back, she slid it down toward to his waist. A caress. "Such a beautiful man. Such a gift."

She spoke sincerely. Gently. Reverently.

Mick's gaze rolled around like a horse who'd just discovered he was shut in his stall with a wolf. As her hand moved over the curve of his ass, sliding into a jeans pocket to massage and enjoy, she leaned forward and kissed his shoulder.

"What are you doing?"

"Whatever I want, Mick. You're mine. Your heart, your soul, your body. You said so. Shut the fuck up and let me enjoy them, or I'll gag you."

The cuffs scraped on the table as he shifted, but she ignored that. She put her mouth on his upper torso...everywhere. Soft, teasing licks and kisses. So slow and easy. Taking her time. Not once did she use her teeth. She murmured to him, told him how remarkable she found him, how much she wanted him, how much she needed him.

With every kiss, every loving word, the violent energy in him grew. When she glanced toward his face, his eyes were blue warning lights. He spoke through gritted teeth. "Stop."

"You have a safe word," she said indifferently. "Use it."

Though if he did, she was going to ignore it. *Far as I'm concerned, CNC is status quo for us.* She'd take him at his word. If he used a safeword, it wouldn't be a medical emergency. It would be his attempt to control things, stop where the session needed to go. Where he needed to go.

She intended to cut him open. When the poison poured forth, he'd be waterboarded by his feelings. She was going to let him know she had him. All of him.

"What do you know about sadists, Mick? Tell me."

His lip curled, showing a hint of those gritted teeth. "You latch onto what your sub doesn't want. What he fears most. I told you I want pain. Not fear."

"And I told you I don't give a shit what you want. This is what you fear. Gentleness. Kindness. You didn't expect to ever have to put up with this from me, did you?" Her tone got cooler. "But I'm not here to perform for you. You give me all of you, or nothing. What I want is what matters. Ask me what I want, Mick."

He shuddered as she kissed his shoulder blade, following the X cut she'd made on him. He had a death grip on the edge of the table, and she heard it creak alarmingly. "What do you want, Mistress?" His voice was grim. A threat, rather than a question. She ignored that, too.

"To break you into a thousand pieces, boil them down, drink them in, make you a part of me, so I know every single dark space inside you. This is a very dark one. The darkest. Pain and violence armors you, but tenderness and praise from your Mistress…that's a reminder you don't get to have any armor with her."

Imposing it on him, watching how it was breaking him apart, infused her sadistic side with a deep joy. While the woman in her, the one who had so many feelings for him, stayed watchful, telling him with her touch, *You're all right. You can be an ugly, hot mess, a dangerous disaster. I know how to handle all of it.*

"When you let me go, you better be able to fucking run."

She laughed against his skin, nuzzled him. "If you catch me, overpower me, you know what will happen. You'll back off and kneel to me. Which is what you should do. Always."

Instead of gripping his hair as he might have expected, she stroked it and blew a playful breath into his ear. "Because I own you, Mick. Don't try to control me. You try to fit me into a mold that you can handle, I'll always see that coming. You wanted a Mistress who can see you. I see you, Mick."

"Fucking bitch. Let me go."

She slid her hand under his hips to run the heel of her hand over his cock. Caressed and teased. "Hate me, Mick. Chase me. Try to catch me. But I'm not the one running. You are."

He bucked against the table then, almost dislodging her. "Don't do this chickenshit soft stuff. Why are you doing that? That's not what you want or like."

"Telling a Mistress what she wants and likes." She made a clucking noise. "That always goes over well."

It was a newbie mistake, which told her he'd never let himself go down this road. If a Mistress had tried it, misreading him, he'd been able to detach, politely thank her for the session and seek one out who'd give him the physical pain he wanted.

He couldn't detach from her. He hadn't from the first time he'd met her. She finally saw it, knew it, owned it.

Gloried in it, even as it tore her to pieces and remade her.

She kept kissing him. Featherlike touches of her mouth, easy caresses over every scar, old and new, ones she'd inflicted and ones he'd earned other places.

The quivering increased, and he cursed her in earnest, trying to keep his mind from being dragged where she was taking it. He couldn't. He was no more immune to her knowledge of him than she was to his.

It started to kick in, that reaction a man couldn't stop. Something inside would crack and then break loose. They'd howl, fight, sometimes panic, but it would very quickly be replaced by rage. That was the kind of man she chose. They didn't know the flight part. Only the fight.

She'd always stayed outside the wind tunnel, her goal to prove she could unlock the dark rooms of a man's soul before she quietly shut the door again, leaving him intact.

Not this time.

Because of that decision, her heart was breaking. It was taking all her focus to keep her hands from trembling and the ache out of her voice as she murmured to him. It stabbed her soul, seeing his desperation go beyond what he could contain merely because he couldn't bear gentleness. Or care.

Nobody understood a hardcore masochist's relationship with pain the way a sadist did. Like an artist did the art, or the cop did the criminal. And vice versa. They understood one another in a way no one else ever would.

He was still cursing her, but his voice cracked. His body bowed upward as if his spine was hardening, drawing him in to himself. The table groaned as his hands gripped the sides and his legs pushed upward against the ropes, the chains. She'd distributed them correctly, though. He couldn't get enough of a leverage point to break anything.

Except himself.

"It's all right." She laid herself over his back, standing between his spread legs, hips against his iron taut backside. She stroked his hair, her mouth by his ear. "It's all right, Mick. Everything you are is in my hands. It's safe. Trust me. Be mean, be angry, be violent. It doesn't matter. You come back to my hands. My care."

My love.

"I can't...I can't take any more. It's killing me, Mistress. I won't safeword, but I can't bear it. It's the worst pain I've ever felt. Let me go. *Let me go.*"

The last part went from a plea to a snarl, a demand, and his teeth snapped close to her cheek. She raised her head in time to avoid it, straightened and stepped back. She watched him struggle, fight the table. Snarl and shout at it. Curse it, curse her.

She waited him out, pulse beating high in her throat. When he stopped, his muscles were still rigid, his thighs trembling from the strain on his bent knees. His chest expanded and contracted, and he dipped his chin to find her, one hostile blue eye riveting upon her through mussed hair.

He was coming apart. When she put him back together, it would send the message that she was responsible for both states. She'd never been a nurturer, but it didn't matter. She would do anything to help put him back together. It would be her strength that would provide the glue, make him accept the loving with the pain. His phenomenal inner strength would help him bear the pain.

Her faith in that strength would help her bear hers.

"You done yet?" she asked, her tone neutral.

He pressed his forehead to the table. She saw perspiration on his shoulders. He nodded, though she knew he was lying, telling her what she wanted to hear.

Moving to her bag, she removed the strap-on harness and laid it next to him so he could see it. It was the one with the spikes embedded into the pelvic piece. She fitted a dildo into the opening, using her own mouth to lubricate it. She took it almost all the way down her throat, then back up again.

He was in a wild, broken state, but he was still in there, enough to appreciate the tease. She laid a hand over his. "Easy," she murmured. "It's all right."

She hadn't been careful enough, or maybe she'd wanted him to have the test. He latched onto her wrist, his grip as unyielding as his cuffs. "I can break your fucking arm from this position." His voice had that hair-raising coldness to it.

She pressed against his hold, brought herself right to his mouth and breathed on his lips. "Do it, then. Show me what a tough guy you are. I won't lift a hand against you, Mick. Am I not worth the same protectiveness as your little bird subs, because I'm a cold bitch of a Mistress?"

"Goddamn you." His facial muscles twitched, but his grip had loosened, so she pulled free. She'd have bruises there, in the shape of his fingerprints. That was okay.

She didn't mind bearing his marks.

Going under the table again, she released the rope between his legs long enough to slip the button of his jeans, work them and his underwear down to his thighs. His erection jutted out, hard and thick, and she teased it playfully with her mouth, tasting the fluid on the tip.

He groaned, jerked. Sent more creative oaths her way.

"You need to listen to your cock, Mick," she advised, blowing a heated puff of air on the sensitive head. "It's fine with anything I do to you. More than fine."

Because she wanted to experience that girth and length in a more tactile way, she put her mouth over it and took it down to the hilt, gripping the base as she sucked and tasted.

Just as she'd told the vendor. Two hands worked best.

His hips jerked against his restraint, trying not to thrust. Either he was being stubborn, not wanting to respond because he was pissed, or he had a submissive's innate understanding that he didn't ever thrust into his Mistress's mouth when she gave him the honor of putting her lips on him. He was probably telling himself it was the first, when it was more of the second.

She slid her mouth off of him and replaced the rope, this time without any denim protection. Indulging her normal inclinations, she put an extra jerk into the cinch, the prickly hemp pressing between his balls.

When she emerged, she donned the strap-on where he could see her. She noted anger, confusion and deeper things.

Moving behind him, she slid her hands over his ass, squeezing his buttocks, playing in the seam, then opening him up with her thumbs. She put one foot against the inside of his left ankle. "Spread for me," she said, "And lift your ass."

Slowly, his feet adjusted, and he complied. She bent and put her mouth on his buttock, teasing him there, too.

"Mistress."

It was muffled, the tone slightly less *I'm going to fucking kill you.* "What is it, Mick?"

"Will you...I know it's about what you want, and I don't direct this. But can you...bite me?"

He turned his head in her direction, and the glimmer of humor in his gaze, the stark pain, almost made her lose her resolve to see this through.

"No. Not right now." She pushed the slick head of the dildo between his buttocks, seating it at his opening. Moved in circles, spreading that oil, pushing in a little more each time, prepping the way for the train to head down well-greased tracks. "You don't do this that often, do you?"

"No."

She put her hand on his back, found the tension there. "Have you *ever* done this before me, Mick?"

He dipped his head to the right, away from her, and his fingers curled on the edges. "No."

"To yourself?"

"No. Don't...don't stop."

It wasn't the act making him more tense. It was the question, and what his answer revealed. He hadn't tried to hide it from her, and she gave him credit for that, because he could have, making it far more painful. What he wanted.

It added ammunition to her assault on his defenses. She withdrew and caressed his ass. Moved that touch up his spine, over every bump, the muscles on either side.

All hers. All of it hers. She thought that during a session sometimes, but when she did, it was always very "in the moment." Tonight she was forging a permanent chain. No matter where he was, no matter how far, the links would hold.

She picked up the lubricant and eased the tip inside him to apply more. She chose her anal lubricants like cooking spice. Her mildest form still had a faint burn. She considered it a "hair of the dog" thing, so the sub would be gradually prepped for her "hotter" oils.

Kissing the middle of his back, she put the head of the dildo back at his opening and began doing that circling again, the slight press forward.

"Just do it," he said, a hoarse growl.

"Keep trying to order me about," she purred. "I'll go slower."

She slid her nails over his buttocks, scraping his flesh, leaving more marks. She let the dildo slide out, then rubbed it up and down the channel between his buttocks, teasing his rim. Setting her teeth to his nape, she bit him, just as he'd asked her to do. A gentle, small nip.

A huff of frustration broke from his lips. She was able to push her arm between his bound body and the table, sliding across his chest, fingertips teasing his nipple and tugging chest hair. "Mistress…Cyn…"

"Shut up, Mick. No more talking. No hiding, no trying to direct things. What's boiling up inside of you is painful, terrifying. You want to prove you serve me? That you're committed to me, now and always? It's more than words. You accept it, face it, let it happen. And trust that as you go down that well, I'm holding the rope. I won't let it go."

A note vibrated from him, an erratic hum. It was from that song *Gone, gone, gone…* and then a snippet of that other one. *So caught up in you…* 38 Special.

Not wanting to get himself free of the "little girl" who had him down on his knees.

Her man used music to help him get through things. That was acceptable. She liked hearing the strain in the mash-up of notes.

She adjusted the dildo at his rectum once more and began to ease in. She'd had sessions where she'd forced it, torn sensitive but healable tissue. But that wasn't what he needed. More importantly, it wasn't what she wanted.

Fucking hell, he was tight. But it made sense. He had superhuman stress management skills, and that stress had to go somewhere. Apparently, it went into having an ass so tight it would give a pencil claustrophobia.

She started matching him with her own song. "Rainbow" by Kacey Musgrave. One night, while they all sat on Ros's back porch, Neil had been holding Abby on his lap. She hadn't had a particularly good day, and he'd been crooning it to her as the others talked and relaxed, cocooning her with the comforting proximity of family.

No matter how terrible life could get, no matter how many times the storms came back, there would always be the rainbow, there was always a port in the storm, even if you had to look for it a really long time.

Like ten years.

She made it that last inch, spikes pressed against his buttocks. "I'm inside you, Mick." She leaned against his back and gripped his strong throat, stroking his windpipe, squeezing as she drew back and returned, easing in. His powerful body was trembling, partly because his ass would be burning, partly for far deeper reasons. When she adjusted to put her other hand around his cock, he was stiffer and thicker than when she'd started.

She increased the force of her penetration and the spikes on the strap-on's panel pushed against flesh. Just like the cane or switch, a pause between pain and relief could intensify both. Now, at last, she'd give him pain, and see what battle it set off inside him.

She wanted a grid of her puncture marks on his ass when she was done. She started to thrust harder, short, firm strokes. It changed the impact of those studs on sensitive nerve endings. His breath got ragged as her arousal built, his back bowing as he pushed into it, head down.

"Christ...Mistress. Fucking hell..."

She put a palm in the center of his back, and he stopped pushing against her, registering the warning.

She pumped his considerable size in her hand as she kept fucking him. "You better not come, Mick. Not until I say so. No condom. You'll spew all over your nice couch and this floor. You'll be cleaning long after I go to bed to dream nice dreams of you."

That same desperate half chuckle answered her, but the note of it said he was floundering in the waters she'd stirred up. The spikes would help restore the tether back to himself, but what she wanted was him tethered to her. She slowed down, eased back so he couldn't feel the spikes and trailed her fingers down his spine. Slow and easy again.

His body stiffened at the decision, but rather than snarling at her, this time he drew that deep breath. It caught, shuddered, but he managed it.

"Good man," she murmured. "Rest. Just let it rest. I'm going to enjoy you, enjoy how close you are."

She drove in a little deeper, stroking her knuckles down his sides, and watched them heave like he'd been running. "Beautiful man. Gorgeous man. Heroic, strong, brave."

He froze. "Stop it. Don't do that shit."

"Would it be easier if I was mocking you? It's me believing it that bothers you?"

"It's not true. You know it's not...don't. Please." His back flattened out as he lowered his head, pressed it to the table. "Cyn...please don't."

She held him as tight as the length of her arm and the barrel size of his torso would allow as he shuddered.

It would have been better if he'd been at least a partially shitty person. Like she was. But he wasn't. He wasn't even a tenth of a shitty person. What was it Tyler had said, about how Mick handled truth and lies?

He never confuses the two.

"Okay. But one thing is true, Mick. You saved me. You're the hero of *my* story. That belongs to me, and you're not allowed to deny it. All right?"

He paused, went very still. She waited him out.

At long last, he nodded. Accepting that much.

As she'd expected, he'd pulled on the cuffs until his wrists were red. Blood seeped from the left one where the scraping had broken through. Since she'd had him in cuffs several times, and she'd done things that had made him fight them, every time, it was no surprise to see it.

She straightened and began to stroke in and out again. She kept his cock in a possessive, pinching grip, her free fingers digging into his balls around the rope. Both a help and a tease to that release that wanted to boil forth. The strap-on had a clit stimulator, and it was pushing her up higher, too. But it was his response to her, how he was coming apart and surrendering to her, that was the real stimulus. His pain was giving way to deeper feelings, beyond pleasure.

What was beyond pleasure? Bliss. Peace. A place to land.

She let the climax have her as she pumped into his beautiful ass, slamming those spikes against it. Her head tipped as she cried out, her body going rigid. She arched back, came forward, working herself into him until she took everything she wanted.

Satisfying, but not close to the intensity of the climax she'd give herself from other means.

Because of that, she didn't indulge the aftershocks. After she eased the dildo out, she unbuckled and set the strap-on aside. She released the rope from between his legs and removed the layers wrapped over his body. When she untied the knot holding his cuffed wrists taut at opposite ends of the table, she didn't unthread the rope from the bracelets.

"Lie down on the floor on your back, Mick."

It was an awkward descent, and she cupped a hand behind his head and put a hand at his waist. Making sure the former didn't hit the table, and to aid the strength of his aching knees on the way down. A concussion wouldn't suit her plans.

He was rigid with the effort to control the release pulsing in his turgid cock. She relished watching his struggle as she looped the rope around the center post to secure his cuffed wrists there.

Mick was stretched out on the floor, arms above him. He held onto the chain attached to the cuffs, his grip suggesting the links would leave marks in his palms.

She stripped off the rest of his clothes then removed her shirt, slow, letting her hair fall back to her shoulders, bare except for bra straps. She slid them off her arms, the drape pulling on the cups, teasing him with what was almost fully exposed.

"I like the way you look at me, Mick."

He was beyond words, but his need conveyed all the words she desired. She liked the hungry silence.

She slid her foot over his cock, playing with it, pressing on it, watching the flex in his thighs as he took the teasing threat and swallowed back a groan. Then she shed her jeans and filmy underwear. The only thing left was today's jewelry, her skeleton cross. She'd left his on him as well.

Okay, yeah, for the two of them maybe it was like the broken coin thing. She wouldn't tell him that, though.

She opened a condom and rolled it over his thick length before she straddled him. Gripping his cock and holding his gaze, she lowered herself, her ready, wet cunt taking him in. She caught her lip in her bottom teeth, enjoying his size, and wanting him to see that. Clutching him with her internal muscles, she dragged that friction along his length.

"Tell me how much you want to come, Mick."

"I want to see you come again first," he managed.

"You won't last that long."

"I want to last that long. I want to see you come in that deep...way you do. Where everything else...goes away, and it's just...you. And me."

She leaned forward, upper body bathed by his heated breath as she untied the rope and pulled it free from the cuffs. She sat back. "Give me your hands. Behave and be polite, or you get nothing."

His eyes still had that wild look, but the wry tilt to his mouth told her he had enough restraint not to leap upon her. When he presented his hands to her, fingers half-curled, a sign of his agitated state, she'd pulled the key off the couch cushion where she'd left it. She unlocked the cuff on his right hand and tossed that set to the side. She then unlocked the open cuff of the left side and bound both his hands together.

His fingers curled over hers as she did all of it, touching her however he could, but he stopped himself from gripping her. Trying to behave.

She strung the key on her necklace, her hands not entirely steady as she refastened it. Fortunately the act drew his gaze to the tilt of her breasts, because if he had noticed the trembling—and his hands hadn't been bound—she expected he would have tried to help her. He was like that.

She cupped his bound hands, bringing them up so she could put her mouth on his wrist, tasting the blood, soothing the scrape with her tongue. His cock pulsed inside her, his eyes half closing. His jaw was so rigid she had a mild concern the muscles might get permanently locked in that position. "Sit up," she ordered.

When he did, she guided his arms over her head and down, so his hands rested on her buttocks. His eyes lifted to hers, alive with a hope and need that gave her own voice a slight break. Her body was shaking, too.

"Take me to the bed, Mick. Give your Mistress pleasure."

She put her hands on his shoulders as he got his legs under him. He pushed up with an impressive display of strength, though he rested his ass on the couch for a beat, her still on his lap. The change of position had made them come apart, but that would be fixed. He kissed her sternum, and she threaded her fingers in his hair, holding him there.

His arms tightened around her, then he rose, carrying her to the main bed in the back. He eased her down on it, removing his arms from around her so she could slide back and make room for him. He got onto the bed, knees planted between her legs, loose and open. His gaze devoured what she revealed. When he began to lower his head, she put her foot on his chest.

"Not right now. Put yourself inside me." She braced her feet and bent her knees. "I want to watch."

He sat back on his heels. Then, using one of the bound hands, he guided himself to her opening.

She pushed up on her toes to take him in. Once he was in her channel, he released himself and gripped the edge of the skylight frame above, as if his arms were bound over him.

"Fuck me, Mick," she said breathlessly.

He used his hold on the frame to begin to thrust. Raising her hips further, she completed the lock. Stroke, retreat, stroke, retreat. She slid her gaze over his flexing hips, his abdomen and chest muscles, the scar and skeleton necklace she'd left upon him. Then back up to absorb his expression as the arousal built where she wanted it to go.

His gaze was on her breasts again. "I want your mouth there, Mick. Come down."

Holding his weight off of her, he curved his bound hands around one breast. He squeezed gently, fondled it as he put his mouth over the jutting tip. As she curled her hand into his hair, an easy sigh left her. She rode the powerful waves of arousal as he suckled her.

When he moved to the other tip, he was careful not to catch it with the chain connecting the cuffs. He took his time, his mouth drawing upon the nipple, shaping and teasing, licking and pulling, as long as she wanted.

Finally, she gripped the chain between the cuffs and guided him so he lay upon her, his hands above her head.

"Fuck me, Mick," she ordered. "Take me home."

She'd thought about taking off the cuffs, but in the end, no. They both wanted the reminder. Mistress and sub. Here she held the control, and he served, because he needed to serve her. And that need was clean.

She'd reminded him why. She was the one he'd saved without having to sacrifice anyone else. Before he'd learned that all heroes—a name he'd never give himself—had ghosts and nightmares.

Otherwise, they weren't really heroes.

"Oh…" The climax came fast, a much more intense rush. She wrapped an arm around his back, legs over his hips and flexing buttocks. "Come with me, Mick. Let me feel it."

He obeyed, but only after the first cry tore from her, her body melding with his, pushing into his strength. He moved his hands behind her head to cup her skull. He poured his need into her, and she gave him hers.

It took a while for the world to settle. He kept stroking inside her, their gazes locked, except for when their mouths met, or his lips touched her face. Or when she did the same, her hands moving over him.

No words exchanged, but so much said. She was glad she'd strung that key on her necklace. She had him give her his wrists, and removed the cuffs. He seemed tense when she examined the damage, but she wasn't going to allow any backward steps.

She put her mouth upon them again, making him accept her gentleness. When she at last released him, he pushed open the skylight so the night air could cool them, and lay next to her. She shifted to her hip to face him.

He fingered her necklace, the key on it. "You should keep the key on it," he said.

"As a reminder of tonight?"

"Maybe."

They were quiet for a while, and then he spoke again, his gaze holding hers. "If the worst happens to me, I'll still come home to you, Cyn. You'll feel it. In your heart and soul."

"You assume I have either of those."

"I know you do. Because you've given them to me, too."

CHAPTER TWENTY-ONE

It was the morning he was supposed to take Cyn to the airport. That was enough reason to consider the day shit, but the text he'd just received confirmed it.

Mick sat down on the folding chair by the fire pit to re-read the brief paragraph. *Well, fuck.*

It wasn't the first time he'd had to weather a volcanic eruption of shit hitting a fan the size of a wind tunnel. Or regroup and make a plan work. Usually he only had the space between two rapid, *oh shit* heartbeats, so he'd consider this amount of lead time a luxury.

He'd figure it out. He refused to lose a single moment to really *be* with her before he dropped her off.

And no matter how bad my day is, it's nothing next to how bad every *day is for those I work for.*

But for this morning, Cyn was his only boss.

The thought helped him smile a little. Not much, but it was something.

"Problem?"

He'd heard her approaching and had already risen from the stoop, turning as she appeared in the motorhome doorway and asked the question. No surprise, she looked damn good. Those form-fitting belted jeans, her boots, a flowing top with angel sleeves that draped her wrists. It was the first time he'd seen her choose sleeves, except when she'd taken his shirt. Which she refused to give back, to his amusement—and deep pleasure.

A long silk cord held that rune-looking stone she'd hit his balls with, that first night they'd seen one another again. His girl could be so sentimental. That necklace framed the shorter one, her skeleton cross. The handcuff key was still on the chain with it.

She had her hair loose and curly, the way he liked it, her eyes bright and sharp. To him, she always looked like a honed knife, ready to cut into a man's flesh and take pleasure in his pain. He wondered if Billy Joel had met Cyn in the creative ether where "Stiletto" had been written.

"Yeah." He pocketed the phone as she reached the ground and put her packed bag next to her. Curling his fingers into her hips and belt, he tugged her closer. She leaned against him, a welcome, solid presence. "I have to let you leave."

"You don't *let* me do anything, Mick."

She was teasing him, but her assessing look said she wasn't missing a thing. Still, he didn't want her to carry more worry than he'd already given her. He wrapped his arms around her. "I know you're not a hugger, but let me hold you a minute."

She slid her arms up under his, palms pressed to his back, her face against his throat. "Damn, this is going to be difficult," she muttered.

"Yeah, it is. I'm sorry. I'm supposed to bear all the pain in this relationship."

"That's crap." She eased back. "Tell me what's going on, Mick. Something's bugging you."

"It's about work. Something I can't share."

She kept looking at him. *Fuck.* He'd promised her he wouldn't lie, and he *could* share the high-level details. "Someone joining me for my upcoming meet has to bail. The buyer."

Goddamn, they'd put so much work into making this come together. If he showed up without her, the chances of getting the intel he'd hoped for would be far less likely. But rescheduling wasn't an option when months had gone into paving the way for a major trafficking player to be present at the meet.

"Is her backing out a warning flag for your own cover?" Cyn's expression was gripped with concern. He appreciated the love, but could reassure her on that point.

"No. She's like me. She's posing as a buyer, not an actual one. A few months back, I told Tyler I needed a straw man, or in this case a woman, to pose as a lucrative buyer. He pulled the right strings. She's a retired undercover. If she's having to pull out at the last minute like this, it's something that can't be avoided."

Her note had been necessarily brief, but she'd included the key intel that it was personal, not professional. The cover identity hadn't been burned. Personal meant an urgent medical issue, for her or a family member. Ruptured appendix, broken leg, car accident. Though he hoped she and her loved ones were all right, his concern took a back seat to the need to rearrange the pieces on the chess board.

"I can work it that she trusted me to be her proxy, and get some of what I was hoping to get." He flashed teeth. "I'll be extra charming."

Cyn didn't smile. "Is the meeting going to be a long one?"

"No." He picked up her bag and nodded toward the car he'd borrowed from the campground owner to take Cyn to the airport. A hundred bucks plus a tank of gas had made that happen. "It's basically a press-the-flesh, making sure the money and merchandise on either side is as real as promised."

The cover was that the buyer represented interests that wanted a regular monthly supply line. If the goods onsite right now met her approval, she'd buy some or all of them, and discuss the details of future deliveries. Mick had told Salazar the buyer expected a discount in exchange for her guarantee of monthly orders the same size or larger.

That was what had set the stage for the meet with the higher-up in the food chain. If she was the real deal, she expected the respect of that face-to-face. On their end, they'd want to verify she wasn't trying to screw them, brokering a better price for a one-time deal.

It would take a lot of charm for Mick to get the higher-up to negotiate with him like he would her. Even if he managed it, the guy wouldn't be likely to hang out and chat with a middleman, revealing details Mick was hoping to learn.

Still, he'd take what he could get.

"Ready to go?" he asked Cyn.

In answer, she took her bag from him, pivoted, climbed the steps of the motorhome and vanished. When she re-emerged, she stuck her empty hands in her back pockets, arching her back, and lifted her chin. "I'll do it."

No fucking chance. But because he'd spent ten plus years learning how to contain his strongest emotional reactions, he managed to sound admirably calm. "No. Are you willing to risk your people, your family?"

"What's the danger of that, for one in-and-out meeting at the ass-end of Texas?"

"It can be zero. Or skyrocket to a hundred percent with one unexpected variable."

"We can change my appearance. I was raised on the streets, Mick. I ran drug deals and fought in turf wars. Not long, but long enough. I've done used car sales and marketing work of all kinds. I know what qualities a buyer and seller have, regardless of the product. I also don't freak out under pressure or threat of violence. What skills am I missing?"

"She's a trained agent. You aren't."

"That's an evasion, not an answer." She crossed her arms, planted her feet shoulder width apart, and used the same reasonable tone, the obstinate woman. Her mind worked too much like his. "Most undercovers start with very little experience; what's most important is they're adaptable, cool headed, and keep an eye on the ball."

And were fucking lucky at the right moments. He eyed her.

"How do you know that?"

"Because one of my regular subs at Progeny was an undercover. We talked a lot, after sessions."

"So what happened to him?" He could play the same read-my-face game she could, and had latched onto the *was*. No man who wanted to be her submissive for more than one session walked away. Unless he had to do so. "He's fucking dead, isn't he?"

Cyn knew all his points were valid, but so were hers. So she abandoned that tactic and put it to him straight. "I want to see what you do, and how you do it."

"Watch a documentary about human trafficking," he retorted. "I can recommend several. Once you're on the plane."

Anger surged. She was going to say something nasty, goad him into a fight, into saying yes. Before she could get the first word out, he'd seized her upper arms and put her against the side of the motorhome, effectively pinning her.

She could try defensive maneuvers to break the grip, but his deadly expression dove right into her head and told her he would be three steps ahead of anything she could try. It made his point brilliantly, but he had more to add to it.

"Are you under the impression I'm not a man?"

"What?"

Bruising fingers bit into her biceps, but his eyes held her just as effectively. "You think because of the things we do together, I'd let you bully me into a situation where you could be tortured, raped or killed? That I would tolerate you being put at risk like that? I would fucking throw you over my shoulder, tie you up and stuff you into a closet to keep you out of harm's way first."

Maybe she couldn't physically match him in this mood, but she had other strengths. She pushed against his hold, meeting his menace with a kiss-my-ass expression. "Try it, and you'll lose body parts that would severely impact your usefulness to me."

They stared at one another. As the scathing sarcasm penetrated, Mick's hold eased. He put her feet on the ground and stepped back. Ran a hand over his face. "Fucking hell. No. Just no, Cyn."

She was aware of his protective instincts, how strong they made his current wall of resistance. There was only one way to get through it. "You aren't the only one haunted by your choices. I don't know where my siblings are. Maybe they're living a daily hell somewhere halfway around the world, or their bodies are buried with no marker, forgotten forever. My brothers and sisters."

"Cyn…"

She went toe to toe with him, staring up into his resolute face, that dangerous expression. "I have the right to pay for my sins. You mire yourself in evil with the hope that it's doing some good, though you never get to see it when it does. I want one chance to help, to stand side by side with you and see your life through your eyes."

"No."

Her fists clenched, but she took a breath. "You need a ballsy bitch who will pass as a supplier of high-grade tail. You tell me, truthfully, that she had some skill that would make this go sideways if I'm in her shoes instead, fine. I'll accept it and get on the plane. But if not…"

She touched his rock-hard jaw. "Fate, the fucking sadist of all sadists, brought us together twice now. Can you really say it isn't driving this, too?"

Mick muttered an oath and moved away. He kicked a rock so hard, it whistled away into the woods. "Goddamn you."

He put his hands on his hips. She stayed silent and still. No matter his reaction, she knew the feel of the shift, when a client started to see things her way.

Mick would fight it with a will as formidable as her own, but the detached part of his mind that made it possible to do what he did was already putting the variables into the picture

394

to see if they could accomplish what was needed. That was why he'd cursed her.

"You know if something happened to you, I couldn't take it. I literally wouldn't…"

At the break in that last syllable, she came up behind him and put her palm on his shoulder.

Under his shirt he carried her marks, front and back. She knew what she was asking of him, and she was doing it without apology or shame, because she'd told him the truth. She thought of those babies every day. Even when she pretended she didn't.

"Then think it through, and come up with a plan that works," she said quietly. "One that does what needs to be done, and brings us back here, to have more canned cheese and stale chips."

He turned and gave her a grimly humorous look. "Was it that bad?"

She shuddered. "They call me a sadist, and yet you made me eat that as a snack in bed last night."

He snorted. "You were hungry, and you wouldn't let me run out to get something I didn't dig out of my pantry. By the way, you'd still love me, even if I had no cock."

She sniffed. "Let's not test the theory."

He put a hand on the side of her throat, his thumb beneath her ear, stroking. The gesture was possessive and overly firm, fueled by frustration.

"Strangling a woman usually works better with two hands," she advised.

"It's why I'm touching you with only one. Too tempting otherwise." He sighed. "I haven't agreed to anything, but follow me."

He led her back into the motorhome, pointing her to the couch behind the table. When she sat down and slid out of the way, he knelt and removed the aisle panel. Bracing her elbows and leaning forward, she saw the vehicle's internal workings, a nest of wires and mechanical parts. Mick pointed to a circular disk no bigger than a quarter, nested among them. He put his thumb on it. A beep, and he'd lifted the whole slab of mechanics free, a false floor. There was another panel beneath it, with a code.

"Put in the wrong one twice, and it destroys everything inside," he told her.

Making sure she was watching closely, he typed in the code. C, I, S, S, Y. Followed by a ten-digit alphanumeric combination she expected had no correlation to anything. The man held onto what mattered, at the same time detaching himself from it. He had her repeat it to him twice, to make sure she memorized it. But after she satisfied him on that, she had a more personal question.

"You weren't taunting me that night. You do use Cissy as a safeword. Why?"

Mick rested his hand on top of hers on the table, a loosely entwined knot of fingers. "Before I left town, I visited her grave a lot."

"Why?"

"You know why. It was why you left the necklace there, knowing I might find it. It was a way to connect to you. I also thought you might want someone to keep it cleaned up. Until I left."

He sat down on the couch, at the other side of the table. His thumb stroked her wrist, back and forth over her pulse. "I swung back to the area a couple times. On the last visit, I discovered you'd moved her. I wouldn't let myself dig out where. It was enough to know you'd found a better place to take her, which meant you were in a better place."

He took his hand away, knelt over the safe again and showed her the contents. Guns and other weapons, money, passports, ID, files. He picked out a Walther, the same brand as her concealed carry, but this was a full-sized 9mm with an extended 15-bullet magazine. Mick handed it to her, with several clips and a holster.

"No serial number on it. Nothing you carry should be traceable to who you are." He tossed a folder onto the table next to her. "That's her identity. Memorize it, make it you. If you have to improvise and add to it, it can't conflict with what's already part of it. I'll test you on it, extensively. You have to prove to me you can become her. You can't break character, not once, so adapt it to your personality traits." His serious lips quirked. "Fortunately, ballsy bitch fits the general MO."

"What's step two?"

"Asking yourself this question and giving yourself an honest answer. Do you think you could sit by and let your mother sell those babies now?"

"No. I'd..." She stopped. It was the same type of question she'd given him. Did he think he could have sex with an unwilling girl to maintain his cover, if it was demanded of him now?

His knowing look matched his uncompromising tone. "The person you have to be is the person who would sell those babies to the highest bidder and reward herself the same night with a steak dinner for the cut she'd earned."

She knew she'd gone a little white-faced when he sat down on the couch across from her again, pushed the folder away and gripped her hands. "You don't have to do this, Cyn," he said fiercely. "You've paid for your sins. You were a child, raised by a monster, and you got out, long before most people would have had the strength or courage to do so."

She pulled away and paced to the front, sitting down in the driver's seat to put some distance between them. "You know she had at least one more after I left? Before the one that thankfully killed her?"

"It doesn't matter. Cyn..."

She shook her head. "It does matter. I stopped by because I did sometimes. Not for her. I'd sit in Cissy's old room and think I could still smell her. On one of those visits, I could tell she was pregnant again. I was no longer eight, and Cissy was no longer there. Nothing to blackmail me with. Maybe she saw what was going through my head on it. She told me she missed Cissy and me, that she might keep this one. She asked for my help."

Her lip curled, self-loathing. "Because of that, I came around more often, for the next few months. I wasn't an idiot. Or told myself I wasn't. I could see she was hiding it from the neighbors, like she always did. I convinced myself if I stuck close enough, I could keep her from giving it away. That maybe I could save that one. I would take the baby from her if I had to, care for it. Then she had him, and for a couple weeks, it was like she was going to keep him."

She paused, remembering the day her mother had gone into labor. At two in the morning. "I delivered that one."

At his surprised look, she shrugged. "Cissy taught me. We delivered two together, but this was the first one I delivered on my own."

She could still remember the weight of the baby in her hands, the tiny mouth and hands.

It *did* matter. It was important for him to understand. This wasn't a passing fancy, *hey, let me go help Mick on some crime gig.* Even if the opportunity presented itself only minutes ago, the more she thought about it, the more certain she was she had to help. Had to do something.

"Yeah, I could claim that my raising mindfucked me. That I'm innately distrustful of the law and had all I could do to survive myself. But this time I'd had a plan to get the baby away from her, but I let myself be convinced she was going to keep him. That he was going to be ours. Or rather, mine, the way I'd been Cissy's."

She swallowed, looked away. *Damn it, hold it together.*

"I came by a few days later, bringing some stuff for the baby. He was gone, and the bitch just shrugged it off. Said her contact, the trafficker, had just 'stopped by,' and offered her more than she could turn down."

"What did you do?"

"I beat the shit out of her," Cyn said flatly. "Forced her to tell me where the baby had gone. But except for the satisfaction of making her bleed, it didn't matter. The moment I'd left, saying I'd be back in a few days, she'd put it in play. The baby was on a plane going overseas that same night, well out of my reach and resources, and she had a nice wad of cash."

Cyn shifted her attention to the front window. The motorhome faced a bank of pine trees. Her heart tightened as she saw a squirrel race up the trunk of one. Like the squirrel she'd seen out Ros's window.

"I told her that if I ever heard she was pregnant again, I'd turn her in. When she told me she'd say I helped her sell the babies, I told her I didn't care. She didn't believe me, but I didn't get to prove it to her. When I found out she was pregnant again, it was the day she died in the hospital from the abruption."

Mick held out a hand. "Come sit with me. I mean it. Don't make me come over there and get you."

She gave him a dubious look, but rose. He guided her onto his knee, looping an arm around her hips, lacing his other hand with hers. She leaned into him, feeling like she could do that. They sat still for a few minutes, then she spoke quietly.

"I'll have your back, Mick. You know I can do it. Otherwise you wouldn't be showing me all this."

"Yeah. Doesn't mean I like it. I have one condition." He threaded his fingers into her hair and tugged the curls. "When this is done, I get to strip off that belt you're wearing and beat your ass with it. Not my usual preference, but at the moment, it's a pretty strong fantasy. Maybe top of my list."

Despite the seriousness of things, she felt amusement, and a little tingle at his determined tone. She gave him her best bitch look.

"If you think you can do it without incurring permanent injury, give it a shot." She held his other hand against her chest. "But what will work better is me doing it to you. Then I'll wrap that belt around your throat while you kiss me. You can prove to me you value my mouth more than air. I'll straddle you, move that belt to your shoulders, which I will make sure are throbbing with pain, and ride you the way I want."

Heat flickered through his expression, and their hands tightened, matching determination and desire. "I'm not sheltered, Mick. I'm definitely not soft. The only thing in life that scares me is finding out my soul is as stained as my mother's. Give me a chance to prove to myself it isn't, in a way that matters. And let me stand with you, at least this once. Whatever happens, happens. But I don't like to lose. If I'm breathing, I won't fail you."

He squeezed her waist, then spoke gruffly. "Study the folder. I'll be back."

"Where are you going?"

"For a walk. To get ready. And get in character."

He shifted her to the cushion beside him and rose to restore the panel. "I'll also pick up a few things to change your look. Later today we'll go get the untraceable car we'll be using."

He moved to the door. At the bottom of the steps, he leaned back in. "When I return, Cyn, I'll be that guy. You might not like what you see."

"I hope not. Just as I hope you won't like who I am." She held up the folder. "But we're pretending."

"No. We're not," he said. "That's the only way it works."

400

CHAPTER TWENTY-TWO

Lookout cameras had marked the silver Mercedes when it was several miles away from the compound. It only slowed when it approached the gate to the warehouse and surrounding buildings, enclosed by chain link fencing and barbed wire. The sun-faded sign out front indicated the business was a scrap metal company. A handful of cars were parked inside the fence, along with a scattering of heavy equipment and a container truck.

As the car pulled up to the security guard's hut, the woman driving wore large dark glasses. Her moist lipstick reminded the guard of an apple, the darker kind. Her hair was pulled back in a straight cosmopolitan style, held that way with lots of product. The black streaked with red gave her a vampiric look. The hands on the wheel were slim, nails painted black. Her elegant brown slacks, short-sleeved jacket and white blouse were business attire, though she showed a tempting hint of bra lace at the vee neckline.

Mickey Cosgrove, whom the guard knew and was expecting with the female buyer, was in the passenger seat. He wore his shoulder harness openly with his preferred Glock. The woman was likely also armed, but that was status quo in their world. Mickey had his hand propped on her headrest in a familiar way.

Lucky Mickey, if he was getting to tap that ass. "How's it going, Mickey?" the guard asked.

"Too fucking hot, Bert. As always." Mick scratched his groomed beard and plucked at the open collar of his dress shirt. He wore that skeleton necklace he always wore, that the guard thought was pretty cool. The woman wore an elegant gold chain and matching earrings. "Hate this fucking state," Mickey continued. "Going to move to Alaska one day, get

401

some sled dogs and an Eskimo woman, to fuck and cook for me."

The man grinned. Same old Mickey. "Kat Greenwood?" His gaze shifted to the woman.

She gave Bert a thorough up and down. Then ignored and dismissed him. Bitch. But as long as her money was good, who the fuck cared?

Mickey confirmed her identity, so Bert waved them through. Even if she was a buyer, Miss Uptight Bitch was in for a surprise if she gave the big boss attitude. Though it was the first time Bert had ever seen him face-to-face, it was clear he didn't take that kind of shit.

Bert didn't bother to hide an unpleasant grin. Greenwood goosed the Mercedes forward, spinning the back wheel so dust shot into his gatehouse. As he cursed her, she tossed him a smile in her side mirror.

Cyn returned her attention to the road ahead, though she caught Mick's approving look. A deliberate reassurance for her, she was sure, because this was the easy part. The tough, impossible-to-rattle bitch was a role she'd played for a long time.

When Mick had returned to the motorhome, he had a changed walk and attitude, which indeed turned him into a different person, though nothing about his basic physical features had been modified.

He'd helped her change her look, too, but physically as well as mentally. Hair dye, makeup applied to subtly alter the shape of her face, different jewelry and clothing choices, made Cyn see a stranger in the mirror. As he tested her knowledge of the folder contents, over and over, she fully transformed into Kat Greenwood. He sprang all sorts of scenarios on her to test it, knowing the folder contents well enough to play the role himself—if he'd had a vagina and the figure for it.

He'd told her if ever they were in a precarious situation, he'd give her all the information she needed. He'd proven he meant those words.

She pulled up in front of the warehouse as a man there pointed to where he wanted her to park. Because her preparation had included a detailed description of all the players, she knew the man who opened her door was Hector Salazar.

"Hola, Señorita Greenwood," he said. "It is a pleasure to have you here."

She ignored him the way she had the gate guard, refusing his hand out of the car as she emerged and moved around him to survey the area.

Hector coordinated with those who brought the "product" in through Mexico. Such language established detachment and protected the traffickers from listening devices or being overheard in public areas.

Hector got compensated on both ends, by the families and individuals wanting into the country, and by the organization who paid him to dupe them into believing they were coming for legitimate work and a chance at a new life. He was also in charge on site until they were distributed to their buyers. Once it arrived at the compound, the product was sorted. Men and older, less attractive but able-bodied women would go to labor jobs across the country. They would be told they could earn their freedom by working off the debt they still owed, because the "costs" of getting them here had somehow doubled. Or tripled.

The younger men and women were sold into sexual slavery. Some would be placed in wealthy homes under the guise of domestic labor, cooking and cleaning services, or nanny work. Others would go straight to underground brothels and rarely see the light of day or any freedom again.

This outfit didn't deal with pre-pubescent children, a dubious blessing. Mothers and their offspring under a certain age were sent to other locations. The separation from fathers and older children gave their captors additional leverage. If those here didn't do what was required of them as domestic or manual laborers, or as sex workers, those absent family members would suffer.

She saw Mauricio Condes, who handled contracts with buyers. His brother, Javier, was in sales, finding those buyers. The armed men sitting or standing around the property, passing time playing cards or kicking around a soccer ball, handled a variety of tasks. Feeding, watering. Beating, violating or conditioning as needed, under Hector's direction, to teach obedience.

By process of elimination, she'd found the man this whole meet was about. He waited inside a courtyard formed by two of the outbuildings. The tall man had patrician looks, silver hair and an expensive but way-too-warm suit for the weather. He'd dealt with that by sitting under a pavilion tent with a woman fanning him. A naked woman.

You've got to be fucking kidding me.

The girl, probably around sixteen years old, had dull eyes, shiny hair, and a firm body. A standing mechanical fan with a mister added to the air movement. In front of the man was a table with a decanter and three tumblers, one already poured. He was sipping from it.

He rose at their approach, nothing if not courteous. She affected an annoyed look at the naked girl, then glanced at Mick. He shrugged.

She stalked toward the pavilion. Mick kept to a sauntering pace, but she caught the look he sent to Hector, as if to say, "Women? What can you do?"

Hector made a muffled snort of agreement.

"Miss Greenwood," the man at the table said politely, in perfect but accented English. She had no illusions about how far his courtesy extended. Only to the heights of the stack of money he expected from their association.

"Ms.," she corrected. "I've divorced three husbands for being weak jackasses. I've earned the title."

Amusement glittered in his gaze. He turned to Mick. "Mr. Cosgrove, a pleasure to make your acquaintance. You've proven very useful to our operations."

Mick inclined his head. "You make money, I make money, and the world keeps turning. We don't anticipate keeping you long, sir. Miss Greenwood□—"

"Ms.," she snapped. "Or Señora. As you well know. And it will take as long as required to assure myself this operation will provide my customers what they need."

Hector stepped forward, a point in a triangle between her and the other man. "Señora Greenwood, Señor Rodriguez is here as a courtesy. He appreciates your business, but you represent your employers. You are not the big fish, señora. You only represent the *men* who are." He flashed his teeth. "So don't be a *puta*."

One of Rodriguez's men moved to her left side to reinforce the threat. Cyn narrowed her eyes at Hector. "Fuck you and your whore of a mother."

Hector gave the man a slight nod. When he reached for her, Cyn backstepped, elbowed his gut and brought her knuckles up to the bridge of his nose. When he stumbled, she pivoted to seize his wrist, wrenching the hand so he dropped to his knees. Though he tried to shake the grip, he was unsuccessful. She made her hold more painful. She'd break it if he kept moving.

He was a trained fighting man, so he got the message. He went still.

Hector hadn't moved, and Rodriguez was watching the scene with a neutral expression. Mick stood calmly, but he'd moved his hand to his gun.

"Our relationship is a good one," he told Hector. "She represents a lot of money. Be patient."

Cyn gave Hector an icy smile, then glanced down at the man. When she pressed the hand back another half inch, a grunt broke from his throat. "Do I look like that naked piece of ass over there, a sheep you can fuck without permission?"

405

"No."

"No, what?"

"No, señora."

"All right, then." Cyn released him with a shove and returned her attention to Rodriguez, ignoring the man and Hector. "I represent clients, Señor Rodriguez. I head up my own operation. I didn't suck a dick to get here, and if this nest of machismo can't behave like they would toward any other client, then several other operations are interested in my business. The Chinese market is your biggest competitor, and they're very respectful."

Rodriguez raised his brow, glancing toward Mick. Mick nodded, confirming she wasn't bluffing. Which meant they thought Mick was pretty much their man, even if he'd been willing to come to her aid.

"Ms. Greenwood, you are an intelligent woman," Rodriguez said. "I am sure you recognize a test."

"I do. Doesn't mean I don't get tired of the shit. Now, I assume you were going to pour me a drink."

Rodriguez gestured to the seat across from him and picked up the decanter. As he filled the two empty glasses, Kat Greenwood and Mickey Cosgrove sat down to talk business with him.

Mick took the lead, injecting subtle cues Cyn used to guide the conversation and get Rodriguez talking. She eased from ballsy bitch into business associate, with the right dose of mysterious strong female with a killer body. Her direct glance wasn't diluted by the green contacts he'd provided her. The confidence was all her own.

She'd made it clear she could be this, and her story had convinced him of it, but it was unsettling, how well she shrugged on the role. He knew what it cost, having to play this part in such a way that it wasn't play, and she'd been born into those circumstances.

He hated having her here. He was used to having to stand by while the defenseless suffered, keeping his eye on the end goal, but there was a reason he kept this world strictly separate from whatever personal life he could maintain. If he didn't, it caused a bloody car wreck in his psyche.

When they'd tested her with that rear attack by one of Hector's thugs, it was all he could do not to lunge forward or overreact. She'd handled herself well.

But if her credentials had been doubted, it wouldn't have been a test. She would have been overpowered and taken down. With Rodriguez here, Hector wouldn't take chances.

Once they sat down, she was pure corporate executive. She discussed high level details of her client base, the kind of "product" they were seeking. She ably answered Javier and Mauricio's questions, with a few careful inputs by Mick, and confirmed the protections her network had in place, to keep things from coming back to bite them in the ass.

The seamless way she let Mick fill in information on the "nitty gritty" when she was sipping her drink had to be drawn from how she and the other TRA women worked together to impress a new client with a marketing package.

"I am not one to tell you your business," Rodriguez said, "but be aware that Soong, one of those 'polite' Chinese distributors, has diversified into the baby trade. He collects women with the right physical characteristics, and inseminates them to produce highly marketable infants. Twenty to thirty at a time."

At Cyn's disinterested look, he spread out his hands. "I did not want you to do business with him blind. While he may have other services compatible with your interests, a child trade operation that extensive carries much higher risk of law enforcement exposure in the States. I myself find the idea of selling children reprehensible."

Mick could only imagine what was going through Cyn's mind, after the information he'd shared about this operation. Probably something along the same lines of what went through his own. *You fucking hypocrite. You may not sell them, but you're happy to use them as blackmail. Or sell them once they reach the ripe old age of twelve.*

"I appreciate your concern for my operation and clients." Cyn put the right touch of sincerity and cynicism in the response. He bet she'd been a champion car salesperson.

Rodriguez rose. "We will see the product now. If this selection meets your requirements, we will handle the wire transfer and transportation arrangements for them."

Cyn stood and tilted her head toward Mick, an imperious gesture to "follow along." As he and Hector fell in behind her and Rodriguez, Hector chuckled and spoke low.

"I think she has you sucking *her* dick, *mijo*."

Mick snorted. "Stroking egos has its rewards. You know that. But I draw the line at sucking dick. Eating pussy is a different matter."

Hector sighed. "You should have been here when this group was prepared. Sweet, young and tight."

"You know I don't stick my dick in merchandise."

"Eh, you don't need more pussy anyway. It's obvious you're fucking her." Hector grinned. "Or rather, she's fucking you."

Mick shrugged. "She likes her pleasures, and has no interest in anything beyond that. Once she's done, honest-to-God, she tells me to shut the fuck up, bring her a drink and leave her alone. No cuddling, no clingy emotions."

"Women. Heaven and hell." Hector sent Cyn's ass a speculative look. "I should offer up my services."

"Good luck. She fucks me when we have time to kill. She says I'm better than her vibrator, but she prefers higher class cock when she's at home."

They'd reached the warehouse door. As they entered, the smell of cleaning products touched Mick's nose. They would have hosed everyone down and made them presentable for the buyer. He'd seen it all before, but Cyn hadn't.

She was one of the toughest women he'd met, but he knew other things about her. *Hang in there, baby. Be Kat Greenwood. Don't be Cynbad Marigold.*

Afterwards, he'd let her rage, take it out on his flesh. Or throw up and he'd help her scrub this filth off of her. Whatever she needed.

Then he'd be out of her life.

She'd said she wanted him to come back to her whenever he could, but after seeing this, would she feel the same? Could *he* come to her, knowing she'd seen it? The invitation and promise were there, but he couldn't wash off that stain. Not as long as he needed the camouflage it provided.

He could tell himself he'd come to her years down the road, when he couldn't do this anymore. But that day would never come.

The day they killed him was the day he'd stop.

Inside the warehouse were conveyors and big dumpsters, offices and other trappings to maintain appearances. Hector went behind one of the dumpsters and opened a door marked *Supply Closet*. Inside, it looked like one, shelves stocked with toilet paper, office supplies, and small machine parts. Tubs of peppermint candy.

At the rear was a bolted door. Mick assumed the shelf next to it could be pushed in place to cover it. Using a ring of keys hung on the wall, Hector opened the door.

The back of the warehouse was a false wall. Someone observant might note the difference in outer and inner dimensions, but since they put effort into the scrap metal business cover and didn't exactly get drop-in business, it was more likely to be overlooked.

The space held a handful of cells. Men were separated from older women, and attractive young women and teenagers of both sexes were separated from the rest. That group huddled in the back of their cells, taking advantage of what little shadows were there, because they'd been stripped naked, probably right before this meeting. Their hair had

409

been brushed, but the girls wore no makeup. Their value had to be confirmed without concealment.

"Get up and present yourselves," Hector commanded in Spanish. Two of the armed men had accompanied him here, and they fanned out to either side of him, reinforcement of the order.

It didn't seem needed. The young women and teenagers scrambled to obey even faster than the rest, lining up in three rows, the middle one two steps off center from the front and back rows, so no one was hidden. Backs straight, hands at their sides, eyes down.

It mocked the true joy of a submissive, presenting themselves for a loving Dominant. Kat—because he knew it was better to think of her as that person right now—took in the sight, her face a blank wall. Mick was ready to say something to nudge her into action, but before he could, she paced closer to the cell holding the sex trade candidates. Her green eyes marked each teenager or young woman, noting their attributes, the way they stood.

"All of you. Eyes up. On me. Let me see what's going on in those pretty heads."

Most complied, though some seemed to struggle with it. At least one girl's eyes burned with hatred.

"We've had to work on her," Hector said, as if he anticipated Kat's displeasure.

Kat shrugged. "There are always buyers who like the ones who fight. If I'm good at my job, I match her to the right one and make more money."

Keeping the same gradual, unhurried pace, Kat moved to the men's and older women's cells, continuing to examine them the way Rodriguez and his men expected. She commanded a few to demonstrate their physical ability by performing push-ups or some jumping jacks. One or two she had turn around to see them from all sides.

Mick moved in lockstep with her, two steps to her right, so she knew he was with her. He noted a half dozen small rooms along the far wall. Places to take individual prisoners for various types of "conditioning." Several were equipped with cots.

Kat would have noted that, too, but she was studying the male prisoners. "My main interest is in the younger ones," she said casually, "but I have a client in California who could use two dozen workers. He overworked his last group, didn't hydrate or feed them properly. Fortunately, he has more money than sense."

"Our favorite kind of buyer," Rodriguez noted.

"*Puta.*" A man in the front of the cell spat through the bars, the saliva splattering the toe of Kat's shoe.

"*No, mijo,*" an older woman cried out. The women around her clutched her arms, shushing her with anxious looks toward the dispassionate jailors.

Kat merely raised a brow. But Hector stepped up to the bars, drew his gun, and fired a bullet into the man's head.

It happened in a blink, but as Hector was moving, so was Mick, already closing the distance between him and Cyn. Before the shot stopped echoing through the warehouse, he'd pulled her behind him.

Several women screamed. The men jumped back as the body fell, the fear in their faces mingled with helpless rage.

Mick felt Cyn's rapid pulse under his hand, but her gaze remained locked on Hector and the fallen man behind him.

Hector waited, gun still raised, until he saw all of the more volatile feelings swallowed, masked. When he spoke, his tone was even, reasonable. "You were each told a third act of disobedience would be punished this way. This was his third. This is to help you, to keep you from making unwise choices." He holstered the gun.

Rodriguez had come to Cyn's side. "If we have a man's wife, daughter or mother here…" Rodriguez paused to look at the woman who'd cried out. The women around her shrunk from his regard. "She is raped before him as he is

411

whipped. This already happened with this man. He is too hard-headed."

Cyn's pulse under Mick's hand slowed, evened out. When she stepped away, she was Kat again.

"Was hard-headed," she said flatly. "What kind of whip is used?"

"A bullwhip. Hector is a fair hand with it." Rodriguez sent Mick a speculative look. "I have never seen Mick move so quickly to defend a client. It is…unexpected."

Kat tossed Mick a scornful look. "It's totally expected. When a woman fucks a man to scratch her own itch, he becomes protective. Which is fine, as long as he doesn't associate it with the delusion of possession."

She turned her back on Mick. As he aimed a killing look at her, Hector suppressed a grin. But then she turned that scornful look on him.

"I know how to use a bullwhip myself. If it's not getting the job done, you need some lessons. As the target. You just killed a man who could have made me money. I also have clients who put men like him into cage matches."

"You are an interesting woman, Señora Greenwood," Rodriguez said. "I think I like you."

She ignored that and went back to corporate mode. "This is an adequate first shipment. I'll take all of them. If you can offer double the numbers and a few tweaks to the composition each month, we can proceed."

Rodriguez's lips almost disappeared into his goatee as he pressed them together, his eyes gleaming with approval. "Good. Let us go into the fresh air and finalize our business."

His nose had wrinkled as the scent of the dead man's released bowels had begun to drift their way. With a nod of assent, Kat and the rest followed him back through the storage room and warehouse, and out to the courtyard.

Mick saw Cyn's nostrils flare as she drew in the air. She'd lifted her sunglasses in the warehouse, but as she dipped her head and put them back in place, the green irises and dark pupils were emerald shards.

He should not have fucking brought her here. She'd said this was a way to atone. He stood by what he'd told her. She had not a damn thing to atone for. Though she'd vehemently disagree, she'd been one of the people in those cells, no matter the different circumstances. Bearing the ghosts of her past was enough penance.

Hector spoke to one of his men. Mick picked up some of the exchange, so when Salazar fell into step next to him, he gave him a curious look. "Who did you tell him to put back into the cells?"

Hector shrugged. "A girl not for sale. If you can swing back after you drop *Señora* Greenwood off, you will see. There is a betting pool. Chavez has a pet tiger he's been keeping hungry. We're taking bets on how long she lasts."

Mick kept his tone low, though his choice of words told Hector he hadn't yet forgiven Kat's shot at his manhood. "Not to agree with queen bitch, but it seems like a waste. Even the damaged ones are usually good for something."

"She has something wrong in her head." Hector rapped his knuckles against his temple. "Our doctor looked at her, and she's not faking. She sees monsters and goes berserk. We drugged her at first, but now that we know she has no value, we just knock her out when she gets too loud."

Hector nudged Mick as his phone started to buzz. "She fights like a wildcat, though. We intended to shoot her and dump the body, but Chavez mentioned the tiger. Who knows? She may scare the beast, despite his hunger. Chavez will have to make her bleed to give the *gato* courage."

Hector pulled out the phone as he spoke, but when he read the series of texts, his expression went hard and blank. He came to a full stop, reading the text more carefully. Pocketing it with a stream of muttered Spanish curses, he quickened his pace, closing the distance between him and

Rodriguez. He issued a curt *"perdón,"* to Cyn before he pulled his boss aside.

In the swift exchange that followed, fury gripped Rodriguez's features. Mick shifted closer to Cyn. She glanced at him. Tension was a screw drilling itself into his abdomen. Had his cover been blown? Or Cyn's?

Hector had dismissed Mick *and* Cyn when he bolted to his boss. Plus, it had been a very long time since Mick had had that concern. He was embedded so deeply it was hardly a consideration.

Showing why he was in charge, and conscious of the need to preserve a lucrative business relationship, Rodriguez banked his anger with effort and turned to Cyn. "Ms. Greenwood, you have my sincerest apologies. A competitor is on their way to seize the cargo. We will be outnumbered and outgunned, so retreat is our best option. You will have your requested shipment next month, you have my word."

Anger and intense annoyance gripped Cyn's features, "Kat's" expected reaction. But before she could say anything, Rodriguez had turned to Hector. Because "competitor" meant another cartel.

"Fold up the tents. Burn it all. They can do the clean-up and pay off the cops."

"Wait a fucking minute." Mick spoke as if he'd read the order from Kat's furious countenance. He was a broker defending his client. And his commission. "We can take custody now. She'll wire you the money. I'll vouch for it."

"No." Rodriguez responded. "You will not get out ahead of them. They will kill you and take the cargo." His gaze slid over Cyn. "Or make you part of the cargo. This is not about money. It is about territory and respect. We paid them to allow us to be here, and they are reneging on the agreement."

His expression sent a direct warning to Mick. Kat could show her ass and have a tantrum, but she'd do it while they headed to the Mercedes. Much as Rodriguez wanted her business, if Mick or "Kat" caused too much of a problem, Hector would be told to shoot them where they stood.

"Your next shipment will have double the discount you requested, Ms. Greenwood," Rodriguez said. "As long as you adhere to the terms of the agreement we outlined. Hector will coordinate it with Mick. You have seen our merchandise, so I trust you and I will not need direct involvement next time. My presence was likely noted."

"So you fucked up, and I'm paying the price." Kat raised a brow. "I'll wire you the money, including enough to pay for that tractor trailer over there." She dipped her head toward the container truck. "We'll drive them out and take our chances."

"I'm not allowing another cartel to take what belongs to us. This is how we teach them not to interrupt a business transaction."

Rodriguez gestured brusquely at Hector. "Make sure they get safely off the property, which means immediately. I will depart for my plane. You know how to handle things."

He moved toward a white Escalade, already populated with a driver and men to provide him firepower. One of them held the door for him, then jumped into the back seat.

Hector jerked his chin at the Mercedes. "Get out of here, Mickey. See you down the line." The wry tone said he didn't envy Mick, having to deal with "Ms. Greenwood's" temper on the drive.

He strode toward the waiting men, barking orders in Spanish. Three disappeared into one of the smaller buildings, reappearing with spray cans of accelerant and bales of newspaper. Whether the invader was law enforcement or a double-crossing competitor, they were prepped for the evacuation plan. The others were checking their weapons.

"What are they doing?" Cyn said. She'd been following Mick's lead, moving toward the car, but her steps slowed as she put together what he already knew.

He gripped her arm and pulled her into motion. "Keep walking."

They reached the Mercedes, but there she dug in her heels, horror gripping her features. "No, Mick," she said low, urgent. "We can't let them do this. They can be bought off, right? He's gone."

"Hector can't. He'll shoot us if we interfere."

Mick reached under the steering wheel and popped the trunk. When he straightened, Cyn pulled him around to face her. It was a good thing they'd anticipated her temper, because her body language reflected it. Even through the sunglasses, her eyes were warrior fierce.

"I know you've had to watch terrible things, over and over," she hissed. "Stand by and let them happen. But not this. If you do, you will have no soul left. None. Neither of us will. We might as well burn with them."

The Escalade was bumping down the road, a mile off now. Twilight was making it harder to distinguish the car from the dust obscuring it, but it was clearly making speed.

"I need you to move so I can get to the trunk," Mick told her.

He didn't wait for her reaction, bodily moving her out of his way. She might have resisted, but even in crisis, his Mistress paid attention, keeping her brain working.

His was working, too. Everything...all of it was in his head. So many images, so many variables. What standing by and doing nothing would mean. What not standing by and doing nothing would mean.

He'd learned to focus on the end goal, which always had to be worth it, no matter what damage it did to his gut, which had been so chewed to hell he was surprised he had one left. But like the two dead girls, a lot of casualty events happened outside his reach, or before his reaction was called into play. Even things like Hector shooting the man in front of him. No choices there, nothing that would help.

That was a far cry from bolting while sixty people were burned alive in one go, while he had time to react.

While he had time to do something about it.

Cyn had followed him to the trunk. "Throw a fit," he told her. "Make a scene. Give me some cover."

Her gaze flickered, her only acknowledgement before he snapped, "Fuck you, Kat. It's business. You'll make one less pile of money this month. Big fucking deal."

"You son of a bitch. You told me this crew was reputable. I should have known better than to get in bed with Mexicans. The Chinese gangs can at least keep their inner office bullshit contained."

As she spat at him, he pulled away the floor of the trunk and lifted out an AK and a second 15-capacity mag Glock.

Though he already carried a weapon, he put the strap of the AK around himself, tucked the additional handgun into the back of his belt, and closed the trunk. "Pull your weapon and follow my lead. Look like you want to join in the fun."

He headed toward the warehouse. "Hector," he called out, holding the AK by the trigger guard, the butt tucked under his biceps as the muzzle pointed toward the sky. "Hold up."

The handful of men with Hector paused at their boss's quiet word. Four were missing, having taken the accelerant and newspaper inside. When Hector gave the AK a curious look, Mick responded with an eye roll Cyn couldn't see, because she was following a couple steps behind him. "She wants to put a bullet in a few. She likes first shooter games. You mind?"

He kept moving forward, fifteen feet, ten feet…

"Too late, man, they're already back there, spraying the gas. No sparks. Maybe□—"

Mick dropped the muzzle of the readied weapon and opened   fire.

CHAPTER TWENTY-THREE

He swept it across the handful of men. They lived by violence, and he couldn't give them time to rally and return fire. He heard the Walther and saw one drop who'd stumbled from the AK but hadn't gone down. Cyn had made sure he fell.

Pain seared through his shoulder as Hector hit him with a shot from the ground. Even with several bullets in his torso, the tough bastard wasn't out of commission. No surprise on his face at Mick's betrayal, nothing but dispassionate reaction, get the job done. It was the life he lived.

No longer. Hector jerked backwards as a bullet punched a hole in his forehead. Cyn was at Mick's left side, her hand on his shoulder and eyes alive with fury.

That was his Mistress. She responded to fear with rage.

"I'm all right. Shit." Smelling smoke, he realized the gunfire outside had prompted the men to start the fire inside. They probably thought the cartel had arrived. "They'll be coming out to help Hector and the others. Four of them. Be ready."

He barely had time to speak the words and back off, her at his shoulder, before the men burst out. They were already firing. Gun fights were way faster than in the movies.

Mick used the AK to take down two. He hit the third when the fourth fell from Cyn's tight cluster in his chest, but the third man had had a chance to fire before Mick's repeat fire ended him.

Mick's heart choked him when Cyn stumbled back, blood blooming on her thigh.

"*Cyn.*" He was at her side in a blink, supporting her around the waist before she could fall.

"We're good. If I can move, it's okay." She was grimacing, but the bullet had hit a couple inches above her

418

knee and to the outside. Likely muscle or bone impact but no major arteries. Still, he tore a section of his shirt and quickly tied it above the bleeding wound, ignoring the snarl of his own shoulder wound. He refused to cut it any slack. *Not when our Mistress is hurt. Shut the fuck up.*

Cyn was looking toward the building. No visible fire yet, but the acrid smoke smell was unmistakable. "Come on, we don't have time."

Mick bent to Hector's body and fished out the bulge of keys he'd noted there earlier. He hoped to God one of them belonged to the tractor trailer. He handed them to her. "Get to that truck and move it away from the warehouse. Keys might be in it, or on this ring. Be ready to load them up. I'll open the cells."

"I'll help□—"

"Help by getting the goddamn truck," he snapped. "Do you know how to drive one?"

"Yes."

"Good. Get ready to convince a bunch of scared people to get into it."

"The cartel□—"

He tossed her his phone, handed her the AK and his guns. "Look for Orchid Master, and text him 911. It's our best hope, and it's a goddamn slim one. Look in the trunk and pull out the rest of the weapons there."

He headed into the warehouse without looking back.

The smoke drifted past the equipment and dumpsters, white tendrils. The bastards had started the fire in the area of most importance to them. He ran toward the supply closet.

The outer door was closed. He tested the knob and found it wasn't yet hot. However, when he yanked it open, way more smoke billowed out. They hadn't closed the door to the cells. He heard panicked screaming and charged through, greeted by flame and human terror. They'd doused the walls, the newspaper bales and guard's desk, but they hadn't sprayed the people, the easiest way to ensure there was no salvageable "cargo" for the oncoming cartel.

Possibly because they'd heard the shots, thrown down a match and come running to the aid of their fellow thugs.

And though they'd kept accelerant and fuel on standby, and probably gone over the steps, they'd either never run through an actual drill on how to set and start a fire so it burned everything up fast, or it had been so long they hadn't remembered the basics.

The oversight would give him valuable minutes, but only minutes. The flame was working its way up portions of the walls.

The men's cell was closest. The dead man had been moved to a corner, hands over his breast in a semblance of dignity. Mick met the gaze of a man who looked like he still had his wits about him, and spoke in rapid Spanish. "There's a truck outside. We'll get you out of here and somewhere safe. I swear it. Go out the door I came through and head for the front."

As the man answered with a startled nod, Mick was moving to the wall. He engaged the master release on the cell locks. As he shouted out what he'd told the man, to exit out the front, people started streaming forth. Ones afraid of the building flame were ushered through the fiery obstacle course by stronger, more determined companions. Heat was building, joining the smoke in filling up lungs and throats.

After the "inspection," the younger women and teens must have been tossed a pile of clothing, because the boys were wearing jeans, the girls in loose dresses that hung on their bodies. They gathered the skirts close or covered their mouths with the hems, some sharing the cloth with the boys, coughing into it.

He kept calling out the same direction, like a macabre flight attendant, until someone started screaming. His gaze snapped to the middle cell. Through the thickening smoke, he realized it wasn't empty. A young woman was crouched at

420

the back. An older woman hovered protectively over her, trying to get her to her feet.

The young woman was the one shrieking. "The monsters are here. They're here."

The girl they'd intended to feed to the tiger, he assumed.

As the people were running out the supply closet door, more oxygen was being pulled into the room. The flames danced higher. They were above them, dropping lit pieces of ceiling material. Mick beat out one on his shoulder and pushed his way through a lingering handful of people, trying to help the two in the cell. "I've got them," he shouted. "Go. Get the others into the truck. We have no time."

He covered his nose and mouth with his shirt as he crouched next to the old woman, who must be the grandmother. She was trying the "come with me and we'll run away from the monster" logic. The girl was too far into the episode, so frenzied she looked close to a seizure.

She struck out at him with flailing fists. "You're all monsters," she screamed.

"Tell me something I don't know," Mick muttered. Grabbing her by the arm, he yanked her to her feet. Even with her screeching, he was far stronger and more determined. He hoisted her into a fireman's carry, hands clamped on her wrists and leg. Fortunately, the older woman didn't need his help. Her eyes were squinted against the smoke like his, her mouth in a determined set.

He gestured to her to lead them out, but they reached the closet too late. The fire was consuming the space, blocking their path. He smelled burning peppermint. The heat was enough to blister the skin even as they stood back from it.

When he heard the sound of glass, Mick looked up. The rotting frame of the upper windows had weakened enough to give way. Wood and glass fell into the eager fire.

He always noted exits and entry points, and though their current visibility was crap, he knew there was a rear exit to the building. Mick told the grandmother that in Spanish and took the lead. As he made his way to a wall, since they could no longer see through the smoke, he guided her hand to his belt, a mute direction to hold onto him so they didn't get separated.

He followed the wall past the men's cell, cursing as he hit a stack of chairs and a group of boxes, fuel waiting for the fire to reach it. The girl kept thrashing. He did his best to protect her head while moving forward.

Here. He'd found it. But hope was dashed when he tried to push the door open. A chain was holding it on the outside. He could hear the rattle as he shoved against it, see it through a meager crack. Though the sudden blast of mostly smoke-free air was welcome, the oxygen would call to the fire, like a dog whistle to a pack of hounds.

The woman had one hand on the girl, one on his belt. The girl chose that moment to bite his shoulder, hard.

I'm used to that, honey. By someone with far sharper teeth than you have.

He thought he was on fire. His clothes felt like they were burning him. The woman was coughing harder, her hand on him faltering. He backed up and kicked the door. It rocked but didn't budge. Mick put the girl down, keeping a clamp on her arm as he kicked and kicked. It might be chained, but it was held in place by a frame that he refused to let stand. He was getting lightheaded.

Then he heard a shout, a command to wait. The man he'd first told to guide the others out appeared in that slender crack. He held a tire iron. A moment later, he broke the chain and yanked open the door, just as the older woman collapsed.

No way, abuela. We're all getting the hell out of here.

The man was of the same opinion, stepping past Mick to pick her up. A billow of hot air and smoke shoved them into the world.

Fortunately, the need to cough lessened the girl's screaming and struggling. They covered the distance from the back of the building to the truck in a matter of a few seconds, Mick hauling the girl, the man carrying the grandmother.

Cyn had put the semi out of range as he'd directed. But the bulk of their intended passengers weren't in it. They milled outside the open trailer door.

No matter how convincing Cyn could be, one, she wasn't fluent in Spanish, and two, fifteen minutes ago she'd been the enemy. They wouldn't know if this was truly an attempt to rescue them, or just a transfer to a new prison.

Some of them had bolted. He saw them making their way across the open scrub. The cartel would hunt them down. He couldn't do anything about that. But he could help the ones still here.

Mick turned to the grandmother. As the man holding her put her down onto her feet, Mick spoke fast. The man's gaze shifted to the older woman, awaiting her verdict. The people closest also watched the exchange.

In every group crisis, there was always a person or persons who became the de facto leader because of his or her wisdom, or level headedness under extreme duress.

Noting that, Mick directed the stream of words at her alone. Gripping the cross around his neck, he lifted and thrust it at her. What it meant to him was the same as it would have been to others, without the skeleton. *Have faith, abuela.*

Through watery eyes, she gazed at him. Then the grandmother lifted a hand and pointed to Mick and Cyn. "*Amigos.*" At the truck. "*Vamos.*"

He and Cyn loaded them in as fast as humanly possible. While they did, Mick kept an eye on the sky and the road. Twilight was taking its damn time about giving way to the concealment of full dark.

The man who'd helped him got into the truck last. Cyn had piled the weapons from the Mercedes near the wheel, so Mick handed him two guns and several of the grenades. "Keep everyone calm," he told him in Spanish. "The door will unlock from the inside. If I hit the horn one long blast, or if you think we've been overwhelmed, jump out and do your best to get away. Most won't, but it's better than none."

The man had a scar across the bridge of his nose and the weathered look of someone who'd spent his life working in fields. He didn't know how to use the gun, but the man next to him did. Mick gave them both instruction on the grenades. Before he shut the door, he saw the grandmother next to the girl again. She was holding and rocking her. She met his gaze before he shut them in.

He hoped he didn't have to add them to the list of faces that haunted him.

Coming back around to the front, he found the driver's seat occupied. "You need to keep your hands free for our defense," Cyn told him. "I can drive."

"Technically, you're driving our biggest defensive weapon," he pointed out. "How the hell do you know how to drive a semi?" Though he didn't doubt that she did. She knew how to fight, handle a gun, conduct a business meeting, sell a client a marketing package, and raise orchids.

"I'll tell you when we're not outrunning a cartel."

"Shit. Here I was, thinking we had time to get drive thru for sixty cheeseburgers. And one vegan patty."

It was second nature for him to quip under stress. She looked startled by it, but she put the truck in gear as if she'd been driving a semi her entire life, and they trundled forward, the engine rumbling.

"Don't use the lights," he told her. "If it gets dark enough, we might be able to get off on a side road before the bad guys show up, and they'll overlook us as they pass by."

Another slim-as-shit possibility.

Then that possibility died. The compound was a half mile in their rearview mirror when headlights popped up on their horizon. A whole stream of them. Enough twilight was left for him to make out the silhouette of two Humvees, a van and a couple flatbed trucks. They'd be bristling with armed passengers. Spotlights topped the two flatbeds, and they were

424

using them. Within a couple minutes, they'd be within their scope.

"Stop the truck," he told her. "We let them out, we all run. I'll blow up the truck and you get as far as you can."

"No. I'm staying with you. We provide cover fire together. Two's better than one."

"Cyn."

As she switched off the ignition, she gave him a look so calm, it was as if they were sitting in his motorhome at the campground. "I never expected to live this long, and if even a handful of them get away, that's worth dying for."

It wasn't like the movies, where there was time for meaningful monologues. He made decisions fast, going with his chewed-up gut. It was better that way, because otherwise his worry about what could go wrong, how she could be hurt, would get them all killed. Or pull him down with despair, knowing the worry no longer mattered.

Mick grabbed the remaining grenades and shouldered the AK as they exited the truck. Cyn stuck the couple extra mags for her gun in the pockets of her slacks.

In the desert twilight, the red dye in her hair was even redder. Her eyes were alive and hard, sparkling with adrenaline. Fear would be buried somewhere deep, an inevitable reaction to facing death, but she wouldn't let it control her.

She was right, that she never would have convinced him to let her do this if he hadn't known, in that same deep-down place, that she could handle it. But he wished that deep-down place had shut the hell up. Or he'd ignored it.

They'd reached the back of the truck, his hand on the latch to open it, when clipped and rapid gunfire rat-tat-tatted holes through the fabric of the air. Followed by an explosion that blasted his eardrums and vibrated through their feet, rocking the truck.

He jerked Cyn further behind it. Then he heard what had been masked by the truck engine and the gunfire. A helicopter.

Moving as one, they reached the corner of the truck and peered around it.

The front vehicle of the convoy was on its side, and on fire. The explosion. The one second in line had crashed into it, and was still intact, but the flames…

Mick pulled Cyn back again as it ignited, a second boom rippling the sides of the truck's trailer, like a light wind over a curtain.

The copter banked and swung around. A second one passed over him and Cyn. *Chop, chop, chop,* loud enough to vibrate the bones. Its lights blinked in the dusky gloom. Mick noted the spark of Venus in the sky. It would be bright at full dark.

But for now he was able to see the man sitting in the open doorway of the bird, holding the launcher that had taken out the first vehicle. A young-looking soldier, wearing fatigues and a helmet with a visor, so Mick couldn't see his face. No identifying markers on the helicopter, but if they'd stopped the oncoming cartel response, they were the good guys.

The post-sunset grey and black streaks in the sky mixed with billowing smoke. He and Cyn moved back to the corner, guns ready. Mick saw the convoy's rear vehicles turning around, to face the way they'd come. Blue and red lights sparked over the horizon. Realizing they were blocked, the battle-hardened men in the convoy were preparing to engage.

The cop cars slid left and right, and officers emerged, taking cover behind the vehicles as they returned fire. Mick pulled Cyn back again. Too close to friendly fire.

The cartel was in a weak position and knew it. So Mick kept sharp watch around the side of the truck, and saw when a few smarter men abandoned the vehicles and headed in their direction.

"Three incoming. Two on this side, one on the other."

"Want to switch?"

He stifled a snort. Even as she tossed out the jibe, Cyn was moving to the opposite corner. When his two were close enough, he squeezed and dropped them fast, then spun to her side. She'd already fired. He reached her in time to see her target fall and stay down, though in that same blink he'd had his gun arm stretched out, parallel to hers, back pressed against her shoulder blade, just in case another shot was needed.

She touched her temple to his jaw, a brief contact and acknowledgement of the backup.

One of the helicopters passed again, then hovered, gusting air over them as it laid down a blast of warning fire in front of the truck. Cartel members were putting their guns down, raising their hands and dropping to their knees. Some tried running off the road and into the scrub, hoping to be lost in the dark.

The cops had K-9 units and would track them down. The desert terrain extended for miles, and when the sun came up, dehydration would get them if they didn't surrender.

Even with all the evidence that things had resolved in their favor, Mick didn't relax his guard. Not until he saw the movement around those cartel vehicles contained by the police, and was certain the few rabbiting were too busy being chased to circle back.

The police were advancing past the convoy toward the truck, ordering anyone listening to step out and show their hands.

Cyn had holstered her weapon. She had his hand, was holding it tight. It was an unusually sentimental gesture for her, but their fortunes had shifted from certain death to a just-at-the-right-moment arrival of the good guys. While fucking fabulous, it was also jarring, like riding a roller coaster with no shocks.

427

Mick put the AK on the ground, and holstered his Glock. Then he gripped the back door latch and called out, so the men would know it was him, and opened the panel.

They were ready, guns lifted and grenade pins hooked over knuckles. Mick leaned an elbow against the door, and nodded to the man who'd saved his life with a tire iron. "Esta bien," he said. "Todos están a salvo."

You're all safe.

Years ago, when Tyler and Mick had discussed him using that 911 text, Mick had been sure it would be too late to do him any good. The point would be to have Tyler swoop in and do damage control.

No one was Superman.

Mick was revising that opinion. Apparently, his handler's capabilities were as endless as Cyn's marketable job skills. He'd be visiting a Hallmark store soon to find a thank you card. Maybe he'd go for one of the expensive ones that played music when opened. The Superman theme song.

Since Cyn liked Hallmark movies, maybe she had a reward points card. She'd probably knee him in the balls for asking. Then hand over the card.

The helicopters never landed. Since the police didn't ask Mick about them, he assumed the birds had whatever official capacity needed to be accepted by the border agents.

Since they usually needed all the help they could get, they weren't likely to look a gift horse in the mouth. Especially when they were going to get credit for busting up a human trafficking deal involving a truckload of people.

They hadn't known that right off, though. Before the cops reached them, Mick had called out and stepped from behind the truck with his hands raised. He'd repeated, over and over, that he had victims in the back, and an unarmed woman standing to his right.

He refused to let her step out, even when they insisted. Not when that many guns were pointing their way.

When they circled wide and had both him and Cyn in their sights, the cop in the lead gave them a close look. "They're ours," he told the others, and gun muzzles lowered.

His gaze shifted behind them, to the frightened truck occupants. Mick had had them relinquish the guns and grenades and put them in a neat and very visible stack on the ground. In accord, he and Cyn had also put themselves between the people and the oncoming firepower.

"Shit," one of the agents murmured.

Mick explained the situation, which kicked off a lot of next steps. Fire trucks were arriving to handle the convoy and warehouse blazes, but the border agent-in-charge radioed in a request for more medical support. As the victims were encouraged to come out of the truck, they were carefully watched by the armed agents. "Trust but verify" was a way to prevent nasty surprises—and to stay alive. Once it was clear no one in the truck was a threat, the people began to be treated like survivors.

By that time, an army of emergency vehicles had arrived.

As Mick answered the agent-in-charge's initial questions, he picked up some information of his own. Tyler's tapdancing had him and Cyn as undercover agents working with an unnamed but valid organization. "I'll still want to question each of you further," the AIC said. "But first you need medical care. Ma'am, you need to sit down."

"Don't mind if I do." Cyn dropped to the ground.

Shit. Mick spun and caught her before she landed too hard on her ass. Blood from the gunshot wound had soaked the slacks around the entry point. It wasn't life-threatening, else Mick would have already had her in the first ambulance, but adrenaline was sliding away, and Cyn was feeling it.

"Being shot hurts," she informed him. "Not the good kind of pain."

429

"No, it isn't." The hand he passed over her hair shook a little. All that stiff goop he'd put in it had held astonishingly well. He missed her curls. The large sunglasses were up on her head, but he put them back down as the AIC waved over EMTs. "Keep those on while they get you to the bus. Don't remove them until you're inside."

Though they were currently in front of the truck, the cartel members were still here. Stretched out on the ground, their wrists zip-tied, but eyes free to roam. With the disguising measures Mick had taken, Cyn shouldn't be recognized from a passing glance, but he wasn't taking chances. Her face was memorable.

She touched his shoulder around the entry wound. "You've been shot, too, you know."

"Yeah. It's not bad."

"You've been shot enough to know the difference between good and bad?"

"Pretty much. If you fall down and stop breathing, it's bad."

She looked at the ground. "I fell down."

He stroked her arm. "You're still breathing fine."

A bullet in the leg was nothing to mess with. But if it had hit a major artery, she would have bled out already. He didn't let his mind dwell there. He was a master at keeping anything out of range that didn't serve the moment's needs, but touching her, her eyes on him, was making that difficult.

File it, manage it, deal with it later.

"Put your arms around my neck," he told her.

"You are not carrying me when you have a bullet in□—"

He picked her up and carried her to the nearest ambulance, where they'd just put the gurney out. They saw him coming and removed the go bag so he could put her on the mattress. "Shut up, Mistress," he murmured. "How are you supposed to kick my ass if you don't let them take care of you?"

Her hand was on his face, her eyes full of a reaction to that. "Not now," he told her. "I can't...not now."

He didn't know what would happen if he let it out here. He bottled the rage, the fear, all of it. When this was done, he'd bring it to a remote campground, and let the primal take over.

Would he tell Cyn about the day he'd stripped naked, rolled in mud and run with wolves? Or startled a young grizzly into bolting away from him when he charged him screaming, daring him to take Mick on?

She'd tell him he was a fucking idiot. No argument. If it had been a mother with cubs, he would have been lunch meat. But he'd dreamed of being wrapped in those arms, the talons raking across his flesh, the blood-tinged breath coming in for the kill, his head dropped back to take it.

Giving the mother grizzly his ferocity and then yielding to her judgment.

If he had a guardian angel—and today his looked a lot like Tyler Winterman—the angel probably wondered what he'd done to be saddled with a crazy bastard like Mick.

"Mick." Pain shot through his shoulder. Despite the startled look from the tech, Cyn had put her thumb on the chunk of flesh the graze had taken and pressed down. Proof that she'd said his name a couple times and resorted to other measures to bring his attention back.

Mick put his hand over hers. "I'm here."

Cyn moved her touch to his collarbone, her bloodstained thumb rubbing a caressing track over the first scar she'd given him and hooking the necklace. His flesh tingled under the contact, helping to ground him further. "Go get checked out, or I will make you get on this gurney instead," she said.

God, a smile hurt worse than the wound. He put his head down against hers. The techs had cut her pants away to reveal the blood-smeared thigh and an oozing bullet hole. When she stiffened against the pain, hers hurt him far worse than his own ever could.

"Sir, you need to give us room."

"Back the fuck off," Cyn told the tech.

The pain of a laugh would surely kill him. So Mick brushed his mouth over hers and stepped back, giving her hand a quick squeeze. "Mick," she warned.

"Yes, ma'am. I'm headed for the nearest available person with a paramedic go-bag. Stolen or not."

He gestured to the EMTs. "Don't let her near anything sharp. And she bites."

The promise of retribution flashed through her gaze, but he moved out of range. He knew to stay within her line of sight as he reached the triage area. The people in the truck were being assessed by the army of emergency personnel. They'd separated out the ones in the worst shape, and the schizophrenic girl had been mercifully sedated. She was on a gurney, her grandmother hovering close as another EMT checked her nose and mouth for smoke exposure.

"Sir, let's take a look at that shoulder. Were you exposed to the fire?"

Mick shifted away from the male EMT and pointed at his female partner. She'd just finished an assessment of the tire iron man and was directing him toward the area where those who were in good shape were being given bottled water, energy bars, and a place to sit and wait for the next step.

Experienced enough to read his patient—or warned by that look in Mick's eyes—the male EMT pointed his partner to Mick.

As Mick took a seat on the open back of the ambulance and let himself be examined, he noted the EMT working on Cyn had returned to the leg after evaluating the rest of her. So the leg was the worst of it. From the paleness of her cheeks and the set of her mouth, the bullet might not be life threatening, but it was lodged somewhere painful. They'd immobilized the limb and would soon be transporting her. Or they'd better be, if they didn't want him up their asses about it.

His EMT cleared him with the usual "recommend you go to the hospital" spiel. He gave her a courteous but dismissive nod. "Got it."

The Hispanic woman had a chunky build, sharp brown eyes and abundant, gray-streaked hair pulled back in a ponytail. "I know you cop types think you're invincible, but just sit here a few minutes. You've done enough for one day."

"Honey, I have three more raids and a shootout scheduled before midnight."

Her lips quirked and she pointed a finger at him. "Sit and stay," she ordered and moved off, shouldering her bag.

"Yes, ma'am," Mick murmured absently. Two cops were with Cyn now, one of them the agent-in-charge. Because Mick had coached her enough for the meet with Rodriguez, he had no doubt she'd know what pieces of the truth to share.

During his assessment, a prison van had been brought to transport the surviving cartel members. They were gone. In the distance, he saw the flashing lights of the fire trucks, grouped around the warehouse. They were getting it under control, though the air was still smoky. Eyes and throats were going to be raw tomorrow. He could no longer see flames, except for the occasional spout as they overhauled the building.

Two buses rolled up. The ambulances had had to skirt the damaged vehicles, but since then the cops had pushed them to the side to clear the road for the buses. They would transport the ambulatory victims to health centers and temporary shelters.

News vans had arrived some time ago, but were being held behind a police barricade. The network helicopters kept passing over, though. Bright lights had been set up on scene by the cops, but Mick was out of the direct glare and kept his head down. He'd secured a spare bill cap from one of the cop cars to shadow his face.

The AIC was done with Cyn and headed his way. Captain Weatherby, according to his bulletproof vest patch, looked like he was former military. His squinted, steel-colored eyes had seen things as bad as expected for this job.

"Surprised you didn't have someone watching me to keep me from bolting from this shitshow," Mick observed.

The captain's response proved he didn't miss much. "You aren't going anywhere she isn't. So why waste the manpower?"

"She okay?" In the list of emotions Mick was having to keep under tight wrap, his objection to not being right up on her was at the top.

"She's going to need to go to the hospital, because the bullet needs to be removed, but she's stable for right now."

"Lodged in the muscle?"

"Yeah. She told the tech she'd take off a testicle if he gave her anything beyond aspirin. She also won't answer any questions about you. Says we have to ask you directly, and if we give you a hard time, she'll gut us in ways turkeys have nightmares about during the holiday season." Humor passed through his gaze. "That's a quote."

Hearing that helped, but knowing the kind of pain she had to be enduring didn't. Mick rose as the EMTs started to move Cyn into the bus. "If you have questions for me, I'll be at the hospital. We were working undercover, it went south when the cartel stabbed our contact in the back, and tried to swoop in and take his cargo. We got in the middle."

The captain glanced toward the victims being moved toward the buses. "According to them, you two kept them from being burned up as collateral damage."

"Will they be sent home?" The captain had to fall in next to him as Mick strode toward the ambulance. Cyn was saying something and gesturing in his direction. The look on her face said the EMT was about to be in the kind of trouble Weatherby had described.

434

"The ones who want to go," Weatherby said. "Those who came here thinking they could find work, we'll try to get them legitimate work visas."

Though the people getting on the bus had been checked out, most moved as if they were in shock, overwhelmed.

Would the dull eyes of the young women and teens ever be bright again? Could they laugh or smile without fear hovering in the shadows?

At least they'd have the chance to find out.

The older woman was being helped into the ambulance that contained her granddaughter. The girl appeared to be sleeping, though her brow was creased, her body twitching. Her grandmother bent over her, smoothing her brow.

As if feeling Mick's regard, she raised her head and met his gaze. Masking the sudden tightness in his chest with a cough, he turned away.

He'd never been present for the victories, such as they were. The good feelings didn't do him any favors. They piled on top of the other things, putting weight on his chest. He needed to breathe through that, or some overeager EMT would decide he was having a heart attack.

He reached Cyn's side before she could lunge off the gurney at the EMT. She was bristling like a pissed-off badger. "For the last fucking time, I'm not going without him," she said.

Mick risked losing a hand by putting it on her shoulder. "You're not going with me. I'm going with you." He hoped. "If you're nice, they'll give you the bullet when they dig it out. You can string it on the same necklace where you keep the fingerbones and teeth of your past victims."

She eyed him, but her expression eased. Yes, they had given her aspirin, but it was nowhere near enough for the pain she was in. Perspiration was on her forehead, and he knew that twitchy, just under the skin look.

"Can't you give her something more?" he demanded, already knowing the answer.

The EMT pointed at her from a safe distance. "She won't let me."

She wouldn't want her senses to be dulled. He got that, but he moved a hand to her face. "I'm here now," he told her. "I'm okay. Let them give you more."

"I'm fine." Cyn's searing gaze went back to the hapless EMT. "He rides with us."

"Would I dare say no?" The man responded dryly. He pointed Mick to the bench inside the bus, tacit acceptance and hope in the gesture, that he would keep the badger from bloody mayhem.

"I'll see you at the hospital," Weatherby told Mick.

Because Cyn was stable, the EMT shut the doors and joined his partner in the front. It was an open area where he could monitor Cyn from the passenger area, which gave Mick a little bit of privacy with her.

When he clasped her hands, the convulsive grip confirmed his assessment. "Let them give you some more pain meds," he reiterated.

She shook her head. "I'm fine."

"Yeah, you are. Draw one of those deep breaths with me, then. Let it out. Easy."

She complied without protest, telling him how much she was hurting. Damn stubborn woman. "So you didn't answer my question. How the hell do you know how to drive a semi?"

"Truck driving school, when I first came to NOLA and was looking at my employment options, beyond the car dealership. Ros also had Lawrence give me combat driving lessons for a birthday gift. How to ram barricades and squash people." Her strained voice held a note of pride. "The police arrived before I could show off my skills."

As she spoke, a shift happened. Her grip on him tightened, knuckles whitening. Her eyes went glassy, and she started to shake.

Shit. In a heartbeat, he was holding her. He didn't care how mad she got. But she didn't object, which told him two things. How deeply she was rattled, and how much she trusted him. She let herself be held as she tried her best not to hyperventilate.

"Been a while since I've done that," she muttered. "Fight for my life or someone else's. I'm out of practice."

"Hey, just like riding a bike. You did great."

She started laughing, and as she did, tears rolled out of her eyes. She didn't notice until he brushed them away, and she looked mortified. Then pissed.

"If you tell anyone I cried, I'll shoot you and make it look like a suicide. I'll put you in women's underwear, too."

He touched her cheek with a knuckle. "Make it something frilly. You know I like to look pretty."

At the hospital, they took her away from him to work on her leg. When he was pacing the waiting room floor for the hundredth time, he got company.

Tyler looked the same in a hospital as he did at the flower festival, in a firefight, or anywhere else. A confident man who had enough money to wallpaper the planet, carrying a mantle of lethal calm developed from years of operating in worlds as grim as those Mick inhabited now.

He sat down in a chair, straightening his legs and crossing his ankles. "She going to be okay?"

"Yeah." On his hundredth lap, some of it had caught up to Mick. All the things that could have gone wrong. How much of a fucking idiot he was, letting her do what she'd done. But if she hadn't been along, not only would he be dead, but a lot of innocent people as well. Getting those people out had required two sets of hands.

"So what are you going to do now?"

Mick gave Tyler a puzzled look. "Wait for her to feel better, then get her back on a plane to New Orleans. This will take a while to sort itself out, but in a few weeks, they'll have another shipment coming. In the meantime, I can head out to southern California to dig into the shit there, get some communication lines started."

"You're done, Mick."

Mick's gaze snapped to his handler. "What?"

Tyler's amber eyes were steady. "Twenty cartel members saw you talking to border agents. Weatherby's solid, but even he'd tell you to assume at least a couple of those agents are dirty. You were treated like an undercover on scene. Plus the victims will remember what you did for them and talk. Not to betray you, but it will get through the grapevine and the result will be the same."

Mick had already been putting together ideas on how he'd cover that. He wasn't worried about Cyn. Disguising her and not giving the cops her real identity had taken care of that. Mick had known some could be on the cartel's payroll.

Once she was back in New Orleans, she was safe.

"I can work it out."

"Not with me." Tyler's tone wasn't unkind, but it was implacable enough to pull Mick's attention out of his own head to focus on the man's resolute expression. "You had a good run. You've accomplished more than anyone ever thought possible. You want to keep working in this field, there are other ways. Special investigation teams and agencies in the New Orleans area who work with the police and SBI could use someone with your knowledge."

"I'm not done." The panic that bloomed in his chest startled him. It felt like he was about to be pushed into a pitch black zero gravity place, no sense of up or down, walls or ceilings. No stars to light his way.

"Would it be easier if someone had put a bullet in your brain today?" Tyler asked pleasantly.

Yes. Don't do this to me.

The words didn't make it to his lips, but Tyler's gaze told him they didn't have to. Mick swallowed, forced himself to sound casual. He'd eventually talk some sense into Tyler if he played along.

"Why New Orleans?"

Tyler lifted a brow. "Where else would you be? That's where she is."

Rubber-soled shoes squeaked to a stop in the waiting room doorway. Mick saw a male doctor standing there. "Jane Doe?" he said without a flicker of irony.

"Yeah." As Mick closed in on him, the doctor took a wary step back. He wiped the killing look from his face and managed the right tone. Mostly. "Tell me she's okay."

"Yes. Bullet's out and wound is dressed. We were able to convince her to let us do it with anesthesia." Poise restored, the doctor's tone suggested that "convincing" had taken slightly more effort than his patient load for the month. "She's a little out of it, but should be able to leave tonight, which she stressed was her preference."

An understatement of astounding proportions.

"She'll need some PT to condition that leg properly during the healing process," he added, "so we'll send a copy of her records and our notes with her. She's in recovery. The nurse will come get you when she's ready to go."

"Okay. Thanks, doc. Does she need a wheelchair? Crutches?"

"Probably a cane to give her additional support. You can pick one up at a local pharmacy." Humor crept into his tired voice. "When she was still under the effects of the anesthesia, she called me a sissy when I asked her if she was comfortable. She also mentioned her birthday is coming up and she expects a strawberry cupcake. With vanilla frosting."

"Okay." Mick wanted to smile, but couldn't. The doctor left him, shoes squeaking across shiny clean tiles.

Tyler cleared his throat. "Mick."

"I got it," he said. "Just...let's talk in a few days. Okay?"

"Okay." Tyler rose. Mick didn't turn in his direction. When Tyler put his hand on Mick's shoulder, he flinched, but the other man didn't lift it.

"Go home with her, Mick. Take a few days. Take a week, a month. Believe me when I say I know how damn hard it is to change paths from something like this. But it's what has to happen now. You were reaching the C-4 end of the lit fuse. Deep inside you, you knew."

His tone hardened. "I know what exit strategy you planned on. Now you have a different one. One I hope to God you'll realize is better."

Mick went rigid. Tyler took his hand away, but he wasn't done. "All these years, you've never fixated on one woman. Suddenly, you have. If you don't recognize that as a message from something bigger than all of us, then you're already brain dead. No bullet required."

"Funny," Mick murmured. Cyn had pointed toward the same thing, to justify how she'd ended up joining him on what Tyler wanted him to believe was his last job.

Fate. It always came back to him serving the Fates. Those heartless, beautiful sadists.

"You know where I am," Tyler said. "Reach out in a few days and let me know how you're doing. Whatever you need, you've earned all the help I can give you. To follow that new track." He paused.

"Tell your Mistress I wish her the best. And remind her what I told her about orchid care."

CHAPTER TWENTY-FOUR

Mick told Cyn he'd drive her home to New Orleans. He wouldn't say if he was staying. He didn't say much of anything, though he was solicitous of her every need. He told her the doctor had recommended PT. Jon Forte's wife and submissive, Rachel, was a physical therapist. Cyn would hit her up and see what exercises she should do.

Mick had given her Tyler's message about orchid care. She'd been thinking about it a lot, while also thinking about Mick. Last night she'd sent a one-line text to that number Tyler had given her. She wasn't sure if he'd already discarded the phone attached to it, but she did it anyway.

He's done, isn't he?

The response came back a half-hour later. *Yes. I've told him. Tread carefully.*

She'd never been fond of being careful. In her experience, it didn't give her the desired results.

Now she sat in the passenger seat watching Mick drive as she scrolled on her phone. His mind looked like it was a million miles away. But whenever she moved the slightest bit, his attention was on her, making sure she was okay.

She'd finished with her work email some time ago, and had instead been looking for something else. She lifted the screen to show it to him.

He glanced at the screen. "I can have you home tonight."

"I know. I want to stay here instead. We have the time, right?"

"Yeah. I guess. Sure."

She let it go for another few minutes. They were passing through forest, marsh, forest, marsh. Open fields. More forest. He was right. She could be home in a couple hours. But she wasn't crossing New Orleans' city limits with this unresolved.

"Talk to me, Mick."

"I don't want to talk."

"Since when do you refuse a direct command?"

His jaw hardened and this time his eyes didn't leave the road. "Since I don't want to talk about fucking anything. My letting you top isn't a constant. You're smart enough to know that, to not pull some shit like that."

"'Letting me' top. Interesting."

He swore and pulled off onto a side road, a service entrance to a local state park. When he switched off the engine, he shifted to face her. "Stop playing with my head and just say what it is you want to say."

"Your cover's been blown, and you can't do this anymore. You're as fucked up as you can be right now, and you need to work through it."

"Thank you. Didn't realize you were a therapist. Maybe you can leave TRA and pursue a career as a professional Domme. One of those who helps sad bastards work through their shit by letting you piss on them."

She unbuckled her seatbelt. He'd gotten her a cane—a sparkly black and silver one from the drugstore—but the limp wasn't that bad, and she didn't need it for this. Unless she decided to bash him in the head with it.

When she lunged at him with an open palm, he grabbed her wrist, but his head really was fucked if he'd fallen for the distraction, the idea she'd respond to the insult with a weak-assed slap. She punched him with the free hand, snapping his head to the left.

He surged up, pushing her into the aisle of the camper. While it would have been a better strategy to have him stop the motorhome and lure him outside, where she had more room for this fight, she wouldn't waste time on that.

She hooked his ankle and they crashed to the floor, him hitting his shoulder on the table as he twisted, trying to protect her from the impact. Despite his obvious anger, he had his arm around her, hand up to protect her skull. She landed beneath him, but most his weight came down on his knee, hard enough she heard the pained grunt.

She seized his hair, yanked. "I can feel how much you need to run me down, Mick. You want something to hunt and fight. I can't give you the hunt, but I can give you a fight."

She struck at his face again, brought her knee up. He wrenched away, so she found thigh muscle instead of testicles. He seized her shoulders and gave her a sharp shake. "You're going to hurt your leg," he snarled. "Stop it. Stop being a bitch."

"That's what I am, Mick. Always." Even while glaring at him, her hands went to his belt, unhooked and stripped it off. It drew his attention, made him slower to push her away, so she got the button of the jeans unhooked, the zipper halfway down, before he knocked her touch aside. "I'm 'letting you' top me, aren't I?" she hissed. "You can't take anything I don't want to give you. You're not wired that way."

She wrapped her legs over his back, ignoring the bolt of pain through her thigh. She wore her short knit skirt, because it lay more comfortably over the taped bandage than slacks or jeans. She grabbed one of his hands, shoving it beneath the hem. "So fuck me. Show me who's boss. Show me I can't get into your head just because I want to. That you're in control of your whole universe. Even when it's burning down, you can get it up and show me you're in charge. Totally in control."

He slammed his mouth down on hers, and she bit him, as he would expect. She wanted to draw blood and she did. He leaned into it, his whole body rigid, holding her down like he was a block of concrete. Her internal organs felt compressed, everything aching, but she wouldn't be the one to give, even if he crushed her.

Proving it, he cursed and shoved himself back on his heels. In the next blink, she was alone. As he refastened his jeans, he exited the motorhome so violently it rocked.

443

Bastard. He knew she couldn't move fast. Still, she grabbed the cane and the other thing she thought she might need, managing to reach the ground before he'd made it too far down the service road. If he thought she was going to chase *him*, he was delusional.

She lifted the gun she'd pulled from her bag and took aim.

The warning shot kicked up the ground fifteen feet to his right. He started away from it and spun, shock on his face.

"If you try to run from me, I will actually shoot you," she said. "In the leg, so we'll match."

He stared at her. After three pregnant seconds, he moved in her direction, his steps as precise as those beats of time. She evaluated his state of mind, had a moment where she thought she might need to shoot him before he did her actual physical harm, but then he was in front of her. He wrapped his fingers around her wrist as he took her Walther. He put it carefully on the stoop, as if he didn't trust either one of them with it.

Then he faced her. "I can't bear it, Cyn. I won't be able to bear it. Not doing it. As long as I was working, I could stay ahead of it, stay ahead of this."

He struck his forehead with the heel of his hand, like a double tap from a fatal bullet. He lowered a clenched fist to his side. "If I always had some way of going forward, it was okay. You can't…there's no way… You can leave, but you don't leave, you see? Too many people lost, because I had to let them lose."

He dropped to his knees, not because he was kneeling to her, but because that concrete weight she'd felt upon her was holding him down as well. He gave her a helpless look, a man she'd never seen look helpless. "I don't know what to do. I know Tyler is right. I know it. There's all forms of cowardice, Mistress, and on this, I'm a coward. I wish I'd been burned alive in that building, or shot in the head. When

I wake from nightmares, at least the ghosts standing around my bed know I'm still trying to do something. Now…"

His half laugh, so miserable and hopeless, squeezed her heart with dread. "I don't know."

I wish I'd been shot in the head. He meant it. He was in that kind of pain.

It took her back to Cissy in the bathroom. He knew what those words meant to her, so the fact he couldn't stop himself from saying them wasn't intended to hurt her. It was stark honesty.

It was also an unconscious plea for help.

She limped to him. He was staring at the ground, so she touched his jaw, insisting that he look at her. He resisted, but in the end, he did it. She could tell he liked looking at her, finding some measure of peace in what he saw there.

That was a start. *The* start.

"It takes time, Mick. It hurts like a bitch. When my life started to be more than survival, my sold siblings set up house inside everything I did. They were out there in the world, no way of finding or helping them, especially with my mother dead and gone. She wasn't exactly a record keeper."

She let the unsteadiness enter her voice, because this wasn't a moment to hold it all in, and he was protective of her. She didn't mind embracing that, using it to draw him out of his head. "I held some of them, Mick," she reminded him. "I remember the way they looked at me, the way all babies do. The rage I feel, the sadness, the things that sabotage my happiness…I know those demons you're talking about. I've walked that path, but I also kept walking, to where I am now. If you trust me, I can help you do it, too."

She had tears on her face. His own expression had softened, the pain still there, but she'd reached him. She could give him more, if she could find the courage to do it.

If she'd had those children in her arms again, she would have done everything to fight for them. Go to the police, her and Cissy serving time with her mother. It wouldn't matter. It was nothing next to the cost of doing too little and living with it. And Cissy would have lived.

She wasn't losing Mick. If she let him disappear from her life, she would. Because she had no doubt she was in a war for his life, and this was only the first battle. He was an incredibly strong man, but one with a wound infected enough to kill him.

So she cut herself open and let all the pain, pain as overwhelming as his, come out.

"I need you, Mick."

His gaze snapped up, captured by those four words.

"I need you to love me. To be mine. To fight with me, to let me give you the pain you need, because it speaks to my own, locks together with it."

His hands were on her hips, holding her. They stayed that way for several silent moments. Seeing the struggle inside him, she steadied herself. "That is one hundred percent an order. I will beat you to death with a shovel and bury you in my backyard, rather than let you leave."

His eyes sparked, mouth tightening, but it was against the pain of an unexpected smile. "I'll try, Mistress," he said. "I swear I'll try, best as I can."

She slid her arms around his shoulders as he put his face to her midriff. He was so tense, everything held inside. She knew how to help with that.

"I'll punish you for the ones who haunt you. I'll help you put the ones you saved on the opposite side of the scale, not for balance, but for perspective, breathing room."

He nodded. As she let more tears fall on his head, she made an additional, silent promise. *And I will love you for being the kind of man who had the courage to do all of it.*

There were rare people in the world, those who tried to help, to fix, because something inside them was so strong they couldn't resist that call. They knew their life's purpose. That mandate filled up every square inch of space. The mandate *was* the person.

446

She'd had enough selfishness to save herself. To give herself happiness and a life worth living. Up until Mick, she hadn't apologized for that, had stood stubbornly against her ghosts. She'd tried to believe she was living the life Cissy and the others might have lived, if they'd been given the chance. The way she lived was an attempt to honor their lost lives.

Mick had implied she'd been as much of a victim as they'd been. Victim wasn't a word she accepted for herself, but in the context of helping him, she'd come to grips with it, without letting it become her identity.

While on a bus, a person was called a passenger. But when she decided to get off, and made that happen, not by waiting for the driver to stop, but by marching up there and forcing open the doors, leaping free, even if the bus was still in motion, she was whatever the hell she wanted to be.

She had to help him find something else he could be as well. Because for the first time in her adult life, she loved a man enough to bear the terror of losing him. Or of him changing into something she could no longer love.

She wasn't worried about the latter. Mick didn't know how to be anything but who he was. She also loved him so fiercely she wasn't letting anything take him away from her. Even himself.

She whispered that to him. And then whispered something else. "I'm your Mistress. You've done all you can this way. It's time to find another way. We'll find it, together, but first you have work to do."

He had to reclaim his soul. It was going to be a hard road, but she'd move into his head and share that space. She'd demand a key, the bigger half of the closet, his bed, and everything else. Take over and let him know everything he had was hers.

She knew what it was to have nothing, so she took very good care of what she'd earned the right to call hers.

Mick lifted his head, showing her those beautiful, dangerously still and haunted eyes. "My pain doesn't deserve to be special, Mistress."

She touched his face with a rare feeling of tenderness. "It is to me. And I'll decide what you deserve."

The place she'd told him she wanted to spend the night was in a heavily wooded park that offered few amenities. Just campsites barely carved out of the forest, buffered from one another by extensive trails and the dense nature she didn't care for. In this case, she sacrificed comfort for the privacy she knew they'd need.

Because it was a nice night, Mick set up a screened gazebo with a canvas floor, so no bugs could get in and bother them on the wide bedroll he stretched out and outfitted with pillows and blankets. He dropped the top flap so they could see the sky through a block of screen. She could tell how weary he was, but suspected he wanted the feeling of the outside space, and had taken the extra steps for her comfort.

She had him lie down fully clothed, and put herself in his arms, settling in as they closed around her. He let out a sigh as she stroked a hand under his shirt, over his abdomen, the waistband of his jeans. She wasn't going to initiate sex, not yet. For now, she just lay with him, and let whatever feelings needed to be spoken have space to come to the surface.

"I told myself the reason I never defined myself as a sub was because I don't overanalyze anything," he said at last. "It gets in the way, and it's usually wrong, making assumptions about yourself or anyone else. We're too complicated to narrow down to one thing, and so simple the reasons seem too obvious and get overlooked."

"So what was the actual reason?"

He paused. "You know how a lot of people, even in committed relationships, fantasize about the perfect lover? The one who can make them see stars, and cherishes them, makes them feel wonderful and special, like they deserve that feeling?"

"Yes. I find them annoying."

His chest vibrated with a chuckle. "You really are a bitch. My bitch. Don't get your hackles up. It's not a possession thing. More like saying you're my queen."

"And you're the country I rule. I like that." Her hand slid down, cupping him through denim to give him a bruising squeeze before she tapped his thigh. "Plenty of territory to explore and claim."

"Nice ego stroke. Thanks, Mistress. I noticed you have Hallmark movies. Some of them are the romance kind."

"I will deny that under torture, but since you've actually seen them, yes."

He chuckled again, then quieted for another few moments. "What I fantasized about was being the one who could give a Mistress that, keep giving it to her, learning what she needed and wanted. I imagined a Mistress who'd want all that from me, who could guide me to that place with her, because it only works if you come to it together."

He lifted a shoulder. "You can't become someone's real fantasy from the outside. It has to be from the heart and soul, and you have to earn her trust, little by little, to get there. Once you're there, you're already halfway to being what she needs you to be, if you know what I mean. The rest evolves over time. Trying to define that on the front end…it limits it. Narrows your vision so you don't see the road you're supposed to go down. Does that make sense? I didn't want to call myself something and miss that turn."

She'd lifted her gaze. His blue eyes were still sad, but the faint smile that crossed his face gave her hope. "A few years ago, I was in traffic, and saw this woman ahead of me. She was turning her neck this way and that, like she'd been driving a while. Rubbing it with one hand. The shirt she wore was scooped in back, so I could see some of her back and shoulders. It reminded me of you in the cemetery, when you put your head down and looked so weary."

She remembered that night, the cold. She hadn't showered in two days. She'd felt like what she was, a feral thing ready to fight whatever threatened her.

"I wanted to put my hands on her," Mick said. "Massage her neck and shoulders, give her comfort, not asking anything in return, just giving her that moment. On the big stage, letting her know she wasn't alone in the world. On the small one, just help the aching neck feel better."

He had that ability. On big and little stages. She'd never been the kind of Mistress who imagined a live-in sub, all the benefits to it. But when she had the thought and attached it to Mick, it became far more interesting.

Definitely not Hallmark, but something that fit them.

"Being a cop again is one choice, but I don't think it's the right one for me." He'd taken a turn back to his main conflict, but she knew it was all connected. "Good cops can find that balance between following the rules and helping, dealing with what's not right or fair. They can get up the next day and keep doing the job. I couldn't."

His gaze was distant, away from the fire and this moment. "Weirdly, anything that happened to me, being shot, beat up, all of that passed in a blink. Watching someone else suffer, nothing else in this world is as endless."

She pushed herself up on one elbow, resting her hand on his chest and gazing down into his face. "Mick. That song you're always humming. 'Gone, Gone, Gone.' Do you get an image in your head when you're hearing it?"

His eyes cleared, curious. "Yeah. I do."

"What is it?"

"A beer commercial." His lips tilted in that faint smile. "Something that reminds me of a Christmas beer commercial. I see a hammock between two palm trees, on some deserted tropical beach. There's a little house nearby, decorated in Christmas lights. You and I are lying in the

450

hammock. There's a breeze. We're sleeping, holding onto one another. The way the hammock is moving, the waves on the shore, they match the song's rhythm."

"A rope hammock."

"Yeah."

Like in her backyard, where she could order him to restrain himself using the diamond-shaped openings, and enjoy herself. Thoroughly. He'd filled in a nice setting around it.

Mick shifted so they were on their sides, facing one another. He touched her thigh with gentle fingers. As she watched, he rested his palm over the skirt fabric and the bandage beneath.

"You're all muscle and silky flesh," he noted. "Not as wiry as you were as a teen, but you don't let your soft spots give a man too much."

"I don't give a man too much of anything. He'll get spoiled."

Another smile and he bent forward, pressing his mouth to her thigh. He held that way until her hand came to his hair, fingers digging in.

"I want something, Mistress. I want it bad."

"Tell me what it is, and I'll tell you if I'm in the mood to be kind."

"I want to give you pleasure, Mistress. Let me eat your pussy. Make you sigh in that deep way you do when I give you what you want."

She stroked his hair, making him wait for her answer. He put his forehead above the bandaged area, his breath warm through cloth. Waiting without expectation, showing he knew the decision was all hers. Even as his mouth teased her with its proximity.

She shifted, so he lifted his head. She hooked the leg over his shoulder, spreading her thighs, a nonverbal assent.

He moistened his lips. "May I remove your clothes, Mistress?"

The nearest campsite wasn't close, and it hadn't been occupied. Not that either of them was that modest. If someone saw them, fine.

Just don't fucking interrupt.

"Only the skirt and shoes. And take off your shirt first." She did her shirt herself, arching to pull it over her head and leaving her in the pink lacy underwear she was wearing.

"Yes, I do occasionally wear pink," she informed him. "It looks good with my brunette coloring."

"It surely does."

She cocked her head in her best coquettish look—which wasn't that convincing—and ran a finger along the center of his chest. "Does this fit reverse Daddy Dom? Daddy better eat me just right, or he'll find out what a spanking feels like from his little girl?"

He laughed, making her heart do a hard somersault. Hope could hurt, but she'd accept that kind of pain.

As his gaze traveled back down her body, he slid his hands to her hips, then up under her back. He rose, impressing her with his balance. Her other leg was hooked under his arm as she rode his shoulder, perched like a queen on the throne his shoulder could provide. The bullet graze that had taken flesh hadn't seemed to bother him. "The circus might be another career option," she noted.

Another smile as he took her to the side of the motorhome. She could grip some of its various protrusions to anchor herself, arch herself into his mouth. But she changed her mind, wanting to give him more.

"Take me to the bed, Mick. I want you to serve me there."

"Any way you want, Mistress. Anywhere you want."

He had to put her down, but he gripped her hand to lead her up the steps and inside, down the aisle to the bed. Lifting her at the waist, he put her on the mattress. She braced a foot against the door frame that allowed the area to be a private sleeping quarters. The other she slid over his shoulder again.

452

"You can put your mouth and tongue under the silk if you can get it there without the help of your fingers," she said. "But you better not rip it."

He gave her a flash of wolfish teeth, telling her that she might be punishing him for that. She could accept that.

He worshipped her thighs with his mouth, endless strokes and teasing touches, while she sank into it, no desire to rush. She also sank into the idea of a man from whom she could demand more than two hours of her time. If she wanted him to worship her body with his mouth all damn night long, he'd do it. She could devote herself to experiencing it.

It would also remind Mick there was more than one form of service that could demand his attention, his energy, in a way that mattered. In the service of love, of caring for the person who'd told her she needed him.

Just as much as he needed her.

His mouth hovered over her cunt, came in close, the moistness shivering through her. Probing with his tongue under the elastic, he found her folds, the slickness of her body. He pushed the underwear out of his way with his mouth and nose so he could put his lips fully over her, suck on her. A tiny nip with his teeth here and there gave her a shiver, a rush of pleasure as a nip became a full clamp. His teeth held her as his jaw tightened to increase the pressure on her labia. While holding her in that grip, his tongue slid over the compressed, swollen tissues, again and again. Pleasure rocketed through her. She tugged hard on his hair, pressing against his grip on her thigh.

"Oh…" Her hand fisted on the covers, the blankets that smelled like him. She'd make them smell like her, one of many ways she'd wind herself around him. Every thought of her, every memory, every word, would form the bonds that held him to her.

She brought both hands back to her upper body and cupped her breasts, playing over nipples taut behind pink lace. Those fierce blue eyes followed the motion even as his mouth kept cherishing her, driving her. She would writhe and dance, play with herself, tempting him with the sight. Everything she did had his attention as he performed as she desired, with full enthusiasm, his mouth teasing, tasting.

She opened the front clasp of the bra, pushing the cups away. "Come suck me, Mick."

He moved up her body, and as he did, she adjusted her knee to rub it against his arousal, pleased with what she found. His eyes sparked in the dim light before he dipped his head to draw her right nipple into a forceful suckle. He gripped her knee, holding it in place against him as he worked his hips, letting her feel his length.

When he let her go, she opened her legs, hands guiding him to rest his chest and upper abdomen against her wet center as he settled to feast. She made herself stay still, didn't grind against him, a sure way to make her climax. She didn't want to go there yet.

She moved to his shoulders, thumb brushing the scar she'd given him before she slid her palms over his back, feeling the healing impression of the X. Any time it threatened to disappear, she'd open it up again, so he'd bear that brand from her, too. Always. She dug her nails into it, and earned a harsh groan even as his service to her breasts didn't slacken.

Not until she put a hand on his jaw, breaking the contact. "I want you inside me."

He sat back only long enough to open the jeans, shove them down, and don a condom.

"Soon as you test clean, nothing is between us ever again," she told him. She had no doubts about his fidelity. None.

His eyes flared with heat, and she clasped her legs over his hips, urging him fully onto the bed with her. As he braced his hands by her shoulders, she put her palms on his face, holding them both still. Vibrating with need, but waiting, gazes locked.

She tightened her legs, drawing him into her, inch by inch, until they were fully joined. His face was set with self-restraint. Wanting to test him, she lay back and began to undulate on his length, a slick up and down. Her fingers dug into his braced arm, telling him to stay still.

"Look down, Mick," she said in a throaty voice. "Watch how my cunt slides down over your cock, leaving you so slippery. All the way...back up."

"Christ. Mistress."

"Stay still."

She kept doing it while he shuddered, while his muscles stood out on his arms and chest, a feast for her eyes. Finally, she let go, the climax rolling through her while he had to stand fast and watch it happen.

Her servant. Her sub. Her slave.

She said all those things to him, watched him come apart behind his eyes, needing that possession with an intensity she would never take for granted. She'd respect it in ways he couldn't yet imagine. In ways they'd explore together.

She brought him down to her. When he slid his arm beneath her and held her tight against his chest, she folded hers over his back.

"Beg me to come," she whispered.

"Please let me come inside you, Mistress. And when I can do it with nothing between us, I'll mark you as mine, too."

Her lips curved against his rough cheek. "You'd get a punishment for that if you weren't trembling, your voice full of such need. Come for me, Mick."

He thrust into her in one violent stroke, making her glad he was holding onto her so securely. As he lifted his upper body to work himself in her, she put her hands on his chest, curled her fingers into rough hair and heated flesh, and watched the climax roar over him. The groans were torn from deep inside.

She met him thrust for thrust. The motorhome rocked, the mattress pressing into her sides as he thrust her into it. An aftershock made her gasp with pleasure. When he finished, her body milked his cock until there was nothing left. At least for a little while. He'd proven he had impressive recovery time. And stamina.

The man was committed to doing a thorough job on any assigned task. Going above and beyond expectations.

The thought had some sobering implications, taking her back to how this had started. And why. "You're mine, Mick," she said softly. "I won't let you go."

He had his head down beside hers, so she couldn't see his face. She put both her hands over his skull, cradled it. The flesh stretched over bone on the right side was rough beneath the hairline, another harrowing scar. "You serve me. Your pain, your love. Tell me you understand," she whispered. "Look at me."

When he did, he braced himself above her again. His eyes still had that weary look, but they also held what they'd just shared, and a deep need to be with her. A passion to be right here, together. The possibilities had sunk into him, which was what she'd wanted to happen. Another step in the right direction.

"Tell me you understand," she repeated.

The answer came slow. "I'm afraid I'll fall apart and hurt you, Mistress. I'm going to become a fucking mess before anything gets better."

If they get better. He didn't say that part. He knew she wouldn't let him, though he probably didn't know why.

She wasn't going to let it be true.

"You will never hurt me as much as I can hurt you, Mick. That's a promise."

His lips curved. "Now that's the *kindest* thing you've ever said to me."

CHAPTER TWENTY-FIVE

"I can't believe I decided to do this. We're cancelling. I'm taking them to dinner at whatever restaurant they want. I'll even cover the bar tab."

Cyn reached for her phone, but Mick had already nicked it off the counter. For the next few moments, they played an entirely childish game of keep-away, him transferring it from one hand to another, around his back and over his head, as she grabbed for it, tried to be mad and stop laughing all at once.

"Give me that, you maniac." She punched him in the side, but he spun on his toe like a quarterback, dodging behind the kitchen island. He went left when she went right.

"Not until you say you're sticking with the plan. If we have to eat all this food, you'll be too stuffed to demand over-the-top sex."

"I'm not worried. I'll make you do all the work. Give it back, or you'll serve us dinner in one of those little maid outfits. Just a cap and apron. A transparent apron."

"No high heels?" He dodged her again.

"If you twist an ankle, you'll be no good to me."

"Sure I will. You'll just twist it harder and my screams will make you laugh."

She vaulted over the corner of the counter and almost snagged him, but he spun away and faced her at the opposite end. He tossed the phone up and caught it, giving her a wink. The bastard was far too fast. "I'm surprised you didn't try to get me to wear something like that to clean the house."

They'd done that chore together, swapping out song preferences on the music player. He'd turned Gretchen Wilson's "Redneck Woman" up to full volume and told her it was her theme song.

Hell, yeah.

She kept a neat place, so it wasn't a lot of work, but she'd wanted to take extra care with the crevices, cleaning dust that might have settled on upper shelves. He'd handled those. She'd demanded he be shirtless, because she could. Seeing her carved X sliding over the back muscles, his ass tightening in his just-right-fit jeans, made dusting far less of a chore.

It even took care of her anxiety for a while. But the time of reckoning was at hand, and it was back full force. Ros, Abby, Skye and Vera were coming to her house for dinner.

She'd placed a catering order with the vegan restaurant she liked. The women had been there before, so they knew excellent meatloaf could be made without meat, and desserts didn't need dairy to be decadent. They even went to the establishment on their own now. Skye had mentioned Tiger liked the fried tofu fingers.

The prepared dishes and sides delivered in aluminum pans only required heating in the oven to be served. The dessert was a vanilla layer cake with raspberry filling, dusted with coconut flakes. She'd made it herself.

The thought of the cake brought something deeper and more troubling to mind, and ended the game. With a sigh of annoyance—with herself—she gave up on getting the phone and left the kitchen, stepping out onto her screened porch.

She heard him put the phone back down on the counter, the creak of the door as he came out to join her. While she gazed at her backyard, he slid his arms around her waist and put his jaw against hers, a faint rasp against her skin before his mouth found her throat. He gripped her hips but didn't say anything. As a coping mechanism, the teasing had gone as far as it could. Now it was time for something else.

He'd been here for three and a half weeks. During that time, they'd learned a lot of things about each other. Some things they anticipated and some they didn't.

What she hadn't expected was finding things out about herself she didn't know, just by being with him. It was the same for him. That mirror could unbalance them both, some days more than others. It could have resulted in sniping or defensiveness. Instead, for the most part, they clasped hands and walked forward into that new terrain.

Adam and Eve, checking out Eden for the first time. When he'd framed it that way, she'd lifted a brow. "Just don't claim it was my fault when you decide to bite the apple."

He'd grinned and spread out his hands. "I'm just a simple servant to my Mistress's desires."

She rolled her eyes. "That is so not true. I have the bruises to prove it."

But not many. He was powerful and strong, and when they sparred, he had moves she'd never encountered. But she was learning, particularly on the nights that they went to parks to do primal play. Places they could slip in after dark without notice.

One night he'd caught up to her at a creek. She'd dashed across and lost her footing on a tricky, slippery rock.

As she'd gone down, headed for a bed of the sharp-edged things, there'd been time for him to register what was about to happen, but no time to stop it. Only to get in the way.

He'd lunged at her, a tackle where he grabbed her around the waist. When they toppled, his back took the brunt of the impact. She fell safely on him.

She'd confirmed he hadn't broken anything, that what he had was a shredded shirt, and a bruised and cut back. Then she'd read the light in his eyes.

She'd shoved him back against the rocks. The sound of ripping fabric cut through the gurgle of the water. She wrapped the fluttering pieces, still attached to the shirt, over her knuckles and rode him in the shallows, cold water sliding over her thighs and ankles. He cupped her knees in his palms, protecting her from the rocks, which also allowed her to pin his hands down. His gleaming eyes devoured her. She found her climax and commanded him to do the same. Blissfully joined, no condom separating them.

Later, at home, she'd tended the cuts, kissed the bruises. Held him to her, wrapped both arms around him as he shuddered, resisting the tenderness but not fighting her. Kindness was going to be difficult for him for a long time to come. Which gave her every reason to keep inflicting it upon him. The sadist in her sensed the well of suffering it tapped, the fear and dread of what it made him face. She would live up to the promise she'd made, to him and herself.

If loving you is the most painful thing for you to bear, then that gives me all the more reason to do it.

She'd whispered that to him. He'd nodded, gripped her hand on his chest, bowed his head over it. Even as he bowed his will to hers.

She'd never had a sub who needed her on so many levels, conscious and unconscious. It made it different. And fucking difficult to organize her feelings in the careful way she normally did. That could be dangerous, but danger was his freaking comfort zone.

He knew how to be what she needed, too. Like now. He wouldn't let her push him away when she faced something difficult, thinking she had to bear it all alone.

If her temper flared over it, as it often did, he proved himself just as stubborn as she was. *If I have to let you cut me to ribbons to love you, then that gives* me *all the more reason to do it.*

"We're a Hallmark couple," she decided. "Positively sappy."

"Absolutely." He turned them so they could look back into the house, toward the kitchen and dining area. "The table settings look good. That Martha Stewart magazine idea worked."

"You did hide them? My current and back issues."

"Safely under your mattress. The kids will never find them there."

She elbowed him. "Oh God, Mick. Why did I agree to do this?"

"You didn't agree to anything. You invited them." He gave her a serious look. "You're not giving away this part of yourself. You're inviting them in to share it."

He touched her face, his expression shrewd, caring. Understanding. "You're in control, Mistress."

The rumble of a motorcycle told her the moment to back out had passed. "She's early. That bitch."

"That smart bitch. They know everything. It's why you like them. You're a know-it-all Domme, too."

She narrowed her gaze. "Skye likes those fussy lime wine coolers."

"On it." He tapped his head. "I've memorized all vital intel. There will be no screw ups. At least not on my part."

He backpedaled as she tried to punch him again. "Go greet your guests. I'll get the appetizers. Good thing we got a double order of those fried tofu fingers, if Tiger's the first one here."

"Tiger isn't staying. He's just dropping her off."

His brow lifted. "I thought..."

"You assumed. It's just the women tonight."

"But you ordered enough food□—"

"To take home for their men. I'm a good hostess."

Without explaining further, Cyn moved into the house, headed for her rarely used front door. His speculative gaze followed her.

Remembering that tonight was about more than her decision to host a dinner actually helped settle her nerves. Both things had been set in motion earlier in the week.

Right after the executive staff meeting.

"So the monthly get-together is at my place," Ros said. "Anyone have any requests? Big Macs? Caviar?"

They were lingering in the top floor board room. Bastion had recorded the action items and headed for his desk. He'd informed them he was leaving promptly at five—for a damn change—to hear a new band on Frenchmen Street. More importantly, he was meeting a couple of submissives there who appreciated music. And him.

"Um…"

Cyn never said "Um." Never. All gazes swung toward her. Horrifyingly, her heart rate accelerated, and her breath tried to go short. She blurted out the words like acid reflux. "I can take a turn."

Despite all that, she hoped she seemed outwardly calm. She met Ros's gaze. "Unless you've already planned something special."

"No. I haven't."

They could have made a big deal about going somewhere they'd never been invited. But this was why they were her family, and such good Dommes to the men they chose. They knew when someone was vulnerable, even if just by doing something anyone else did without a second thought.

"That would be lovely," Ros said smoothly. "You'll need to text us the address."

"Okay. Just the four of you. Mick will be there."

Full stop, as the significance of the directive gripped the table. "Are you sure he's ready?" Skye signed first. "We know it's been rough."

Yeah, it had been.

Mick had already bolted twice. She hadn't gone after him. The first time, he'd returned after twelve hours.

The second had been three days.

"Do it one more time," she told him, "And I will chain you up in my shed."

She wasn't going to lose him to his demons.

But the threat wasn't why he hadn't done it since. She'd put him through a grueling beating that night, one that evened them both out, supposedly. But later that night, he'd woken to find her in her yard, digging a hole for plants she didn't have, the helpless worry so unbearable she had no outlet for it other than the physical rending of the earth. Until he appeared and she turned the anger on him.

He'd held onto her as she struck at him. He'd known that, for once, she wasn't looking for a fight. They'd ended up kneeling together on the dirt. "All right." His voice was raw. "I won't do that again, Mistress. I won't leave you."

He'd let her put a location app on his phone, so if he needed some time to himself, and was too deep in his head to call or send a text, she'd know he was somewhere close by. Like at the park, or the Audubon Zoo. He liked watching the elephants. It told her he was taking time, not taking off.

He wouldn't consider therapy, and she was the last person to push it, but she'd spoken to Abby about Dr. Mo, aka Maureen Whisnant, the woman who'd helped Abby with her schizophrenia. Sometime in the future, maybe Mick would find his way to her. Right now it was just day by day.

"It's not about him being ready," Cyn answered Skye's question. "It's about me."

Ros smiled, her gaze serious. "So it's time."

"Yes. I'm certain."

"Good." Proving the importance of the declaration, Abby's gaze held Cyn's for a full few seconds before it slid to the left, but she held on at Cyn's earring. "So were we. But I won the bet on when you'd figure it out."

Cyn made a face, and everyone chuckled. Except Vera. She had her head bent over her tablet.

"Vera?"

The HR manager lifted her head, her pale gray eyes thoughtful. "I'm so glad for you."

"Do you have a concern?" Ros asked.

"Would it matter?"

The uncharacteristically edgy response startled Cyn, but she met Vera tone for tone. "Yes. I don't give a shit what the whole world thinks, about how I live my life or the choices I make. But you're my family. Your opinion matters."

463

Regret crossed Vera's face. "When you and Mick are together, it's obvious. We all saw it, the moment you crossed paths at the club. His darkness concerns me, because it's deep." She gave Cyn a pointed look. "You got shot while you were on a camping trip with him."

"Please. Everyone here knows I don't need a man's help to get myself shot."

Vera sighed, rubbed her forehead. "He's going to take a lot of healing."

"And I'm not the nurturing type?" Cyn's fingers curled defensively on the table. She wasn't in the habit of disguising her reactions in this company. She wouldn't now.

"The healing fits the patient." Vera met her gaze. "I think you're exactly what he needs. What I hope you know is that you have a whole team to help you."

Proposing dinner at her place should have confirmed Cyn's understanding of that point. However, insightful as ever, Vera had recognized a lack of direct acknowledgement.

Okay. Take the final step. Cyn swallowed. "It's been difficult to invite you all to my home. I'm sure you all figured out why a long time ago."

No disagreement. They waited for her to continue. Her emotions surged. Cyn guessed it showed how much her and Mick's relationship had advanced in just three weeks that her first thought was wishing he was here, at her back.

He couldn't be. Not for this. But she had support just as strong, right in front of her.

She normally expressed her affection by giving them a lot of shit, but this moment brought raw and painful things to the top, knotted with a history of professional success, personal triumphs and stumbles.

Every revelation about loyalty, friendship and what family could be when you created it, rather than letting others set the terms, had been hard-won for Cyn. Up until this moment, she'd held back on full trust, even as she'd known she'd walk through fire and break through chest-high ice for every woman here.

"I'm inviting you because it's time to let that wall fall. I don't need it anymore. I'm also inviting you because of Mick."

She looked toward Vera. "It *is* hard. Hard to find I've let someone inside me so deeply that I've handed him the ability to tear me to pieces. With his pain, of all things. Knowing I have you at my back, to help me put myself back together, so I can keep putting him back together, until he gets through the worst of this...I need you. I need you to know that. And I need him, more than I've ever needed anyone or anything in my whole life."

Vera's initial reaction may have unsettled her, but her response now left no questions. She reached over and captured Cyn's hand in an unbreakable grip, her fingers strong and steady. "Don't cry," her friend teased her. "You'll scare us all to death."

"I'll scare me to death." Cyn held the hand a nice long moment, letting Skye take her other one. Ros and Abby had the expression they'd so often given each woman when she hit a crisis.

Anything you need, we're here.

When Cyn released Skye and Vera, she pulled out her phone and sent a group text. "That's my address. I don't want to hear a damn word about it, by the way," she warned. "Yes, it's in the suburbs."

"We figured it was a cottage deep in the forest, where everything was made of candy." Skye used a monotone, Jenna Ortega Addams Family "Wednesday" voice. "To lure children."

Cyn rolled her eyes. She could draw a deep breath again. Obviously realizing it would help her if they behaved as if nothing momentous had happened, everyone rose with their usual chatter. It brought the meeting to an official end. Vera left the room first. She met Cyn's gaze before she

465

disappeared, and though the smile was warm, there was something…sad in it.

It wouldn't be until later that Cyn would reach a astonishing thought about that. Only Cyn and Vera had been left in the single life, and they'd known it was just a matter of time for Vera. She wanted to settle down, have a couple kids. She wasn't actively seeking it, but when the time came, she'd welcome it.

Cyn had been sure it would happen for Vera, while she'd never expected it for herself. When the others went off at the end of the night, Vera would usually stay to have an extra drink with her, but Cyn had thought through what it would feel like when that wasn't the case. Not in a worried-that-she'd-feel-alone way. It would just feel different. Being on her own, figuring out her own shit, because she could take care of herself—Cyn was good with that.

No. Cyn had to be mistaken about that expression. Vera was a "things happen when they're supposed to happen" kind of person. Serene and balanced. Spiritual. She liked her life, her club regulars.

But it had never occurred to Cyn, to any of them, what Cyn choosing Mick meant.

Vera hadn't expected to be the last to find the man she wanted to call hers forever.

☒

But it had only been a moment, and Vera had been her usual normal self ever since, enough to have Cyn doubting her impression.

And tonight was about other things.

Skye was getting off the bike from behind Tiger. As she handed him her helmet, he hooked an arm around her neck for a kiss. Her hands slid over his thigh and hip before she backed off with a smile and headed for the door. Tiger stowed the helmet and nodded to Cyn, then exited the driveway, the engine roaring in a way as head turning as the man himself.

Skye came up her walkway, her attention on the house, the potted flowers on the stoop. The cheerful welcome flag with gnomes on it. Her face wreathed with a grin.

"Shut up," Cyn said. "Damn chatterbox."

Skye's smile grew deeper. "Does Mick know it's just us girls?" she signed.

"He does now."

"Think he can keep his balance?"

"Absolutely. Until I knock him off it." In the right ways.

She brought Skye in, and Mick greeted her with an affectionate cheek kiss, one-armed hug, and the wine cooler. The others arrived shortly thereafter. Cyn had braced herself for teasing, but though she was ribbed, it was in amiable, low-key ways, like Skye's nudge about gnomes.

She discovered a quiet pride as they asked for the tour, and she showed them the things she'd done to make the house a home. Looking at the landscaping and gardening work she'd done, Vera, their vegetable expert, asked her about the soils she was using for her flourishing flower beds. Inside, Ros complimented Cyn on her living room photo montage, created out of recycled wood. It showed pictures of all of them, at Abby's wedding and other social occasions.

Through it all, Mick moved among them, making sure the women had full drinks and access to appetizers. She really should have gotten him that apron, but there was something distractingly masculine about a well-dressed man who tended to the needs of female guests with warm smiles and a deep voice.

He wore slacks and one of his blue dress shirts. Her necklace gleamed against his tanned skin, while his groomed beard coaxed her to stroke its softness. He'd brushed his hair so the top strands fell over his brow in their appealing, rakish way. That mysterious gaze, holding a hint of the unsafe man he could be, added to the appealing package.

467

He wasn't a service sub, but after she'd told him it would just be the women, he'd quickly adapted, and proved himself good enough to earn approving looks. Though they'd keep their hands to themselves, she was tossed more than one teasing look about how damn sexy he was.

In his mind, he'd be going over all the possible reasons she hadn't told him it would only be the women. She was sure he wouldn't guess the why of it—but he was good at waiting to see how an unexpected situation unfolded.

When they sat down for dinner, he didn't join them. He bent to brush his lips across her temple. "I'll be in the kitchen if you want anything, Mistress."

As he departed, Skye picked up her plate and fanned herself with it, then used it as a shield to deflect the dinner roll Cyn pelted at her, starting the meal with laughter. While they filled their plates, there was easy conversation about the food, as well received as she'd expected. It moved forward along a female, meandering path, through work, personal lives, clients and family. More about Cyn's house, her interest in gardening.

However, as the meal drew to a close, Ros met her gaze, a question. Anticipation slid through Cyn as she nodded. She'd told them she wanted the formal acknowledgement, but had left it to them to choose the look of that, for the same reason she'd opened her home. She trusted them. They would know what was needed.

Mick had reappeared to clear the table and bring out coffee and dessert. He waved away offers to help.

"I'm gaining job experience. Waitstaff is looking good. With my fabulous ass and New Orleans' endless supply of bars, I'll make enough in tips to earn a decent living."

In reality, he and Tyler had spoken a couple of times. Cyn suspected Mick would eventually end up helping several of those task forces who could use his expertise. He might travel to those locations to give his insights, and monitor the progress on certain ops. He might even train others to go undercover, or be a handler like Tyler.

He wasn't ready for it yet. He needed to get his head on straight first, and Tyler had bluntly told him that sign-off would come from her, not Mick himself. Though Mick hadn't responded well to that, Tyler didn't budge.

It would take time, but he'd get there, she knew it. Though Mick had kept moving to stay ahead of the darkness within him, at his core he was also a man who could get restless if fixed in one place. When he balanced out, she could handle him being on the road, doing the things that mattered to him.

As long as he always came home to her.

"Mick, before we do coffee and dessert," Ros said smoothly, "we'd like to handle something else first."

Cyn gestured to the place by her chair. "Come stand over here," she told him.

His wariness amused her. He wasn't into being shared, nor being treated blatantly like a sub in front of others, outside of a formal club session. With the look she gave him, she conveyed her respect for that, even as she was telling him to get over it for a few minutes.

He stood beside her chair and spoke with forced ease. "Sure. What's up?"

Ros rose and folded her hands, meeting his gaze. "Each man who has come into our circle belongs to one of us. He also belongs to all of us. Family, not just the traditional definition, but as it's defined by Dominants and submissives. They are under our protection and guidance. They can look to us for that, wherever it's needed."

"I don't understand," he said slowly.

"I think you do." She arched a fine brow. "I expect you've even asked Lawrence, Neil or Tiger about it in some roundabout way, because you're a perceptive man."

"Roundabout" was the right word. Cyn doubted any of the men had spoken overtly of it. Their experiences had been very personal and different for each of them, fitting the relationship they had with the Mistress in question.

Mick looked toward Cyn. She saw the concern in his gaze, that darkness. *I'm not ready, I'm not worthy of this. I will let you down.*

No, you aren't. But yes, you are worthy. And no, you won't let me down.

"This isn't a decision for you to make," she said. "It's mine. Whatever happens between you and me will happen. But I'm certain of my feelings on this, and toward you. That's what this is about, Mick. They're letting you know that they support that. They support us."

The understanding penetrated his defenses. His tensions eased as what she was telling him took root and rocked his world, making his gaze on her soften.

Cyn was reinforcing before witnesses what she'd only intimated in private. *I want you for my own. Not for a session, not until we hit a bad patch. But always. Through everything.*

"You love me and you want to serve me. Is that true? It's the only question that matters."

"Yeah, it is. If I can..." He shook his head. "Yeah. Yes, Mistress."

Abby had excused herself from the table earlier. Now a silver box rested by her plate. She picked it up and passed it down to Cyn. When Cyn removed the top, Mick's gaze fell upon it at the same time hers did.

The man's bracelet was made of antique gold links, separated by four black disks. Each disk was flanked by square cut crystals, in seven different colors. A flat, rectangular lock hooked onto one side of the bracelet, waiting to be fastened to the opposite end.

"Our initials are engraved on the disks," Ros said. "And each of us chose a word to put on the back."

"Faith," said Vera.

Skye made a sign with her hands. "Courage," Cyn supplied.

"Loyalty," said Ros, meeting his eyes.

"Trust," Abby finished.

"The crystals are the colors of the chakras," Vera said. "They help with balance and healing. Peace of mind."

"The lock is Cyn's, of course," Ros smiled. "It also has a word on the back of it. *Mistress*. A reminder. You are hers exclusively," she gestured to Cyn, "but your wellbeing is owned by all of us. Do you understand?"

Slowly, Mick nodded. Cyn took the bracelet out and turned it over, reading the words. His gaze dropped to look at it, then he reached out and touched it, their fingers brushing. "I'm honored," he said. "And a little terrified."

"There's a key to the lock in there," Ros said to Cyn. "But we had five made." Her gaze shifted to Mick. "We all have one. Another part of the message, reinforcing it."

She picked up an envelope Abby had put beneath the box. "Our family has expanded these past few years," she noted, glancing at Skye and Abby. "Cyn respects your privacy, Mick, but we haven't been oblivious to the difficulty of these past few weeks, the drastic changes in your life. We recognized a way for us to help."

He shifted uncomfortably, but when Cyn reached out and clasped his hand, it helped him settle.

It's okay, she thought. *They're family. You'll learn, just like I did, that it's not something to be antsy about.*

Ros opened the envelope and unfolded the handwritten paper. "This is a letter to you, from Lawrence. He wrote it with Tiger and Neil's input." Her gaze softened as she skimmed her man's words. It told Cyn that it was the first time her boss was seeing them herself.

Ros cleared her throat. "I'm going to read it aloud, because, like the bracelet, it's a gift that should be witnessed."

Mick kept his hand in Cyn's, their grip tight.

471

Mick,

Love for a Mistress is something that can't be defined. They demand we give them everything, but we want to protect and cherish them, so how do we reconcile that when we have bad shit to work out inside ourselves? When the load is way more than what we want to put upon them?

Though they're strong and willing enough to take it all, and we know sharing it with them is important, a man, and a submissive, has a mandate of his own. Healing, living with yourself, loving her, all of it requires a place to stand on your own feet and fight it out with those demons.

You have those places with us. Neil will take you out into the bayou where he's found peace, after being in places no one would ever want to know about.

I'll take you on workouts with me and Max, another former SEAL, and we'll sweat you down to the bone. It helps, I promise.

Tiger has spare bikes and knows all the backroads, where you can open up and roar. It's where he came to grips with the violence that dictated the first part of his life and almost kept him from ever finding his Mistress.

Cyn noted Skye's soft smile, the tightening of her fingers against the elbows she had resting on the table. Abby had her head dipped, listening, her lovely hazel eyes thoughtful. Vera's expression was impossible to read, until she looked toward Cyn and gave her a look of deep love and understanding. Unconditional support.

In those places, you can fight it out, find your peace. And always come back to her arms.

You're not alone, man. Never again.

472

Ros read the last few lines with some emotion in her voice, then folded up the paper. "I will leave this here. It's yours."

Mick couldn't seem to speak for several moments. "Thank you," he said at last. He made an oddly formal gesture, a slight bow to the whole table, before he met Cyn's gaze. Emotional overload was threatening, but neither of them ever flinched from pain, did they?

Mick, masochist that he was, decided to exacerbate it.

"Loving someone isn't easy, but you never really stop loving someone." His voice was thick. "Even when you fall out of love with someone, you love them for the memories you made. I came from a broken home, like a lot of people." His gaze swept the table and came back to Cyn. "What I learned from watching my parents before I lost them was this. Even worse than the falling out of love was the constant disappointment they dished out to one another. Disappointment is what builds up over time and sucks the heart and soul from you, even if you stay together."

He took a breath. "I'm pretty fucked up right now. I know that. I promise all of you I'll do my very best to serve her the way a Mistress like her should be served. With my last breath, with the last drop of blood. With my last smile or laugh, with the last good feeling I have on this earth. It will all be about and because of her."

When he came back into her life, there'd been an energy that bound them. It had been growing ever since, and now she felt it intensify and spread throughout the room, as her sisters bore witness to what he was pledging. It also felt like it was just the two of them, in that crazy way the romances talked about.

She lifted the bracelet. He dropped to a knee and offered his arm. As she bent her head over the bracelet so she could attach the lock, she felt his breath on her ear, the tension vibrating through him. "I expected it to be made out of barbed wire," he murmured.

473

She bit back a smile. "I have a cock ring made out of that. Thanks for reminding me."

He huffed a chuckle across her neck, and she closed her eyes, tightening her hand on his arm. He sobered and his hand was on her shoulder. "Mistress."

She was okay. She was remembering that long ago night when he'd destroyed her mother's grave for her. How he'd tended Cissy's headstone, then gone out into the world to make a difference. For people like her, Cissy and her siblings.

They knew she wasn't demonstrative, and what she was about to do might put them all into shock, but that wasn't what mattered.

She clicked the lock shut. Then she lifted her face, so close to his. "I love you, Mick," she said. "All those things on the disk—loyalty, courage, trust and faith. Give me those, and I'll give you the same."

She fished the key out of the box, holding it out to him. "You hold onto this," she said. "It will always be your choice to take it off or not."

He shook his head. Leaning forward, he slid his hands under her hair and unclipped the skeleton necklace she wore. He took off the cuff key she'd put there that night in the motorhome, and replaced it with the bracelet one. He pocketed the other key before putting the necklace back on her, cupping her throat.

"My Mistress of the Hunt," he said. "Whichever direction the chase takes, or how far away I am, it never changes that. I'm yours."

She met his lips with her own, gripping his wrist as she did. The links of the chain bit into her palm, and into his wrist. Maybe she'd add a loop of barbed wire to the design.

When she drew back and took a deep breath, she saw the humor in his eyes, as if he'd read the thought. And anticipated what she'd do next.

"Enough of this shit," she said. "Who wants cake for dessert?"

WANT MORE? While we're waiting for Vera's story, how about a **FREE** gateway-to-series from another of Joey's contemporary works? You encountered **Tyler Winterman** in this book, and you can download his and Marguerite's love story (his "angel") for free!

CLICK TO READ NOW
ICE QUEEN or
https://dl.bookfunnel.com/oc9uxd0wy7

Note: If you'd like to read **Matt Kensington** and **Savannah's** story, it's also a **FREE** first-in-series for the Knights of the Board Room. This series inspired the Mistresses of the Board Room spin-off!

CLICK TO READ NOW
BOARD RESOLUTION or
https://dl.bookfunnel.com/ns4cw7rwsr

Reading this in print format?
Look for it at your favorite book vendor or use the typed-out BookFunnel link above (books not free at Nook).

ABOUT THE AUTHOR

Having penned over fifty acclaimed BDSM contemporary and paranormal titles, which includes six award-winning series, *Joey W. Hill* has been awarded the RT Book Reviews Career Achievement Award for Erotic Romance. A submissive herself, Hill brings authenticity to her intensely emotional love stories.

She is grateful for the support of a wonderful and enthusiastic readership, which allows her to live on her beloved Carolina coast with her even more beloved husband and menagerie of animals.

- On the Web: https://storywitch.com
- Twitter: https://twitter.com/JoeyWHill
- Facebook: https://facebook.com/JoeyWHillAuthor
- Facebook Fan Forum:
  https://facebook.com/groups/JWHMembersOnly
- MeWe: https://mewe.com/i/joeywhill
- GoodReads:
  https://www.goodreads.com/author/show/103359.Joey_W_Hill
- BookBub: https://bookbub.com/authors/joey-w-hill
- Amazon: https://amazon.com/Joey-W-Hill/e/B001JSCIW0

ALSO BY JOEY W. HILL

Natural Law

Ice Queen

Mirror of My Soul

Mistress of Redemption

Rough Canvas

Branded Sanctuary

Divine Solace

Worth The Wait

Truly Helpless

In His Arms

Ignition Sequence

Naughty Bits Series

Naughty Bits

Naughty Wishes

Vampire Queen Series

Vampire Queen's Servant

Mark of the Vampire Queen

Vampire's Claim

Beloved Vampire

Vampire Mistress *(VQS: Club Atlantis)*

Vampire Trinity *(VQS: Club Atlantis)*

Vampire Instinct

Bound by the Vampire Queen

Taken by a Vampire

The Scientific Method

Nightfall

Elusive Hero

Night's Templar

Vampire's Soul

Vampire's Embrace

Vampire Master *(VQS: Club Atlantis)*

Vampire Guardian *(VQS: Club Atlantis)*

Vampire's Choice

<u>*Non-Series Titles*</u>

Chance of a Lifetime

Choice of Masters

If Wishes Were Horses

Medusa's Heart

Make Her Dreams Come True

Snow Angel (short story)

Submissive Angel

Threads of Faith

Unrestrained

Virtual Reality